Peter Tremayne is the fiction pseudonym of a well-known authority on the ancient Celts, who utilises his knowledge of the Brehon law system and 7th-century Irish society to create a new concept in detective fiction.

Sister Fidelma made her first appearance in 1993 in short stories. This is her fifth appearance in novel form. Peter Tremayne's previous Sister Fidelma mysteries, ABSOLUTION BY MURDER, SHROUD FOR THE ARCHBISHOP, SUFFER LITTLE CHILDREN and THE SUBTLE SERPENT are also available from Headline and have received the following praise:

'The Sister Fidelma stories take us into a world that only an author steeped in Celtic history could recreate so vividly – and one which no other crime novelist has explored before. Make way for a unique lady detective going where no one has gone before' Peter Haining

'Definitely an Ellis Peters competitor . . . the background detail is marvellous' *Evening Standard*

'I believe I have a *tendresse* for Sister Fidelma. Ingeniously plotted . . . subtly paced . . . written with conviction, a feel for the time, and a chill air of period authenticity. A series to cultivate' Jack Adrian

'A triumph! Tremayne uses many real characters and events as background . . . bringing the ancient world to life . . . The novels are admirable' *Mystery Scene*

'A fast-moving whodunnit thriller . . . Unputdownable' *Irish Democrat*

'Sister Fidelma . . . promises to be one of the most intriguing new characters in 1990s detective fiction' *Book & Magazine Collector*

Also by Peter Tremayne from Headline

Absolution By Murder
Shroud for the Archbishop
Suffer Little Children
The Subtle Serpent
Valley of the Shadow

The Spider's Web

Peter Tremayne

HEADLINE

First published in 1997
by HEADLINE BOOK PUBLISHING

First published in paperback in 1997
by HEADLINE BOOK PUBLISHING

10 9 8 7 6 5 4 3 2

ISBN 0 7472 5287 4

Printed and bound in Great Britain by
Clays Ltd, St Ives plc

HEADLINE BOOK PUBLISHING
A division of Hodder Headline PLC
338 Euston Road
London NW1 3BH

For my good friend
Terence,
The Mac Carthy Mór, Prince of Desmond
51st generation in unbroken male line descent from
King Eoghan Mór of Cashel (d. AD 192)
who has welcomed Sister Fidelma
into his family ancestry!

'Laws are like spider's webs: if some poor weak
creature come up against them, it is caught;
but a bigger one can break through and get away.'

– Solon of Athens
(b. c.640 BC – d. after 561 BC)

HISTORICAL NOTE

The events of this story occur in the month known to the Irish of the seventh century as Cét-Soman, which was later called Beltaine, the month of May. The year is AD 666.

Those readers who have previously encountered the adventures of Sister Fidelma will already know of the differences between the seventh-century Irish Church, now popularly called the Celtic Church, and that of Rome. Much of the Irish liturgy and philosophies were different. It has already been made clear that the concept of celibacy among the religious was not a popular one at this time, either in the Celtic Church or even in that of Rome. It must be remembered that in Fidelma's era many religious houses frequently contained both sexes and the religious often married, raising their children in the service of the Faith. Even abbots and bishops could and did marry at this period. An appreciation of this fact is essential to an understanding of Fidelma's world.

Allowing that most readers will find seventh-century Ireland a pretty unfamiliar place, I have provided a sketch map of the kingdom of Muman. I have maintained this name rather than the anachronistic term which was formed by adding the Norse *stadr* (place) to Muman in the ninth century AD which produces the modern name of Munster. As many seventh-century Irish personal names may also be unfamiliar, I have, as a means of assistance, included a list of principal characters.

It may enhance readers' appreciation to know that a *cumal* used as a monetary unit was equivalent to the value of three milch cows. Used as a unit of land measurement, a *cumal* was the equivalent of 13.85 hectares.

Lastly, readers will remember that Fidelma operates in the ancient Irish social system with its laws, the Laws of the Fénechus, more popularly known as the Brehon Laws (from *breaitheamh* = a judge). She is a qualified advocate of the law courts, a position which was not at all unusual for women in Ireland at this time.

PRINCIPAL CHARACTERS

Sister Fidelma of Kildare, a *dálaigh* or advocate of the law courts of seventh-century Ireland
Brother Eadulf of Seaxmund's Ham, a Saxon monk from the land of the South Folk

Cathal, abbot of Lios Mhór
Brother Donnán, a *scriptor*
Colgú of Cashel, king of Muman and Fidelma's brother
Beccan, Chief Brehon, or judge, of Corco Loígde

Bressal, a hostel keeper
Morna, Bressal's brother

Eber, chicftain of Araglin
Cranat, Eber's wife
Crón, daughter of Eber and his tanist or heir-elect
Teafa, Eber's sister
Móen, a blind, deaf, mute

Dubán, commander of Eber's bodyguard
Crítán, a young warrior

Menma, head stableman at the *rath* of Araglin
Dignalt, the stewardess
Grella, a servant

Father Gormán of Cill Uird

Archú, a young farmer of Araglin
Scoth, his fiancée
Muadnat of the Black Marsh, his cousin
Agdae, Muadnat's chief herdsman and nephew

Gadra, a hermit

Clídna, a brothel keeper

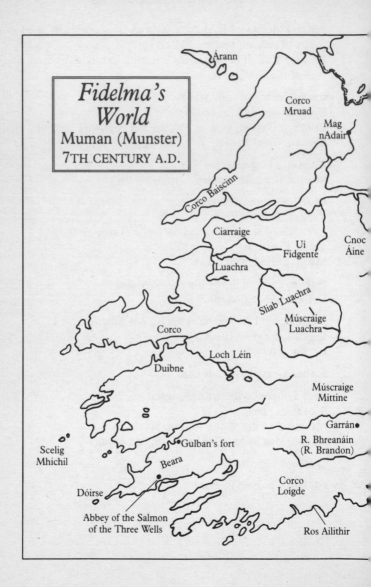

Árann

Corco
Mruad

Mag
nAdair

*Fidelma's
World*
Muman (Munster)
7TH CENTURY A.D.

Corco Baiscinn

Ciarraige

Ui
Fidgente

Cnoc
Áine

Luachra

Sliab Luachra

Múscraige
Luachra

Corco

Loch Léin

Duibne

Múscraige
Mittine

Garrán●

R. Bhreanáin
(R. Brandon)

Scelig
Mhichil

Gulban's fort

Beara

Corco
Loígde

Dóirse

Abbey of the Salmon
of the Three Wells

Ros Ailithir

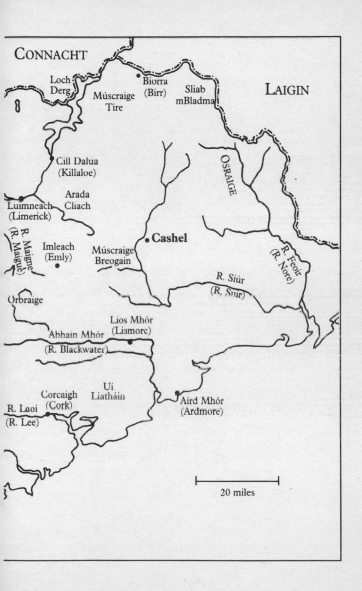

CONNACHT

Loch Derg

Biorra (Birr)

Múscraige Tíre

Sliab mBladma

LAIGIN

Cill Dalua (Killaloe)

Arada Cliach

Luimneach (Limerich)

R. Maigue (R. Maigue)

Imleach (Emly)

Múscraige Breogain

OSRAIGE

Cashel

R. Siúr (R. Siúr)

R. Feoir (R. Nore)

Orbraige

Lios Mhór (Lismore)

Abhain Mhór (R. Blackwater)

Uí Liatháin

Corcaigh (Cork)

R. Laoí (R. Lee)

Aird Mhór (Ardmore)

20 miles

Chapter One

Thunder was rumbling around the high bald peaks of the mountains which spread from the central summit of Maoldomhnach's Hill, from which they took their name. An occasional bright flash silhouetted the rounded height, causing shadows to flit briefly across the valley of Araglin within its northern foothills. It was a dark night with storm clouds clustering and racing across the heaven, tumbling over each other as if blown in disarray by the powerful breath of the ancient gods.

On the high pastures, the shaggy-coated cattle huddled together, some bellowing fretfully now and then, not just to comfort themselves from the threatening storm but to warn one another of the prevailing scent of ravening wolves whose hungry packs haunted the dark woodlands which bordered the high meadows. In a corner of the pastures, well away from the cattle, a majestic stag stood as an anxious sentinel over his hinds and their calves. Now and then he would thrust his elaborately antlered head skyward and his sensitive nostrils would quiver. In spite of the darkness, the heavy clouds and threatening storm, the beast sensed the approach of dawn beyond the distant eastern peaks.

Below in the valley, by the dark, gurgling ribbon of a river, a group of unfortified buildings stood in complete darkness. No dogs were stirring at this hour and it was still too early for the cocks to herald the approach of a new day. Even the birds had not begun their dawn chorus and were still sheltering sleepily in the surrounding trees.

Yet one human was stirring at this dark hour; one person was

1

awakening at this hour of stillness when the world seemed dead and deserted.

Menma, the head stableman to Eber, chieftain of Araglin, a tall, ponderous man with a bushy red beard and a fondness for liquor, blinked and threw off the sheepskin from his straw palliasse bed. The occasional flash of lightning lit his solitary cabin. Menma groaned and shook his head as if the action would clear it from the effects of the previous night's drinking. He reached to a table and, with shaky hands, fumbled for the flint and tinder to light the tallow candle which stood upon it. Then he stretched his cramped limbs. In spite of his excessive drinking, Menma was possessed of a mysterious in-built sense of time. All his life he had risen in the dark hour before dawn no matter the lateness of the hour at which he had tumbled, in drunken stupor, into his bed.

The big man began his ritual morning cursing of all creation. Menma had a fondness for cursing. Some people began the day with a prayer, others by performing their morning's ablutions. Menma of Araglin began his day by cursing his master, the chieftain Eber, wishing upon him all manner of deaths by choking, by convulsion, by mangling, by dysentery, by poison, by drowning, by smothering and by any other means his meagre imagination could devise. And after he had exhausted such manner of ill-wishing on his master, Menma continued cursing his own existence, his parents for not being rich and powerful; cursing them for being only simple farming folk and thereby ordaining for him a role as a lowly stableman.

His own parents had been simple labourers on their richer cousins' farmsteads. They had not succeeded in life and had ordained Menma's own menial existence. Menma was a jealous and bitter man, unhappy with his lot in life.

Nevertheless, he rose automatically in the darkness of the early morning and drew on his clothes. He never bothered to wash nor comb the matted tangle of his shoulder-length, red-coloured hair and the great bush of his beard. A gulping draught of *corma*, the sickly mead that always stood in a jug by his bedside, was all the cleansing he deemed necessary to prepare him for the day. The stench of his body and garments proclaimed, to those near enough to inhale their malefic odour, that Menma and cleanliness were not compatible.

He shuffled to the door of his cabin and peered out, blinking up at the darken sky. The thunder still rumbled but he instinctively knew that it would not rain that day in the valley. The storm was on the other side of the mountains and moving along them east to west, keeping parallel to the valley of Araglin. It would not cross northward over the mountains. No; it would be a dry day even if cloudy and cool. The clouds obscured the stars so that he was unable to be precise about the time but he sensed, rather than saw, the pale line of dawn just below the distant eastern peaks.

The *rath* of the chieftain of Araglin still slumbered in the darkness. Although this was no more than an unfortified village, it was courtesy to call the dwelling of a chieftain a *rath* or fortress.

Menma stood at his door and now he began to softly curse the day itself. He resented the fact that everyone was able to sleep on but that he had to be the first to rise. And when he had finished with the day there was Araglin itself to be cursed and he did full justice to his scanty vocabulary.

He turned back into his cabin for a moment and blew out the candle before beginning to shuffle along the track that led between the peaceful buildings towards the chieftain's stables. He needed no candle for he had often walked that path before. His first task would be to turn the horses out to pasture, feed the chieftain's hunting hounds, and then to oversee the milking of the chieftain's cattle. And by the time the horses were out in the pasture and the hounds were fed, then the women of the household would be awake and coming to attend the milking. Milking was not a man's job and Menma would not demean himself by doing it. But there had been a cattle raid in the valley recently and Eber, the chieftain, had instructed him to check the milch herd before each milking. It was an affront to the honour of the chieftain that anyone would dare steal even a calf from his herd and Eber had been furious at the news that cattle raiders were threatening the peace of his clan lands. His warriors had scoured the countryside for the culprits but without success.

Menma approached the imposing dark outline of the hall of assembly, one of the few great large stone buildings within the ancient *rath*. The other stone building was Father Gormán's chapel. The stables were at the back of the rounded construction, just behind the guests' hostel. To approach the stables, Menma had to trudge a circular path around the wooden extensions to the stone hall which housed the private apartments of the chieftain and his family. Menma glanced at the buildings in jealousy. Eber would still be snoring in his bed until well after dawn.

Behind his veil of beard, Menna grinned lewdly. He wondered if anyone was sharing Eber's bed that night. Then he frowned angrily. Why Eber? Why not him? What was so special about Eber that he had wealth, power and was able to entice women into his bed? What fate had made him a humble stableman? Why . . . ?

He paused in mid-stride, head to one side.

The darkness seemed soundless. The *rath* continued to slumber. High, high up among the distant hills came the long, drawn out howl of a wolf breaking the silence. No; it was not that which had caused him to halt. It had been some other noise. A noise he could not quite place.

He stood for a moment more but the silence remained. He was just about to dismiss the half heard sound as a trick of the wind when it came again.

A low, moaning sound.

Was it the wind?

Menma suddenly genuflected and shivered. God between him and all evil! Was it one of the dwellers in the hills? The people of

4

the *sidh*; the little folk in search of souls to carry below into their dark caverns?

There came a sudden shriek, not loud but sharp enough to make Menma start, his heart increasing its beat for several seconds. Then the low moaning came again. This time it was a little stronger and more sustained.

Menma looked around him. Nothing stirred among the dark shadows of the buildings. No one else seemed to have heard the noise. He tried to locate its origin. It came from the direction of the apartments of Eber himself. In spite of its ethereal quality, Menma could now identify it as human in origin. He sighed in relief for, as brutal in his views of the world as he was, nevertheless, it did not bode well to go up against the folk of the *sidh* if they were intent on soul-stealing. He glanced quickly about. The building appeared dark and tranquil. Was Eber ill? He frowned, undecided what to do. Eber was his chieftain, come what may, and Menma had a duty to his chieftain. A duty which not even his bitterness could cause him to neglect.

He cautiously made his way to the door of Eber's apartments and tapped softly.

'Eber? Are you ill? Do you require assistance?' he called gently.

There was no reply. He tapped again, a little louder. When there was still no response, he summoned courage and lifted the latch. The door was not secured, not that he expected it to be. No one secured their doors in the *rath* of the chieftain of Araglin. He moved inside. He had no trouble adjusting his eyes to the darkness. The room which he had entered was empty. He knew from previous experience that Eber's apartments consisted of two rooms. The first room, in which he stood, was called 'the place of conversation', which was a private reception room for the chieftain, where he discreetly entertained special guests, away from the public gaze of the hall of assembly. Beyond this room was the chieftain's bed chamber.

Menma, having ascertained the first room to be empty, turned towards it.

The first thing he noticed was a glow of light from beneath the door. The second thing that registered with him was the rising sound of the moaning beyond the door.

'Eber!' he called sharply. 'Is there anything wrong? It is I, Menma the stableman.'

There was no reply and the moaning sound did not diminish.

He moved across to the door and rapped sharply.

Hesitating only for a moment, he entered.

A lamp was lit on a small table. Menma blinked rapidly to adjust his vision. He was aware of someone kneeling by the bed, someone in a hunched posture, rocking back and forth and whimpering. They were the source of the low moaning sound that he had been hearing. He was aware of the dark stains on the clothes of the figure. Then his eyes widened a fraction. They were blood stains and there was something flashing and glinting in the lamplight, something that the person was clutching in their hands. It was a long bladed dagger.

For a moment, Menma stood immobile, fascinated by the spectacle.

Then he realised that there was a second person in the room. Someone was lying in the bed beside which the moaning figure was kneeling.

Menma stood a pace forward.

Sprawled on the bed, naked except for the coverlets twisted around him, was the blood-smeared body of Eber the chieftain. One hand was thrown casually back behind his head. The eyes were wide and staring and seemed alive in the flickering of the lamplight. The chest was a mess of bloody wounds. Menma had seen enough animals slaughtered not to recognise the jagged tearing of injuries caused by a knife. The knife must have been frenziedly plunged, again and again, into the chest of the chieftain of Araglin.

Menma half raised his hand to genuflect but then dropped it. 'Is he dead?' he demanded hollowly.

The figure beside the bed continued to rock back and forth moaning. It did not look up.

Menma took another step forward and gazed dispassionately downwards. Then he moved closer, dropping to one knee and reaching towards the pulse in the chieftain's neck. The body already felt cool and clammy. Now that he looked more closely into the eyes, and the lamplight played no tricks with them, he could see that they were set and glazed.

Menma drew himself up and stared down in distaste. He hesitated, feeling that in spite of the evidence of his eyes, he had to make sure that Eber was dead. He raised a foot to nudge at the body with the toe of his boot. There was no response. Then he raised his foot and lashed viciously out at the side of the body. No, he was not mistaken. Eber, the chieftain, was dead.

Menma turned his gaze to the still moaning figure, which was still clutching the knife. He began to laugh harshly. He suddenly realised that he, Menma the stableman, was going to be rich and powerful just like the cousins he had envied all his life.

He was still chuckling when he left the chieftain's apartments and set off in search of Dubán, the commander of Eber's body-guard.

Chapter Two

The tolling of the deep baritone bell of the abbey signalled the reconvening of the court. It was early afternoon but the atmosphere was not warm. The cool grey granite walls of the building protected the interior from the sun. The small side chapel of the abbey, which had been given over to the legal hearings, was almost empty. Only a few people had taken their seats on the wooden benches there. Yet until the previous day the chapel had been filled to bursting point with supplicants, with the accused and their witnesses. But this afternoon, the last of the cases to be heard before the court was scheduled for judgment. Justice had already been dispensed in the numerous matters that had been previously heard.

The half a dozen or so participants in this final affair of the court rose respectfully as the Brehon, the judge, entered and took a seat at the head of the hall. The judge was female, in her mid- to late-twenties, and she wore the robes of a sister of the religious. She was tall, with attractive features, red hair tumbling from beneath her headdress. The colour of her eyes was difficult to identify exactly for they appeared ice blue on occasions or, at times, held a strange green fire depending on her moods. Her youthful appearance did not accord with the general idea of an experienced wise and learned judge but, over the last few days, as she had examined and shifted evidence in the various legal claims, this youthful looking woman had impressed those appearing before her with her knowledge, logic and compassion.

Sister Fidelma was, in fact, a qualified *dálaigh*, an advocate of the law courts of the five kingdoms of Éireann. She was proficient to the degree of *anruth* which meant that she could not only plead cases before judges but, when nominated, she could sit to hear and adjudicate in her own court on a range of applications that did not require the presence of a judge of higher rank. It was as a judge that Fidelma had been chosen to preside over the court at the abbey of Lios Mhór. The abbey lay outside 'the great fortification' after which it took its name. Lios Mhór stood on the banks of the impressive river simply known as Abhainn Mór, 'the great river', south of Cashel, in the kingdom of Muman.

The *scriptor* of the abbey, who acted as the clerk of the court and kept a record of all its transactions, remained on his feet while Fidelma and the others seated themselves. He had a melancholy voice which caused Fidelma to think he would do well as a professional mourner.

'This court is now in session. The claim of Archú, son of Suanach, against Muadnat of the Black Marsh continues.'

As he sat down, he cast an expectant glance towards Fidelma and raised his stylus, for the record of the proceedings was made on wet clay inset in wooden frames and at the end of the sessions these records would then be transcribed to more permanent form in vellum books.

Fidelma was seated behind a large ornately carved oak table, her hands placed palm downward before her. She leant back in her chair and looked steadily round at those who sat on the benches in front of her.

'Archú and Muadnat, please come and stand before me.'

A young man rose hastily. He was no more than seventeen years old, his expression eager, like a dog seeking a favour from a master, mused Fidelma as she watched him hurry forward. The second man was in his middle years, old enough to be the youth's father. He was a sombre faced man, almost dour in his expression. There was little humour in his countenance.

'I have listened to the evidence presented in this case,' Fidelma began, glancing from one to another. 'Let me see if I can put the facts fairly. You, Archú, have just reached the age of seniority, the age of choice. Is this so?'

The youth nodded. Seventeen years was the age, according to the law, when a boy became a man and able to make his own decisions.

'And you are the only child of Suanach, who died a year ago? Suanach, who was daughter to Muadnat's uncle?'

'She was the only daughter of my father's brother,' affirmed Muadnat in a gruff unemotional tone.

'Indeed. So you are cousins to each other?'

There was no answer. Obviously there was no love lost between these two whatever their relationship.

'Such close relatives should not need recourse to law to settle their differences,' admonished Fidelma. 'Do you still insist upon the arbitration of this court?'

Muadnat sniffed sourly.

'I have no wish to be here.'

The youth flushed angrily.

'Nor I. Far better it would have been for my cousin to do what was right and moral before it reached this pass.'

'I am in the right,' snapped Muadnat. 'You have no claim on the land.'

Sister Fidelma raised her eyebrow ironically.

'It seems that is now a matter for the law to decide as neither of you appear to agree. And you have brought the matter before the court so that it may make that decision. And the decision that this court makes on the matter is binding on you both.'

She sat back, folded her hands in her lap and examined each of them carefully in turn. There was anger in both of their storm-ridden faces.

'Very well,' she said, at last. 'Suanach, as I understand it, inherited lands from her father. Correct me if I am wrong. She later married a man from beyond the seas, a Briton called Artgal who, being a stranger in this land, had no property to bring into the marriage.'

'An impecunious foreigner!' grunted Muadnat.

Fidelma ignored him.

'Artgal, who was Archú's father, died some years ago. Am I correct?'

'My father died fighting the Uí Fidgente in the service of the king of Cashel.' It was Archú who interrupted and the boy spoke proudly.

'A mercenary soldier,' sneered Muadnat.

'This court was not asked to make a judgment on the personality of Artgal,' Sister Fidelma observed waspishly. 'It is asked to adjudicate on law. Now, Artgal and Suanach were married . . .'

'Against the wishes of her family,' interposed Muadnat again.

'I have already discerned that much,' Fidelma agreed blandly. 'But married they were. On the death of Artgal, Suanach continued to work her land and raise her son, Archú. A year ago, Suanach died.'

'Then my so-called cousin came and claimed that all the land was his.' Archú's voice was bitter.

'It is the law.' Muadnat was smug. 'The land belonged to Suanach. Her husband being a foreigner held no land. When Suanach died, then her land reverted to her family and in that family I stand as her next of kin. That is the law.'

'He took everything,' the youth complained bitterly.

'It was mine to take. And you were not of the age of choice anyway.'

'That is so,' agreed Fidelma. 'For this last year, under the law, as senior member of your family, Muadnat has been your guardian, Archú.'

'Guardian? Slave master, you mean,' scowled the youth. 'I was forced to work on my own land for nothing more than my keep; I was treated worse than a hired worker and forced to eat and sleep in the cattle-pens. My mother's family do not even accord me the treatment they give to those they hire to work the land.'

'I have already noted these facts,' Fidelma sighed patiently.

'We have no legal obligation to the boy,' grunted Muadnat. 'We gave him his keep. He should be grateful for that.'

'I will not comment on that,' Fidelma replied coldly. 'The sum of Archú's case against you, Muadnat, is that he should inherit some of the land which belonged to his mother. Is this not so?'

'His mother's land returns to her family. He can only inherit that which belonged to his father and his father, being a foreigner, had no land in this country to leave him. Let him go to his father's country if he wants land.'

Fidelma continued to sit back in her chair, hands before her, her gaze now concentrated on Muadnat. Her fiery eyes had become slightly hooded and her expression seemed purposely bland.

'When a person who is an *ocáire*, that is a small farmer, dies, then one seventh of the land is subjected to tax and paid to the chieftain for the upkeep of the clan territory. Has this been done?'

'It has,' interrupted the *scriptor*, looking up from making his record. 'There is a disposition to that effect from the chieftain, Eber of Araglin, sister.'

'Good. So the decision that this court has to make is now a straightforward one.'

Fidelma turned slowly to Archú.

'Your mother was the daughter and only child of a small farmer, an *ocáire*. On his death she stood as female heir and is entitled to a life interest in her father's land. Normally, she cannot pass this land on to her husband or sons and on her death it reverts to the next of kin within her own family.'

Muadnat drew himself up and for the first time his disgruntled features loosened in a satisfied expression. His eyes darted triumphantly at the younger man.

'However,' Fidelma's voice suddenly took on an icy note which cut through the hall of the abbey, 'if her husband was a foreigner, and in this case he was a Briton, he would have no land within the clan territory. He can therefore leave nothing to his son. In these circumstances, the law is clear and it was our great judge, Bríg Briugaid, who set the judgment which became the law on this matter. That is, in such circumstances, the mother is entitled to pass on the land to her son but with qualification. Of her lands, she can only bequeath land to the value of seven *cumals* which is the minimal property qualification for an *ocáire* or small farmer.'

There was a silence as both plaintiff and defendant tried to understand the judgment. Sister Fidelma took pity on their puzzled expressions.

'The judgment is in your favour, Archú,' she smiled at the young man. 'Your cousin occupies the land unlawfully now that you are of age. He must relinquish to you an amount of land to the extent of seven *cumals*.'

Muadnat's jaw dropped.

'But . . . but the land scarcely extends seven *cumals* as it is. If he has seven *cumals* there will be nothing of it left for me.'

Fidelma's voice took on the manner of a master lecturing a pupil.

'According to the *Crith Gablach*, the ancient law, seven *cumals* is the property qualification of an *ocáire* which is the right of Archú to receive,' she intoned. 'Further, for acting in violation of the law to the extent that Archú had no recourse but to come before me with this claim against you, you must pay a fine of one *cumal* to this court.'

Muadnat's face was white. His expression had become a mask of rage.

'This is an injustice!' he growled.

Fidelma met his fury calmly.

'Speak not of injustice to me, Muadnat. You are kin to this youth. When his mother died, it was your duty to nurture and protect him. Yet you sought to deprive him of his lawful dues, sought to make him work for you without payment, forcing him to live in worse conditions than a slave. I doubt whether you have an understanding of justice. It would be justice if I made you pay further compensation to him for what you have done. As it is, I am tempering justice with mercy.'

The words came coldly from Fidelma, causing the dour faced man to blink as if physically assaulted by the flood of her contempt. He swallowed hard.

'I will appeal to my chieftain, Eber of Araglin, against this ruling. The land is mine! You have not heard the last of me.'

'Any appeals can only be directed to the chief judge of the king of Cashel,' interrupted the *scriptor* dryly, as he finished writing the judgment. He laid down his stylus and endeavoured . to explain to the disgruntled litigant. 'Once a Brehon makes a judgment, it is not up to you to rail against the Brehon. If you want to object, then you must do so in the proper manner. In the meantime, Muadnat of the Black Marsh, you must obey the judgment and withdraw from the land leaving your cousin Archú to occupy it. If you do not, within nine days from now, you may be physically evicted. Is that understood? And your *cumal* fine must be paid by the rising of the next full moon.'

Without a word, Muadnat turned and strode silently and swiftly from the chapel. A short man, with a small, wiry frame and a shock of chestnut hair, rose and joined him sheepishly in the exodus.

Archú, his expression showing that he was scarcely able to believe the ruling, leaned forward across the table and held out his hand, grabbing Fidelma's own and pumping it rapidly.

'Bless you, sister. You have saved my life.'

Fidelma smiled thinly at the enthusiastic young man.

'I have merely given judgment according to the law. Had the law been otherwise, I would have had to give judgment against you. It is the law which speaks in this court, not I.'

She disengaged her hand. The young man seemed hardly to have heard her but, still grinning, turned and hurried to the back of the chapel where a young girl rose and almost ran into his arms. Fidelma smiled wistfully as she observed the way the two youngsters clutched at each other's hands and gazed upon one another.

Then she turned quickly to her *scriptor*.

'I believe that was the last case we had to deal with, was it not, Brother Donnán?'

'It was. I shall record the judgments later today and ensure that they are announced in the appropriate manner.' The *scriptor* paused, coughed slightly and lowered his voice a little. 'It seems that the abbot is standing by the door waiting to speak to you.'

He indicated with a nervous gesture of his head towards the doors of the chapel. Fidelma turned. Indeed, the broad shouldered figure of Abbot Cathal was standing at the door. Fidelma immediately rose and made her way to him. She noted that the abbot seemed somewhat preoccupied.

'Are you looking for me, Father Abbot?'

Abbot Cathal was a well-built, muscular man of middle age; a man who carried himself with a military stamp for, as a youth, he had trained as a warrior. He was a local man who had left the military life to be taught under the guidance of the blessed Cáthach at Lios Mhór and risen to be accepted as a most accomplished teacher and abbot. The son of a great war chieftain, Cathal had distributed all his wealth to the poor of his clan and lived in the simple poverty of his order. His simplicity and directness caused him enemies. Once a local chieftain, Maelochtrid, had him imprisoned on a trumped up charge of practising magic. Yet on his release Cathal had forgiven him. That was the nature of the man.

Fidelma liked Cathal's gentleness and lack of vanity. It contrasted pleasantly to the arrogance of office which she so often encountered. Cathal was one of the few men of the church whom she would unhesitatingly call a 'holy man'.

'Indeed, I was looking for you, Sister Fidelma,' the abbot replied with a swift but warm smile. 'Has the court finished its deliberations?'

His voice was softly modulated, almost bland, yet Fidelma detected that something unusual had happened to bring him in search of her.

'We have finished pronouncing judgment on the last case, Father Abbot. Is there a problem?'

Abbot Cathal hesitated.

'Two riders have arrived here at the abbey. One of them is a foreigner. They have come from Cashel in search of you.'

'Has anything happened to my brother?' demanded Fidelma sharply in response to the first thought which crossed her mind, sending icy fingers of fear clutching at her. Had something happened to her brother, Colgú, the newly installed king of Muman, the largest of the five kingdoms of Éireann?

At once Abbot Cathal looked contrite.

'No, no. Your brother, the king, is safe and well,' he reassured her. 'Forgive my clumsiness of expression. Come, follow me to my chamber where you are awaited.'

Her curiosity aroused, Fidelma hurried as sedately as she could along the corridors of the great abbey beside the taller figure of the abbot.

From a small slumbering backwater, Lios Mhór, the great house as it was called, had risen into prominence when Cáthach of blessed name moved from Rathan to establish a new community of religious only a generation before. Within a short time, Lios Mhór had become one of the foremost ecclesiastical teaching centres to which flocked students from many lands. Like most of the great abbeys of Ireland, it was a mixed house, a *conhospitae*, in which religious of both sexes lived, worked and raised their children in the service of Christ.

As they made their way through the cloisters of the abbey, the students and religious respectfully stood aside to allow the abbot's passage, heads bowed in deference. The students were young men and women from many nations who came to the five kingdoms to receive their education. At the door of the abbot's chambers,

Cathal halted and opened it, ushering Fidelma inside.

A large, elderly man of imposing appearance was standing beside the abbot's table. He turned with a broad smile on his face as Fidelma entered. He was still handsome and energetic looking in spite of his silver hair and obvious advanced years. He wore a gold chain of office over his cloak. Had not his physical appearance distinguished him, his chain of office proclaimed him as a man of rank.

Fidelma recognised him at once.

'Beccan! It is good to see you again.'

The Chief Brehon returned her smile. He came forward and took both her hands in his.

'To meet with one who is the subject of affection as well as professional esteem is always a matter of joy for me, Fidelma.'

His expression and warmth of his greeting were not matters of protocol but of genuine emotion.

Fidelma was aware of a hollow cough behind her and she turned with a look of inquiry. The figure of a brother of the cloth stood with hands folded into his homespun brown woollen robes. His tonsure was different from the tonsure of the blessed John, as worn by the religious of the five kingdoms of Éireann. It was a Roman tonsure. His face was solemn but his dark brown eyes contained a twinkling mirth as he bowed his head in greeting to her.

'Brother Eadulf!' breathed Fidelma quickly. 'I thought you were in attendance on my brother in Cashel?'

'That I was. Yet there was little to do at Cashel and when I heard that Beccan was coming here in search of you, I offered to accompany him.'

'Coming to find me?' Fidelma suddenly remembered the words of the abbot. 'What is amiss?'

She swung round to the elderly Brehon. Abbot Cathal went to seat himself behind his desk while the Chief Brehon addressed Fidelma.

'There is some disturbing news, sister,' Beccan began solemnly. Then he shrugged and smiled apologetically. 'Forgive me, first I should say that your brother rests well in his capital of Cashel. He sends his warmest greetings to you.'

Fidelma did not bother to explain that Abbot Cathal had already assured her of her brother's safety.

'Then what is the disturbing news . . . ?'

Beccan paused a moment as if to gather his thoughts.

'Yesterday afternoon there came to Cashel a messenger from the clan of Eber of Araglin.'

The name was immediately familiar to Fidelma and it took her a moment to register that the name had occurred in the very last case which she had judged that afternoon. Eber was chieftain of the area from which Archú and his compassionless cousin had come to plead before her.

'Go on,' she prompted guiltily for Beccan had paused again when he observed that her thoughts were wandering

'The messenger reported that Eber had been murdered along with one of his relatives. Someone was caught at the scene of the crime.'

'What has this to do with me?' Fidelma asked.

Beccan made a gesture with his hand as if to express apology.

'I am on my way to Ros Ailithir, on your brother's business. It is urgent business and I cannot afford the time to journey to Araglin and conduct a proper investigation. Your brother, the king, was concerned that this matter should immediately be investigated and that justice be dispensed. Eber of Araglin has been a good friend to Cashel and your brother thought it fitting that you . . .'

Fidelma could guess the rest.

'That I go to Araglin,' she ended with a sigh. 'Well, the business here is concluded and I was planning to join my brother in Cashel tomorrow. I suppose that it matters little if I arrive a day or so later than I expected to. Yet, I do not fully understand, what is there to investigate in Araglin if the culprit is already caught, as you say? Is there some doubt as to his guilt?'

Beccan shook his head firmly.

'None that I know,' he assured her. 'I am told that the murderer was caught with a dagger in his hand and blood on his clothes as he stood over the body of Eber. Your brother, however . . .'

Fidelma grimaced wryly.

'I know. Eber was a friend to Cashel and justice must be seen to be done and done fairly.'

'There is no Brehon in Araglin,' interposed Abbot Cathal, in order to explain the position. 'It is more a matter of ensuring that justice is properly conducted.'

'Is there any reason to suspect it might be otherwise?'

Abbot Cathal spread his hands as if to imply the question was not so clear cut.

'Eber was, by all accounts, a very popular chieftain with a reputation for kindliness and generosity. He was apparently well liked by his people. There might be a tendency to punish the culprit without recourse to justice and the strict letter of the law.'

Fidelma gazed into his troubled eyes for a few moments. Cathal knew the mountain people around Lios Mhór better than most for he was one of them. She nodded briefly in acknowledgment of his concern.

'I have had an example in my court of how at least one man of the clan of Araglin has little respect for the law,' she mused. 'Tell me more about the people of Araglin, Father Abbot.'

'Little to tell. They are a close-knit people who are usually resentful of outsiders. Eber's clan lives mainly in the mountains around a settlement which is called the *rath* of the chieftain of Araglin. The lands stretch to the east along the Araglin river which flows through the glen. It is rich farmland. Eber's clan keep themselves to themselves and distrust strangers. It will not be an easy task that you undertake.'

'You say that they have no Brehon? Have they a priest?'

'Yes; Father Gormán is to be found at the *rath*. There is a chapel there which is called Cill Uird, the church of ritual. He has lived twenty years among the people of Araglin. He was trained here, at Lios Mhór. You will doubtless find him of valuable assistance to you although he has certain dogmatic views on the propagation of the Faith which you might find yourself in conflict with.'

'How so?' inquired Fidelma with interest.

Cathal smiled disarmingly.

'I think it better if you discover for yourself so that I do not bias you one way or another.'

'I suppose he is an advocate of Roman custom,' Fidelma sighed.

Abbot Cathal grimaced.

'You are very discerning, sister. Yes. He believes the Roman ways are better than our native customs. He has some support in this for he has built a Roman chapel at Ard Mór which is becoming renowned for its opulence. Father Gormán seems to have rich supporters.'

'Yet he still dwells in such an isolated spot as Cill Uird,' remarked Fidelma. 'That is curious.'

'Do not look for mysteries that do not exist,' rebuked Abbot Cathal, though with a smile. 'Father Gormán is a man of Araglin but believes in propagating his interpretation of the Faith as well.'

Beccan was regarding her doleful countenance with amusement. He shook his head playfully.

'The trouble, Fidelma of Kildare, is that you are too good at your profession. Your wisdom is becoming a by-word throughout the five kingdoms of Éireann.'

'The thought does not please me,' muttered Fidelma. 'I serve the law not for personal esteem. I serve it to bring justice to the people.'

Beccan took her irritation in good spirits.

'And in doing so, Fidelma, you are known as a just person with an ability to solve contentious conundrums. In the wake of your successes comes your reputation. You must accept that with good grace. But now . . .'

He turned decisively to Abbot Cathal.

'I must be on my way for I wish to get to Ard Mór before nightfall. *Vive valeque*, Cathal of Lios Mhór.'

'*Vive, vale*, Beccan.'

With a quick smile to Fidelma and a nod to Eadulf, the elderly man was gone, leaving the room almost before they had realised he had departed.

Fidelma turned to Brother Eadulf curiously.

'Are you not continuing the journey with Beccan? Where do you go from here, Eadulf?'

The dark-eyed monk, who had shared many of her adventures, was indifferent.

'I thought that I would accompany you to Araglin; that is if you have no objection. I would be interested in seeing a part of this land that I have never seen before.'

Fidelma's lips quirked in a mischievous grin at Eadulf's diplomatic reply which was obviously framed to placate any inquisitive thought that the abbot had.

Eadulf was a hereditary *gerefa* or magistrate of his people, the South Folk Saxons. He had been converted to the Christian faith by an Irish missionary, Fursa, and sent to the great colleges of Éireann for his education, studying firstly at the monastery of Durrow and then at the famous college of medicine at Tuaim Brecain. Then Eadulf had left the Church of Colmcille for the Church of Rome. He had become secretary to Theodore, the new archbishop of Canterbury, appointed by Rome. Theodore sent him back to Ireland as an emissary to Fidelma's brother Colgú of Cashel. Eadulf was perfectly at home in the five kingdoms, whose language he spoke fluently.

'You may join me and welcome, Eadulf,' she replied softly. Then: 'Have you a horse?'

'Your brother kindly loaned me a mount for this journey.'

Usually the religious did not ride on their journeys. Fidelma's ownership of a horse was merely a recognition of her rank and her office as a Brehon of the courts of law.

'Excellent. Perhaps we should make a start upon our journey immediately. There are still many hours of daylight left.'

'Would it not be wiser to wait until dawn tomorrow?' asked Abbot Cathal. 'You will not get to Araglin by nightfall.'

'There is bound to be a hostel along the way,' replied Fidelma with easy assurance. 'If there is a possibility of preemptive action against the accused by Eber's people, without them waiting for the matter to be dealt with by law, then the quicker I get to Araglin, the better.'

Cathal agreed, albeit reluctantly.

'As you will, Fidelma. But the mountains are no place to be caught abroad at night without shelter.' The abbot, however, was only too well aware that he was not talking to a simple religieuse but to the sister of his king. What she decided was not something he could challenge with any authority. 'I will get one of our brothers to prepare food and drink for your journey and see that your horses are watered and saddled.'

Abbot Cathal rose and left the room.

As the door shut behind him a metamorphosis overcame the solemn features of Fidelma. She wheeled round and caught the hands of the Saxon monk. There was a bubbling humour in her green-blue eyes. The natural expression of merriment on her fresh, attractive face would make even the most sombre of religious wonder why such an alluring young woman had taken up the life of holy orders. Her tall, yet well-proportioned figure seemed to express a desire for a more active and joyous role in life than that in the cloistered confines of a religious community.

'Eadulf! But I had heard that you were on your way back to the land of the Saxons?'

Eadulf's expression reformed itself in an embarrassed grin at her enthusiasm at seeing him again.

'Not yet awhile. When I heard that Beccan was coming to find you, in order to send you on this journey to Araglin, I told your brother that I would like to see something of the country and the law in operation. It gives me an excuse to stay a little longer in this land.'

'It is good that you have come. If the truth be told, I was so bored here in Lios Mhór. It will be good to get up into the mountains; into the sweet air and have someone to talk with about this and that . . .'

Eadulf laughed. It was a pleasant, good-natured laugh.

'I have learnt what your sort of talk means,' he replied pointedly.

This time it was her turn to laugh. She had missed the debates which she used to have with Eadulf. Missed the way she could tease Eadulf over their conflicting opinions and philosophies; the way he would always rise with good humour to the bait which she threw at him. Their arguments would rage but there was no enmity between them. They learned together as they examined their interpretations of the moral principles of the founding fathers of their Faith and passionately contested their ideas of life.

Eadulf was suddenly serious as he gazed at her animated features.

'I, too, have missed our talks,' he said quietly.

They stared at one another in silence and then the door opened abruptly and Abbot Cathal came in. They moved apart in embarrassment.

'It is done. The food will be ready. In fact, you are in luck. I am told that there is a farmer from Araglin who is just about to start on his return journey there. He can guide you on your way.'

Fidelma regarded him hesitantly.

'A farmer? Is he young or middle-aged?' she queried cautiously.

Abbot Cathal stared perplexed for a moment and then shrugged.

'He is young. There is a young girl with him as well. Does this have some relevance?'

'In this case, it does not matter.' Fidelma shook her head with solemn amusement. 'But had the farmer been an older man then I think it might well have made a difference. You see,' she decided to explain to the clearly puzzled abbot, 'I have just made a judgment against a middle-aged farmer – one Muadnat. He might not take kindly to my company.'

Abbot Cathal still looked bemused.

'But all must accept the judgment of law.' He seemed unable to contemplate the concept that a judgment under the law could cause any resentful emotions.

'Not everyone accepts it in good grace, abbot,' replied Fidelma. 'But now I think that it is time that Brother Eadulf and I were on our way.'

Abbot Cathal appeared reluctant to let them depart.

'This may be the last time we see each other, Fidelma; at least for a while.'

'Why so?' she asked curiously.

'Next week I shall be setting out on a pilgrimage to the Holy Land. It has been my ambition for many years now. Brother Nemon will take my place as abbot here.'

'The Holy Land?' Fidelma sounded wistful. 'That is a journey that one day I, too, hope to make. I wish you great joy of the journey, Cathal of Lios Mhór. May God be on every road you travel.'

She held out her hand to the abbot who took it and clasped it firmly.

'And may He continue to inspire your judgments, Fidelma of Kildare,' the abbot replied solemnly. He smiled at them both in turn and half raised a hand in blessing. 'To the end of the road – peace and safety.'

Chapter Three

In the flagged courtyard of the abbey, they found the young man, Archú, with the girl who had been with him in the chapel. They were waiting impatiently, seated in the shade of the cloisters. Nearby two horses stood already saddled. Archú stood up and approached Sister Fidelma as she appeared. He still reminded her of an eager puppy awaiting his master's pleasure.

'I am told that you need a guide to take you to the land of Araglin, sister. I am pleased to be able to offer my service to you since you have restored my land and my honour.'

Fidelma shook her head, restraining a smile at his youthful dignity.

'I have told you before, the law was the only arbiter in that matter. You owe no debt to me.'

She turned as the young girl now approached, eyes down cast. She was attractive, slim and fair-haired and Fidelma estimated that she was no more than sixteen years of age.

Archú introduced her with a self-conscious air.

'This is Scoth. Now that I have my land, we are to be married. I shall ask our priest, Father Gormán, to arrange it as soon as we get home.'

The young girl blushed happily.

'Even had the judgment gone against you, I would still have married you,' she rebuked him gently. She turned to Fidelma. 'That was why I followed Archú here. It would not have mattered to me which way your judgment went. Truly it would not.'

Fidelma regarded the young girl gravely.

'But it is just as well, Scoth, that the judgment went well. Now

27

you are to marry an *ocáire* and not a landless man.'

In turn, Fidelma introduced Brother Eadulf to them. One of the brothers had been packing food and drink for the journey into the saddle bags of the horses and now came forward leading the two mounts by their bridles. She noticed that Archú and Scoth each carried a bundle and a blackthorn staff. She realised that there were no other horses in the courtyard and it was clear that they had no mounts, not even an ass to ride.

Archú noticed her frown and correctly guessed what was passing through her mind.

'We do not have horses, sister. There are horses on the farm in Araglin but, of course, I was not allowed to take them for the journey here. And my cousin, Muadnat,' he hesitated and his pronunciation of the name was tinged with bitterness, 'has already left with Agdae, his chief cowman. So we must return as we came . . . on foot.'

Fidelma shook her head gently.

'No matter,' she replied cheerfully. 'Our horses are strong mounts and you are but small extra weight. Scoth can ride behind me while you, Archú, can get up behind Brother Eadulf.'

It was mid-afternoon when they turned through the large wooden gates of the monastery and walked the horses along a path by the broad river with the mountains rising immediately to the north of them.

Archú, seated behind Eadulf, pointed across his shoulder.

'Araglin lies up in those mountains,' he called eagerly. 'We will have to rest somewhere in their midst tonight but you will be in Araglin before midday tomorrow.'

'Where were you planning to spent the night?' asked Fidelma, as she turned her horse across the narrow wooden bridge which spanned the great river in the direction of the tall northern peaks.

'Within a mile or so we'll leave the northern road to Cashel and begin to ascend through hilly country towards the land of Araglin, along the west side of a small river that rises in those mountains,' replied Archú. 'It is heavily wooded country. Along that path there is a tavern should you wish to spend the night there. We should reach there just before nightfall.'

'Then the next day's journey will be easy,' chimed in the girl, Scoth, from behind Fidelma. 'It will be but a few hours' ride across the head of the great glen and down into the valley of Araglin which takes you straight to the *rath* of the chieftain of Araglin.'

Brother Eadulf turned his head slightly.

'Do you know why we are heading there?'

Archú contrived to shrug on his perch behind the monk.

'The Father Abbot did tell us the news from Araglin,' he replied.

'Did you know Eber?' asked Fidelma. The youth had not seemed unduly alarmed that his chieftain had been murdered. She was interested by his lack of concern.

'I knew *of* him,' Archú admitted. 'Indeed, my mother was related to him. But most people in Araglin are related in some way. My mother's farm was in an isolated valley known as the valley of the Black Marsh, which is some miles from the *rath* of the chieftain. We had little cause to go to the *rath* of the chieftain. Nor did Eber ever come to see my mother. Her marriage to my father was not approved of by her family. Father Gormán came to visit us now and then but never Eber.'

'And you, Scoth? Did you know Eber?'

'I was an orphan, raised as a servant on Muadnat's farm. I never was allowed to go to the *rath* of the chieftain, though I saw Eber several times when he came to feast or hunt with Muadnat. And once he came to Muadnat's farmstead some years ago to raise the clan to battle against the Uí Fidgente. I remember him as being in the same mould as Muadnat. I have seen him drunken and abusive.'

'My father, Artgal, answered his call and went off to fight the Uí Fidgente but never returned,' added Archú angrily.

'So there is little you can tell me about Eber?'

'What is it that you wish to know?' asked Archú with interest.

'I would like to know about the sort of person he was. You say that you have seen him drunk and abusive. But was he an able chieftain of his people?'

'Most people spoke well of him,' Archú offered. 'I think he was well-liked but when I sought advice from Father Gormán, about making a legal claim against Muadnat, he advised me to take the claim to Lios Mhór rather than appeal directly to Eber.'

Fidelma found this a curious piece of advice for a priest to give. After all, the first step in any litigation was an appeal to the clan chieftain; even a petty chieftain of a small sept had the right to make an initial judgment. She was reminded that Beccan had mentioned that Araglin did not have a Brehon to advise on the law, so perhaps Father Gormán's advice was sound enough and not a reflection on the prejudice of Eber.

'Did Father Gormán offer any reason why you should appeal directly to Lios Mhór?' she asked.

'None.'

'Isn't it curious that two people can be raised in a clan territory yet hardly see the chieftain of their clan?' Eadulf questioned.

Archú laughed disarmingly.

'Araglin is not some small territory. You could easily get lost among the mountains. Indeed, you might dwell all your life there and not meet the neighbour on the other side of the hill. My farmstead,' the boy paused and savoured the phrase, 'my farmstead, as I have said, is in an isolated valley and there is only one other farmstead in it, the farm of Muadnat.'

Scoth sighed deeply.

'It is to be hoped our lives will be different now. I hardly knew the countryside beyond Muadnat's kitchen.'

'Why didn't you run away from Muadnat then?' asked Fidelma.

'I did as soon as I was of legal age. But where could I go? I was soon brought back to his farmstead.'

Fidelma raised her eyebrows in astonishment.

'Were you taken back by force? By what right did Muadnat

force you back? You were not one of the unfree class?'

'Unfree class?' interposed Eadulf. 'Slaves, you mean? I did not think there were slaves in the five kingdoms.'

'There are not,' replied Fidelma immediately. 'The "unfree class" is the class who have no rights at all within the clan.'

'What are they but slaves?'

'Not so. They consist of those who were prisoners, taken in war, hostages and cowards who deserted their clan in time of need. They also include law breakers who could not or would not pay the compensation and fines judged against them. These are deprived of all civil rights but not excluded from society. They are placed in a position where they have to contribute to its welfare. Of course, they could not bear arms or be elected to any office within the clan.'

Eadulf pulled a face.

'It sounds like slavery to me.'

Fidelma showed her annoyance.

'The "unfree class" are divided into two groups. One group can rent and work on the land and pay taxes while the other are those who are untrustworthy and in constant rebellion against the system. Anyone in either position can redeem themselves by working until the fines are met.'

'And if they are not met?' queried Eadulf.

'Then they remain in that position, without civil rights, until they die.'

'So their children become slaves?'

'Not slaves!' Fidelma corrected again. 'And the law states "every dead person kills their own liabilities". Their children become full citizens once again.'

She caught the smile of amusement around Eadulf's mouth and wondered whether he was using her tactic of playing devil's advocate in order to provoke her. She had often used this stratagem to bait Eadulf in the past about his beliefs. Could it be that Eadulf had finally learnt a more subtle humour? She

31

was about to say something when the girl, Scoth, intervened.

'I was not of the "unfree class",' she said hotly, reminding them of the origin of the discussion. 'Muadnat was simply my legal guardian and had control of me until I reached the age of choice. He had no hold on me after that but I had nowhere to go. I left his farmstead but there was nowhere I could get work and so I had to return.'

'Things will be different now,' Archú insisted.

'Well, I would caution you to beware of Muadnat,' Fidelma advised. 'He struck me as a man who harbours grudges.'

Archú agreed emphatically.

'That I do know. I shall be watchful, sister.'

The track along which Fidelma and Eadulf guided their horses began to rise more rapidly up into the hills, away from the stately pushing river, upwards towards the more towering rounded bald peaks of the mountains, which poked up from the skirting forests. The lower periphery of the hills was thickly forested but the track across the mountain had been used for countless centuries so that the trees fell away on either side leaving a fairly clear roadway which even a good sized wagon could traverse in dry weather.

The air was still, the quiet broken only by the heavy snorting breath of the horses as they moved upwards. Now and again they could hear the excited yap of wild dogs and the protesting howl of a wolf, warning against intrusion into its territory.

The sun was already dipping below the peaks to the west and long shadows were spreading rapidly. As the sun began to disappear, the air turned chill. Fidelma was reminded that tomorrow would be the feast in remembrance of Conláed of blessed name, a skilled metalworker of Kildare who had fashioned the sacred vessels for Brigid's monastery. She must remember to light a candle in his name. But the thought caused her to acknowledge that they were already into the month regarded as the first month of the summer period which ended with the feast of Lughnasa, one of the popular pagan festivals which the new Faith had been unable to abolish. The horses climbed slowly and deliberately and Eadulf began to cast nervous glances towards the glowing tip of sunlight behind them to the west.

'It will be dark before long,' he observed unnecessarily.

'It is not far now,' Archú assured him. 'See that bend in the road to our right? We take the small path there, leaving this main track, and moving higher into the mountains along the side of the stream which crosses our road there.'

They fell silent again as they turned into the dark oak forests where there was now room for only one horse to tread the clearly unfrequented path. One behind the other the two horses plodded through the narrow defile amidst sedate oaks and tall yews. A further hour passed. Twilight descended rapidly.

'Are you sure that we are on the right path?' demanded Eadulf, not for the first time. 'I see no sign of a tavern.'

Patiently, the youth, Archú, pointed forward.

'You will see it once we reach the next bend in the track,' he guaranteed the Saxon monk.

It was beyond dusk now; in fact, it was almost dark and they could barely see the turning along the tree lined path. Although there were no clouds in the sky, the trees also hid a clear view of the night sky. Only a few bright stars could be clearly seen through the canopy of branches. Among them Fidelma noticed the bright twinkling of the evening star dominating the heavens. They had been climbing along this mountain path for a full hour, wending their precarious way through the darkening trees which oppressed them on every side. They had encountered no one else on the road since they left the main thoroughfare. Even Fidelma was beginning to wonder whether it was unwise to press further. Perhaps it would be better to halt, prepare a fire and make the best of it for the night.

She was about to make this suggestion when they came to the bend in the path. It abruptly opened out into a broader track.

They saw the light as soon as they reached the bend.

'There it is,' announced Archú with satisfaction. 'Just as I said it would be.'

A short distance ahead of them, by the side of the track, a lantern flickered from the top of a tall post on a short stretch of *faitche*, or lawn, which stretched to a stone building. Fidelma knew that, according to law, all taverns or public hostels, *bruden* as they were called, had to announce themselves by displaying a lighted lantern all through the night.

They halted their horses by the post. Fidelma saw, incised in the Latin script on the wooden name-board below the lantern, the name '*Bruden na Réaltaí*' – the hostel of the stars. Fidelma glanced up to the sky, for the canopy of branches no longer obscured it, and saw the myriad of twinkling silver lights spread across the heavens. The hostel was aptly named.

They had barely halted when an elderly man threw open the door of the hostel and came hurrying forward to greet them.

'Welcome, travellers,' he cried in a rather high pitched voice. 'Go inside and I will attend to your horses. Get you in, for the night is chill.'

Inside, the hostel seemed deserted. A great log fire was crackling in the hearth at one end of the room. In a large cauldron, an aromatic broth simmered above the flames, its perfume permeating the place. It was warm and comforting. The lanterns were lit and flickering against the polished oak and red deal panels of the room.

Fidelma's eye was caught by a table on one side of the room on which, at first glance, seemed to be a scattered assortment of common rocks. She frowned and stooped to examine them closely, picking up one and feeling its heavy metallic weight. The rocks were polished and appeared to be placed as someone might arrange ornaments to give atmosphere to the room.

Shaking her head slightly in perplexity, Fidelma led the way to a large table near the fire but did not sit down. Hours in the saddle made her appreciate the comfort of standing a while.

It was Archú who approached her nervously.

'I am sorry, sister. I should have mentioned this before but neither Scoth nor I have any means to pay the hosteller. We will withdraw and camp the night in the woods outside. That was what we were going to do. It is a dry night and none too cold in spite of what our hosteller says,' he added.

Fidelma shook her head.

'And you an *ocáire*?' she gently chided. 'You have wealth enough now that you have won your plea to the courts. It would be churlish of me not to advance you the price of food and lodging for the night.'

'But . . .' protested Archú.

'No more of this,' Fidelma interrupted firmly. 'A bed is more comfortable than the damp earth and this simmering broth has a wonderful, inviting aroma.'

She gazed with curiosity around the deserted hostel.

'It seems that we are the only travellers on this road tonight,' Eadulf observed as he sprawled on a chair near the fire.

'It is not a busy road,' Archú explained. 'This is the only road which leads into the country of Araglin.'

Fidelma was immediately interested.

'If that is so and this is the only hostel along the route, it seems odd that we have not encountered your cousin Muadnat here.'

'God be thanked that we have not,' muttered Scoth as she took her seat at the table.

'Nevertheless, he and his companion . . .'

'That was Agdae, his cowman and nephew,' supplied Scoth.

'He and Agdae,' continued Fidelma, 'left Lios Mhór before us and they would surely have taken this road if it is the only one to Araglin.'

'Why worry about Muadnat?' Eadulf yawned, his eyes coveting the broth.

'I do not like questions that are unresolved,' Fidelma explained in a vexed tone.

The door opened. The elderly man appeared. They could see

in the light of the room that he was a man of fleshy features, greying hair and a pleasant manner that befitted his calling. His face was red, round and wreathed in a permanent smile.

He regarded the company warmly.

'Welcome again. I have stabled and attended your horses. My name is Bressal and I am entirely at your service. My house is yours.'

'We will require beds for the night,' Fidelma announced.

'Certainly, sister.'

'We will also require food,' added Eadulf quickly, looking longingly at the simmering contents of the cauldron once again.

'Indeed, and good mead to slack your thirst, no doubt?' agreed the hostel keeper breezily. 'My mead is regarded as the best in these mountains.'

'Excellent,' agreed Eadulf. 'You may serve . . .'

'We shall eat after we have washed the dust of travel from us,' Fidelma interrupted sharply.

Eadulf knew that it was the Irish custom to have a bath every evening before the main meal of the day. It was a custom that he had never really grown accustomed to for the ritual of daily bathing was not a practice of his own people. However, here it was regarded as a lack of social etiquette not to bathe before the evening meal.

'Your baths shall be prepared, but they will take a little while for I have no other help but my own two hands,' Bressal explained.

'I do not mind a cold bath,' Eadulf offered quickly. 'I am sure Archú is not bothered about a warm bath.'

The youth hesitated and shrugged.

Fidelma's mouth turned down in disapproval. She believed in the correct ritual of purification.

'Scoth and I will help Bressal heat the water for our baths,' she volunteered. 'You may do as you think fit,' she added with a glance of reproof at Eadulf.

Bressal spread his arms apologetically.

'I regret the inconvenience, sister. Come, I will show you the way to the bath house. For you, brother, there is a stream running beside the hostel. You may take a lamp with you, if it is your wish to bathe there.'

Archú picked up a lamp, although he looked somewhat reluctant having heard where the site of the bath house was located.

'I will carry the lamp,' he offered.

Eadulf clapped him on the shoulder.

'Come, little brother,' he encouraged. 'A cold wash never hurt anyone.'

It was over an hour later before they finally sat down to eat. The broth was of oatmeal and leeks enlivened by some herbs. And there was a dish of trout to follow; trout caught in the local stream, served with freshly baked bread and honey sweetened mead. Bressal was no novice when it came to cooking.

He kept up a lively conversation as he served them, recounting local pieces of information. But it was clear that he was isolated and he had certainly not yet heard of the murder of the chieftain of Araglin of which young Archú informed him, wishing to establish his new found position as a man of status in Araglin.

'Are we the only travellers on this road tonight?' Fidelma asked during a lull in the conversation.

Bressal pulled a face.

'You are the only travellers to stop here during the last week. Not many traverse this particular road to Araglin.'

'Then there are surely other roads?'

'Indeed there is one other. A track which runs from the east of the valley along which one might reach the south, Lios Mhór, Ard Mór and Dún Garbháin. This road is merely the one which joins the great road that runs north to Cashel or south to Lios Mhór. Why do you ask, sister?' There was a glint of curiosity in the hostel keeper's eyes.

Archú was frowning.

'I was told that this was the only road to Lios Mhór.'

'By whom?' demanded the hostel keeper.

'Father Gormán of Araglin.'

'Well, the eastern road is the quicker road to Lios Mhór,' Bressal insisted. 'He should know better.'

Fidelma decided to change the subject and indicated the collection of rocks on the side table. 'You have a curious collection of ornaments there, my friend.'

Bressal was dismissive.

'Not mine. I did not collect them. My brother, Morna, is a miner, working in the mines which lie to the west of here on the Plain of Minerals. He picked up these rocks during his work. I keep them for him.'

Fidelma appeared to be very interested in the rocks, picking them up and turning them over in her hands.

'They are very intriguing.'

'Morna has been collecting them for years. It was only a couple of days ago that he came here, full of excitement, saying that he had discovered something that would make him rich. He had a rock with him. How a rock would make him rich I do not know. He spent a night here and left the next day.'

'Which was the rock he brought with him?' Fidelma asked, intrigued as she ran her eye over the collection.

Bressal rubbed the back of his head.

'I confess that I am not sure now.' He picked one up. 'This one I think.'

Fidelma took it and held it in her hands, turning it over. To her untrained eye it was just an ordinary piece of granite. She handed it back to the hostel keeper. He replaced the rock on the table.

'Can I get you anything else before you retire for the night?' he asked, turning to the company.

Archú and Scoth decided to retire while Eadulf asked for another cup of mead and announced he would sit by the fire awhile longer. Fidelma sat talking to Bressal for hostel keepers were always a good source of information. She turned the conversation to Eber. Bressal had only seen Eber half-a-dozen times passing from his territory on the road to Cashel. He had little knowledge to form an opinion of him, though he said that he had heard mixed opinions of the man. Some thought he was a bully while others praised him for his kindliness and generosity.

It was still early when Fidelma announced that she would retire to bed. Bressal had allocated Fidelma a corner of the main sleeping area which consisted of the entire top floor of the hostel. It was a curtained off space, for it was unusual in tiny hostels to find separate rooms for those spending the night. The bed was no more than a straw palliasse on the floor and a rough woollen blanket. It was clean, warm and comfortable and she would ask no more.

It appeared to her that her head had barely lain on the straw when she was startled awake. A warm hand was gripping her arm and squeezing gently. She blinked and began to struggle but a voice whispered: 'Hush. It is I.'

It was Eadulf's voice.

She lay still, blinking a moment.

'There are some armed men outside the hostel,' Eadulf continued, his voice pitched so low that she could barely hear it.

Fidelma was aware that the window was filled with a curious grey light and while, through its uncurtained aperture, she could still see one or two tiny bright points of stars reluctant to leave the sky, she realised that dawn was not far away.

'What is it that worries you about these armed men?' she demanded, following Eadulf's example and keeping her voice low.

'The sound of horses woke me fifteen minutes ago,' Eadulf explained quietly. 'I peered out and saw the shadows of half a dozen riders. They rode up silently but did not come to the hostel. They hid their horses in the woods beyond and took up positions among the trees before the hostel door.'

Fidelma sat up abruptly. She was wide awake now.

'Outlaws?'

'Perhaps. It seems to me that they mean no good to this hostel for they all carried bows with them.'

'Have you alerted Bressal?'

'I woke him first. He is downstairs securing the doors in case we are attacked.'

'Has he been attacked before?'

'Never. Sometimes the richer hostels along the main road between Lios Mhór and Cashel have been attacked and robbed by groups of outlaws. But why would anyone choose this isolated hostel to rob?'

'Are the youngsters awake?'

'The youngsters? Oh, you mean Archú and Scoth. Not yet. I came . . .'

There was a curious whooshing sound from outside and Fidelma momentarily caught the smell of fire. A second whoosh barely registered on her ears as an arrow sped through the window and embedded itself in the wall beyond. Straw, fastened around the arrow, had been set alight. Now there came the sounds of a man calling orders from outside.

Fidelma leapt from her bed.

'Wake the others. We are being attacked.' The last sentence was unnecessary as another flaming arrow flashed into the room and embedded itself into the floor. She ran forward and grasped it, without concern for the hungry flames. She turned and threw it through the window before reaching for the first arrow and sending it after the other through the window. Turning again, she grabbed her robe and dragged it over her head. Almost without pausing, she pulled down the curtained partitions in case an arrow ignited them. Archú, awakened by Eadulf, came running forward to help her.

'Stay here,' instructed Fidelma. 'Keep down but if any lighted arrows land in the room make sure the flames are put out.'

Without waiting for a reply she turned away and hurried down the stairs into the main room.

40

Bressal, the hostel keeper, was busily stringing a bow. It was clear that he was unpractised for he was clumsy.

He glanced up, his usually cheerful face was creased with anger.

'Outlaws!' he muttered. 'I have never known outlaws in these woods. I must defend the hostel.'

Eadulf now came racing down the stairs.

'You said that you saw these men,' Fidelma greeted him. 'How many did you estimate there are?'

'About half a dozen,' replied Eadulf.

Fidelma compressed her lips so hard that they almost hurt. She was trying hard to think of a means of defending the hostel.

'Do you have any other weapons, Bressal?' Eadulf demanded. 'We have nothing to defend ourselves with.'

The hostel keeper stared at him in surprise that a man of the Faith should be asking for weapons to defend himself with.

'Quickly, man!' snapped Eadulf.

Bressal jerked in obedience.

'I have two swords and this bow, that's all.'

Eadulf eyed the bow speculatively. It looked a good one, made of yew, strong and pliable, so far as he could judge.

'How well can you use that?'

'Not well,' Bressal confessed.

'Then give it to me. Take a sword.'

Bressal was bemused.

'But you are a brother of . . .'

It was Fidelma who cut him short by stamping her foot.

'Give the bow to him!'

Eadulf almost grabbed the bow from his hand and strung it with an ease born of long experience.

'Give me one of the swords,' Fidelma instructed as Eadulf tested the string. There was no time to explain to the astounded hostel keeper that as daughter of a Failbe Flann, king of Cashel, she had grown up using a sword almost before she had learnt to read and write.

Eadulf took the handful of arrows that were on the table.

'Is there a back door?' he questioned.

Bressal gestured wordlessly in the direction of the rear of the hostel.

Eadulf and Fidelma exchanged a quick glance.

'I mean to sneak out the back and try to circle behind these carrion,' he replied in answer to her silent question.

'I'll come with you,' replied Fidelma at once.

Eadulf did not waste time arguing.

Fidelma glanced to Bressal.

'Our young companions are above and will attempt to put out the lighted arrows that fall into the room. You stay here and do the same but be sure that you bar the door after us.'

Bressal said nothing. Events were happening too quickly for him to protest.

Eadulf, with bow and arrows, followed by Fidelma, gripping the sword which Bressal had thrust into her hand, moved to the back door. Bressal unbarred it and, looking swiftly out, motioned to them that it was safe to leave. Eadulf hastened across the yard into the trees beyond. Fidelma followed a moment later, thanking the saints that the attackers, whoever they were, did not have the sense to completely surround the hostel.

Once into the cover of the woods, Eadulf moved cautiously, swinging around the hostel towards the roadway which ran in front of it. They could see several more arrows had been released towards the front of the hostel, one or two falling onto its thatched roof. Soon the place would be ablaze unless the attack was quickly beaten off.

The air was cold but the light was sharp now as the sun began to rise.

Fidelma, peering through the cover of the trees, saw the shadowy figures in the underbrush opposite. She knew enough to realise that they were not professional warriors for they made no good use of the cover and were shouting to each other thus revealing their positions. It was clear that they did not expect any real opposition from the hostel keeper and his guests. It occurred to Fidelma that it was curious that they did not simply burst into the hostel and rob the occupants, if that was their intention. It seemed as if they merely wanted to burn the place down.

Eadulf had strung an arrow and was waiting the next move.

Fidelma's eyes narrowed.

One of the men, shooting the flaming arrows into the hostel, stood up to aim, presenting a clear target in the early morning light. Fidelma touched Eadulf's arm lightly and gestured towards the figure. She had no wish to kill anyone, even though the man seemed intent on destroying the hostel, but it was too late to instruct Eadulf how to ply the bow.

Eadulf raised the bow and aimed quickly but carefully. She saw his arrow embed itself in the shoulder of the man, the shoulder of the bow arm. She could not have done it better. The assailant gave a sudden scream and dropped his own bow, clasping his bleeding shoulder with his other hand.

There was a momentary silence.

Then hoarse voices cried out demanding to know what the matter was with the man. Someone ran towards the injured attacker through the trees, making a noise that any real warrior would be ashamed of. Eadulf had strung a second arrow and silently asked a question of Fidelma with a glance. She nodded.

A second bowman had appeared by the side of the injured man.

Eadulf took aim and released another missile.

Again he aimed carefully and hit the bow arm, his arrow striking the man's shoulder. The second man yelled more in surprise than in pain and began a furious cursing.

A third voice cried out in panic: 'We are being attacked. Let's go. Go!'

There was a clamour, the frenetic whinny of horses and the two injured men turned and stumbled, moaning and cursing, through the trees. Eadulf strung a third arrow.

Out of the surrounding forests came a small band of horsemen, urging their mounts to breakneck speed towards the narrow path ahead. Fidelma saw that, as Eadulf had said, there were no more than half a dozen men. She spotted the two injured men, precariously mounted. They came charging down the road, passing close to where Fidelma and Eadulf had taken up their positions. Eadulf was about to spring out at them, but Fidelma held him back.

'Let them go,' she instructed. 'We have been lucky so far.' Indeed, she uttered a prayer of thanks for professional fighting men would not have been so easily routed.

She stared up as the attackers rode by her and noticed the last man in the cavalcade, a burly man with a large reddish beard and ugly features, crouching low over his horse's neck. Eadulf had half raised his bow but let it drop with a shrug when he realised the rider failed to present a good enough target.

The band of horsemen quickly disappeared along the path and into the forests.

Eadulf turned to Fidelma in bewilderment.

'Why did we let them go?' he demanded.

Fidelma smiled tightly.

'We were lucky. If they had been warriors we would not have come away so lightly. Thank God that they were a group of cowards, but if you corner a coward, like a small frightened animal, he will fight savagely for his freedom. Besides, our attention is needed at the hostel. Look, the roof is already alight.'

She turned and hurried to the hostel, calling out to Bressal that the attackers had fled and to come out to help them.

Bressal found a ladder and within moments, they had formed a chain, passing buckets of water up to the thatch. It took a while but eventually the fire was doused and the thatch just damp and smoky. Bressal, gratefully, took a flagon of mead and poured cups for them all.

'I have to thank you for saving this hostel from those bandits,' he announced as he handed them the drink.

'Who were they?' demanded young Archú. 'Did you see any of them close to, sister?'

'Only a glimpse,' confessed Fidelma.

'At least two of them will have painful shoulders for a while,' Eadulf added grimly.

'This area is a poor part of the country,' Archú reflected wonderingly. 'It is strange that bandits would attempt to rob this hostel.'

'Rob?' Fidelma raised an eyebrow slightly. 'It seemed to me that they were trying to burn it down rather than rob it.'

Eadulf nodded slowly.

'That is true. They could have come up quietly enough and burst in, if they had wanted to simply rob the hostel and its guests.'

'Perhaps they were just passing by and seized the opportunity on the spur of the moment without any thought of a plan,' Bressal offered the explanation but his tone did not carry conviction.

Eadulf shook his head.

'Passing by? You said yourself that this road is not one used frequently and that it only leads in and out of Araglin.'

Bressal sighed.

'Well, I have never been attacked by outlaws before.'

'Do you have enemies, Bressal?' Eadulf pressed. 'Is there anyone who would want to see you driven out of this hostel?'

'No one,' affirmed Bressal with conviction. 'There is no one who would profit in any way by the destruction of this hostel. I have served here all my life.'

'Then . . .' Eadulf began but Fidelma interrupted sharply.

'Perhaps it was just a gang of plunderers searching for easy pickings. But they will have learnt a lesson for now.'

Eadulf looked as if he were about to say something but, catching Fidelma's eye, he clamped his jaw shut.

'It was lucky that you were here,' Bressal agreed, not noticing this interplay. 'I could not have beaten off the attack by myself.'

'Well, it is time to break our fast and be on our way,' Fidelma replied, realising that the morning hour was growing late.

After breakfast, Archú announced that he and Scoth would part company with them. The way to Archú's farmstead could be reached from this point without going towards the *rath* of Araglin. Archú and Scoth offered to spend an hour or two with Bressal helping him clean the hostel and repair the thatch while Fidelma and Eadulf continued on towards Araglin.

It was Bressal who suggested Fidelma and Eadulf might like to keep the weapons they had borrowed from him.

'As you have seen, I am not proficient with weapons. From what you tell me, these bandits rode off in the direction of Araglin and you do not want to encounter them unarmed along the way.'

Eadulf was about to accept the weapons but Fidelma pressed them back on Bressal with a shake of her head.

'We do not live by the sword. According to the blessed Matthew, the Christ told Peter that all who take the path of the sword shall perish by the sword. It is better to go into the world unarmed.'

Bressal grimaced wryly: 'Better to go out into the world able to defend yourself against those who are prepared to live by the sword.'

It was not until they were well on the path to Araglin that Eadulf challenged Fidelma on her unspoken interruption when he was about to voice his suspicion as to the origin of the attackers.

'Why did you not want me to point out what was only logical?'

'That the so-called bandits were probably from Araglin itself?'

'You suspect Muadnat, don't you?' he said, nodding agreement.

Fidelma repudiated the idea.

'I have no reason to suspect him. To bring up the question might put fear into Archú and Scoth unnecessarily. There are many other possibilities. Bressal might not be telling the truth when he says he knows of no enemies. This may, indeed, be simply an attack by illogical bandits. Or the attack may well have something to do with the death of Eber.'

The other possibilities had not entered Eadulf's mind but he was not convinced.

'You mean that someone involved with Eber's death could be trying to prevent your investigation?' he asked sceptically.

'I put it forward as an alternative to what you are suggesting, Eadulf. But I do not say that it provides the answer. We must be vigilant but assumptions without evidence can lead to a dangerous path.'

Chapter Four

The morning was warm and sunny as Fidelma and Eadulf made their way serenely through the tree crowded forest and emerged on a hillside track which gave a spectacular view across a valley about a mile in width, through which a sparkling silver river ran. While clumps of trees stood here and there, it was clear that the valley had long been cultivated for the woodlands which encircled the bald mountain tops had been cut back and a boundary of yellowing gorse stood between the cultivated fields and pastureland and the converging trees.

The ribbon of the river cut through the bright green of the valley pasture. The beauty of the place caught at Fidelma's breath. In the distance she could see a group of reddish-brown dots and as she focussed she saw a majestic red deer, a stag by his antlers, guarding a group of hind, some with small calves at their feet, brown little objects with white spots. Here and there, throughout the valley, were small grazing herds of cattle, moving slowly on the open pastureland around the stone bordered fields. The valley looked lush and enticing. It was rich farming country and the river, judging just by the run of it, would be replete with salmon and brown trout.

Eadulf leant forward in his saddle and surveyed the landscape approvingly.

'This Araglin appears to be a paradise,' he murmured.

Fidelma pursed her lips wryly.

'Yet there is a serpent in this particular paradise,' she reminded him.

'Perhaps the richness of this land could be a motive for murder?

A chieftain who has this wealth must be vulnerable,' Eadulf suggested.

Fidelma was disapproving.

'You should know our system well by now. Once a chieftain dies, the *derbfhine* of the family have to meet to confirm the tanist, the heir-elect, as chieftain and appoint a new tanist to the chieftainship. Only an heir-elect would benefit and so they would be the first to be suspect. No; it is rarely possible for someone to be murdered for their office.'

'The *derbfhine*?' queried Eadulf. 'I have forgotten what that consists of?'

'Three generations of the chieftain's family who elect one among them as the tanist and confirm the new chieftain in office.'

'Isn't it easier that the oldest male child inherit?'

'I know the way you Saxons deal with inheritance. We prefer that the person best qualified become chieftain rather than an idiot, chosen simply because they are the eldest son of their father,' declared Fidelma.

She looked across the valley and pointed.

'That must be the *rath* of the chieftain.'

Eadulf knew that a *rath* was a fortification but the group of buildings in the distance, some almost hidden among several tall beeches with their new brilliant green leaves, and several still flowering yews, was not a fortress. Yet the buildings were quite extensive, like a large village. Eadulf had seen many powerful chieftains living in stone built fortresses, in his travels in the five kingdoms, but this *rath* had the appearance of just wooden farm buildings and cabins. Looking more closely, he could see a few stone buildings among them, one of which was obviously the chapel of Cill Uird. He could also see, close by the chapel, a large round stone construction which he presumed was the chieftain's assembly hall.

His expression must have shown his surprise for Fidelma explained: 'This is farming country. The people of Araglin have the mountains as their protection. In turn they are a small community which threatens no one so there has probably never been a need to build a fortress to defend them against enemies. Nevertheless, in politeness we call a place where a chieftain dwells his *rath*.'

She nudged her horse forward and started down the mountain slope towards the valley bottom, towards the distant river and the *rath* of the chieftain of Araglin.

The track led across an open stretch of country running down the hillside. By the side of it stood a tall cross of carved granite. It stood nearly eighteen feet in height. Eadulf halted his horse and gazed up at the cross in admiration.

'I have never seen anything like this before,' he observed with a degree of awe which caused Fidelma to glance at him in amusement.

It was true that there were few such spectacular, high crosses in the kingdom. Its carved grey stone depicted scenes from the gospels, picked out in bright painted colours. Eadulf could identify the scene of the Fall from Grace, Moses smiting the Rock, the Last Judgment, the Crucifixion and other incidents. The summit of the cross was shaped as a shingle roofed church with gable finials. Carved at the base were the words '*Oroit do Eoghan lasdernad inn Chros*' – a prayer for Eoghan by whom the cross was made.

'A spectacular border mark for such a small community,' Eadulf observed.

'A small but rich community,' Fidelma corrected dryly, nudging her horse to continue its passage along the road.

It was noon when they grew near the *rath*. A boy, herding cattle, stopped to stare at them with open-mouthed interest as they passed. A man busy hoeing out the hairy pepperwort that had invaded his cereal crop paused and leant on his hoe, regarding them curiously as they rode by. At least, unlike the boy, he gave them a cheery greeting and received Fidelma's blessing in return. Dogs began to bark from the buildings ahead of them and a couple of hounds ran out towards them, yelping as they came but not threateningly so.

A well-constructed bridge of oak crossed the swiftly flowing river to the *rath* on the far bank. Now that they had come closer to the *rath*, Eadulf observed that between the river and the buildings there had once been a large earthen bank that encircled the buildings, though it was now overgrown with grass and brush, almost part of the verdant fields around. There were several sheep grazing in its depression. It showed that the buildings had once, long ago, been fortified. Now they were surrounded by wicker walls, interlaced pieces of hazel wood which, Eadulf guessed, were more to keep out roaming wolves or wild pigs than any human aggressor. A large gate in the wicker fence stood wide open.

The hooves of their horses struck hollowly on the wooden planking of the bridge as they crossed the river. They started up the short track to the gates.

A figure emerged between the gates; a muscular man yet beyond his middle years, with sword and shield, and a well-cut black beard flecked with silver, who stood in the middle of the path and regarded them with narrowed speculative dark eyes but with no hostile expression on his features.

'If you come in peace there is a welcome before you at this place,' he greeted them ritually.

'We bring God's blessing to this place,' returned Fidelma. 'Is this the *rath* of the chieftain of Araglin?'

'That it is.'

'Then we wish to see the chieftain.'

'Eber is dead,' replied the man, flatly.

'This we have already learnt. It is to his successor, the tanist, that we come.'

The warrior hesitated and then said: 'Follow me. You will find the tanist in the hall of assembly.'

He turned and led the way through the gates directly towards the large round stone structure. The doors of the building faced straight onto the open gates and had obviously been positioned for a purpose. No visitor to the *rath* could avoid it. It had been designed to impress. And, as if to add to the importance of the building, the stump of what must have been a great oak tree stood to one side of its main door. Even foreshortened, it stood twelve feet high and the top of it constituted a delicately carved cross. Even Eadulf knew enough of the customs of the country to realise that this was the ancient totem of the clan, its *crann betha* or tree of life, which symbolised the moral and material well-being of the people. He had heard that sometimes, if disputes arose between the clans, then the worst thing that could happen would be a raid by the opposing clan to cut down or burn their rivals' sacred tree. Such an act would demoralise the people and cause their rivals to claim victory over them.

There was a wooden hitching post nearby. Fidelma and Eadulf slid from their horses and secured them. Several people within the *rath* had paused in their work or errands and stood examining the two religious with idle curiosity.

'We do not often get strangers in Araglin,' the warrior remarked, as if he felt the urge to explain the behaviour of his fellows. 'We are a simple farming community, not often troubled by the cares of the outside world.'

Fidelma felt no reply was needed.

The complex of buildings spoke of prosperity. They spread in a great semi-circle behind the stone building of the hall of assembly. There were stables and barns, a mill and a dovecot. Beyond these was a perimeter of several small wooden cabins and domestic dwellings which constituted a medium-sized village not to mention the house of the chieftain and his family. Fidelma mentally calculated that some dozen families must dwell in the *rath* of Araglin. Most impressive was the chapel, standing next to the assembly hall, with its dry stone and elegant structure. This, Fidelma noted, must be the church of Father Gormán called Cill Uird, the church of ritual.

The middle-aged warrior had gone to the wooden oak doors of the building. From a niche at the side of the doors he took a wooden mallet and beat at a wooden block. It resounded hollowly. It was the custom of chieftains to have a *bas-chrann*, or hand wood, outside their doors for visitors to knock before gaining admittance. The warrior vanished into the interior, closing the doors behind him.

Eadulf glanced at Fidelma.

'I thought such ritual only applied at the homes of great chieftains,' he muttered.

'Every chieftain is great in their own eyes,' Fidelma responded philosophically.

The doors reopened and the middle-aged warrior motioned them inside. They found themselves in a large single room of impressive proportions which was panelled by polished deal and oak. Along these panels hung shields, highly burnished pieces of bronze, some brilliantly enamelled. A few colourful tapestries were draped here and there. The floor was of oak planking, dark and ancient. There were several movable tables and benches. At one end stood a raised platform, no more than a foot high, on which was placed a magnificently carved oak chair adorned with the pelts of some animal. It was inlaid with polished bronze and some silver.

Although it was daylight outside, there were no windows within this great hall but several oil lamps, hanging from the beams, caused shadows to flicker and dance throughout the room and this effect was enhanced by a fire crackling in a hearth at one side of the room.

The warrior instructed them to wait and then withdrew leaving them alone.

They stood quietly, examining the opulence of the room carefully. If the room was meant to impress it certainly impressed Eadulf. Even Fidelma admitted to herself that the hall would not be out of place in her brother's palace at Cashel. Only a few moments passed before a lithe figure emerged from behind a tapestry curtain at the back of the raised platform and came to stand before the ornate chair. In the smoky atmosphere, Fidelma saw the figure was that of a young woman, scarcely more than nineteen years of age. She had corn-coloured long tresses and pale blue eyes. That she was attractive, there was no doubt. But the features seemed rather too hard for Fidelma to feel comfortable with them and the blue of the eyes was too cold. The mouth was set just a little too thinly so that the overall impression she had was of a person of unbending severity of nature. All this Fidelma deduced by a quick glance.

Fidelma noticed that she wore a dress of blue silk and matching shawl of dyed wool fastened with an elaborate gold brooch. She held her hands folded demurely before her. The young woman stood examining them with a questioning expression.

'I am Crón, tanist of the Araglin. I am told that you wish to see me?'

Her voice, though a mellow soprano, was not welcoming.

Fidelma hid her surprise that one so young could be chieftain-elect of a farming clan. Rural communities were usually conservative as to who they approved of as civil leaders over them.

'I believe that my arrival is expected,' she replied. She kept her tone formal.

The blonde-haired girl's face remained blank.

'Why should I be expecting members of the religious at this place?' she countered. 'Father Gormán fulfils all our needs in the matter of our Faith.'

Fidelma stifled a low impatient sigh.

'I am a *dálaigh* of the courts, asked to come to this place to investigate the death of Eber, your former chieftain.'

Crón's set expression flickered for a moment and then reformed into its expressionless rigidity.

'Eber was my father,' she said quietly, the only expression of emotion. 'He was murdered. It was without my approval that my mother sent to the king in Cashel requesting a *dálaigh*. I am capable of conducting an inquiry into this matter myself. However, I hardly expected the king of Cashel to answer me by sending one so young and presumably without knowledge of the world outside a religious cloister.'

Brother Eadulf, standing just behind Fidelma, saw her shoulders stiffen and tensed himself waiting for the inevitable blast of wrath from Fidelma. Instead, her voice remained calm, almost too calm.

'The king of Cashel, my brother Colgú . . .' Fidelma paused to allow the emphasis of her words to sink in. 'My brother asked me to come here to take personal charge of this matter. You may have no fear that I am without knowledge. I am trained to the level of *anruth*. I am tempted to believe that my years and experience will be in excess of your own, tanist of Araglin.'

The level of *anruth* was only one degree below the highest award that the secular and ecclesiastical colleges of Ireland could bestow.

There was a silence as both women stood regarding each other, cold blue eyes gazing deeply into sparkling green ones, each face a mask without emotion. Behind those masks, minds rapidly made assessments of the strengths and weaknesses of each other.

'I see,' Crón said slowly, putting a wealth of emotion in the pronouncement of the simple phrase. Then she returned to her sharp manner. 'And what is your name, sister of Colgú?'

'I am Fidelma.'

The cold gaze of the blonde woman now turned quizzically to Eadulf.

'This brother appears to be a stranger in our land.'

'This is Brother Eadulf . . .' introduced Fidelma.

'A Saxon?' queried Crón in surprise.

'Brother Eadulf is emissary of the archbishop of Canterbury at my brother's court in Cashel. He has been trained at our colleges and knows our country well. But he has expressed an interest to see how our legal processes work.'

It was not the entire truth but it would do for Crón.

The chieftainess regarded Eadulf sourly, inclining her head in greeting, no more than for etiquette's sake, before turning back to Fidelma. She made no attempt to invite them to sit neither did she attempt to do so herself.

'Well, this matter is a simple one. I, as tanist, could have dealt with it. My father was stabbed to death. The killer, Móen, was discovered still standing over his body with the knife in his hand, Móen's hands and clothes were covered in my father's blood.'

'I am told that someone else was also found dead at the same time?'

'Yes. My aunt, Teafa. She was found later. She had been stabbed to death, too. Móen had dwelt in her house and had been raised by her.'

'I see. Well, I shall wish to gather the basic facts. But, firstly, perhaps you would instruct someone to show us to your guests' quarters where we may clean ourselves after our journey? Food would not go amiss as it is after midday. When we have washed and eaten then we can start to question those involved in this matter.'

A flush crossed Crón's features at thus being instructed in her duties as host for such an action could be regarded as an insult had it been uttered by anyone of lesser rank than Fidelma. There was a steely glint in the cold blue eyes. For a moment Eadulf was sure that the young tanist was going to refuse. Then she shrugged and turned to a side table on which stood a small silver handbell. She picked it up and tinkled it loudly.

A moment or so passed in uncomfortable silence before an elderly woman, slightly stooped with greying hair, though it had once been fair, appeared through a side door. Her features were gaunt, the skin yellowing where once it had been tanned by a life spent mainly outdoors. The eyes were pale and suspicious. They darted here and there like the eyes of a nervous cat. In spite of her age, she gave the impression of strength, a woman used to the harsh life of farming. Her broad hands bore the callouses of years of toil. She moved with an anxious gait to Crón and bobbed her head.

'Dignait, please see to the needs of our . . . guests. Sister Fidelma is here to investigate the murder of my father. They will require accommodation, water to wash and food.'

The woman, Dignait, glanced towards Fidelma and Eadulf. Fidelma had the momentary impression that her eyes were startled and fearful. Then it was as if the lids hooded them.

'If you will both accompany me . . . ?' Dignait invited them almost woodenly.

Crón turned away with a suspicion of a sniff.

'When you are ready,' she called over her shoulder as she began to walk back towards the curtain behind her chair of office, 'I will explain to you the details of what took place.'

Dignait conducted them through a small side door out of the hall and across an open yard to the guests' hostel. It was a simple, single storey wooden building at the back of the hall of assembly, consisting of a single large room, partitioned into several sleeping cubicles by simple screens of polished deal. Behind each screen was a pallet of straw. A carved log of polished wood served as a pillow, a linen sheet and woollen rugs provided the bed coverings. Dignait ensured that they approved of the comfort of their beds. An open section of the building stretched before the cubicles, containing several benches with a table where guests could eat and which generally was used as living quarters. There was a hearth but no fire had been lit. When Dignait remarked on this fact, Fidelma said the weather was too clement for the need of a fire.

The wash room and privy were found beyond a second door at the far end of the guests' house. The door was marked with a small iron cross. Fidelma presumed that this was a sign of the work of Father Gormán for the privy was called a *fialtech*, or veil house, by certain religious who had picked up the concept from Rome. They believed the Devil dwelt within the privy and it became the custom to make the sign of the cross before entering it.

When Fidelma pointed out the needs of their horses, Dignait assured her that she would asked Menma, who was in charge of the stables, to wash and feed them.

Fidelma then expressed satisfaction with the accommodation but called Dignait to stay a moment when she would depart. Dignait seemed to pause with obvious reluctance.

'You must have been in service here for many years,' Fidelma opened the conversation.

The old woman's expression increased in suspicion. The eyes continued to be hooded but she did not refuse to answer.

'I have served the family of the chieftain of Araglin for just over twenty years,' she replied stiffly. 'I came here as servant to the mother of Crón.'

'And did you know Móen? The one who is accused of killing Eber?'

For a second Fidelma thought she saw that flicker of fear again.

'Everyone in the *rath* of Araglin knows Móen,' she commented. 'Who would not? Only a dozen families live here and most are related to the other.'

'And was Móen related to everyone?'

The old stewardess shivered perceptibly and genuflected.

'He was not! He was a foundling. Who knows from whose womb he sprang or whose seed cursed the womb? The lady Teafa, peace be upon her misguided soul, found him as a baby. That was a day of ill-fortune for her.'

'Is it known why Móen would kill Teafa, then, or Eber, the chieftain?'

'Surely only God would know that, sister? Now forgive me . . .' She turned away abruptly to the door. 'I have work to see to. While you have your wash, I will instruct Menma about your horses and see that food is brought to you.'

Fidelma stood staring at the closed door for a few seconds after the old woman had hurried away.

Eadulf looked questioningly at her.

'What troubles you, Fidelma?'

Fidelma lowered herself into a seat, reflectively.

'Maybe nothing. I have the distinct impression that this woman Dignait is afraid of something.'

Chapter Five

When they had cleansed themselves of the dust of the morning's travel and had eaten the midday meal, they returned to the hall of assembly and found Crón, who had been forewarned of their return, awaiting them. She had seated herself in her chair of office while seats had been arranged facing her below the dais.

Crón rose unwillingly as Fidelma and Eadulf entered. It was a small but reluctant token of respect due to the fact that Fidelma was the sister of the king of Cashel.

'Are you refreshed now?' queried Crón as she motioned them to the seats prepared for them.

'We are,' Fidelma replied, as she seated herself. She felt slightly irritated for she disliked being placed in a position where she had to look up to where Crón sat. Fidelma's rank as a *dálaigh*, and the degree of *anruth*, allowed her to speak on a level with kings let alone petty chieftains; and even in the presence of the High King at Tara, she could sit on the same level when invited and converse freely. Fidelma jealously guarded the observances of such etiquette but only when others made a point of their position which overlooked her status. However, there was no way of asserting her correct standing at this moment without causing outright hostility, and she wanted to be able to collect the facts of the case. So she resigned herself to the situation.

Eadulf followed her example and sat in the chair next to her, raising his interested gaze to the young female tanist.

'Now we may listen to the facts, as you know them, concerning the death of your father, Eber,' Fidelma said, leaning back in her chair.

Crón settled herself a moment, inclining forward a little in her chair, hands folded together, and allowed her eyes to focus on some object in the middle distance, between Fidelma and Eadulf.

'The facts are simple,' she intoned as if the subject wearied her. 'Móen killed my father.'

'You were witness to this act?' Fidelma prompted sharply after Crón made no attempt to amplify her statement.

Crón frowned in annoyance and glanced down at her.

'Of course not. You called for the facts. I gave them to you.'

Fidelma allowed her lips to thin in a smile.

'I think that it is best, and it serves the interests of justice, for you to tell me how this affair unfolded but from your own perspective only.'

'I am not sure that I know what you mean.'

Fidelma disguised an expression of impatience.

'At what point did you know that Eber had been slain?'

'I was awakened in the night . . .'

'Which was how many days ago?'

'It was six nights ago. Just before sunrise if you want me to be precise.'

Fidelma ignored the sneer in the young woman's voice.

'It is in everyone's interest in this matter to be as precise as one can,' she replied with icy politeness. 'Continue. Six nights ago you were awakened. By whom?'

Crón blinked as she picked up on the acid sweetness of the tone. It was clear that Fidelma was not going to be intimidated by her. She hesitated and then shrugged as if she conceded the skirmish of wills to Fidelma.

'Very well. Six nights ago I was awakened shortly before sunrise. It was the commander of my father's bodyguard, Dubán, who woke me. He had . . .'

'Merely confine yourself to what he actually told you,' cut in Fidelma in sharp warning.

Crón's voice came almost between clenched teeth. 'He reported

that something terrible had happened to Eber. He said that he
had been slain by Móen.'

'Were those the exact words he used?' Eadulf could not resist
posing the question.

Crón glanced at him with a frown and turned back to Fidelma
without deigning to reply.

'I asked him what had happened and he told me that Móen had
stabbed my father to death and that he had been caught in the act.'

'What did you do?' Fidelma asked.

'I rose and asked Dubán what he had done about Móen. He
told me that Móen had been restrained and taken to the stables
where he has been kept ever since that night.'

'And then?'

'I asked Dubán to fetch Teafa.'

'Teafa? Your aunt? Why would you do that?' Fidelma knew
well that both Crón and Dignait had told her that Teafa had raised
Móen from babyhood but she wanted to go over the story fact by
fact.

'I was told that Móen was raging and Teafa is . . . *was* the only
person who could handle him.'

'Because Teafa raised him?' queried Fidelma.

'Teafa has taken care of Móen since childhood.'

'And how old is Móen now?' demanded Eadulf.

Crón was about to ignore him again but Fidelma raised an
eyebrow in query.

'It is a valid question,' she said pointedly.

'Twenty-one years old.'

'He is an adult, then?' Fidelma was surprised. From the way
Crón and Dignait had been speaking of him, it had sounded almost
as if Móen was but a child. 'Is he a difficult person?' she hazarded.

'That will be for you to judge,' replied Crón sourly.

Fidelma bowed her head and conceded the point.

'That is true. So you felt that Teafa might be able to calm
Móen? And what happened then?'

'Dubán found . . .' Crón hesitated and rephrased her response pointedly. 'Dubán returned within a few minutes and told me that he had discovered Teafa's body. She had also been stabbed to death. Móen had clearly killed her first before . . .'

Fidelma raised her hand to interrupt.

'I am to be the judge of what happened. This is your speculation. We will proceed as the law tells us to.'

Crón sniffed in annoyance.

'My so-called speculation is correct.'

'That we shall eventually see. What happened after Teafa's death was reported to you?'

'I went to rouse my mother and tell her the news.'

'Your mother?' Fidelma leaned forward with interest. 'Eber's wife?'

'Of course.'

'I see. Then she did not know of the death of her husband at this time?'

'I have said as much.'

'But this event happened before sunrise. Where was your father found?'

'In his bed chamber.'

Fidelma followed the logic grimly.

'Then your mother was not with Eber?'

'She was in her own bed chamber.'

'I see,' Fidelma said softly. She decided not to press the point. 'And what happened after that?'

Crón shrugged almost indifferently.

'Little more that bears relevance. Móen, as I have said, has been safely locked away. Without my knowledge, my mother sent a young warrior named Crítan to Cashel to inform the king of the tragedy. She apparently thought a Brehon should be sent to investigate rather than let her daughter exercise the role of tanist. My mother did not want me to be tanist.'

Fidelma noted a slight bitterness in the girl's voice.

'Crítán returned two days ago to say that the king was sending someone. Thus we buried my father, as custom dictates, in our mound of chieftains. Teafa also. In accordance with the law I, as heir-elect, have taken charge. I could have dispensed justice as well without all these complications.'

'That is not so, tanist.' Fidelma's voice was soft but firm. 'You will not be chieftain until your *derbfhine* meets to confirm you in office and that is not for twenty-seven days after the death of the chieftain. A qualified Brehon needs to be the authority in such an investigation.'

The young tanist made no reply.

'Well,' Fidelma said at length, 'the facts seem clear as you have presented them. Did Dubán make the discovery of your father's body himself?'

Crón shook her head.

'It was Menma who heard his death cry and burst into my father's chamber to discover Móen in the act of slaughter.'

'Ah. Menma. And who is Menma?' queried Fidelma, trying to remember where she had heard the name before.

'He is the head of my father's,' Crón paused and corrected herself, 'head of *my* stables.'

Fidelma remembered that Dignait had mentioned the name.

'So far as your own knowledge is concerned,' Fidelma continued after a moment, 'the facts of this matter are clear and simple? You have not been troubled or mystified by them?'

'There is no mystery. The facts are clear.'

'What reason do you offer as to why Móen would kill both Eber and Teafa?'

The reply came without hesitation.

'No logical motive. But then logic would not be part of Móen's world.' Her voice was bitter.

Fidelma tried to fathom her meaning.

'As I understand it, Teafa had raised Móen from a baby. He had much to be grateful to her for. Are you saying logic did not

65

play any part in this deed? Then what do you ascribe the motive as, for surely there must be a motive?'

'Who can tell what passes in the dark still mind of one such as Móen?' replied the tanist.

For a moment, Fidelma wondered whether to press her for an explanation of her choice of words. She felt that she should not bias herself before she had spoken with Móen. However, there was one person to see before she spoke with Móen and that was the person who had discovered him in the act of killing Eber.

'I will now speak with Menma,' she announced.

'I could save you trouble,' replied Crón sharply, 'for I know all the details of this matter as Menma and Dubán told them to me.'

Fidelma smiled tightly.

'That is not the way a *dálaigh* works. It is important that I gather the facts at first hand.'

'What is of importance is that you pronounce the legal punishment that Móen must suffer. And pronounce it soon.'

'So there is no doubt in your mind that Móen did this deed?'

'If Menma says that he found Móen in the act of doing it, then he did so.'

'I do not question it,' Fidelma said, rising to her feet, with Eadulf following. Fidelma turned to the door.

'What will you do with Móen?' demanded Crón, nonplussed, for she was unused to people rising in her presence and leaving before she had formally dismissed them.

'Do?' Fidelma paused and gazed back at the tanist for a moment. 'Nothing, as yet. Firstly, we must speak to all the witnesses and then hold a legal hearing, allowing Móen to make his defence.'

Crón startled them by letting out a peal of laughter. It sounded slightly hysterical.

Fidelma waited patiently for it to subside and then asked: 'Perhaps you will tell us where we may find the man, Menma?'

'At this hour you will find him at the stables just beyond the guests' hostel,' Crón replied, between giggles.

As they were about to leave the hall of assembly, Crón managed to control her amusement and called to stay them a moment more. She became serious.

'It would be a wise course to give judgment in this matter as soon as possible. My father was well liked among his people. Kind and generous. There are many among my people who feel that the old laws of compensation are inadequate to cope with this crime and that the words of the new Faith, the creed of retribution, are more suited. An eye for an eye, a tooth for a tooth, burning for burning. If Móen is not dealt with swiftly by you, there may be willing hands to exact justice.'

'Justice?' Fidelma's voice was icy as she spun to face the young tanist. 'You mean mob vengeance? Well, as chieftain-elect of this clan . . . presuming that you are confirmed in office by your *derbfhine* . . . you may pass this word on from me – if anyone lays hands on Móen before he is tried and judged in accordance with the law, they will find themselves being judged in turn. I promise that, no matter what station they hold in life.'

Crón swallowed hard as she met the cold blast of anger from the religieuse.

Fidelma returned the gaze of the hostile blue eyes of the woman with equal coldness.

'One more thing, I would like to know,' she added. 'Who has preached a creed of retribution in the name of the Faith?'

The tanist thrust out her chin.

'I have already told you that we have only one person here who attends to the needs of the Faith.'

'Father Gormán?' offered Eadulf.

'Father Gormán,' confirmed Crón.

'This Father Gormán seems out of step with the philosophy of the laws of the five kingdoms,' Fidelma observed quietly. 'And where is this gentle advocate of the Faith to be found? In his church?'

'Father Gormán is visiting some outlying farmsteads. He will be back here tomorrow.'

'I shall look forward to meeting with him,' Fidelma replied grimly as she led the way from the hall.

It turned out that Menma was a heavy-set man who had ugly features and a bushy red beard. They found him sitting on a tree stump in front of the stable buildings, honing a billhook with a stone. He paused and looked up as they approached. His expression was one of cunning. He rose slowly to his feet.

Eadulf heard Fidelma give a sharp intake of breath and glanced at her in surprise. She was examining the fox-like features of Menma with curiosity. They came to a halt before him. Eadulf was aware of an awesome rancid smell. He gazed distastefully at the man's dirty matted hair and beard and shifted his position slightly for the breeze seemed to blow the stench of the man against him.

Menma gave an occasional tug at his red beard as he stood before Fidelma.

'Do you understand that I am an advocate of the law courts, charged by the king of Cashel to investigate the killing of Eber?'

Menma nodded slowly.

'I have been told, sister. The news of your coming has quickly spread here.'

'I am told that it was you who discovered the body of Eber?'

The man blinked.

'It is so,' he said after a moment's reflection.

'And what is your task at the *rath* of Araglin?'

'I am head of the stables of the chieftain.'

'Have you served the chieftain long?'

'Crón will be the fourth chieftain of Araglin that I have served.'

'Four? That is surely a long service.'

'I was a young lad in the stables of Eoghan, whose life is remembered by the high cross which marks the clan lands on the road from the high mountains yonder.'

'We have seen it,' affirmed Eadulf.

'Then there was Eoghan's son, Erc, who died in battle against the Uí Fidgente,' Menma continued as if he had not heard him. 'And now Eber has passed to the Otherworld. So I am serving his daughter Crón.'

Fidelma waited a moment but there was no further response. She suppressed a sigh.

'Tell me the circumstances of your finding Eber.'

For the first time the pale blue eyes of Menma seemed to focus with a slightly puzzled expression.

'The circumstances, lady?'

Fidelma wondered if the man were slow-witted.

'Yes,' she said, trying to be patient. 'Tell me when and how you discovered the body of Eber.'

'When?' The muscles in the broad face of the man creased the features. 'It was the night when Eber was killed.'

Brother Eadulf turned aside to hide his amusement.

Fidelma gave an inward groan as she realised the type of person she was dealing with. Menma was slow-witted. Not a half-wit but merely someone whose thoughts moved laggardly and were ponderous. Or was he being so purposely?

'And when was that, Menma?' she coaxed.

'Oh, that was six nights ago now.'

'And the time? At what time did you find the body of Eber?'

'It was before first light.'

'What were you doing at the chieftain's quarters before first light?'

Menma raised a huge, gnarled hand and ran his fingers through his hair.

'It was my task to turn out the horses to pasture and oversee the milking of the cattle of Eber. It is also my task to slaughter the meat for the chieftain's table. I rose and was making my way to the stables. As I walked by the chambers of Eber...'

Fidelma leant forward quickly.

'Do I presume that to traverse the path from your cabin to the stables, you have to pass Eber's apartments?'

Menma stared at her in surprise as if he failed to understand why she needed to ask the question.

'Everyone knows that.'

Fidelma forced a small smile.

'You will have to be patient with me, Menma, for I am a stranger here and do not know such things. Can you point out Eber's apartment from here?'

'Not from here but from there.'

Menma raised his billhook and indicated the position with the blade.

'Show me.'

Reluctantly, Menma led the way from the stables around the back of the guests' hostel, along the granite wall of the hall of assembly to a well-trodden path between the buildings. Eber's apartments were apparently on the opposite side of the assembly hall to the guests' hostel. He again indicated with the blade of his billhook. There were a series of wooden structures built around the hall of assembly, between the wall of the assembly hall and the stone building of the chapel. Menma indicated one of them.

'That is Eber's apartments. There is the door by which I entered but there is another which connects his rooms from the inside to the hall of assembly.'

'And where is your cabin?'

He indicated with the billhook again. Fidelma acknowledged that one path for Menma to traverse to the stables would certainly lead him by the stone chapel, passing Eber's apartment. She had not really suspected the accuracy of Menma but merely wanted to get the geography fixed firmly in her own mind.

'Who does the milking here?' she asked as they walked slowly back to the stables.

She wondered if Eadulf realised that it was unusual for a man to be involved in the milking. In most farming communities, people arose at sunrise and the first tasks of the day were for the head of the stables to let out the horses into the pasture and for the women to milk the cows. It was therefore strange that the keeper of the chieftain's stables would oversee the milking as well as release the horses.

'The women always do the milking,' replied Menma, unperturbed.

'So why did you have to supervise them?'

'It has been so for the last few weeks,' Menma frowned. 'There has been some cattle stolen from the valley and Eber asked me to check his herd each morning.'

'Is the theft of cattle an unusual occurrence? Were the thieves ever caught?'

Menma contemplated the question, rubbing his bushy chin thoughtfully.

'It was the first time anyone had dared rob the clan of Araglin. We are an isolated community. Dubán searched for days but lost the track of the thieves in the high pasture.'

'How so?'

'There were too many animal tracks up there.'

Fidelma felt a twinge of frustration. Drawing information from Menma was like drawing teeth. 'Continue. It was just before first light. You were on your way to oversee the milking of the cattle and were passing Eber's cabin. What then?'

'It was then I heard a moaning sound.'

'Moaning?'

'I thought Eber must be ill and so I called out to ask if he was in need of help.'

'And what happened?'

'Nothing. There was no reply and the moaning sound continued.'

'So what did you do?'

'I entered his apartments. I found him in the bed chamber.'

'Was it Eber who was moaning?'

'No, it was his killer, Móen.'

'And you saw Eber's body immediately?'

'Not at first. I saw Móen kneeling by the bed, clutching a knife.'

'You said it was before sunrise. Therefore it must have been dark. How could you see in the interior of Eber's bed chamber?'

'A lamp was lit. By its light I saw Móen clearly. He was crouching over the bed. I saw the knife in his hand.'

Menma paused and his features twisted in an expression of distaste as he remembered the scene.

'By the light of the lamp I could see the knife had stains on it. I saw stains on the face and clothes of Móen. It was only when I saw the naked body of Eber, stretched across the bed, that I realised that the stains were blood.'

'Did Móen say anything to you?'

Menma sniffed. 'Say? What could he say?'

'You accused him of killing Eber?'

'The fact that he had done so was surely obvious? No, I went immediately in search of Dubán.'

'And where did you find Dubán?'

'I found him in the hall of assembly. He told me to continue my tasks, seeing to the horses and cattle, for animals cannot wait on the whims of men.'

'Móen was left alone during this time?'

'Of course.'

'You did not think that he would run away?'

Menma seemed perplexed.

'Run where?'

Fidelma pressed on.

'What happened then?'

'I was leading out the horses when Dubán and Crítán came to the stables with Móen.'

'Crítán? Ah yes; I believe he is the warrior who rode to Cashel?'

'He is one of Dubán's warriors,' Menma confirmed.

'What then?'

'They brought Móen to the stables where he was shackled by

72

Crítán. The stables have to serve as a prison for we do not have any other suitable place of confinement in Araglin.'

'Móen offered no explanation nor defence about the killing? Did he even admit the killing?'

Menma looked bewildered.

'How could he say anything? As I say, it was obvious to everyone what had happened.'

Fidelma exchanged a glance of surprise with Eadulf.

'So what did Móen do? Did he resist imprisonment?'

'He struggled and whimpered as Crítán shackled him. Dubán then went to rouse Crón to tell her the news.'

'I see. And you have had no more contact with Móen since he has been locked away?'

Menma shrugged.

'I see the creature when I go to the stables. But Crítán attends to him. It is Crítán and Dubán who tend to him.'

Fidelma nodded thoughtfully.

'Thank you, Menma. I may have need to ask further questions of you. But now I will speak with Dubán.'

Menma gestured to the stable entrance where they could see the middle-aged warrior who had greeted them on their arrival in conversation with a younger man.

'There are Dubán and Crítán.'

He made to leave but Fidelma stayed him.

'One more thing. Do you usually rise before first light to attend to the horses?'

'Always. Most people here are up at sunrise.'

'Did you rise before first light this morning to attend to the horses?'

Menma frowned.

'This morning?'

Fidelma tried to control her irritation.

'Did you attend to the horses this morning?' she repeated sharply.

73

'I have told you, each morning before first light I attend to them.'

'And what time did you go to bed last night?'

Menma shook his head as if trying to remember.

'Late, I think.'

'You think?'

'I was drinking until late.'

'Was anyone with you?'

The brawny man shook his head.

When he had gone she glanced at Eadulf who was staring at her, obviously perplexed.

'What had Menma's actions this morning to do with the murders of last week?' he demanded.

'Did you recognise him?' Fidelma asked.

Eadulf frowned.

'Recognise who? Menma?'

'Yes, of course!' Fidelma was irked at Eadulf's slowness.

'No. Should I have done so?'

'I am positive that he was one of the men who attacked the hostel this morning.'

Eadulf gaped in astonishment. It was almost on the tip of his tongue to say 'Are you sure?' but he realised that it would merely bring forth an angry retort. Fidelma would not say she was positive, if she were not.

'Then he was lying.'

'Exactly so. I swear he was the same man. You will recall that the attackers rode close by us. I observed one of them with particularly ugly features and a bushy red beard. I do not think that he saw me to recognise me again. But it was Menma.'

'It is not the only mystery here. Why is it that everyone is accepting Móen as guilty but making no effort to discover why he killed Eber and the woman Teafa?'

Fidelma gave him an approving nod at the aptness of the observation.

'Let us go and see how Menma's story accords with that of Móen.'

They walked across to the two warriors standing by the stable doors. The younger man, scarcely more than a youth, had dirty fair hair and rather coarse features, and was lounging against the door post. A round shield hung loosely from his shoulder and he wore a workmanlike sword at his left side. Both men had turned to watch Fidelma and Eadulf approach. The younger warrior did not shift his lounging attitude as he stared with unconcealed curiosity at Fidelma. Silence had fallen between them.

'Are you truly the Brehon?' The question was uttered by the youth. His voice sounded as if he suffered a perpetual sore throat. Fidelma did not reply but showed her disapproval of his greeting by turning her attention to the middle-aged warrior.

'I am told that your name is Dubán and that you command the bodyguard of the chieftain?'

The burly warrior shifted uneasily.

'That is so. This is Crítán, who is one of the guard. Crítán is . . .'

'Champion of Araglin!' The young man's voice was boastful.

'Champion? At what?' Only Eadulf could tell that Fidelma was irritated by the pomposity of the youth as she acknowledged him.

Crítán was not deflated by her question.

'You name it, sister. Sword, lance or bow. I was the one sent to Cashel to inform the king. I think he was impressed with me. I mean to join his bodyguard.'

'And does the king of Cashel know of your great ambition?' she asked. Fidelma's expression did not alter. It was impossible to tell whether she was amused or angry at the youth's impertinence. Eadulf decided that she was scornful of the boy.

Crítán did not hear the irony in her voice.

'I have not told him yet. But once he knows of my reputation, he will accept my services.'

Fidelma saw that Dubán looked uncomfortable at his subordinate's bragging tones.

'Dubán, a word with you.' She drew him aside, ignoring the piqued expression on the youth's face.

'You realise that I am an advocate of the courts?'

'I have heard as much,' agreed the commander of the bodyguard. 'The news of your coming is now common knowledge in the *rath*.'

'Good. I now wish to see Móen.'

The warrior jerked a thumb across his shoulder to the closed stable door.

'He is in there.'

'So I am told. I will wish to question you on your part in discovering the body of Teafa but at this moment I shall deal with Móen. Has he said anything since you detained him?'

She was confounded by Dubán's expression of confusion.

'How could he do that?'

Fidelma was about to reply but decided it was better to see Móen before pressing any further.

'Unlock the door,' she instructed.

Dubán motioned to his boastful subordinate to do as she bid. Inside, the stable was dark, dank and stale.

'I'll get a lamp,' Dubán said apologetically. 'We have no place to confine prisoners and so we turned out the horses which Eber kept here and put them in the pasture. This has been converted into a prison.'

Fidelma sniffed disapprovingly as she peered into the blackness.

'Surely there must have been somewhere better to confine him? This place reeks enough without the added indignity of darkness. Why wasn't a light left for the prisoner?'

The young warrior, Crítán, chuckled loudly behind her.

'You have a wit, lady. That is rich!'

Dubán gruffly ordered the youth to return to his post outside and then shuffled into the darkness. Fidelma and Eadulf, as their eyes adjusted to the gloom, could see the shadowy outline of his figure bending over something, then they heard a sound as he struck a flint and a spark caught an oil wick which began to glimmer. The warrior turned with a lamp in his hand. He beckoned them further inside the cavernous stables and pointed to the far corner.

'There he is! There is Móen the killer of Eber.'

Fidelma moved forward.

Dubán held up the lamp as high as he could in order to shed its light around the smelly interior. In the far corner was what seemed, at first, to be a bundle of clothes. Dirty, smelling rough homespuns. The bundle twitched and a chain rattled. Fidelma swallowed hard as she saw that the clothes were, in fact, the covering of a man who was shackled by the left foot to one of the support posts which held up the roof of the building. Then she saw a tousled head raise itself with a jerky motion, back towards her, and it seemed as if its owner was listening, the head slightly to one side. A strange whimpering sound came from it.

'That is the creature, Móen,' Dubán said hollowly at her shoulder.

Chapter Six

Fidelma could not restrain the shudder which passed through her as she gazed on the grotesque figure.

'God look down on us! What is the meaning of this? I would not keep an animal in such conditions, much less a man, even one suspected of murder.'

She moved forward and bent down to touch the shoulder of the crouching form.

She was unprepared for what happened next.

The figure jumped at her touch with an anguished howl. It scurried away on all fours like an animal, moaning, until the length of the chain attached to its ankle caused it to jerk to a halt. It fell; fell full-length on the dirty straw of the floor, and lay there, at the same time raising both hands as if to protect its head from a blow. Pausing in that position only for a moment or so, it scrambled up and turned to face them. Fidelma and Eadulf were unprepared for what they saw; the eyes were pupilless, wide staring white orbs.

'*Retro Satana!*' It was Eadulf who breathed the words, raising a hand to genuflect.

'Satan it is, brother,' Dubán agreed in humourless tones.

The figure was that of a male. It was so covered in dirt and excrement, the hair so wild and matted, that they could not clearly discern its features. Fidelma had the impression that it was not elderly. Then she recalled that Crón had said that Móen was only twenty-one years old. The mouth was a wide slobbering aperture and a terrible moaning noise continued to issue forth. But it was the eyes that held the attention of both Fidelma and Eadulf. Those

79

pitiful white opaque orbs with scarcely any sign of a pupil at all.

'Is this Móen who is accused of killing Eber and Teafa?' whispered Fidelma aghast.

'Indeed it is.'

'Móen,' muttered Eadulf grimly. 'Of course! Doesn't the very name mean one who is dumb?'

'You have the right of it, brother,' agreed Dubán. 'Dumb has he been since he was found and given a home by the lady Teafa.'

'And sightless?' queried Fidelma, staring in horrified pity at the figure crouching before her.

'And deaf,' Dubán added grimly.

'And it is claimed that such an unfortunate could kill two healthy beings?' breathed Fidelma in disbelief.

Eadulf stared at the creature with distaste.

'Why were we not told about the condition of this person before?'

The warrior looked surprised.

'But everyone knows Móen. It never occurred to me that . . .'

Fidelma silenced his protests.

'No. It is not your fault that I have not been informed before now. Let us be perfectly clear; am I to understand that it is this deaf, dumb and blind creature who is charged with the slaughter of Eber and . . .'

She paused for the figure had moved cautiously forward and was holding his head up like an animal, his nostrils flaring. He was sniffing. Fidelma stared down at him as he approached near to her on all fours.

'I would stand back a little, sister, for he smells people even if he can't see or hear them,' warned Dubán.

It was too late, for a cold, dirty hand suddenly stretched out and touched Fidelma's foot. She started back in alarm.

Móen stopped abruptly.

Dubán moved towards him, one hand holding the lamp while the other was raised as if to strike the unfortunate.

Fidelma saw the action and reached out a hand.

'Do not strike him,' she commanded. 'You cannot strike one who cannot see the blow.'

Indeed, it was just as well for Móen was sitting his face upturned and now he had raised his hands, waving them in curious motions before him.

Fidelma shook her head sadly.

'Ignore him, sister,' muttered Dubán, 'for he is cursed by God.'

'Can you not have him cleaned at least?' demanded Fidelma.

Dubán looked astonished.

'For what purpose?'

'He is a human being.'

The warrior grimaced sarcastically.

'Not that you would notice it.'

'According to the law, Dubán, you have already committed an offence by mocking someone who has a disability.'

The warrior opened his mouth to protest but Fidelma went on grimly, 'I want him clean before I next see him. You may still confine him but he must be given food and water and be cleaned. I will not see one of God's creatures suffer this way. Whatever they have been accused of.'

She turned on her heel and strode from the stable. Eadulf hesitated a moment; he felt an unease as he watched the bitter emotions chase themselves across the middle-aged warrior's face as he stared after Fidelma.

Fidelma was standing outside breathing deeply as if in an effort to control her anger. There was now no sign of the other warrior, Crítán. They hesitated a moment before walking slowly in the direction of Eber's apartments.

'One cannot blame Dubán,' Eadulf tried to act as conciliator. 'And remember, this poor creature, as you call him, did kill Eber, his chieftain.'

He almost winced as Fidelma's green eyes suddenly blazed at him with an angry fire.

'Móen's guilt has first to be proved. He is a human being and has the same rights before the law as everyone else. In the meantime there is no excuse to treat him as if he were less than an animal.'

'True,' conceded Eadulf. 'He should not be treated in such a way but . . .'

'He has a right of defence before being judged guilty or not.'

Eadulf raised a shoulder and let it fall in an expressive gesture.

'Deaf, dumb and blind, Fidelma. How can one communicate with such a being in order to find out what defence they can present?'

'If there is a defence, I shall find it. But he will not be condemned without a fair trial. On my oath as an advocate of the laws of the five kingdoms, I shall ensure it.'

There was an awkward silence and then Eadulf asked: 'Is there really a law imposing penalties on anyone who mocks the disabled?'

'I do not make up laws,' Fidelma replied stiffly, still irritated. 'Heavy fines can be imposed on anyone who mocks the disability of any person from an epileptic to a lame person.'

'It is hard to believe, Fidelma, even though I had studied in this land of yours, I am still a prisoner of my own culture. In our society we recognise that man is a cruel creature and that God often ordains him to live short and brutish lives. It is in the holy order of things that, in the violence of nature, man has a violent path.'

Fidelma stared at him in surprise.

'You have seen the alternative in our society, Eadulf. You surely do not believe that the Saxon way is the only way?'

'Any way is only transitory. Life is subject to sudden change. On every side there is pestilence, famine, oppression, violence from personal or political enemies. We resign ourselves to the dispensation of the inscrutable will of the Father in the heavens where all our security lies.'

Fidelma shook her head.

'Time to argue such a philosophy later, Eadulf. Our laws and the way we conduct our lives is surely an argument against the manifold misery of life you accept in your land? But before we debate the subject, there is this matter to be resolved. And it is a difficult one, Eadulf, and I need your support. Once I have gathered the evidence, and if the blame does lie at the door of this unfortunate then I will have to decide whether he has any legal capacity in law. Such a disabled person is not subject to distraint and one has to act against the legal guardian. So we must discover who is the legal guardian of this creature, Móen. Ah,' she paused and rubbed her head, 'I must try to recall the words of the text *Do Brethaib Gaire . . .*'

'What is that?' demanded Eadulf.

'On the judgments of maintenance which is a tract on the kin's obligation to care for its incapacitated members. The first part deals with the care of the deaf, blind and dumb.'

Eadulf was always bemused by the Irish laws of compensation to the victim and their family even for murder. In his land of the South Folk, the death penalty was enacted even for thieves and those who harboured and supported them. Murderers, traitors, witches, absconding slaves, outlaws and those who protected them could be hanged, beheaded, stoned, burnt or drowned, while lesser penalties consisted of mutilations; the cutting off of hands, feet, nose, ears, upper lip or tongue, even blinding, castration and scalping as well as branding and scouring. Eadulf knew that the Saxon bishops preferred to mete out the punishment of mutilation rather than death for it gave the sinner time to repent. But these Irish with their refusal to accept the satisfying concept of revenge but who talked of compensating the victim by putting the wrong-doer to useful work . . . well, it was humane but he often wondered whether it was an appropriate justice.

A call halted them as they passed around the grey granite of the hall of assembly.

It was Dubán hurrying after them. There was still a degree of hostility in his eyes but his features were more controlled.

'I have given orders to Crítán to carry out your instructions, sister. Móen will be made presentable for your . . .' He fought for the right word. 'To your sensibilities.'

'I had no doubt that you would do so, Dubán,' Fidelma replied quietly.

The elderly warrior frowned, trying to detect what hidden meaning might lurk in her voice. However much he was affronted by Fidelma's criticism, he had apparently been told to follow her instructions.

'Crón has charged me to attend you during your stay in the *rath* of Araglin and carry out any other directions you might give.'

'I see. Well, we are on our way to Eber's apartments to examine where Menma found the body with the wretched Móen.'

'Then I shall be your guide,' offered Dubán, moving off to lead them to the building which Menma had already pointed out. It was a single storey affair like most of the wooden buildings within the *rath*.

The door led into an easily recognisable reception room where the chieftain could dine and entertain in private when not using the hall of assembly. This room was connected to the hall by means of a door hidden behind a tapestry which Dubán indicated. There was a cauldron in a hearth, a table and chairs. The dead chieftain's weapons hung on the wall with trophies of the hunt. Rugs and tapestries gave a warmth to the room. A wooden panelled wall and door divided it from what was obviously the bed chamber. The sleeping arrangements were simple, a large straw palliasse on the floor with rugs. Fidelma saw the bloodstains on them but did not comment. A table stood nearby on which an oil lamp stood.

'Is that the lamp which was lit when Menma entered?'

'Yes,' Dubán confirmed at once. 'The room has not been disturbed since the . . . the tragedy. The lamp was still lit when I came here with Menma. Móen was kneeling just there,' he indicated with his hand, 'just by the bedside.'

'Had he made any attempt to leave?'

'Oh no.'

'So he made no attempt to run away before you came?'

'Run away? Deaf, dumb and blind as he was?' Dubán laughed dryly.

'Yet deaf, dumb and blind as he was, you tell me that he was able to enter here and kill Eber,' mused Fidelma, examining the room. Before he could respond she instructed him: 'Tell us what happened from your viewpoint.'

'As commander of the guard, I was on watch that night.'

'This is an isolated *rath*. Surely there is no need to mount a watch for you have the natural protection of the mountains around this valley?'

Dubán nodded morosely.

'Yet a few weeks ago we had cattle-raiders in the valley, sister. Eber asked me to set a watch.'

'Ah yes, of course. And you were on watch during the night when Eber was murdered?'

Dubán looked chagrined.

'To be truthful, as daylight approached, I had fallen asleep on the seat within the entrance of the assembly hall. Menma had to rouse me. He told me that he had found Eber dead and Móen was the killer. I came here with him without delay and I saw the body of Eber sprawled in the bed, just as Menma described. There was blood all over the place and you can see where it has dried. Móen was crouched as I have indicated. He still had the knife in his hand, it was stained with blood, and his clothes were all bloody as well.'

'What was he doing?'

'Just rocking back and forth and moaning to himself.'

'And you were able to observe this clearly because the lamp was lit? What then?' encouraged Fidelma.

'I told Menma to carry on with his duties and went to fetch

Crítán. But he was already coming to relieve me of the watch. We took Móen to the stables and shackled him and I went to inform Crón.'

'Ah yes, Crón. Why did you not inform Eber's wife first? Would that not have been the correct procedure?'

'Crón is tanist, the heir-elect. With Eber dead, she was now chieftainess-elect of Araglin. It is correct that she should be informed first of all.'

Fidelma silently agreed with Durbán's interpretation of the protocol.

'And then?'

'When we started putting the shackles on Móen, he began to struggle and cry out. I told Crón so and she instructed me to fetch Teafa. I went to her chambers.'

'And found her dead?'

'I did.'

'I am told, Teafa was the only person in the *rath* of Araglin who could calm Móen, if "calm" is the right word.'

'She was. She had looked after him since he was a baby.'

'And she was Eber's sister?'

'She was.'

'So Móen was not her own child?' Fidelma was puzzled about the relationship.

Dubán was firm.

'No one knows where the child came from. But it was not Teafa's because she would have been seen to be pregnant in the weeks before his birth and she was not. This is a small community. He was a foundling.'

'As it is a small community, it must be known who gave birth to the child?'

'It is not. He was not the child of anyone in the valley. That much is certain.'

'Can you tell me any more? How and why did Teafa come to adopt the child? Who found him?'

Dubán rubbed a finger along the side of his nose.

'All I know is that Teafa went out hunting by herself and she returned some days later with the child. She simply went to the mountains and came back with the new-born babe.'

'Did she explain to anyone how she found it?'

'Of course. She said that she had found it abandoned in the woods. She announced that she would adopt it. I left Araglin only a short while after that event and I was away fighting the wars of the Cashel kings until three years ago. I am told that as the child grew older, the debilities became known. But Teafa refused to give it up. Teafa never married nor had child of her own. She was a warm-hearted person and maybe needed a surrogate child. It seemed that the child and Teafa grew to be able to communicate in some curious fashion. I am not sure how.'

'How long were you away from Araglin then?'

'Nearly seventeen years passed until I returned to serve Eber. That was, as I have said, three years ago.'

'I see. Is there anyone else here in the *rath* who might know more about Móen?'

Dubán shrugged.

'I suppose Father Gormán might know something else which can be revealed now that Teafa is dead. But Father Gormán will not be back for a day or two.'

'What of Eber's widow?'

'The lady Cranat?' Dubán pulled a sour face. 'I am not sure. She did not marry Eber until a year or so after Teafa brought Móen to dwell among us. On my return I observed that Cranat and Teafa did not share the intimacy one might expect between sister and sister-in-law.'

Eadulf leant forward eagerly.

'Are you saying that Cranat did not like Teafa?'

Dubán looked pained.

'I know you Saxons pride yourselves on plain speaking. I thought I had made my view clear.'

'Clear enough,' conceded Fidelma quickly. 'You are telling us that Cranat and Teafa did not get along well?'

'Not well,' agreed Dubán.

'Do you know how long this state of affairs had existed?'

'I am told that they fell out when Crón was about thirteen years old. There was some sort of argument between them and they barely spoke to one another. Certainly about two or three weeks ago I was witness to a fierce argument between them.'

'What was this about?'

'It is not really for me to comment on.' It was clear that Dubán felt that he was resorting to gossip. Fidelma immediately seized on his awkwardness.

'But having said as much, I feel that you should explain yourself.'

'I really don't know the substance except that Teafa was angry, shouting at Cranat, and Cranat was in tears.'

'You must have heard something then. You must have gained some idea as to the cause of the quarrel?'

'Not I. I recall that Móen was mentioned and also Eber. Teafa was shouting something about divorce.'

'She was demanding that Cranat divorce her brother?'

'Perhaps. I do not know. Cranat ran off to the chapel to seek solace from Father Gormán.'

Fidelma made no other comment but stood looking around the bed chamber, examining it minutely before returning to the dividing door and examining the reception room.

'For someone who is deaf, dumb and blind, this Móen would appear to have the gift of moving easily through this *rath*.'

Eadulf came to join her with a frown.

'What do you mean, Fidelma?' he asked.

'Regard these rooms, Eadulf. Firstly, Móen had to make his way here. Then he had to enter, negotiate his way to Eber's bed chamber and enter, take his knife, find his target and kill Eber before the chieftain realised his presence. That not only takes stealth but a talent I would not expect to find in one who is so debilitated.'

Dubán overheard and appeared disapproving.

'Are you denying the facts?' he demanded.

Fidelma glanced at him.

'I am merely trying to ascertain them.'

'Well, the facts are simple. Móen was found in the act of slaughter.'

'Not quite,' Fidelma corrected. 'He was found by Eber's body. He was not actually seen killing him.'

Dubán put his head back and gave a gruff bark of laughter.

'Truly, sister, is this the logic of a Brehon? If I find a sheep with its throat ripped out and sitting by the carcass is a wolf with blood on its muzzle, is it not logical that I should blame the wolf for the deed?'

'It is reasonable,' Fidelma conceded. 'But it is not proof positive that the wolf did it.'

Dubán shook his head in disbelief.

'Are you trying to claim . . . ?'

'I am trying to discover the truth,' snapped Fidelma. 'That is my sole purpose.'

'Well, if it is truth you want, then it is well known in the *rath* that Móen was able to move about without undue difficulty within certain areas.'

'How was this accomplished?' Eadulf was intrigued.

'I presume that he had some sort of memory. He also seemed to smell his way.'

'Smell?' Eadulf's tone was disbelieving.

'You saw the way he used his sense of smell in the stable to identify that there were strangers there. He has developed his sense of smell like an animal. Provided he is placed in certain areas of the *rath* he can find his way within those areas. Everyone knows that.'

'Ah, so it is of no surprise that he was able to negotiate his way here?'

'None whatever.'

Eadulf looked at Fidelma and shrugged.

'Well, it seems there is no mystery then.'

Fidelma did not reply. She was not convinced.

'Where is the knife with which Móen stabbed Eber?'

'I have it still.'

'Has the knife been identified?'

'Identified?'

Dubán sounded puzzled.

Fidelma was patient.

'Has the ownership of the knife been discovered?'

Dubán shrugged.

'I believe it is one of Eber's own hunting knives.' He pointed to one of the walls where a collection of swords and knives hung with a shield. One hanging sheath was clearly empty. 'I saw that one of the knives was missing and I presume that it was the one which Móen took.'

Fidelma moved to examine the place which Dubán indicated. She turned and walked across the room to the main door. Then she stood with her back to it for a moment before making her way around the intervening pieces of furniture towards the knife rack. It was a complicated and indirect route because of the intervening obstacles. Finally, she reached out to the rack, then turned and made her way around a table and bench to the bed chamber door.

She paused and stood looking thoughtful for a moment.

'I will want to see that weapon shortly.'

Dubán inclined his head.

'Good. And now let us see where Teafa was discovered and in what manner.'

Chapter Seven

Dubán escorted them out of Eber's apartments and along the path behind the stables. The track twisted and turned beyond some store houses which stood next to a kiln for drying corn. They crossed a yard, with a well in it, towards a small wicker and wattle covered cabin.

'Teafa had her own cabin,' he explained as they walked, 'away from the rest of the chieftain's family.'

'Did you say that she was never married?' asked Eadulf.

'I did,' Dubán replied. 'Why do you ask?'

Eadulf smiled knowingly.

'It is surely unusual for the unmarried sister of a chieftain to live outside of the chieftain's immediate circle of apartments?'

'She still dwelt within the chieftain's *rath*,' explained Dubán, clearly unsure of the point Eadulf was making.

In the land of the South Folk, women were regarded as the property of the male head of the household until they married and only then would they be allowed outside of the confines of the house of the family. Eadulf suddenly realised that his view was not valid in the five kingdoms.

'What Brother Eadulf means,' interposed Fidelma, 'is that Teafa's cabin is a poor one on the outskirts of the *rath* when she might have been expected to dwell in more luxury within the interior of the chieftain's apartment.'

Dubán grimaced indifferently.

'It was her own preference. I recall that she made that decision just after she had adopted Móen.'

Teafa's cabin appeared to be only a small construction but once inside, Fidelma noticed that it was divided into three rooms. A large room in which Teafa and her charge had obviously cooked, eaten and used as a general living area. In most houses of this size it was called a *tech immácallamae* or 'house of conversation', a common gathering point for a family and their friends. Two doors gave access to bed chambers. It was obvious which room Móen had occupied for it had no window and the light from the open door revealed a simple mattress on the floor with no furniture.

Fidelma was about to turn back when something caught her eye behind the door of Móen's bed chamber.

'Is there a candle or lamp in here?' she asked.

Dubán took up a flint and tinder from a side table and soon had a tall tallow candle spluttering.

Taking the candle, Fidelma entered the room which Móen had occupied, and turned to the area behind the door. To the untrained eye it seemed that there was a stack of firewood piled high there, bundle after bundle, bound with leather thongs.

'Come here, Eadulf,' Fidelma instructed. 'What do you make of this?'

Eadulf moved forward. Dubán followed, peering over his shoulder, and saw the bundles of sticks.

'An odd place to keep kindle for the fire,' Dubán observed.

Eadulf had reached forward and picked up a bundle. The sticks were cut to uniform lengths of about eighteen inches. They were mainly of hazel and some were of yew. Eadulf was examining them closely and, at one point, he unbound a bundle to examine the lengths of stick. Finally he turned to Fidelma. He smiled knowingly.

'It is not often you see such fine specimens outside of the great libraries.'

Dubán looked bewildered.

'What does he mean, sister?'

Fidelma regarded Eadulf with the approval that a teacher reserves for a bright pupil.

'He means that these pieces of kindle, as you call them, are in fact what are known as "Rods of the Poets". They are old books. Look closely. You will see that they are notched in the ancient Ogam alphabet.'

Dubán examined them with intrigue. He clearly had no knowledge of the ancient form of writing.

'Was Teafa a scholar then?' asked Eadulf.

The warrior shook his head in bewilderment.

'I don't think she pretended to be but I believe that she was well versed in the arts and poetry. If so, she probably knew the old alphabet so it does not surprise me that she had these books here.'

'Even so,' Fidelma reflected, 'I have not seen such a fine collection outside an abbey library.'

Eadulf carefully retied the bundle and replaced it with the others while Fidelma turned back into the main room. She crossed to the second sleeping chamber. Teafa's room contained more ornaments and elaborate furnishing. There was an air of past opulence which a daughter of a chieftain and sister of a chieftain would doubtless assume. The candle now being unnecessary, Fidelma extinguished it with a swift breath. She turned to Dubán.

'So once you had reported the death of Eber to Crón and she had asked you to fetch Teafa to pacify him, you came directly here?'

'I did. I arrived at the door and found it was partially open.'

'Open?'

'It stood ajar just a fraction – enough for me to sense something was wrong.'

'Why? Surely a door standing ajar is not a sign of anything being amiss?'

'Teafa was fastidious about closing doors.'

'To keep Móen in?' Eadulf hazarded.

'Not exactly. Móen was allowed to move about but, in order for him to be aware of the boundaries of where he was, doors

93

were always kept shut so that he did not pass through inadvertently.'

'I see. Go on. The door was ajar.'

'The place was in darkness. I called out to Teafa but there was no reply. So I pushed open the door and stood for a moment on the threshold. By then the dawn was coming up – it was that period of half light. From that I saw a bundle of clothes, or so I thought, on the floor. As I looked more closely I realised that it was a body. Teafa's body.'

'Show me where.'

Dubán pointed to a place before the hearth whose ashes now lay grey and chill. Fidelma had noticed the pungent smell of burnt wood immediately she had entered the cabin.

'I looked around, found a candle and was able to light it. In fact, the very same candle we used just now. The body was that of Teafa. There was blood all over her clothes. She had been stabbed savagely in the chest, around the heart, several times.'

Fidelma bent down to the floor and could see dark stains that had been caused by blood. At the same time she observed a small burnt area on the floor close by and she realised that it was this that smelled more acerbically than the remains in the fireplace. Nearby this was a stain. It was not a blood stain. She placed a finger on the still damp area and sniffed. It was oil.

'Was anything lying here?' she asked.

'A broken oil lamp,' Dubán recalled after a pause for thought. 'It has been tidied away, I think.'

'Did you get the impression that Teafa had been holding it when she was struck down?'

'I did not think much about it. But now that you mention it, it does seem likely that she was holding the lamp in her hand and dropped it when she was struck down. It must have fallen to the floor causing a small fire to start which, God be praised, did not spread and soon extinguished itself.'

Fidelma gazed thoughtfully at the burnt patch.

'It would have been fierce enough to have burnt this entire cabin had it not been extinguished. And there is still unburnt oil here.' She held out her finger with the tell-tale oil stain on the tip. 'What could have caused it to be quenched?'

'Well, it was out when I arrived here,' Dubán shrugged.

Fidelma was about to rise when she saw a piece of unburnt stick in the fireplace. There was nothing extraordinary about it apart from a few notchings. It was about three inches long and was a piece of hazel. She picked it out of the ashes and examined it carefully.

'What is it?' demanded Eadulf.

'An Ogam wand which has nearly burnt away completely.'

Something had prevented this piece of the hazel from burning, perhaps the way it had fallen from the fire. A few letters remained which made no sense at all. Between the burnt ends she could make out ' . . . *er wants* . . .' But that was all. Why would Teafa wish to destroy this particular wand? Thoughtfully, Fidelma placed the piece of hazel in her *marsupium* and stood up.

Fidelma gave a final glance around the cabin. As with Eber's rooms, it was tidy. There was nothing left in any real disorder. It was obvious that robbery was not a motive here.

'Dubán, you indicated that Eber's wife was not well disposed to Teafa. Did Teafa have a close relationship with her brother?'

'To Eber?' Dubán was evasive. 'She was his sister and we all live in this small community.'

'There was no animosity, no friction, as you claim with Eber's wife, Cranat?'

Dubán spread his hands as if he had decided to give in to a greater force.

'There was . . . I cannot explain it very well . . . a distance between brother and sister. I have a sister of whom I am fond. And even though she is married and with children, I eat often with her family and take her children hunting. Teafa never had a warm relationship with Eber. It might well be that there was some animosity over her adoption of Móen but I could not speak authoritatively.'

'I think that it is time that I spoke with this lady, Cranat,' Fidelma murmured.

'How about the relationship between Teafa and Eber's daughter Crón?' interrupted Eadulf.

'They were polite and there were no harsh words between them. That is about all.'

'Incidentally, how was Móen generally treated in this community?' pressed Fidelma.

'Most people treated him with tolerance; with pity. They had known him since the time Teafa brought him to the community. The lady Teafa was very respected by the people. Eber had time for the boy. But not so Cranat, who refused to have the boy near her. Also Father Gormán forbade the boy to enter his chapel. Crón seemed indifferent to him.'

'In a Saxon community, he would have been killed at birth.' Eadulf was unable to stop the comment which sprang to his lips.

Fidelma drew her brows together.

'A fine Christian attitude to take, no doubt?'

Eadulf flushed and Fidelma felt a pang of regret for the sharpness of her tongue for she had no doubt that Eadulf would have no part in such attitudes.

'People who have physical disabilities may be ineligible for office, may not be king or chieftain, but they are members of the community,' Fidelma explained patiently to Eadulf. 'All other rights are theirs to enjoy, only the person's legal capacity or responsibility is changed depending on their disability. For example, an epileptic is legally competent if they are of sound mind. But a person who is deaf and dumb cannot be subjected to distraint – the plaintiff must take action against their guardian in law.'

'So Móen was not subjected to any inferior position?' Eadulf observed wonderingly.

'Not at all,' replied Fidelma. 'I have already told you that if he were, then Teafa could have taken action under the law, for a heavy fine is levied on anyone who mocks or denigrates the disability of a person be he epileptic, a leper, lame or blind or one who is deaf and dumb.'

'It appears that I have now learnt some law of the five kingdoms,' Eadulf said penitently.

'These are not the laws that our Father Gormán would have us follow,' observed Dubán impassively.

Fidelma turned to him with interest.

'Perhaps you would explain that?'

'Father Gormán preaches the rules of Rome in his church. What he calls the Penitentials.'

Fidelma knew that many of the new ideas from Rome were entering the five kingdoms and some pro-Roman clerics were even attempting to make these new philosophies part of the laws of the kingdoms. A new system of Roman ecclesiastical law was springing up alongside the native civil and criminal laws.

She remembered the comment of Abbot Cathal of Lios Mhór. Father Gormán was a strong advocate of Roman customs and had even built another chapel at Ard Mór from money raised by the supporters of the pro-Roman camp. The conflict among the clerics of the churches in the five kingdoms was becoming bitter. The Council of Witebia, in Oswy's kingdom, where she had first met Eadulf two years ago, had only been a means of making the differences deeper. Oswy had asked the council to debate the differences between the ideas of the church of Rome and those of the churches of the five kingdoms. In spite of the fine arguments, Oswy had decided in favour of Rome which had given support to those clerics in the five kingdoms who wanted to see Rome's authority established there. It was well known that Ultán, the archbishop of Ard Macha, Primate of all five kingdoms, favoured Rome. But not everyone accepted Ultán's authority anyway. There were factions and cliques each arguing for their interpretation of the new Faith.

'And are you saying that Father Gormán disapproved of Teafa's care of Móen?'

'Yes.'

'You said that you thought Teafa was able to communicate with Móen. Could anyone else communicate with him?'

Dubán shook his head.

'No one else, as far as I know, seemed to have any contact with him at all. Just Teafa.'

'So how was Teafa able to make contact with him?'

'Truly, that I do not know.'

'It is a small community, as you say. Surely someone must know what means she used?'

Dubán raised his shoulder and let it fall in an explicit gesture.

A thought then occurred to Fidelma, one she cursed herself for not having thought of before. The idea made her feel cold.

'Are you telling me that Móen does not know what he is supposed to have done, or why he is being held?'

Dubán stared at her for a few seconds and then chuckled sourly.

'Of course he must realise that. He had just killed Teafa and Eber. Why else would he think he was taken and shackled?'

'If, indeed, he had killed Teafa and Eber,' agreed Fidelma. 'But what if he had not? He would not know why or who constrained him. If you cannot communicate with him, how could he know what he is supposed to have done? Has he made efforts to communicate with you?'

Dubán was still smiling, not taking her seriously.

'I suppose he has tried, in his animal-like way, that is.'

'What way is that?'

'He keeps trying to seize our hands and making gestures with his hands as if to attract attention. But surely he knows only Teafa could understand him.'

'Exactly,' Fidelma said grimly. 'Has it not occurred to you that Móen might think that Teafa is still alive and is trying to get someone to fetch her so that he can communicate?'

Dubán shook his head.

'He killed Teafa, whatever you may claim, sister.'

'Dubán, you are a stubborn man.'

'And you appear to be equally as stubborn.'

'Why don't we see if we can communicate with this creature?' Eadulf suggested as a compromise.

'A good suggestion, Eadulf,' agreed Fidelma, turning to lead the way from Teafa's cabin.

Móen was still shackled in the stables but there was a distinct difference. One stall of the stable had been cleaned out. A straw palliasse was laid in a corner and nearby was a jug of water and a commode. Seated cross-legged on the palliasse, though still shackled by one ankle, was Móen.

Fidelma could see at once that her instructions had been carried out. He had been washed. His hair and beard had been cut and combed. Only his white staring eyes, the tilt of his head, marked him out as in any way exceptional from anyone else. In fact, Fidelma reflected sadly, the young man was quite handsome.

As they entered, his nostrils quivered slightly. He turned his head in their direction and it was almost impossible to believe that he could not see them.

'Now,' Dubán asked cynically, 'how are you going to try to communicate with him, sister?'

Fidelma ignored him.

She motioned Eadulf to stay back and moved towards the young man and halted before him.

He started back nervously and once more raised a hand to protect his head.

Fidelma turned and scowled towards Dubán.

'This tells me much about how this unfortunate has been treated.'

Dubán flushed.

'Not by me!' he replied. 'But remember that this creature has killed – twice!'

'There is still no excuse for beating him. Would you beat a dumb animal?'

She turned back to Móen and reached forward with her hand, taking the one he was holding above his head and gently pushing it to one side.

The effect was electric. An eager expression came on the creature's face. His nostrils flared and he seemed to be catching Fidelma's scent.

Fidelma carefully seated herself alongside Móen.

Dubán started forward, his hand on his sword.

'I cannot allow this . . .' he protested.

Eadulf reached forward and held Dubán back. He had a strong grip and it surprised Dubán.

'Wait,' Eadulf instructed gently.

Móen had reached forward with his hand and his fingertips touched Fidelma's face inquiringly. Fidelma sat quietly and allowed Móen to trace her features. Then she held up her crucifix and placed it in his hand. He suddenly smiled eagerly and began to nod.

'He understands,' she explained to them. 'He understands that I am a religieuse.'

Dubán snorted derisively.

'Any animal can understand kindness.'

Móen had reached forward and taken Fidelma's hands. She frowned.

'What is he doing?' asked Eadulf.

'He seems to be tapping on my hand, or drawing some symbols . . .' muttered Fidelma, frowning. 'Strange, I think they must mean something. But what?'

With a quick sigh of exasperation, she took Móen's hand and traced some words in bold Latin characters upon it.

'I am Fidelma,' she pronounced as she traced the characters.

Móen was frowning as he felt her touch.

He gave a grunt, shook his head, seized her hand again and

continued his curious tapping, stroking motion.

'This obviously means something,' Fidelma said in frustration. 'This must be the way Teafa communicated with him. But what does it mean?'

'Maybe it is some code that only Teafa and Móen knew between them,' Eadulf hazarded.

'Perhaps.'

Fidelma halted the rapid movement of Móen's fingers on her hand.

Móen seemed to understand that she could not fathom his means of communication and he dropped his hands to his lap and his face twisted into a mask of misery. He gave a long, deep sigh, almost of despair.

Fidelma felt suddenly overcome with sadness for him and reached out her hand and touched his cheek. It was wet. She realised that tears were coursing down by the sides of his nose.

'I wish I could tell you how much I understand your disappointment, Móen,' she said softly. 'I wish we could speak so that I might learn what has happened here.'

She gripped his hand and pressed it.

Móen seemed to incline his head as if in acceptance of the communication of emotion.

Fidelma rose carefully and moved back to Eadulf and Dubán.

The middle-aged warrior was gazing in thoughtful wonder at the quietly seated figure of the unfortunate.

'Well, I have seen Teafa calm him but never anyone else.'

Fidelma moved away from the stall, with Eadulf and Dubán following.

'Perhaps that is because no one else treats him like a human being,' she observed, fighting down her anger that a sentient being could be treated so badly.

At the door of the stables they encountered the young warrior, Crítán.

The boastful youth with the dirty-coloured fair hair smirked at them.

'You could present him at the palace of Cashel now, couldn't you?' he said, indicating Móen.

Fidelma eyed the young warrior disfavourably. She did not deign to reply.

As she left the stable the youth added derisively: 'Well, at least the creature will look clean and nice when he is hanged.'

Fidelma wheeled round in fury.

'Hanged? Who said, even if he were guilty, that he should be punished by hanging?'

'Father Gormán, of course.' The young man was unabashed. 'He says we should take a life for a life.'

Fidelma looked grim.

'Indeed, as Plautus told us, in his *Asinaria – lupus est homo homini!*'

Crítán screwed up his face.

'I have no Latin or Greek learning.'

'Accepting your belief in the philosophy of mere vengeance, are you so sure that it is Móen's life that should be forfeit?'

For a moment it appeared that Crítán did not fully understand what she meant and then he smiled easily.

'I know Móen was the killer, there is no doubt.'

'No doubt? How can you be so sure?'

'Because I saw him.'

Fidelma blinked, feeling as if someone had dealt her an unexpected blow. Eadulf leaned forward quickly.

'Are you saying that you actually saw him kill Eber?' he demanded.

Crítán grinned knowingly.

'Not actually saw him,' he confessed, tapping the side of his nose with a forefinger, 'but as good as.'

'What is that supposed to mean?' snapped Fidelma. 'You can only say something is certain if you witnessed it.'

Crítán was boastful again now that he had her full attention. 'I witnessed Móen enter Eber's apartments.'

Fidelma allowed her eyes to widen fractionally in surprise. Neither Menma nor Dubán had referred to the fact that Crítán had been in the vicinity of Eber's apartments before the discovery of the body.

'You will have to explain a little more,' she said tersely. 'When did you see Móen enter Eber's apartments?'

'It was the morning when Menma discovered them. About half an hour before I went to relieve Dubán on guard duty.'

Fidelma shot a quick glance of interrogation at Dubán. The senior warrior was clearly bewildered. He was apparently hearing this story for the first time.

'What were you doing abroad so early?' Fidelma asked softly. The young man seemed to hesitate and she continued: 'You must explain if you are to be accepted as a credible witness.'

'If you must know,' Crítán's face reddened and his tone was defensive, 'I had spent the night at a certain place . . .'

'A certain place?'

Dubán suddenly guffawed lewdly.

'I'll wager that he means Clídna's brothel. It is a few miles along the river from here.'

Crítán's mortified face confirmed the fact.

'I was to return to the *rath* before sunrise and had just reached the entrance to the hall of assembly. I saw Dubán sprawled on a bench just inside. He was fast asleep.' Dubán's face reddened but he said nothing. 'Then I saw that creature sneaking along in the shadows. He did not know that I was there, of course.'

'Was Móen alone?'

Crítán grimaced.

'Yes. It is well known that he was able to move freely, blind, deaf and dumb as he was. He seemed to have an uncanny instinct at knowing how to move from one house to another.'

'I see. So he was alone?'

'He was,' confirmed the youth.

'And you saw him enter Eber's house?'

'I did.'

'How?'

Crítán blinked rapidly. 'How?' he echoed the question as if he did not understand it.

'You said that you were at the entrance of the hall of assembly. To see Eber's door you would have had to move some twenty to thirty feet even to see it in the light let alone the darkness.'

'Oh. When I saw him sneaking along I wondered what he was up to. So I waited until he had gone by me and then I followed him.'

'And you saw him enter Eber's apartments? How did he enter?'

'Through the door.' The youth was ingenuous.

'I meant, did he do so with stealth, or did he knock on the door or otherwise attempt to announce his presence? How?'

'Oh, with stealth, naturally. It was still dark.'

'And you saw Móen enter in the darkness. You have good eyesight. What did you do then?'

'I was intent on returning to the warrior's lodge to wash before relieving Dubán,' grinned Crítán. 'I continued on my way. I did not wish to get involved so said nothing when Teafa . . .'

He suddenly paused. A look of uncertainty came into his eyes.

'When Teafa . . . ?' prompted Fidelma. 'When Teafa . . . what?'

'I had returned by the hall of assembly, beyond the stables towards the warriors' hostel, which lies just by the mill house. Teafa's cabin is nearby. As I was passing, she came out with lamp in hand. She was searching for Móen. At first I thought that she was looking for firewood for she had bent down to pick up a stick by her door. Then she saw me and asked if I had seen Móen.'

Fidelma was looking thoughtful.

'Did you tell her where he was to be found?'

'Not I. I did not want to get involved in hunting for the creature. I told her that I had not seen him and passed on. I washed, changed my clothes and then went in search of Dubán. When I found him, he told me what had happened.' Crítán smiled triumphantly at the end of his narrative. 'So there you are. It is clear that Móen killed Eber and Teafa.'

Eadulf nodded reflectively.

'It does seem conclusive,' he acknowledged, glancing at Fidelma.

'Just let me make sure that I have this clear,' she said. 'You saw Móen enter Eber's apartments. They were in darkness. It was before sunrise. How were you able to see Móen enter?'

'Easy to say. My eyes were accustomed to the dark. I had just ridden from Clídna's place in the dark.'

'Then you passed on and came on Teafa standing at her cabin door with a lamp looking for Móen? When you went to find Dubán, perhaps a half an hour later, you learnt that Menma had found Eber and Móen. Why didn't you mention what you had seen?'

'There was no need. There were other witnesses.'

'When did you learn that Teafa had also been killed?'

Crítán was confident.

'After Dubán went to find her to deal with Móen.'

'Thank you, Crítán, you have been of great help.'

Fidelma began to walk at a leisurely pace towards the guests' hostel with Eadulf hurrying at her side.

'Do you need me again today, sister?' called Dubán after them.

Fidelma turned absently. 'I still want to see the hunting knife with which Móen is supposed to have carried out this deed.'

'I'll bring it directly,' the warrior answered.

As they walked back to the guests' hostel, Eadulf waited patiently for Fidelma to make some comment but, as she remained silent, he decided to prompt her.

'I think the evidence is pretty clear. Eye-witnesses and the discovery of Móen with the knife. It seems there is little more to be inquired into. Móen, pitiable creature though he is, is guilty of this deed.'

Fidelma raised her smouldering green eyes to his dark brown ones.

'Quite the contrary, Eadulf. I think that the evidence goes to support the argument that Móen did not commit the murders as charged.'

Chapter Eight

After Dubán had been sent to request a meeting with Cranat, the widow of Eber, word came that she would meet with Fidelma and Eadulf in the hall of assembly within half an hour.

Crón was already there when they entered, seated in her chair of office. Before her, just below the dais, were the same seats as before. This time Fidelma noticed that a second chair had been placed next to Crón's chair of office. Fidelma and Eadulf had barely reached their places when a straight-backed woman entered, with a fixed, unsmiling expression. She did not glance in their direction, nor make any attempt to acknowledge them, but moved forward to the empty chair and seated herself beside her daughter.

For a woman approaching her fiftieth year, Cranat was still handsome. She had kept her figure well. There was something aristocratic about her oval face, her fair skin, white and delicate. Her golden hair had no grey in it but was worn long and flowed down below the shoulders. The hands were well formed with slender tapering fingers. Fidelma noticed that the nails were carefully cut and rounded and artificially coloured crimson. Berry juice dyed the eyebrows black and there was a hint of *ruam*, the juice of sprigs and berries of the elder tree, which highlighted the cheeks with the blush of red. Fidelma noticed that Cranat did not believe in stinting herself when it came to perfume. A heavy scent of roses permeated the air around her. Cranat seated herself in regal posture.

She wore a dress of red silk fringed with gold and bracelets of silver and white bronze adorned her arms while a circlet of gold encased her neck. Clearly Cranat was possessed of wealth and her bearing showed that she was also possessed of status not just the rank of the wife of chieftain of Araglin.

Fidelma stood for a few moments waiting for Cranat to even acknowledge her by raising her eyes.

Finally, it was Crón, the tanist, who ended the silence, speaking without rising from her own chair.

'Mother, this is Fidelma, the advocate who is here to pronounce judgment on Móen.'

Only then did Cranat raise her head and Fidelma found herself staring into the same cold blue eyes of Cranat's daughter, Crón.

'My mother,' went on Crón, 'Cranat of the Déisi.'

Fidelma kept her face a mask. In the introduction, the reason for Cranat's bearing had been explained. Legend had it that during the High Kingship of Cormac mac Airt, the sept of the Déisi had been banished from their ancestral lands around Tara. Some had fled abroad to the land of the Britons while others had settled in the kingdom of Muman where they had split into two further septs, the Déisi of the north and those of the south. That Crón had introduced her mother as 'of the Déisi' meant that Cranat was a daughter of a prince of her people. Even so, it did not excuse the manner in which she had refused to greet or acknowledge Fidelma. Irritation caused Fidelma's face to redden. She had allowed this insult to her rank and position to pass unchallenged once. She could not do it a second time if she were to maintain control of this investigation.

Instead of seating herself, she calmly stepped up onto the raised platform on a level with Crón and Cranat.

'Eadulf, place a chair here for me,' she instructed coldly.

The look of shock on the faces of Cranat and her daughter indicated that they were not used to anyone challenging their authority.

Eadulf, trying to hide a smile of amusement, for he knew how Fidelma liked to make points of protocol when they had been forgotten, hastily seized a chair and placed it where she had indicated. Eadulf knew that ordinarily, Fidelma did not care a jot about matters of privilege and ritual. Only if people used such matters of etiquette to wrongfully assert authority did Fidelma use her own position to put them firmly in their place.

'Sister, you forget yourself!'

It was the first sentence Cranat had uttered, expressed in a scandalised tone.

Fidelma had taken her seat and regarded the widow of the chieftain with a bland expression.

'What would you suggest that I have forgotten, Cranat of Araglin?'

She emphasised the choice of title softly, just enough to make a point.

Cranat swallowed noisily, unable to make any reply.

'My mother is . . .' began Crón but stopped as Fidelma turned to face her. 'Ah . . .' she suddenly realised the point of protocol Fidelma had made. She turned quickly to her mother. 'I have neglected to tell you that Sister Fidelma is not only an advocate but is sister to Colgú of Cashel.'

Before Cranat could digest this information, Fidelma leant forward. She spoke pleasantly enough but her voice was firm.

'The matter of my parentage aside and ignoring the kingship of my brother,' she paused, for this was a direct demolition of Cranat's own royal pretension, 'I am qualified to the degree of *anruth* and may sit in the presence of the High King of the five kingdoms himself and speak with him on the same level.'

Cranat's mouth became a tight thin line. She turned her ice cold eyes to focus elsewhere in the hall.

'Now,' Fidelma sat back and smiled broadly. There was a brisk tone in her voice. 'Now let us leave aside the tedious matters of custom and propriety for there is more important work to do.'

Once again, there was no doubt that Fidelma was rebuking Cranat and Crón for their pretensions and they knew it. They sat in silence for there was no response that they could adequately make.

'I need to ask you some questions, Cranat.'

The woman, sitting stiffly, sniffed. She did not bring herself to look directly at Fidelma.

'Then I am sure that you will ask them,' she replied without humour.

'I am told that it was you who sent to my brother at Cashel to request a Brehon to attend here. I am told that you undertook to send to Cashel without the knowledge and approval of your daughter who is the tanist. Why was this?'

'My daughter is young,' Cranat said. 'She is inexperienced in law and politics. I believe that this matter has to be properly conducted so that no stigma is allowed to attach itself to the family of Araglin.'

'Why might that happen?'

'The nature of the creature who committed the crimes, and the fact he was the adopted son of the lady Teafa, might incline people to speak ill of the house of Araglin.'

Fidelma thought it was a reasonable explanation.

'Then let us return to the morning six nights ago when you heard of the death of your husband, Eber.'

'I have already explained what happened,' interrupted Crón hastily.

Fidelma clicked her tongue in annoyance.

'You have told me of the events as you saw them. Now I am asking your mother.'

'There is little to tell,' Cranat said. 'I was awakened by my daughter.'

'At what time?'

'Just as the sun was rising, I think.'

'And what happened?'

'She told me that Eber had been slain and that Móen had done the terrible deed. I dressed and joined her here, in the hall of assembly. As I did so, Dubán came in to say that Teafa had also been found dead from stabbing.'

'Did you go to see Eber's body?'

Cranat shook her head.

'Not go to pay your last respects to your dead husband?' Fidelma allowed a note of surprise to enter her voice.

'My mother was upset,' Crón intervened defensively.

Fidelma's eyes still held those cold blue eyes of Cranat.

'You were upset?'

'I was upset,' echoed Cranat.

Instinctively, Fidelma knew that Cranat was seizing the easy excuse given by her daughter.

'Tell me why you did not share your husband's sleeping chamber?'

There was a gasp of indignation from Crón.

'How dare you ask such an impertinent . . . ?' she began.

Fidelma swung her head round and regarded Crón with narrowed eyes.

'I dare,' she replied impassively, 'because I am an advocate of the courts and no question that seeks to get to the truth is impertinent. I think, Crón of Araglin, you still have much to learn of the wisdom and duties of a chieftain. Your mother was right to send to Cashel for a Brehon.'

Crón swallowed, her face reddening. Before she could think of a suitable response, Fidelma had already turned back to Cranat.

'Well, lady?' she prompted sharply.

Cranat's icy expression challenged her for a moment but Fidelma's fiery green eyes accepted the challenge and were not cowed. Cranat's shoulders eventually slumped in resignation.

'It has been many years since I shared my husband's bed,' she replied quietly.

'Why so?'

Cranat's hands fluttered in her lap.

'We have grown apart in . . . in *that* way.'

'And this did not bother you?'

'No.'

111

'Nor, presumably, did it bother Eber?'

'I am not sure what you mean?'

'You know the laws of marriage as well as I do. If there were sexual failings between you then either party could have sought divorce.'

Cranat's face reddened.

Crón glanced to where Eadulf was sitting impassively.

'Must the Saxon stay and hear this?' she demanded.

Eadulf, with some embarrassment, began to rise.

Fidelma motioned him to be reseated.

'He is here to observe the working of our legal process. There is nothing to be ashamed at before the law.'

'We had an amicable arrangement,' Cranat continued, realising that she and her daughter had met someone with a stronger will than either of them. 'There was no need for divorce or separation.'

'None? If either of you had become incapable of intercourse, then you could legally divorce with ease. The problems of infertility or impotence are equally covered.'

'My mother knows the law,' interrupted Crón indignantly. 'Can we leave it that my father and mother simply preferred to sleep apart?'

'I will accept this,' Fidelma agreed, 'though it would have been easier to understand if I knew a reason.'

'The reason was that we preferred to sleep alone,' Cranat insisted heavily.

'So you remained partners in everything else?'

'Yes.'

'And your husband made no attempt to obtain a wife of lower status, a concubine?'

'That is forbidden,' snapped Crón.

'Forbidden?' Fidelma was surprised. 'Our laws are quite specific that polygyny is still accepted under the *Cáin Lánamna*. A man may have a chief wife and his concubine who has, under law, half the status and entitlements of the chief wife.'

'How can you approve of that?' demanded Crón. 'You are a sister of the Faith.'

Fidelma regarded her equably.

'Who says that I approve it? I simply tell you of the law of the five kingdoms which operates today. And I am an advocate of that law. I am surprised that here, in such a rural community, there is disapproval of it. Usually, in rural areas, there is much support for the old laws and customs of our people.'

'Father Gormán says that it is evil to have more than one wife.'

'Ah, Father Gormán. Again, Father Gormán. It seems that the good father has a strong influence over this community. It is true that within the new Faith many oppose polygyny but with little success as yet. In fact, the *scriptor* of the law text, the *Bretha Crólige*, actually finds justification for polygyny in the texts of the Old Testament. It is argued that if the chosen people of God lived in a plurality of unions, how can we, gentiles, argue against it?'

Cranat make a curious sound of disapproval, clicking her tongue.

'You may argue your theology with Father Gormán on his return. Eber had no need of other wives nor concubines. We dwell here in an amicable family. And our close relationship has nothing to do with his death for his killer has been clearly identified.'

'Ah yes,' Fidelma breathed, as if she had been distracted. 'Let us return to this matter...'

'I know no more than what I told you,' snapped Cranat. 'I learnt only of Eber's death from others.'

'And, as your daughter says, you were upset?'

'I was.'

'But clear-minded enough to instruct the young warrior, Crítán, to ride to Cashel to request a Brehon be sent here?'

'I was a chieftain's wife. I had my duty to fulfil.'

'Were you shocked when you heard it was Móen who killed your husband?'

'Shocked? No. Sad, perhaps. It was inevitable that that wild beast would turn on someone sooner or later.'

'You did not like Móen?'

The eyebrows of Eber's widow arched in perplexity.

'Like? How could anyone even know Móen?' she demanded.

'Perhaps not so far as "knowing", in the sense of understanding his thoughts, his hopes and ambitions. But did you have any daily contact with him?'

'You would give the creature the same sensitivities as a normal person?' sneered Crón, interrupting.

'Being deprived of sight, hearing and speech does not deprive one of other sensitivities,' corrected Fidelma. 'You, Cranat, must have seen Móen raised from childhood?'

Cranat pursed her lips sourly.

'Yes. But I did not know that unfortunate creature. I have seen pigs grown into sows from little piglets. This does not mean that I *know* the sow.'

Fidelma smiled dryly.

'What you mean is that you looked upon Móen as an animal rather than a human being? Therefore, he was nothing to do with your life?'

'If you say so,' she conceded.

'I am merely trying to understand your attitude to Móen. Let us ask this, then, what was your attitude to Teafa? I am told that she, at least, seemed to communicate with him.'

'Does the shepherd communicate with his sheep?'

'I am also told that you did not get on well with Teafa.'

'Who tells you such scandal?'

'Are you denying that it is so?'

Cranat hesitated and shrugged.

'We have had our differences in recent years.'

'Why was this?'

'She suggested that I should divorce Eber and lose my status as chieftain's wife. I felt sorry for the woman. Though, of course,

114

she brought misfortune upon her own head.'

'Misfortune? Why?'

'She was beyond marriageable age, frustrated with life and had, in her frustration, adopted the foundling, Móen, who could not return the emotions which she demanded from him.'

'Yet she was your husband's sister?'

'Teafa preferred her own company. She sometimes attended religious feasts here but did not agree with Father Gormán's interpretation of the Faith. She was almost a recluse even though her cabin is thirty yards from this very spot.'

'What reason would Móen have to kill her or Eber?'

Cranat spread her arms.

'As I said earlier, I cannot put my mind into the thoughts of a wild animal.'

'And is that how you saw Móen? Simply as a wild animal?'

'How else could you view the creature?'

'I see. Was this the manner in which he was treated by Teafa's family during all these years that he lived in this community? As a wild animal?' Fidelma asked, ignoring Cranat's question.

Crón decided to answer for her mother.

'He was treated like any other of the animals in this *rath*. Perhaps better. He was treated well, not harshly, but how could one treat him otherwise?'

'And, if I have interpreted you correctly, you ascribe his actions, after all these years, to some sudden fit of animal instinct?'

'What else?'

'It requires a cunning animal to take a knife, kill the woman who has been looking after him all his life and find his way to Eber's apartments and similarly kill him.'

'Who said animals were not cunning?' Crón riposted.

Cranat grimaced sourly in agreement.

'It seems to me, young woman, that you are trying to find some way to exonerate Móen. Why is this?'

Fidelma suddenly stood up.

'I am merely seeking the truth. I am not responsible for how you see things, Cranat of Araglin. I have a job to do, according to my oath as an advocate of the courts of the five kingdoms. That task is not merely to establish who is guilty of breaking the law but why the law was broken, in order that the assessment of culpability and compensation are adequately made. And now, I have finished for the time being.'

Eadulf noted the expressions of outrage on the faces of mother and daughter. If looks could have killed, then Fidelma would have been dead before she rose and stepped off the dais. Obliviously, she preceded Eadulf, who had also risen, to the doors of the assembly hall.

Once outside the doors, Fidelma paused. They stood in silence for a while.

'You do not appear to have much liking for Cranat and her daughter,' observed Eadulf dryly.

Fidelma's eyes flashed as she turned to him but then she gave him a mischievous grin.

'I have a grievous fault, Eadulf. Of that I freely admit. I am intolerant of certain attitudes. Haughtiness is one thing that prejudices me against people. I respond in kind. I am afraid I cannot obey the teaching of "turning the other cheek". I find that such a teaching is merely an invitation to further injury.'

'Well, at least you recognise your fault,' replied Eadulf. 'The greatest of faults is to be conscious of none.'

Fidelma chuckled softly.

'You are becoming a philosopher, Eadulf of Seaxmund's Ham. But one important factor we have learnt from this clash of temperaments. Cranat is not to be trusted.'

'Why not?'

'She was too upset to pay her last respects to the body of her husband, to even see the body, but strong enough and devoted to duty to send a messenger to Cashel because she did not trust her inexperienced daughter's knowledge of the law. I find that strange.'

She glanced towards the chapel. Eadulf followed her gaze. The door of the chapel stood open.

'I wonder if the redoubtable Father Gormán has returned?' she mused. Then making up her mind she moved towards it calling over her shoulder: 'Come, let us see.'

Eadulf groaned a little under his breath as he hurried after her for he knew, by the picture he had already built up, the priest was someone who would be a dog to Fidelma's cat.

There were candles lit in the dusk shrouded chapel. The fragrance of incense struck them immediately, permeating throughout the polished deal panelled building. The perfume of it was exceedingly strong. Fidelma glanced quickly around at the opulence of the interior. There were gold-framed icons on the walls and an exquisite silver bejewelled cross stood upon the altar with a plain silver chalice before it. There were no seats within the church as it was the custom for congregations to stand throughout the services. Lighted candles impregnated with perfumes and spices caused the aroma which made them catch at their breath. Certainly Father Gormán boasted an opulent church and congregation.

A man was kneeling at his devotions. Fidelma paused at the back of the chapel, Eadulf at her shoulder. The man seemed to sense their presence for he glanced over his shoulder, turned back to end his prayers and genuflected to the altar. Then he rose to his feet and came to greet them.

Father Gormán was tall, with a slight almost feminine figure but with a dark, swarthy complexion, a fleshy face, thick red lips and receding greying hair that had once matched the blackness of his flashing eyes. There were traces of the handsome youth although Fidelma now had the impression of a dissolute middle-age which seemed at odds with the positive impression she had gathered of a fiery Roman priest. He greeted them in a deep, thunderous voice which still held the promise of hellfire and damnation in it. She noted, though not with surprise, that he wore the *corona spina* on his pate, the mark of a cleric of Roman adherence and not the tonsure of a follower of the Irish church. Curiously, Fidelma noticed that he was wearing gloves of rough leather.

His eyes seemed to soften as he caught sight of Eadulf's own Roman tonsure.

'Greetings, brother,' he boomed. 'So we have one among us who follows the path of real wisdom?'

Eadulf was embarrassed at the welcome.

'I am Eadulf of Seaxmund's Ham. I would never have expected to find so rich a chapel here among these mountains.'

Father Gormán laughed warmly.

'The earth provides, my brother. The earth provides for those with true faith.'

'Father Gormán?' Fidelma interposed before the conversation continued on the course the priest had sent it. 'I am Fidelma of Kildare.'

The dark eyes flashed to her appraisingly.

'Ah yes. I have been hearing from Dubán about you, sister. You are welcome in my little chapel. Cill Uird, I call it, the church of the ritual, for it is by ritual we live the true Christian life. God bless your coming, sanctify your staying and give peace to your departure.'

Fidelma inclined her head in acknowledgment of the greeting.

'We would appreciate a few minutes of your time, father. You have doubtless learnt the purpose of our visit here?'

'I have so,' agreed the priest. He gestured for them to follow him and led them across the chapel to a small side room which appeared to be the sacristy where there was a bench on which was draped a parti-coloured cloak. In front of it was a chair. Wordlessly, he removed the cloak and indicated that they should be seated on the bench while he himself took the chair, removing his gloves as he did so.

'You will forgive me?' he said, catching her inquisitive

expression. 'I have only just returned to the *rath*. I always wear leather to protect my hands when riding.'

'A priest with a horse to ride is unusual,' pointed out Eadulf. Father Gormán chuckled.

'I have rich supporters who have donated a horse for my convenience for it would take many days to administer to my flock if I had to do it all on foot. And now, no more talk of me. I saw you both at Hilda's abbey during the council there.'

'Were you at Witebia?' Eadulf was astounded.

Father Gormán nodded affirmatively.

'Indeed. I saw you both there but you will not remember me. I was finishing a missionary tour with Colmán when I came to Streoneshalh. I was there not as a delegate but merely to listen to my betters arguing the merits of the churches of Colmcille and Rome.'

Eadulf did not disguise his feeling of smugness.

'So you were there when we solved the murder of the Abbess Étain and . . .'

'I was there,' interrupted Father Gormán heavily, 'when Oswy, in his wisdom, decided that Rome was the true church and that those who followed Colmcille were in error.'

'It is already obvious that you follow the dictates of Rome,' Fidelma conceded dryly.

'And who could argue against Oswy's decision once the arguments were made?' replied the priest. 'I returned to this, my parish, and have tried to guide my people, the people of Araglin, along the true path ever since.'

'Surely there are many paths which lead to God?' interrupted Fidelma.

'Not so!' snapped Father Gormán. 'Only those who follow the one path can hope to find God.'

'You have no doubt of that?'

'I have no doubt for I am firm in my belief.'

'Then you are to be envied, Father Gormán. To believe with

such certainty you must surely have begun with doubt. '

'You are not free until you have ceased to doubt.'

'I thought even Christ doubted at the end,' Fidelma pointed out with a benign look that belied her sharp retort.

Father Gormán looked scandalised.

'Only to demonstrate to us that we must remain true to our conviction.'

'Is that so? My mentor, Morann of Tara, used to say that convictions are more dangerous enemies of truth than outright lies.'

Father Gormán swallowed and was about to reply when she raised a hand to still him.

'I did not come to debate theology with you, Gormán of Cill Uird, though I shall be happy to do so once my business is ended. I came in my role as advocate of the courts.'

'About the killing of Eber,' added Eadulf quickly, for he judged that Father Gormán would not be so easily deflected from his course.

Father Gormán looked reluctant for a moment to give up the argument about religion but then bowed his head.

'Then there is little I can help you with. I know nothing.'

'Nothing at all?'

'Nothing.'

'But your church stands a yard or so away from Eber's apartments. I understand that you sleep in this church. Of all the people in the *rath* you were the closest to Eber's apartments. It might be expected that you were best placed to have heard something.'

'I sleep in the room next to this,' Father Gormán said, pointing to a small door behind them. 'But I can assure you that I knew nothing of the killing until I was roused from my sleep by the noise of people outside Eber's apartments.'

'When was that?'

'After sunrise. The people had word of Eber's death and gathered outside his apartments. It was the hubbub of the people which first woke me and I went out to find out what was amiss. I knew nothing before that.'

'I thought Rome offered strict rules as to the time of rising,' Eadulf put in slyly.

Father Gormán regarded him with disfavour.

'You may know, brother, that what is good for Rome is often not good for us in the more northern climes. Rome can say that a religious must rise at a certain hour. That is fine in Rome for the day gets lighter there earlier and there is justification for rising early. But what is the point of a man rising in the darkness and cold of these latitudes because his brothers in Rome rise at that hour?'

Fidelma was smiling broadly.

'So there is some good to be salvaged from the rules of the church of Colmcille?'

Father Gormán's eyes narrowed as her thrust went home.

'You may have your joke, sister. The fact remains that the rules of the church of Rome are the rules as consecrated by Christ . . . in the matter of theology and teaching. We can differ only when geography and climate make them impractical.'

'Very well. I will not argue . . . for the present. You rose just after sunrise and it was only then that you discovered what had happened to Eber. You had been fast asleep all night?'

'I had offered the midnight Angelus and retired to bed. Nothing had disturbed me.'

'You heard no scream or cry for help?'

'I have said as much.'

'You see, when a man is attacked in such a manner as Eber obviously was, it seems to me that he might scream for help.'

'I was told that Eber was stabbed as he lay sleeping. Hardly time for a cry for help.'

Fidelma pursed her lips thoughtfully.

'Hardly time for a cry for help?' she repeated slowly. 'No time to cry out as someone who was blind, deaf and dumb was able to enter the room without disturbing anyone, take a knife and stab Eber savagely several times? All this while, Eber lay in a room with a lighted lamp?'

It seemed that she was speaking half to herself.

'I heard nothing,' Father Gormán insisted.

'Did it surprise you when you learnt that it was Móen who had been found by Eber's body and that he had, according to witnesses, been the killer?'

'Surprise me?' Father Gormán thought a moment. 'No I cannot say surprise was my reaction. Allow a wild animal to run loose in your home and expect it to turn on you and bite you.'

'Is that how you saw Móen?'

'As a wild animal? Yes. I saw that child of incest as no more than a wild beast. I would not allow that child of incest within the walls of this chapel. He was God's accursed.'

'Would you say that was a Christian way of dealing with someone who was afflicted?' interrupted Fidelma in indignation.

'Should I argue with God against His punishment of this creature? Punishment it was, depriving him of that which makes us human. Didn't the Christ tell us: "The Son of Man shall send forth his angels, and they shall gather out of his kingdom all things that offend, and them which do iniquity, and shall cast them into a furnace of fire; there shall be wailing and gnashing of teeth"? God punishes us as much as He rewards us.'

'You seem sure that God created Móen to punish him. Perhaps he created Móen in order to try the extent of our Christian faith?'

'That is an impertinence.'

'You think so? I am often accused of impertinence when people cannot answer, or are unwilling to answer, a question. Poor Móen. It seems that he was not well tolerated in this place after all.'

It was a statement that implied a question.

'Do you rebuke my Christian ethics, sister?' There was a dangerous edge to the priest's voice.

'It is not for me to do so, Father Gormán,' replied Fidelma blandly.

'Quite so!' snapped Father Gormán, misunderstanding her slight emphasis.

'Then you have no qualms in believing that Móen is responsible?' interspersed Eadulf, trying to ease the growing tension.

Father Gormán shook his head.

'What qualms should I have? There were witnesses.'

'But have you never asked what reason Móen must have had to do this?'

'Probably he had several reasons. The creature lives in his own private world, cut off from the rest of us. Who knows his logic, his reasoning? He does not have to have the same reasons and motives that we in this world do. He is of the other world. Who knows the bitterness and hate that he harbours in his world for those more blessed in this one?'

'Then you do allow him some human feelings?' Fidelma thrust quickly.

'I would allow an animal those feelings. Ill-treat a dog, for example, and it may one day turn on you.'

Fidelma leant forward thoughtfully.

'Are you saying that Eber may have ill-treated Móen?'

'I am giving you general reasons not specific ones,' the priest replied defensively.

'Did Teafa ill-treat Móen?'

Father Gormán shook his head.

'No. She doted on the creature. All the family of the chieftains of Araglin are perverse.'

Fidelma quickly took the bait that he had unwittingly offered.

'Are you including Eber in that statement?'

'Him especially. Let us pray that Crón takes after her mother and not her father.'

Fidelma's eyes narrowed.

'Yet many have told me that Eber was kindliness and generosity itself; that he was well respected everywhere in Araglin. Was I told falsely?'

Father Gormán allowed a bitter smile to twist his mouth out of shape.

'Eber had one blessing – he was a generous man. There he departed from the virtues and his life was one long trail of vices. Why do you think that his wife left his bed chamber?'

'I have asked her and she would only say that it was mutually agreed.'

Father Gormán sniffed sceptically.

'I tried to persuade her to divorce him under the law. But she is a proud woman as befits her station as a princess of her people.'

'Why would you want to persuade her to divorce Eber?' asked Fidelma.

'Because he was a man not fitted to marriage.'

'Cranat did not think so, or so she told me. Can you be more explicit?'

'All I can tell you was that Eber was . . .' he shuddered and genuflected, 'forgive me, he was sexually perverse.'

'In what way?' Fidelma pressed.

'Do you mean that he preferred to lie with boys or young men rather than women?' hazarded Eadulf, suddenly seeing a reason why Móen might have killed him. 'Was Eber sexually abusing Móen?'

Father Gormán held up both his hands and his face showed his horror.

'No, not that! No, Eber liked the opposite gender well enough . . . perhaps too well.'

'Ah, I see. And Cranat knew of this?'

'Everyone knew of it. Cranat was the last to know. He had always been like it since he came to the age of puberty. His sisters knew well enough and it was Teafa who finally had to tell Cranat. Cranat told me so. That was when she decided to vacate the marital bed.'

'Why didn't Cranat leave him?'

'Because of her daughter, Crón. Because of the shame it would bring. And there was the fact that Cranat, while a princess of her people, had no money or land to call her own. She married Eber for his money. He married her for her lineage and family connections. Perhaps that is not a good basis on which to form a marriage.'

'I see. But surely, under the law, Cranat was entitled to be rid of him? If Cranat had divorced Eber on the grounds you state then she was entitled to take out of her marriage all that she had brought into it. If this was nothing, then, further, she was automatically entitled, at separation, to one-ninth of the increase of her husband's wealth during marriage. Even if she had no property at the time of her marriage, surely one-ninth of the wealth generated by Eber during the twenty or so years of Cranat's marriage to him would be enough to allow her to live well.'

Father Gormán had a slightly bitter note in his voice.

'That it would. That it would. I could have helped her. But she chose to remain.'

Fidelma regarded him thoughtfully.

'You obviously have great feeling for Cranat,' she observed quietly.

Father Gormán flushed abruptly.

'There is nothing amiss in wishing to correct a grievous wrong.'

'Nothing at all,' Fidelma assured him. 'But this matter would not have endeared you to Eber. I hear, however, that you believe that Móen should be punished to the point whereby his own life is taken in forfeit.'

'Isn't the word of God explicit? If a man destroys the eye of another, they shall destroy his eye. I believe in the full measure of retribution as it is taught by our Faith and Rome.'

Fidelma shook her head.

'Extreme justice is often unjust.'

Father Gormán's eyes narrowed.

'That smacks of the wisdom of Pelagius.'

'Is it wrong to quote the words of a wise man?'

'The churches of Ireland are filled with Pelagian heresy,' sneered the priest.

'Was Pelagius such a heretic?' questioned Fidelma mildly.

Father Gormán nearly choked with indignation.

'You doubt it? Do you not know your history?'

'I know that Pope Zosimus pronounced him innocent of heresy in spite of pressure from Augustine of Hippo who persuaded the Emperor Honorius to issue an imperial decree condemning him.'

'But Pope Zosimus did eventually declare him guilty of heresy.'

'After coming under pressure from the emperor. I hardly call that a theological decision. Ironic he should be condemned for his treatise *De Libero Arbitrio* – On Free Will.'

'So you support a heretic, like most of your Columban breed?' Father Gormán was openly offensive.

'We do not shut our minds to reason, as Rome commands of its adherents,' Fidelma snapped back. 'After all, what does heresy really mean? It is simply the Greek word for making a choice. It is in our nature to make a free choice therefore we are all heretics.'

'Pelagius was full of Irish porridge! He was rightly condemned for refusing to see the truth of Augustine's doctrine on the Fall of Man and Original Sin!'

'Should not Augustine have been condemned for refusing to see the truth of Pelagius' doctrine on free will?' returned Fidelma hotly.

'You are not only impertinent but in peril of your soul.' Father Gormán was red in the face and angry.

Fidelma was not flustered.

'Let us consider the facts,' she rejoined quietly. 'The original sin was Adam's and Adam and his descendants were punished by God for that sin. Is that correct?'

'It was a curse that had been passed on to all mankind until the sacrifice of the Christ redeemed the world,' agreed the priest, his temper simmering.

'But Adam disobeyed God?'

'That is so.'

'Yet, it is taught, God is omnipotent and He created Adam.'

'Man was given free will and Adam, in defying God, fell from grace.'

'This is where Pelagius asked the question: before Adam's fall, could he choose between good and evil?'

'We are told that he had God's commands to guide him. God told him what he should do. But the woman tempted him.'

'Ah yes. The *woman*.' The emphasis was softly made. Brother Eadulf stirred uncomfortably. He wished Fidelma would not chance the Fates by her arguments. He glanced towards her but she was leaning forward, enjoying the confrontation of intellects. 'God was omnipotent and created Adam and Eve. Surely God's will was enough to guide them?'

'Man had free will.'

'So Adam's will, the will of the *woman*,' again the gentle emphasis, 'was more powerful than God's will?'

Father Gormán was outraged.

'No, of course not. God was omnipotent . . . But He had allowed man to be free.'

'Then the logical course of thought is that God, being omnipotent, and thus able to prevent sin, refused to do so. Being omnipotent, He knew what Adam would do. Under our law, God was then an accessary before the fact!'

'That is blasphemy,' gasped Father Gormán.

'There is more, Gormán,' continued Fidelma ruthlessly, 'for if we are to be logical, we can argue that God acquiesced in Adam's sin.'

'Sacrilege!' gasped the priest in horror.

'Come, be logical.' Fidelma was quite unperturbed at his reaction. 'God was omniscient and He created Adam. If He was omniscient then He knew Adam would sin. And if the human race was cursed because of Adam's sin, then God knew they would be cursed. He then created people to suffer by unnumbered millions.'

'You and your finite mind, you cannot understand the great mystery of the universe,' snapped Father Gormán.

'We will not be able to understand it if we choose to obscure the path to that universe by creating myths. This is where I stand with the teachings of Pelagius who was a man of our people, and why Rome has always attacked our churches not only here but among the Britons and the Gauls who share our philosophies. We are a people who question all things and only through our questions can we hope to arrive at the Great Truth and we must stand by the Truth even if we stand against the world.'

She rose abruptly.

'I thank you for your time, Father Gormán.'

Once outside she exchanged a glance with Eadulf.

'So a tiny bit of the mist begins to clear away,' she said with satisfaction.

Eadulf pulled a face. He was bemused.

'About Pelagius?' he hazarded.

Fidelma chuckled.

'About Father Gormán,' she reproved.

'You suspect Father Gormán of some involvement?'

'I suspect everyone of something. But you are right. It is clear that Gormán was, or is, passionately devoted to Cranat.'

'At their age?' Eadulf was indignant.

Fidelma turned to her companion in surprise.

'Love between people can be felt at any age, Eadulf of Seaxmund's Ham.'

'But a woman of her years and a priest . . . ?'

'There are no laws forbidding priests from marrying, not even Rome prohibits it, though I admit that Rome disapproves of it.'

'Are you saying that Father Gormán might have had reason for wishing Eber dead?'

Fidelma's expression was almost impassive.

'Oh, he had a reason right enough. But did he have the means of fulfilling his wish or arranging for its fulfilment?'

Chapter Nine

That evening they bathed and ate their meal alone. Crón had not invited them to dine in the hall of assembly, as protocol would naturally dictate. Eadulf was not particularly surprised at their isolation. When he considered the day's events he realised that if Fidelma had made a friend of anyone in the *rath* of Araglin it was only the poor creature Móen. She had certainly not endeared herself to any of the others. That Crón and her mother, Cranat, did not want to associate themselves with her company was hardly a matter for wonder.

It was a nervous young girl who brought the trays of food to the guests' hostel. She was dark-haired, about sixteen years old, almost unnaturally pale and seemed afraid of them. Fidelma did her best to reassure her by making friendly overtures.

'What is your name?'

'I am Grella, sister. I work for Dignait in the kitchens.'

Fidelma smiled encouragingly.

'Are you happy in your work, Grella?'

The young girl frowned slightly.

'It is the work I do,' she said simply. 'I was raised in the kitchens of the chieftain. I have no parents,' she added, as if this would explain everything.

'I see. You must have been saddened by the death of your chieftain, then, having been raised in his house.'

To Fidelma's surprise the girl shook her head vehemently.

'No . . . no, but I was saddened by the lady Teafa's death. She was a kind lady.'

'But Eber was not kind?'

131

'Teafa was kind to me,' the girl replied anxiously, apparently not wishing to speak ill of the dead chieftain. 'The lady Teafa was kind to everyone.'

'And Móen? Do you like Móen?'

Grella looked puzzled again.

'I was uneasy when he was about. Teafa was the only one who could tell him what to do.'

'Tell him?' Fidelma immediately seized upon the phrase. 'How did she tell him?'

'She had some way of communicating with him.'

'Do you know what it was?' interrupted Eadulf eagerly.

The young girl shook her head.

'I have no idea. Some form of finger-tapping it was said that both understood.'

Fidelma was intrigued.

'Did you ever see it? Did Teafa ever tell you how it was done?'

'I saw her doing it many times but I did not understand it. Perhaps it was just the familiar touch of a hand which calmed him.'

Fidelma was disappointed.

Grella held her head to one side in thought, as if dredging her memories. Then she smiled briefly.

'I recall; she said that it was Gadra who taught her the art.'

'Gadra? Who is Gadra?' Hope sprang up again.

Grella shuddered and genuflected.

'Gadra is a bogeyman. They say he steals the souls of naughty children. Now I must go or Dignait will be looking for me. I shall be in trouble.'

When she had gone they ate, for the most part in meditative silence. Eventually Eadulf felt courage enough to chance her displeasure by raising the matter which had long been troubling him.

'Is it wise,' he asked reflectively, 'to purposefully arouse the ire of everyone?'

Fidelma raised her head from a contemplation of the food on her plate.

'I hear the sound of disapproval in your tone, Eadulf of Seaxmund's Ham,' she observed solemnly, although there was a mischievous twinkle in her eye.

Eadulf grimaced as if in apology.

'Forgive me, but I feel that sometimes a little tact and discretion might achieve the same ends as . . .'

'You think I am unduly rude?' interrupted Fidelma earnestly, like a pupil seeking the advice of a master.

Eadulf felt awkward. He did not trust Fidelma in such a mood and shook his head negatively.

'My mother once told me that you cannot unpick a piece of embroidery with an axe.'

Fidelma stared at him in genuine surprise.

'You have never mentioned your mother before, Eadulf.'

'She no longer lives. But she was a wise woman.'

'I accept her wisdom. Sometimes, however, when you find a thick wooden door of arrogance closed against you, you have to take the axe and splinter it before you can talk to the person inside. Often common courtesy is mistaken by arrogant people for weakness and even sycophancy.'

'Have you really splintered your way through to the truth?'

Fidelma held her head to one side.

'I have managed to get nearer the truth than I would otherwise have done if I had allowed the doors to remain shut. Yet I would agree that the complete truth is still very far away.'

'Then how is it to be reached?'

'When we have finished our meal I shall seek out Dubán. Perhaps we can find out whether this bogeyman, Gadra, truly exists. If he does and is able to show me a means of communicating with Móen then we may be that much nearer the truth. If we can discover what Móen knows . . .'

Eadulf was sceptical.

'It was merely a child's fairy tale. A bogeyman stealing children's souls, indeed!'

'There is usually a truth behind each fairy tale, Eadulf.'

'You are presuming much, Fidelma.'

'How so?'

'You are presuming that this bogeyman exists. You are presuming that the child, Grella, reported correctly that this being, Gadra, taught Teafa a means of communication with Móen. You are even presuming that there *is* some means of communication with the creature. You are further presuming that there is also a mind in that unfortunate being. You are also presuming that he will tell you something that will cast a light on the matter. You are finally presuming that he is innocent.'

Fidelma sat back, placing her hands palm downward on the table on either side of her plate, and regarded Eadulf for a moment or two before responding.

'My presumption is a faith in his innocence. I cannot explain it neither do I have the evidence to demonstrate it. It is a feeling, a belief that what seems false to my senses is, indeed, false. The logic being that which is argued as the truth, yet feels false, is false.'

Eadulf pursed his lips.

'Is it not true that the greatest deception is self-deception?'

'You believe that I am deceiving myself?'

'I am trying to suggest that what seems so, may well be so.'

Fidelma chuckled softly, reached out a hand and laid it on his arm.

'Eadulf, you are the voice of conscience. When I am too enthusiastic, you curb my intemperance. Nevertheless, we shall seek out this Gadra, the bogeyman, if he exists.'

Eadulf sighed.

'I had no doubt that we would,' he said in resignation as she rose and went in search of Dubán.

It was Crítán, standing on guard duty by the stables, who

134

eventually informed her that Dubán was not in the *rath* of Araglin. The brash young man was not very forthcoming for he had to be prompted several times before he explained.

'He had to leave with some warriors and go to the high pastures.'

'Is anything wrong?' demanded Fidelma. 'Why did they ride off at this hour with darkness descending?'

Crítán was sullen.

'Nothing is wrong. You need have no fear while there are men to guard this *rath*, sister.'

Fidelma restrained herself from an angry retort.

'Nevertheless, what caused Dubán to ride off?' she pressed.

'Word came of a cattle raid against one of the isolated farmsteads across the mountains.'

'A raid?' She was interested at once. 'Is it known by whom?'

'That is what they went to discover. Presumably by the same raiders who made a foray into this valley a few weeks ago. I should have gone with Dubán but, instead, I have been instructed to remain here and look after the creature, Móen. It is not fair.'

Fidelma thought the young warrior appeared more like a sulky child than a grown man.

'To be a warrior,' Fidelma said carefully, 'you are not bound by duty unless you have freely accepted it as your obligation.'

Crítán looked annoyed.

'I do not understand what you mean.'

'Exactly so. Tell me, Crítán,' she changed the subject quickly. 'Tell me, does the name Gadra mean anything to you?'

The young man grimaced with ill-temper.

'He is said to be a bogeyman who steals children's souls. People here about use his name to frighten their children.'

'Does he have a real existence?'

'I have heard Dubán speak of him. I do not believe in bogeymen, so once I asked about him.'

'And what did Dubán say?' pressed Fidelma.

'He told me that in his youth, Gadra was a hermit who dwelt

in the mountains and refused to accept the new Faith.'

'Is he still living?'

'It was many years ago. He lived in the forests up in a small mountain valley. I do not know where. I think Dubán might know.'

Fidelma thanked the young man and turned back into the guests' hostel to report to Eadulf.

'What now?' Eadulf asked.

'Now? There is no more to be done than to wait until tomorrow.'

It was well after midnight that Fidelma awoke to hear the sounds of a horse entering the *rath*. She could hear Eadulf still deep in slumber in his cubicle. She rose, draping her cloak around her shoulders, and picked her way, barefoot, to the window which gave a view to the front of the hostel.

A man was dismounting by the gates. By the light of the blazing brand torches, she could see it was the stableman, Menma. She was about to turn back to her bed when a shadow detached itself from the front of the hall of assembly. It moved into the light of the torches and greeted the red-haired man.

It was Father Gormán. His body seemed animated and he waved his arms. His voice was intense but not loud and she could not make out his words.

To her surprise, Menma appeared to be answering with equal vehemence.

Father Gormán was waving a hand towards the guests' hostel. Plainly Eadulf and herself were the subject of their argument. She wondered why?

After a moment or two, Menma yanked at the reins of his horse and drew the beast away from the priest towards the stables.

For some moments Father Gormán stood, hands on hips, staring after Menma. Then he, too, turned abruptly and strode away towards his chapel.

Thoughtfully, Fidelma returned to her bed.

The sun was shining brightly when Fidelma joined Eadulf for the breakfast which Grella had brought. She could feel the warmth of the sun's rays through the window of the guests' hostel. Eadulf had just finished eating and now sat back, allowing Fidelma to break her fast in silence. Only when she had finished did he ask rhetorically: 'Do you think Dubán has returned?'

'I shall go in search of him now and see if he can tell us more about this hermit.'

She instructed Eadulf to see if he could pick up any further information from the inhabitants of the *rath* while she went in search of the warrior.

Fidelma walked from the hostel around the stone wall of the hall of assembly.

The sound of voices and the bark of harsh laughter halted her. The timbre of the voice sounded familiar.

She paused in the shelter of the wall and looked across to the group of buildings from where the sound had emanated. There was a horseman, apparently newly arrived for the dust of travel was still on him. He had dismounted and stood with the reins of his mount over his arm. Fidelma recognised the tall, stocky man at once. It was Muadnat, the farmer, against whom she had given judgment at Lios Mhór. What took her breath away was the figure whom he was clasping in his arms, who was returning his kiss for kiss with the passion of a young girl. She was a tall, fair-haired woman clad in a parti-coloured cloak.

Only when she broke away from the fierce embrace did Fidelma recognise the woman as Cranat, the widow of Eber.

Some instinct made Fidelma move back further into the shadows of the wall in order to examine the burly farmer more closely. For one who had just lost seven *cumals* of land, Muadnat seemed happy as he embraced the widowed chieftainess. It did not need experience to see the easy intimacy between them. Muadnat gave another bellow of laughter, to which Cranat placed a finger against her lips and cast a nervous glance around and then beckoned him in a conspiratorial fashion into the building behind them. Muadnat paused only to hitch his horse to a railing outside.

137

Fidelma waited until they had vanished and then, head bent in thought, she continued her way to the entrance of the hall of assembly. The doors stood open. She did not know what instinct made her hesitate instead of announcing her presence. Then she entered. Maybe she had subconsciously caught the sound of voices and the anxious tone of conversation. The first voice was that of Dubán.

'I think you should be more respectful to her,' he was saying earnestly. 'At least, do not go out of your way to incur her enmity.'

'Why not? She should not be here that long. I think she is exceeding her instructions.'

Fidelma frowned for the second voice was that of Crón. The voices were coming from a side room to which the door stood ajar. Fidelma trod with cat-like silence nearer to the door.

'I know she is Colgú's sister. But do you think he would send her here merely because of that? She is a clever woman. Little escapes those quizzical green eyes.'

'Ah! You've noticed the colour of her eyes?' The retort was sullen. Fidelma's eyes widened as she heard the tone of jealousy in the voice of the tanist.

Dubán responded with a chuckle.

'I've noticed that she is someone not to be fooled with. The less her hostility is aroused the better, pulse of my heart.'

Fidelma blinked at the easy endearment which came from his lips.

'Surely she cannot really believe that Móen is innocent?' Crón's tone was slightly mollified.

'I think she suspects it. Father Gormán believes that she is determined to prove it. He was quite upset when I saw him last night after he had spoken with her.'

'I thought this matter would be easily resolved. If only my mother had let well alone.'

'Nothing is ever easy, my dear. If she does believe Móen is innocent, then she will look elsewhere for those who might have murdered him. You would do well to make her into a friend.'

There was a slight intake of breath.

'She might discover how much I hated my father. Is that what you mean?'

'She will eventually discover how much everyone hated him,' replied Dubán. 'Anyway, you must deal with that idiot Muadnat. He would choose this moment to come to the *rath* to create trouble. Can't you tell him to go away? To return next week when all this is over?'

'How can I do that, my dear? He is not sensitive enough to understand why. He might present problems. No, I must deal with the matter. Tell Muadnat of my decision and tell him to be here in the hall of assembly at noon.'

'Then please treat the sister with more grace.'

'Go now,' came Crón's voice more firmly. 'There is much to do.'

Fidelma quickly retraced her steps, on tip-toe, back to the door. She turned on the threshold, taking the mallet and banging it on the wooden block before entering the hall, as if for the first time. Crón came forwards from the side room. She was alone. She greeted Fidelma civilly enough, although her eyes were guarded.

'I am looking for Dubán,' Fidelma announced.

'What makes you think he is here?' the tanist demanded defensively.

'Surely here is as good a place as any to search for the commander of your bodyguard?' inquired Fidelma innocently.

Crón realised her mistake and forced a smile.

'He is not here at the moment. He was late abroad last night and probably has not risen.' The lies fell easily from her lips. 'If I see him, I shall tell him that you were inquiring for him. Now, if you will excuse me, I must prepare for an important matter.'

Fidelma was not to be dismissed so easily.

'Prepare?'

'I need to sit in judgment today,' Crón replied. 'Minor cases I

139

may judge even if my mother does not approve of my knowledge of the law.'

It was true that a chieftain could act as judge in insignificant cases if they had no Brehon at hand to help them.

'What manner of case?'

'Nothing that would concern you,' Crón replied immediately. Then she caught herself and conceded. 'A case of animal trespass. One farmer of our community claims damages against another farmer of our community. It is a matter that needs to be dealt with immediately for the litigant is in great anger.'

Animal trespass cases were common enough. Damage to either land or crops by the domestic animals of a neighbour was a major source of legal action in any farming community. Neighbouring farmers usually exchanged fore-pledges called *tairgille* to cover potential injury by animal trespass.

In most walks of life the law relied on the use of a pledge to ensure that legal obligations were carried out. Even in Fidelma's own office, being regarded as a professional judge, she had to place, with the chief judge or Brehon of the district, a pledge of five ounces of silver in case of dispute with her judgment. For if her judgment was found faulty by the chief judge, then she had to compensate those she had wronged by a false judgment. The confiscation of her pledge only happened if the litigant expressed dissatisfaction within a given period with her judgment and the chief judge then found her to be at fault. If a judge refused to put up this pledge then they were debarred from further practice in the territory.

It was certainly a trivial matter and one that Crón could adequately deal with. Fidelma was about to make her excuses and leave when a sudden suspicion occurred to her. She swung back hurriedly.

'Is one of the litigants a farmer called Muadnat?'

Crón stared at her in surprise.

'Do you have second sight, sister? What do you know of Muadnat?' she demanded.

Fidelma knew from her startled expression that she was right. Obviously Crón did not know that Fidelma had been Brehon at Lios Mhór. So this was why Muadnat had appeared at the chieftain's *rath*.

'Did you know about Muadnat's case against his kinsman Archú?'

Crón pursed her lips as if this helped her recall a memory. She nodded slowly.

'I know only what local gossip tells me. Muadnat was forced to appear before a Brehon in Lios Mhór and lost a farm that he was claiming.'

'I was that Brehon,' Fidelma announced. 'It was while I was in Lios Mhór that I received word from my brother to come here.'

The blue eyes of the chieftainess regarded her curiously. Fidelma continued.

'Against whom does Muadnat enter into litigation?'

'With Archú again.'

Fidelma's mind worked quickly.

'Can you tell me the details of his argument?'

For a moment it seemed that Crón might refuse and then she appeared to think better of it.

'I think there is a case to be answered by Archú,' she said defensively.

'But the details?' pressed Fidelma.

'Simple enough. Since Archú took over the disputed farmstead by the Black Marsh, he became a neighbour of Muadnat, for Muadnat's lands stretch by his. Muadnat claims that Archú, through malice and neglect, allowed his pigs to stray at night across his boundary fences where they inflicted damage to Muadnat's property. What is more the animals defecated in Muadnat's farmyard.'

Fidelma took a slow breath and exhaled as she considered the matter.

'In other words, if Muadnat speaks the truth about his claims against Archú, then he will be able to demand a great compensation from him?' she asked.

Crón's face indicated that this was obvious enough.

'Muadnat has already pointed that out to me.'

Fidelma was cynical.

'So Muadnat has already checked the law?'

'What are you implying?' demanded the young tanist sharply.

'I am simply making an observation, not implying anything. It is true, however, that if through malice and neglect the animal trespass did happen then the owner of the animals is regarded on the same level as human trespass; if that trespass takes place at night, it doubles the level of the fine; that the animals defecated further increases the amount of compensation. In other words, Archú would have to pay a substantial amount in compensation to Muadnat.'

Crón agreed.

'Probably half or more of what his farm is worth,' she said. 'Unless he has additional value in livestock than just the value of the farm, he will doubtless lose the farm.'

'And we both know that he has not,' replied Fidelma tightly. 'Muadnat will settle for nothing less than the farm.'

'I believe that is the law.'

Fidelma thought carefully before speaking again.

'As chieftain-elect, it is your right and responsibility to sit in judgment in your clan territory – and you may sit alone when there is no Brehon available.'

'I am aware of my rights and duties.' Crón's eyes narrowed a little in suspicion.

'I mean no offence when I ask you, to what level have you studied law?'

'I have studied only the *Bretha Comaithchesa*, the Law of Neighbours, for we are a small farming community and this is the law that most applies here. But I am not qualified in law. I studied at Lios Mhór for only three years to the level of *Freisneidhed*.'

Fidelma nodded slowly. The degree of three years of study was one which most chieftains in the five kingdoms could boast of obtaining. Chieftains had to be educated for they had to fulfil many duties and being a judge of the tribal court was one of them. She realised that Crón was regarding her with some hostility. She would have to be diplomatic, as Eadulf had implored her to be, for her relationship with Crón was already a difficult one.

'Would you allow me to sit with you and advise in this case?'

Crón flushed, thinking some insult was meant.

'I think I am capable of making judgment in this matter,' she responded protectively. 'I have sat and watched my father make judgments many times.'

'I did not say that you were not capable,' Fidelma replied in a pacifying tone. 'But I have a feeling that there is something more here than a simple case of trespass. Remember, I have seen Muadnat attempt to use the law to dispossess Archú before.'

'Wouldn't that make you biased in your judgment?' Crón asked, trying hard to repress the hint of a sneer.

'Perhaps I am biased,' agreed Fidelma benignly. 'But what I suggest, however, is that you make the judgment, while I merely am seated at your side to advise you on any matters of law. I promise you that my advice will be strictly on matters of law.'

Crón hesitated, wondering if there was some hidden meaning to Fidelma's offer.

'The judgment is mine to make?'

'You are the chieftain-elect of the Araglin,' acknowledged Fidelma. 'You will make the judgment.'

Crón thought for a moment. It was true that Fidelma, as a *dálaigh* qualified to the level of *anruth*, one degree below the highest awarded in the five kingdoms, could simply demand to take her seat in judgment. That was the law for, in a place where there was no permanent Brehon, a visiting judge could, depending on their degree of office, outrank a minor chieftain. That Fidelma had asked permission merely to sit and advise was clearly her way of showing that she did not wish to interfere with Crón's authority.

'What could be wrong with Muadnat's plea?' Crón demanded, still defensively.

'That remains to be seen. Muadnat was bitter when the law was pronounced against him and he lost the farm to young Archú.'

Crón accepted this.

'Do you think that Muadnat has concocted this charge then?'

'As you will sit in judgment on him, it is better, perhaps, if I kept my thoughts to myself,' Fidelma immediately replied. 'But let me sit with you and I will advise you merely on the law, and you will judge the facts. My words will be on law, no more. You have my oath on it.'

'Then, to that I agree.' For the first time in the presence of Fidelma, Crón gave what appeared to be a genuine smile of friendship.

'What time is Muadnat to present himself before you?'

'At the midday hour.'

'Then I will go and tell Eadulf.'

'He is an interesting man, that Saxon of yours,' Crón observed slyly.

'Of mine?' Fidelma arched an eyebrow in surprise. 'Eadulf belongs to no woman or man.'

'You appear friendly enough,' Crón replied. 'Surely, the handsome brother does not believe in the ideas that Father Gormán teaches about the servants of God, male and female, remaining in celibacy?'

Fidelma found herself flushing.

She realised that although she had debated all the aspects of Roman teaching with Eadulf they had never touched on the concept of celibacy. While Rome made no hard and fast rule on the celibacy of the religious, it was true that there was a growing number of the clergy who believed in the idea that members of the religious should not cohabit or marry. It was surely such an alien idea to human beings that it would never be accepted.

She found Crón watching her with some amusement.

She thrust out her chin.

'Brother Eadulf and I have been friends, and friends alone, since we met at the council held at Hilda's abbey in Northumbria. That is all.'

It was clear that Crón treated the assurance with some scepticism.

'It is nice,' she observed meaningfully, 'to have such a friend.'

'Speaking of friends,' Fidelma returned slyly, 'I must find Dubán.'

'What is so important that you need speak with him so urgently?' queried the tanist.

'Have you heard of Gadra?'

Crón looked surprised.

'Why do you wish to know about Gadra?'

'So you do know him?' pressed Fidelma eagerly.

'Of course. I have not seen him since I was a tiny girl. I can just remember him. He lived at Teafa's cabin for some years. But he went away again. He is a hermit. Nowadays the young ones think he is just a bogeyman. Because he is a hermit who vanished into the hills, some people use him as a means of scaring children into obedience.'

'Do you know where Gadra may be found?'

Crón shook her head.

'I doubt if he still lives.' She shrugged. 'But if he does then it would take a brave person to go in search of him for it was said he refused to acknowledge the Faith and consorted with evil.'

'Consorted with evil?'

Crón nodded seriously.

'He clung to the faith of our pagan ancestors and they say that this was why he withdrew into the vastness of the dark mountains.'

There was a movement behind Fidelma and she turned to see the middle-aged warrior enter self-consciously.

Dubán glanced from Fidelma to Crón quickly, trying to feign surprise at finding them together, and then raised a hand in salute to his tanist. Fidelma was aware that anyone who could act with such duplicity might well be able to be equally evasive in other matters.

'The talk is of lack of success in your venture, Dubán.' Crón greeted him with a slightly querulous voice as if she had not seen him previously that morning.

The big warrior grimaced, an expression which summed up the futility of his search.

'We scoured the hillside for miles but there was no sign of the raiders. Two cows were driven off from the farmstead of Díoma. We followed the tracks as far as the borders of the Black Marsh but lost them in the forest.'

Crón was clearly troubled by this.

'I cannot remember the last time when brigands were allowed to raid our valley with impunity. They must be dealt with. Our honour is at stake.'

'It shall be done,' muttered Dubán. 'As soon as I have gathered a fresh band of warriors . . .'

'It is futile now. Anyway, we have the legal hearing to consider. Sister Fidelma has suggested that she might sit with me. I have agreed. I have also told the sister that you will be able to help her with some information about old Gadra.'

Crón swung away and left the assembly hall leaving Dubán with an uncertain expression on his face.

'What does she mean?' he asked awkwardly after a moment or two. 'About Gadra, that is?'

'I am told you knew Gadra.'

'Gadra the Hermit,' Dubán acknowledged. 'Yes, I did but that was twenty years ago. He is dead.'

Fidelma had a sinking feeling.

'Are you sure?'

Dubán rubbed his chin reflectively.

'Not sure. But I have not seen him since I left Araglin when I was young. He must be dead.'

Fidelma clung to her course of action.

'Crón said she saw him when she was a young girl; that he came to stay with Teafa in the *rath*. If he were still alive, would you know where he might be found?'

Dubán indicated with a jerk of his head upwards.

'Up in the mountains, to the south. There is a little valley where he used to dwell.'

'Would you take Brother Eadulf and myself to where he might be found?'

Dubán looked confused.

'After all this time. He is probably dead,' he repeated.

'But you don't know for sure?'

'No. But the journey will doubtless be wasted. It is nearly a day there and a day back.'

'Will you take us?'

'I have my duties . . .'

'Crón seemed to indicate that she had no objections to your taking us.' Fidelma felt that she was not distorting the truth. 'Or is it that you have some other objections?'

'But why would you want to see old Gadra? Even if he is still living, he will be an old man. What would he know that would be of help to your investigations?'

'That is more my concern than yours, Dubán,' she replied firmly.

Dubán was reluctant but finally said: 'When would you want to leave?'

'If the court reaches a conclusion soon, we could set out this very afternoon.'

Dubán tugged at his beard thoughtfully.

'The journey will mean at least one overnight encampment, even if we do find Gadra,' he repeated.

'I am used to travel,' Fidelma said pointedly.

Dubán spread his arms in resignation.

'After the court reaches its conclusion then. If Gadra lives then we must respect his right to be a recluse. Only I will accompany you and the Saxon brother. No one else.'

'It is agreed,' Fidelma confirmed as she left the hall.

Outside, she came face to face with Archú's sweetheart, Scoth. The young girl's face lightened as she recognised Fidelma and she caught at both the hands of the religieuse.

'Oh, sister! I prayed that you would not have left here. We stand in great need of your help.'

Fidelma was sympathetic.

'So I have heard. Is Archú here to answer the new charges?'

'He has gone to find accommodation for us.' Scoth was tense and unhappy.

Fidelma quietly took the girl by the arm and guided her towards the guests' hostel.

The young girl gave a painful smile.

'Muadnat is like a battle scavenging crow, waiting for the right moment to swoop on us. We felt that our only hope was if you were still at the *rath*.'

'Well, I am here.'

'Thank God! Had Muadnat been a more careful man he would have discovered this fact. But he was so greedy to seize possession of the land that he came racing to the *rath* little realising that he could have to face your judgment again.'

Fidelma shook her head.

'He doesn't face my judgment. It is Crón, your tanist and chieftain-elect, who sits in judgment here.' Scoth looked aghast and halted in mid-stride, turning to Fidelma.

'But you must sit in judgment. You cannot abandon Archú,' she wailed. 'Crón will look after her own!'

'I have not abandoned anyone, Scoth. Am I to presume, from what you say, that Muadnat has invented this charge of animal trespass?'

'No, he has not.'

It was Archú who spoke and Fidelma turned to find the young man standing behind her.

Fidelma digested his admission.

'Then I am sorry to see you in this plight, Archú,' she replied sadly.

'But you can intervene and dismiss the charge,' Scoth insisted, desperation in her voice.

'Scoth!' Archú was sharp. 'Sister Fidelma is bound by oath to the courts.'

They were standing outside of the guests' hostel and Fidelma gestured for them to precede her inside. Eadulf came forward and greeted them with an exclamation of astonishment. Fidelma explained to him the news before turning to Archú.

'Tell me the truth. You say that Muadnat has not made up this charge against you? That his claim is true?'

Archú was flushed. He gestured helplessly.

'He is too cunning to make up such a charge.'

Fidelma was silent in thought for a moment.

'Then you realise what this means?'

Archú was bitter.

'It means that Muadnat, my dear cousin, will reclaim what momentarily belonged to me. He will take back my mother's farmstead. I will be landless once more.'

Chapter Ten

The proceedings were formal. Crón was wearing a long parti-coloured cloak of office over her dress of blue silk. It was fastened with an ornate gold brooch. Fidelma was amused to see that she wore doeskin gloves on her hands. Among many clans, it was the practice of chieftains to wear parti-coloured cloaks and gloves as badges of office when giving judgments. Fidelma noticed that Crón had been careful, in her dress, her toilet and her choice of perfume for the scent of lavender filled the air. Obviously, Crón took her role as chieftain-elect with seriousness.

Crón sat in her chair of office in the hall of assembly. Beside the ornately carved wooden chair a second chair had been placed on the dais for Fidelma. Dubán stood in front of the platform, slightly to one side, in his official capacity of commander of the guard, while those engaged in the litigation were seated on wooden benches which had been brought forward in front of the dais. Muadnat, with the dark, lean-faced companion who had been at Lios Mhór, were seated to the right while Archú and Scoth were seated to the left with Eadulf. Warriors of Dubán's guard had taken up strategic positions at the rear of the hall. As she came into the hall, Fidelma noticed that Father Gormán was seated towards the back.

As soon as Fidelma had entered and taken her seat next to Crón, Muadnat recognised the religieuse. He was on his feet shouting. 'I protest!'

Crón settled herself and regarded him impassively.

'You protest already? About what?'

Muadnat was glaring at Fidelma and he raised a hand to point a finger at her.

151

'I will not have that woman judging my case today.'

Crón's lips thinned slightly.

'*That* woman? To whom do you refer?'

Muadnat bit his tongue.

'Fidelma of Kildare,' he growled.

'Sister Fidelma is here at my invitation and is a *dálaigh* of the courts of the five kingdoms, learned in law. Is there some reason why you object to her presence, Muadnat?'

Muadnat was still angry.

'I object on grounds of . . . of . . .' He fumbled for the right word. 'On grounds of partiality. She has already shown herself in favour of the accused. She was judge over his claim to lands which belonged to me and gave them to him. I will not have her as my judge.'

'Nor will she be,' Crón replied softly. 'I am judge in this case. Mine is the decision but Sister Fidelma sits to advise on law and she shall do so. Now proceed, Muadnat, with your case if you have one to make.'

Sister Fidelma leant towards Crón and whispered in her ear. Crón nodded grimly and added loudly to Muadnat: 'I have taken into account your verbal insult on a Brehon. This is regarded with utmost seriousness and the offence requires the payment of your victim's honour-price.'

Muadnat's mouth dropped in consternation.

Crón paused to let him dwell on what she was saying. Then she continued: 'As it appears that you have spoken merely in ignorance, Sister Fidelma is willing to forgo the payment. However, she cannot ignore the insult for to do so, according to law, makes her guilty of tolerating the insult and thus losing her honour-price. Some compensation therefore must be extracted from you. We will return to this matter after I,' she paused for emphasis, 'have heard the charges which you wish to bring before me for judgment.'

The big man hesitated, swaying a little as if he had been hit, and then, apparently accepting Crón's ruling and pulling himself together, he stared sullenly in front of him.

'Very well. The facts are simple and I have a witness to the facts – my chief herdsman and nephew, Agdae, who sits with me today.'

He turned and indicated his companion.

'Tell us these facts,' invited Crón.

There was a movement behind the dais and Cranat entered abruptly. She was dressed as opulently as ever. She frowned in annoyance as she saw Fidelma seated in what was doubtlessly considered her rightful place in the hall. She paused in mid-stride but before she could say anything her daughter spoke.

'Mother, you did not tell me that you wished to attend this court?' Crón was clearly annoyed at the interruption to the proceedings.

Cranat glanced to where Muadnat was standing. Did the burly farmer cast her a warning look and give a slight shake of his head? Fidelma could not be sure.

Cranat's mouth drooped in disapproval.

'I will sit and observe, daughter.' She went to a quiet corner where there was an unoccupied bench and seated herself, head held high. She was obviously displeased and perplexed. She said audibly as she seated herself: 'I did not have to seek such permission while Eber was alive.'

'Sister Fidelma, as a *dálaigh*, is here to guide me in law only,' Crón felt she had to explain to her mother before turning back to Muadnat. 'Proceed. You were about to tell me the facts, Muadnat.'

'Easy to tell. My farmland borders on the land now farmed by Archú.'

Fidelma sat expressionless, her sharp eyes watching Muadnat carefully. The big farmer seemed confident enough as he launched into his charges.

'Two nights ago, the pigs that were kept by Archú were allowed to trample through the fence that borders our farmlands. They came at night. They did damage to my crops. One of the hogs fought with one of mine, causing injury. The pigs defecated in my farmyard. Is this not so, Agdae?'

The lean man nodded, almost glumly.

Muadnat went on: 'Every farmer in the land knows the law. I demand the full measure of compensation for this.'

He sat down abruptly.

Crón turned her gaze to Agdae.

'Can you confirm everything that Muadnat has said, bearing witness without fear or favour of Muadnat to whom you are related and for whom you labour?'

Agdae stood up, glanced at Muadnat and nodded rapidly.

'It is so, tanist of the Araglin. It is exactly as my uncle claims it to be.'

He sat down with equal swiftness.

Crón turned to Archú and motioned him to stand.

'You have heard the charges made against you. What have you to say in your defence, Archú? Do you dispute the facts as we have heard them?'

The young man stood up. His expression was one of weary resignation. Scoth caught at his hand as if to give him comfort.

'It is true.' He spoke as if he was filled with fatigue. 'The pigs did escape from my land and crossed into Muadnat's and caused the damage as he said.'

Muadnat's face creased into a broad triumphant smile.

'He admits it,' he observed aloud, as if to emphasise the point to the court.

Crón ignored him.

'Have you nothing to say in your defence?' she pressed.

'Nothing. I had built a temporary pen for the pigs as best I could and found that this had been pulled down. The pigs themselves had not destroyed it.'

Crón leant forward eagerly.

'Are you claiming that the fence was pulled down deliberately?'

'I believe it to have been so.'

Muadnat gave a bark of laughter.

'Desperation forces the youth to lie. You cannot believe that.'

'Do you name the person responsible?' asked Crón. 'If so, you must substantiate that claim.'

Archú looked with hatred at Muadnat.

'I cannot make any such claims. I have no witness to support me. I did not see who damaged the pig pen. I can make no defence.'

'The facts are clear!' Muadnat called impatiently. 'The boy admits them. Give me the full measure of compensation.'

'Have you anything else to say, Archú?' inquired Crón.

'Judge me as you will,' said the youth in resignation, returning to his seat.

It was then that Fidelma leant forward and touched Crón's arm gently.

'If I may be permitted to ask some questions to settle points of law?'

Crón indicated her agreement: 'Proceed.'

'My first question is addressed to Archú. When did you come into legal possession of your farm and the ownership of your pigs?'

Archú stared at her in amazement.

'But you know that,' he protested.

'Answer the question,' Fidelma replied sharply.

'At the time of the judgment which you, yourself, made at Lios Mhór.'

'How long ago was that?'

'Four days ago, no more,' Archú replied, shaking his head as if he thought she had taken leave of her senses.

'And you, Muadnat, do you agree with that?'

Muadnat laughed scornfully.

'You made the judgment for him. Have you forgotten so soon?'

'So Archú has been four days in ownership of the farm? Do you both agree?'

'Yes; the farm is his and the pigs are his and his is the responsibility,' Muadnat grunted, smiling triumphantly at his nephew Agdae who sat nodding his agreement.

'And am I right in suggesting that before Archú owned the farm and the pigs, you, yourself, owned that same farm and the pigs?' Fidelma inquired.

For the first time a flicker of suspicion crossed Muadnat's eyes.

'You know that well enough,' he replied with an attempt at braggadocio but there was a slight uneasiness in his voice.

'Did you farm the land now owned by Archú separately or as one with your adjacent lands?'

Muadnat hesitated again, not really understanding where the questions were leading but suspecting some forthcoming trap.

He appealed to Crón.

'The facts have been laid before you, tanist of Araglin. I do not understand what this woman is seeking to imply.'

'Answer the question,' Fidelma insisted. 'Ignorance of the meaning behind the question is no excuse not to answer a *dálaigh* of the courts. You already stand guilty of insulting my office.'

The sharpness in her voice caused Muadnat to blink and swallow.

He looked appealingly at Crón but the tanist simply motioned him to answer.

'I farmed them as one,' he admitted gruffly.

Fidelma nodded impatiently, as if she had known the answer all along but was merely waiting for him to enunciate it.

'The law states that the boundary fences between farms must be clearly maintained. This is the law under which you seek judgment, is it not so?' she asked.

Muadnat did not reply.

'Did you maintain the boundary fences?'

'The farm that Archú now owns had been mine for years. I removed the boundary fences when there was no need for them to be there.'

'The law found that the farm Archú owns had not been yours and that for the years you had been running it you had done so only as legal guardian of the interests of your kinsman, Archú,' replied Fidelma. 'You admit removing the boundary fences between his farm and your farm?'

Crón was regarding Fidelma with unconcealed admiration as she suddenly caught the trend of the questioning. Her past antagonism with Fidelma aside, Crón was intelligent enough to appreciate Fidelma's sharp mind and legal knowledge.

'Admit?' Muadnat was confused. 'Why leave a boundary between lands which were mine?'

Fidelma allowed a thin smile to hover on her lips.

'You removed the boundary fence?'

'I did.'

Fidelma turned to Crón apparently satisfied.

'I am now willing to advise you on the law, tanist of Araglin, unless you wish more questioning. The matter is clear to me. Do you wish my advice in private or in public?'

'I think the litigants have a right to hear the law,' replied Crón solemnly.

'Very well. Firstly, we learn that Archú became owner *de facto* – that is, in actual fact   of the property only four days ago. Until that time, while owner *de jure* – that is, by right – it was Muadnat who occupied and ran the farm. Muadnat admits that he took down the boundary fences between the two farms. That, under law, is an illegal act, although we may excuse Muadnat because he can argue that he thought he was acting legally.'

Muadnat rose and tried to interrupt.

'You will be silent while the *dálaigh* is giving advice on the matter of law.' Crón's voice was harsh.

Cranat, who had sat like a statue all this time, stirred uneasily.

'Daughter, is there call for such sharpness in addressing one who is your kin and has served your father faithfully?' she protested. 'It shames us before strangers.'

Muadnat had fallen silent and resumed his seat.

Crón looked angrily at her mother.

'I am tanist; a tanist giving judgment. The court must be quiet, mother. This includes you.'

Cranat stared in surprise at her daughter, her mouth snapping shut with an audible sound.

'Proceed, Sister Fidelma,' Crón ordered after a moment. Fidelma went on:

'Secondly, bearing in mind that Archú assumed the ownership only four days ago, one may assume that he has had no time to secure the fences.'

'The law is clear,' cried Muadnat obstinately. 'Time does not matter. He is responsible for the fence.'

'Not so,' Fidelma replied, still speaking directly to Crón. 'Time does matter. The *Bretha Comaithchesa* is exceedingly precise. The possessors of adjacent farms are both responsible for a fence between their property, the fence is the common property so that each must execute their own part of the joint work.' She turned to the burly farmer. 'What have you done to rebuild the common fence which you destroyed in the first place, Muadnat?'

Muadnat was red in the face. He could no longer bring himself to speak. He had the sense to realise that somehow he was losing once more and yet was not possessed of the intellect to understand why.

'None, I presume from your silence,' remarked Fidelma dryly. 'As for time not being a consideration, that time is a principal factor for the law is clear. When a person comes into possession of a farmstead, three days are allowed for marking out the perimeters; in ten days the fence should be completed. No one is directly compelled to raise a fence in that there is no fine if it is not so completed. However, there is indirect compulsion by reason of possible law suits for animal and human trespass.'

Fidelma paused before turning once more to Crón.

'That is the advice I have to give on the matter of law. The judgment is with you, Crón, and has to be made in accordance with the law.'

Crón grimaced wryly.

'Then it is obvious that the judgment must be that Muadnat is unable to proceed in this matter. Archú has had no time, the time allowed by the law, to put up fences.'

Muadnat stood up slowly; he was quivering with outrage.

'But I say he allowed his pigs to trespass with neglect and malice.'

'The neglect cannot be charged,' replied Crón. 'As for malice, I will not entertain that argument. You are equally responsible for the construction of your boundary fence, Muadnat. In fact, Sister Fidelma has shown generosity in her interpretation of the law when she suggests that you be absolved from culpability of the fact that you tore down the boundary fences in the first place. I may not be that generous. Ensure that these fences are raised and by the prescribed time.'

Muadnat was scowling at Fidelma. His hatred was clear. He seemed about to speak when Agdae, his nephew, caught at his arm and seemed to shake his head in warning.

'And one thing more,' added Crón. 'In bringing this serious charge without due consideration of all the implications and of true knowledge of the law, you will pay one *séd* to me and one *séd* to Sister Fidelma for her advice on the law. That fine, either in coin or in the equivalent of two milch cows, will be given to my steward at the end of this week.'

Muadnat half turned to leave when Crón stayed him.

'There is still the matter of the fine for insulting a *dálaigh* which you did at the beginning of this hearing.'

She turned to Fidelma and looked questioningly.

Fidelma's face was expressionless as she replied to Crón's unarticulated question. 'In token of that insult, which in full would be my honour-price, I will allow Muadnat to donate the value of one milch cow to the local church for its upkeep or the equivalent value in labour in repairing the fabric of the building of the church. Whichever he chooses.'

Muadnat almost exploded in wrath.

'Do you think I am blind to your self-interest, tanist?' he shouted. 'Tanist, indeed! Tanist by bribery and corruption. You are no true . . .'

Father Gormán rose suddenly and came forward.

'Muadnat! You forget yourself!' he admonished.

The priest laid a hand on the angry farmer's arm and Agdae assisted in propelling Muadnat out of the hall of assembly. They could hear him shouting even from outside the hall. Cranat waited only a few moments more and then rose, in almost indecent haste, and left the hall.

Crón looked across to where Archú and Scoth were embracing each other and grinning wildly.

'You are dismissed Archú but let me give you some advice . . .'

Archú turned expectantly, trying to reform his features into a more respectful countenance.

'You have an unforgiving enemy in Muadnat. Be wary.'

Archú bobbed his head in acknowledgment of his tanist's advice and then grinned broadly towards Fidelma. He and Scoth joined hands and hurried from the hall.

Crón sat back with a deep sigh and turned to regard Fidelma with some admiration.

'You make the maze of the law texts seem a straightforward path, Fidelma. I wish I had your knowledge and gift.'

Fidelma was indifferent to the compliment.

'That is what I am trained to do.'

'My warning to Archú equally applies to you. Muadnat is unforgiving. He was a distant cousin and friend of my father. Perhaps I should not have been so harsh with him. My mother disapproved of me today.'

'Your mother clearly regards Muadnat as a close friend.'

'A chieftain cannot have close friends. I cannot make judgments based on friendship.'

'You can only do as the law instructs,' observed Fidelma. 'As must I. A Brehon or a chieftain must be above friendships in the interpretation of the law.'

'I know what you say is right. But Muadnat has been a power in Araglin. He also remains a good friend of Father Gormán. They are often together.'

Fidelma was thoughtful.

'You mentioned that Muadnat was a relative and friend of your father, Eber?'

'Yes. They grew up as young men and went off to fight the Uí Fidgente together.'

Fidelma considered the matter a moment. Then she gave a mental shrug. At least Muadnat could not be concerned in her inquiry into Eber's death for he had been in her court in Lios Mhór at the time of his murder. She stood up and glanced to where Dubán had been standing stiffly.

'Perhaps there is now time to go in search of this hermit, Gadra?'

Crón rose. For the first time since Fidelma had arrived at the *rath* she was effusive with goodwill. In spite of what she had said, she seemed to have enjoyed defeating Muadnat and she was flushed with excitement.

'Fidelma, I have seen your diligence with the law. I realise, perhaps belatedly, that you will be equally diligent in discovering the truth behind my father's death. I just wish . . .' It was the nearest that she came to an apology for her behaviour. She hesitated and then continued: 'I would like you to know that I will do all I can to help in your inquiry.'

Fidelma raised an eyebrow in query.

'Is there something more that you think I should know now?'

For a moment, she thought she saw a look of anxiety cross the pale eyes of the tanist of Araglin.

'Something more? I do not think so. I speak merely because I acted too proudly when you came here. Courtesy should be freely given for it costs nothing.'

'If you bear that in mind, then you will become a just chieftain of your people in Araglin,' Fidelma replied gravely. 'And that is more important than a cloak of office.'

Crón looked self-conscious and fingered the golden brooch which fastened her cloak to her shoulder.

'It is the custom, here in Araglin, that all the chieftains and their ladies wear the parti-coloured cloak and gloves as their badge of office.' She smiled briefly.

'It is a great responsibility to be elevated into such a position,' Fidelma observed. 'Sometimes it takes time to adjust to a change in life.'

'It is still no excuse for arrogance. This mention of Gadra reminds me of one teaching he gave when he was staying in the *rath* when I was a little girl. I was small but I remember his words well. He said that the proud place themselves at a distance from others and observing others across that distance they believe that they are little and insignificant. Yet the same distance makes them also appear equally small and insignificant to others.'

Fidelma smiled appreciatively.

'Then Gadra is a man of wisdom. Truly, if you do not raise your eyes you will always believe that you stand on the highest point. Come, Dubán, let us go in search of this sage.'

'If he still lives,' added Dubán pessimistically.

Chapter Eleven

Dubán and Fidelma led the way along the narrow track that wound through the great oaks of the forest which spilled through the mountain passes. Brother Eadulf rode behind them. His eyes were watchful. With all this talk of raiding brigands, it occurred to him that whole warbands could hide in such gloomy places and not be noticed by wayfarers who might pass their concealment within yards and not even notice them, so dense and impenetrable were the rich woodlands that spread across the mountains which surrounded Araglin. So close together did the trees grow that they shut out all sight of the blue canopy of the sky and the warm spring sunshine. The air felt chill and Eadulf observed that few spring flowers were blooming but there were plenty of dark evergreens and plants that liked the cold dark musty atmosphere of the woodlands.

Eadulf rode with watchful eyes but his body was at ease, letting his mount match the leisurely walking pace of the lead horses.

The quiet was almost oppressive. Now and then something rustled through the underbrush and Eadulf had noticed that few bird songs trilled through the woodland.

'A bleak, black place to dwell,' Eadulf called, breaking the silence in which they had ridden since first entering this part of the woodlands.

Dubán half turned with a brief smile.

'It is the nature of hermits to dwell in places that others are not attracted to, Saxon,' he replied.

'I have known healthier places,' Eadulf responded. 'What is the point of dwelling as a hermit if it costs you your health?'

'A good argument, Saxon,' the warrior chuckled. 'Yet they say that Gadra has lived over four score years. And, if he continues to live, I shall be surprised.'

'So you keep telling us,' intervened Fidelma wearily. 'Tell us some more of your knowledge of Gadra. We know he is a hermit and we know that he appears to be a man of wisdom. What else do you know of him?'

'Little to tell. Gadra is Gadra. He has always been the same age to me.'

'Is anything known of his origin?' pressed Fidelma.

Dubán shrugged.

'They say that he was a religious of the pagan times.'

'A Druid?' demanded Fidelma. It was true that here and there among the five kingdoms were still to be found followers of the old gods. Fidelma herself had encountered such members of the recluse; those who still clung to the old ways, the old beliefs. Even Fidelma found herself admiring many of their philosophies. The new Faith of Christ had not been long enough established in the land for the old ways to be anachronistic.

'I suppose one would call him so. We were told stories of old Gadra when I was a boy. He has always been old to us. We were warned to stay away from him because the priest said he performed human sacrifices to ancient gods in these fierce oak forests.'

Fidelma sniffed deprecatingly.

'There is always talk of human sacrifice when one does not understand the truth of a religious cult. The founder of my own house at Kildare, Brigid of blessed name, was a Druidess and the daughter of a Druid. There is nothing to fear from such as they. But tell me more about this Gadra. Is it known when he came to this place?'

'Not in Eber's time, that's for sure,' replied Dubán. 'I think he came when Eber's father was a little boy. He had the gift of healing and of wisdom.'

'How could he have a gift of healing unless he believed in the

True Faith?' interrupted Eadulf a little indignantly.

Fidelma grinned at her companion.

'One cannot argue with such logic,' she replied mischievously.

Eadulf was not sure whether she was making fun of him.

'Does he perform his healing in the name of the Christ Saviour?' he demanded.

'He simply heals those who go to him with affliction. He does so in the name of no one,' replied Dubán. 'Of course, Father Gormán used to denounce any he found who had sought a cure from Gadra. But I have not heard of Gadra for some years now. I say he is dead and we waste time on this journey.'

Eadulf was about to speak further when Dubán suddenly raised a hand to bid them draw rein on their horses.

'I see a clearing ahead. I think we are close to the glade where he once dwelt.'

Fidelma peered forward eagerly.

'Is this the spot where Gadra lives?'

Dubán nodded.

'Stay here. Let me go first,' he said softly, 'for if he still lives, I think he will recognise me.'

He manoeuvred his horse in front of her and began to walk it carefully along the track towards the bright area of the clearing before them.

Fidelma saw that the clearing was only a small glade and she could hear, in the silence of the forest, the gushing and gurgling of a stream. Fidelma thought she saw a wooden building ahead through the trees.

Suddenly Dubán's voice echoed loudly back.

'Gadra! Gadra! It is Dubán of Araglin! Do you still live?'

There was silence for a while.

Then they heard a voice reply. It was a voice of age, yet deep and resonant.

'If I do not, Dubán of Araglin, then it is surely a wraith who answers you.'

Dubán's voice came again, lower in tone. Neither Fidelma nor Eadulf could hear what was being said. After a while, Dubán's voice called loudly upon them to come forward into the glade.

On a level piece of land by a surging, tumbling mountain stream, stood a wooden cabin, well built and thatched. The glade showed signs of cultivation. A small garden of herbs and vegetables and some fruit trees surrounded it. Dubán had dismounted and tied his horse to a nearby bush and was standing a few feet from another figure. He was a short, elderly figure, with a shock of white hair, leaning on a staff of polished blackthorn. He looked, at first sight, frail. But Fidelma realised that the frailness was misleading. He was thin but sinewy. He wore loose robes dyed with saffron and round his neck was a golden circlet bearing ancient symbols the like of which Fidelma had not seen before.

Fidelma swung from her horse and handed the reins to Eadulf and moved forward towards the elderly figure. She halted a few paces away.

'Blessings on you, Gadra,' she greeted, inclining her head slightly.

She found herself looking into a kindly face, whose nut-brown, weather-tanned skin was highlighted by piercing bright eyes. They seemed grey rather than blue. The cascade of snow-white hair surrounded the face. It was shoulder length from the head and merged indivisibly into a silken-like beard that was cut short so that the circlet showed where it hung on his chest. That Gadra was old was not in dispute but it was impossible to estimate his age for his face was still youthful and unlined and only the rounded shoulders gave an impression of the passing years.

She found the face regarding her with good humour.

'You are well come to this place, Fidelma, daughter of Failbe Flann.'

Fidelma started a little.

'How did . . . ?'

She saw the man laughing and she caught herself and smiled sheepishly and shrugged.

166

'What else did Dubán tell you?'

Gadra nodded approvingly.

'You have a quick mind, Fidelma.' He glanced across her shoulder to where Eadulf was tying the horses to a bush. 'Come forward, Brother Eadulf of Seaxmund's Ham. Come forward and let us sit ourselves down and speak for a while.'

Fidelma, as she used to do when she was a young pupil of Morann of Tara, sank cross-legged on the grass before the old man, like a novice before a master. Gadra smiled approvingly. Brother Eadulf, more awkwardly, preferred to prop himself up on a nearby rounded boulder, using it as an uncomfortable seat. Dubán similarly seemed to think his dignity would be affronted to be seated on the ground and found another boulder. Gadra, as if he were still youthful, squatted down on the grass before Fidelma.

'Before we talk,' Gadra began, at the same time raising his hand to finger the golden crescent which hung around his neck, 'does this bother you?'

Fidelma glanced at the emblem.

'Why should it bother me?'

Gadra pointed to her own crucifix.

'Is it not at odds with that?'

Fidelma slowly shook her head.

'Your crescent stood as a symbol of light and knowledge among our people for countless centuries. I have no need to fear it. Why should it offend me?'

'Yet it offends many who embrace the New Faith.'

Eadulf stirred uncomfortably for he found it distracting to be in the company of someone wearing a symbol of a pagan faith.

'You have not embraced the Faith of Christ?' he demanded.

Gadra looked up at him and smiled softly.

'I am an old man, brother Saxon. In me, the ancient gods and goddesses of our people take a long time a dying. Yet I do not grudge you your new ways, your new thoughts and your new hopes. It is in the nature of things that the old should die and the new

167

should live. It is also the danger of this world as well as its blessing. That is the nature of the children of Danu, the Mother Goddess. Life dies and is reborn. Life is reborn and it dies. It is a never ending cycle. The old gods die, the new are born. The time will come when they will also die and new gods will arise.'

Fidelma heard Eadulf's splutter of indignation but she said hastily: 'We are all the prisoners of our times.'

Gadra chuckled approvingly.

'You have perception, Fidelma. Or is it merely sensitivity? Can you tell me what is swifter than the wind?'

'Thought,' replied Fidelma at once, knowing immediately the game that the old man was playing.

'Ah. Then what is whiter than snow?'

'Truth,' she replied sharply.

'What, then, is sharper than a sword?'

'Understanding.'

'Then we understand one another well, Fidelma. I am the repository of the old and much will be lost when I am gone. But that is the way of it. And that is why I have come to the forests to die.'

Fidelma was silent a moment.

'Has Dubán told you the news from Araglin?'

'He has told me who you are. That and no more. That you have come to seek something from me is obvious.'

'Eber, the chieftain of Araglin, has been murdered.'

Gadra did not appear surprised.

'In my time we would celebrate the death of a soul in this world for it meant that a soul was reborn in the Otherworld. It was the custom to mourn birth, for it meant a soul had died in the Otherworld.'

'The death of Eber is of more concern to me, Gadra, for I am an advocate of the courts of the five kingdoms.'

'Forgive me if I spoke as a philosopher. Of course, the manner of his going to the Otherworld is of concern. I presume that Muadnat is chieftain of Araglin now?'

Fidelma stared in surprise.

'Crón is tanist and will be chieftain when the *derbfhine* of her family confirm her as such.'

Gadra gave her a curious sideways glance but made no further reference to Muadnat.

'So Eber is dead? Murdered? And you, child, are a *dálaigh*, an advocate of the courts come to investigate?'

For once Fidelma did not mind being called 'child' by this elderly mystic.

'This is so.'

'What would you have of me?'

'Móen was found by Eber's body with a bloody knife in his hand.'

For the first time, the calm humour of the old man's face was creased by an expression of amazement. But it was quickly gone. He had tremendous control.

'Are you telling me that Móen is supposed to have murdered Eber?' His voice was still composed.

'He stands accused of that murder,' Fidelma confirmed.

'If I had not lived a long life and seen many things, I would say that the boy was not capable of taking life.'

Fidelma frowned, leaning forward.

'I am not sure that I follow. Do you accept that he committed the murder?'

'In special circumstances even the most docile of human beings will turn to kill. Móen is the most docile of human beings.'

Fidelma made a wry face.

'Docile is not a word that others would use.'

Gadra sighed softly.

'Believe me, the boy is sensitive and of a calm nature. I know for I have watched him grow from a baby. Teafa and I taught him all he knows.'

Fidelma regarded the old man for a few minutes.

'You *taught* him?' she prompted with emphasis.

'I have said so. What does the boy say about this charge? What does Teafa say?'

'Móen is one who is deaf, dumb and blind. How can he tell us anything?'

Gadra snorted impatiently.

'Through Teafa, of course. He communicates through Teafa. What has she to say?'

'Ah . . .' Fidelma let her breath expel slowly, regretting that she had not explained fully.

Gadra was looking at her curiously.

'Something has happened to Teafa? I can read that much in your expression.'

'Yes. Teafa is dead.'

Gadra sat very still and upright.

'I will say a prayer for a good rebirth in the Otherworld,' he said softly. 'She was a good woman and possessed of a great soul. How did she die? Was she killed by Eber? Was that when the boy struck back, in defence of Teafa?'

Fidelma shook her head, trying to stop her tumbling thoughts reacting to what the old man had said.

'Móen also stands accused of having killed Teafa, stabbing her with a knife, and then going to Eber's chambers and stabbing him.'

'Can this be true?'

Gadra, in spite of his years of self-discipline, at controlling his emotions, was clearly distressed.

'The accusation is true. But I have come to ascertain the facts.'

'These facts you state must be in error then,' Gadra replied decisively. 'While I can concede that Móen could, if sufficiently provoked, turn on Eber, he would never strike at Teafa. Teafa has been his mother.'

'Sons have killed their mothers before now,' Eadulf intervened.

Gadra ignored him.

'Has anyone been able to communicate with Móen since Teafa's death?'

Fidelma shook her head.

'I was told that only Teafa could communicate with Móen. No one else knew how. He cannot hear, he cannot see and he cannot speak.'

Gadra was sorrowful.

'There are other forms of communication. The boy can touch, he can smell, he can feel vibration. If the fates deny us some of our senses, then we can develop others. So no one has communicated with him since this terrible thing happened?'

'I have been unable. That is why I am here. I have heard that you might understand how this method of communication is accomplished.'

'It is so. As I said, I taught the boy with Teafa. I must come back with you to the *rath* of Araglin at once and speak with him,' said the old man decisively.

Fidelma was surprised. She had been hoping for some advice but never dared to consider that the old man would insist on coming to the *rath* himself.

'If you can accomplish this thing then I will believe in all the miracles without reservation.'

'It can be so,' Gadra assured her grimly. 'Poor Móen. Can you imagine what it must be like for someone imprisoned in such a body unable to know or communicate with those around him? He must be frightened and desperate for he will not know what has happened.'

Eadulf leaned forward again.

'If he is innocent of the accusations then he is going through a terrifying ordeal,' he conceded. 'But someone else at the *rath* must have known how Móen was able to communicate apart from Teafa?'

Gadra glanced across to Eadulf with a shake of his head.

'You are practical, Saxon. The answer to your question is that only Teafa had the patience to learn the skill from me. She might have tried to pass it on. But I do not think she did. I think she felt it better that it was kept a secret.'

171

'Why?'

'That answer has doubtless died with her.'

Gadra rose to his feet and Fidelma followed his example.

'I have no horse,' the old man said, 'so it may take me a while to reach the *rath* of Araglin.'

'You may ride behind either Dubán or Brother Eadulf. There is no problem.'

'Then I will ride with Brother Eadulf,' the old man announced. Eadulf went to get the horses and Gadra lowered his voice to Fidelma.

'Your Eadulf speaks our language well.'

She coloured hotly.

'He is a visitor to our country. A Saxon monk who has been trained in our colleges.' She paused and added quietly, 'And he is not *my* Eadulf.'

The amused bright eyes were suddenly fixed on her questioningly.

'There is a warmness in your voice when you speak of this Saxon.'

Fidelma found her cheeks colouring even more fiercely.

'He has been a good friend to me,' she replied defensively.

Gadra studied her face closely.

'Never deny your feelings, child, especially not to yourself.'

The old man went into his cabin before Fidelma could frame any reply. For a moment she felt annoyed and then she found herself smiling. Pagan or not, she liked the sincerity and wisdom in the old man. She turned to Dubán and found him watching her inquisitively.

'I see that you like the old man in spite of your religious differences.'

'Perhaps the differences are not so much once we remove the names we give to things. We are all sprang from the same common ancestry.'

'Perhaps.'

The old man returned a moment later with a travelling cloak

and a *sacculus*, a bag on a strap strung across his shoulder, in which he had obviously put the items he needed for the journey.

'Tell me, brother Saxon,' he said, as Eadulf helped him to mount the horse, 'I presume my old antagonist Gormán is still at the *rath*?'

'Father Gormán is the priest at Araglin.'

'Not my father,' muttered Gadra. 'I do not object to calling anyone my brother or my sister but there are not many on this earth that I would acknowledge have the right to be called my father, especially one whose intolerance is like a canker eating away at his soul.'

Eadulf exchanged a glance with Fidelma at the old man's vehemence but the Saxon's amusement did not find a resonance in Fidelma's eyes. She was solemn.

'Have no concern of Gormán,' she told the old man, as she swung up on her own mount. 'Mine is the authority by which you come to the *rath* of Araglin.'

Gadra laughed or, at least, his sinewy body quivered with amusement.

'Each person is their own authority, Fidelma,' he said.

They began to make the return journey along the path through the great mountain forests. It seemed that some mutual unspoken agreement caused them to lapse into silence so that only the heavy snorting breath of their horses, treading the forest path, could be heard. Even the dark woods themselves were without sound in spite of the fact that it was still daylight above the gloomy canopy.

Fidelma was head down, deep in thought, trying to puzzle how this old man and, indeed, Teafa, could form any meaningful communication with someone who had Móen's disabilities. She gave up the attempt after a while. The fact that he said he could do so was good enough for her for she accepted without question that Gadra was a man who spoke the truth. Didn't the old wise ones use to say that by Truth the earth endures and by Truth we are delivered from our enemies?

She glanced back to Eadulf and wondered what he was thinking. He must be uncomfortable about the proximity of someone who rejected the New Faith and adhered to the ways of the ancient ones. Gadra had been right in his one word summation of Eadulf. He was practical; down to earth and pragmatic. He accepted what he was taught and once accepted he would adhere to those teachings without question or deviation. He was like a ponderous ship ploughing a stately way across an ocean. If so, then she was a light bark, speeding hither and thither, darting across the waves. Did she do him an injustice? She suddenly found herself remembering a maxim of Hesiod. Admire the little ship but put your cargo in a big one.

She gave a mental sigh and turned her mind back to the task in hand. She reflected on the evidence she had so far heard but at the end of her contemplation she realised there was nothing to be done until Gadra learnt what he could from Móen. Fidelma felt annoyance and, having questioned her annoyance, realised that she was impatient to get back to the *rath* and learn what Móen could tell them. Impatience was, she acknowledged, her biggest fault. She accepted Eadulf's remonstration about her irritability and impatience. But she admitted that a restless spirit was at least a sign of being alive.

She was abruptly aware that Dubán had drawn rein and had raised one hand up to halt them.

He held his head cocked to one side in a listening attitude.

They stayed still for a moment or two. The warrior turned and gestured for them to dismount.

'What is it?' whispered Fidelma.

'Several heavy-shod horses,' replied Dubán in the same soft tone, 'and riders who make little attempt to disguise their passage. Listen!'

She held her head to one side and found she could actually hear voices raised, shouting to one another.

Eyes narrowed, Dubán was looking around him.

'Quickly,' he instructed, still keeping his voice low, 'let us lead our horses off the path into the forest. Through there,' he thrust out a hand to indicate a route, 'there are some rocks behind which we can conceal ourselves.'

Questions rose in Fidelma's throat but she bit them back. When a trained warrior issued such advice it was not her place to debate with him.

They followed him as silently and rapidly as possible from the track into the forest, through the brush to the outcrop of rocks he indicated. Eadulf held the horses with Gadra by his side while Dubán and Fidelma moved to the edge of the rocks and crouched there observing the path.

The sound of a number of men on horseback was now easily identifiable and the noisy laughter and shouting of the riders showed they feared no opposition to their passage through the forests.

Fidelma glanced sideways at Dubán. The middle-aged warrior was frowning as he peered towards the path. He was clearly anxious.

'What gives you concern?' she whispered. 'These are the forests of Araglin and you command the bodyguard of the chieftains. Why are we hiding?'

Dubán did not move his head and spoke softly out of the side of his mouth.

'A warrior is told never to test the depth of a river with both feet.'

He paused, holding his head to one side.

'Listen.'

Fidelma listened to the sounds of the approaching horses.

'I am no warrior, Dubán. What do you hear?'

'I hear the rattle of war harness, of swords bumping on shields, of the tread of heavy-shod horses. It tells me that the riders are armed men. If I see a hound in a sheep pen, I look first to see if it means harm to the sheep.'

He motioned her to silence.

The outline of figures on horseback could be seen through the brush and trees that stood between them and the forest track. There were about a dozen riders. They sat at ease on their mounts. Several of them wore light riding cloaks and carried rounded shields slung on their arms. A few of them carried long pointed spears.

At the end of the column of horsemen, being guided by long lead reins by the last riders, were half a dozen asses, sturdy pack animals, on whose backs were large covered panniers which appeared loaded and heavy.

That the riders had no idea that they were being observed was obvious. Coarse laughter echoed from their ranks and someone was exchanging ribald remarks about some member of the company.

Fidelma's eyes narrowed. Bringing up the rear of this procession, after the asses, rode a man without a cloak. She could make out a bow, slung over one shoulder. But the other shoulder was in bandages with the arm supported by a sling.

She drew in a sharp breath.

The line of horsemen proceeded on its noisy way through the forests. They waited in silence until they could hear nothing more of the riders.

Slowly, Dubán rose to his feet, followed by Fidelma, and turned back to where Eadulf and Gadra stood by the horses.

'I do not understand,' Eadulf said immediately. 'Why do we hide from these horsemen?'

Dubán was absently fingering his black beard.

'I believe that they are the cattle raiders who have been worrying the farmsteads of Araglin.'

'How do you know?' asked Fidelma.

'I saw a body of well-armed men who are strangers in this glen. Why are they here? We know that armed men have been raiding some of our farmsteads. Is it not logical that these are the same men?'

'Logical enough,' conceded Eadulf reluctantly.

'If they were cattle raiders, why are they transporting those heavily laden asses? And to where?'

'This road leads south out of these valleys towards the coast. You can be in Lios Mhór or Ard Mór in a short time from here,' Gadra explained.

'Is this a faster way of reaching Lios Mhór than the road which leads by Bressal's hostel?' queried Fidelma, remembering what Bressal had told her.

'It is a full half a day quicker to reach Lios Mhór by this road than by Bressal's hostel,' confirmed the old man.

'Whoever those men were,' interposed Eadulf, 'surely they would not harm us? I may be a stranger here but this I have learnt, it is not the custom to offer violence to those wearing the cloth of the Faith.'

'My Saxon brother,' Gadra laid a thin hand on Eadulf's arm, 'given a strong incentive, even the most established of customs may be broken. For protection you should rely only on your own common sense and not on what clothes you wear.'

'Good advice,' agreed Fidelma. 'For we have met at least one of these men before.'

Eadulf's eyebrows shot up in surprise.

'We have?' he asked.

'Where?' demanded Dubán.

'The one with his arm in the sling,' went on Fidelma, unperturbed by their consternation, 'was one of those shot by Eadulf two mornings ago when the hostel of Bressal was attacked. The arrow bit deep.'

'Eadulf shot the attacker with an arrow?'

Old Gadra was gazing at Eadulf in unconcealed amazement. Then he began to chuckle.

Eadulf sniffed in annoyance.

'Sometimes I rely on other means apart from the clothes I wear to defend myself,' he said dryly.

177

Gadra clapped him on the shoulder.

'I think I shall like you, brother Saxon. Sometimes I forget the need for the pragmatic. You cannot row across a river unless you have oars to do so.'

Eadulf was not quite sure how to interpret the old man's remark but decided it was meant as something complimentary.

Dubán was still looking serious.

'Are you sure that these are the men who attacked Bressal's hostel?'

Fidelma nodded affirmatively.

'We were witnesses to it.'

'I think we must get back to the *rath* of Araglin as quickly as possible.'

'What of Menma?' Eadulf began, only to be silenced by Fidelma with a look of anger that made him blink.

Dubán turned to him with a frown, missing her warning glance.

'What about Menma?' he asked.

'Eadulf was thinking of the need to protect the *rath* if these bandits attacked,' Fidelma explained hastily.

Dubán shook his head.

'Menma will not be of much help. But there is young Crítán and other of my warriors there. However, those outlaws are riding away from the direction of the *rath* so I would have no concern for the safety of it, brother.'

Eadulf shrugged, realising that for some reason or other Fidelma wanted to keep to herself her belief that Menma had been one of the raiding party at Bressal's hostel. Fidelma gave him a withering look and began to lead her horse after Dubán.

Eadulf realised that Gadra was examining him with a knowing expression.

He turned irritably and began to lead his horse after Dubán and Fidelma, back to the track.

This time Dubán led them at a much faster pace than before, breaking into a canter whenever the path through the narrow defiles and under the low, overhanging branches allowed an easy passage.

It was after some minutes that Gadra, hanging on behind Eadulf, moved his mouth close to his ear.

'Be comforted, my Saxon brother,' the old man called so that only he could hear. 'If you think twice before you speak, you will speak twice the better.'

Eadulf's mouth closed in a tight line and he silently cursed the old man's prescience.

Chapter Twelve

Crítán brought Móen into the guests' hostel which Fidelma had deemed as the most appropriate place to question him, away from the environment of his imprisonment in the stables. Apart from Fidelma and Eadulf only Gadra was there. Dubán was discussing the matter of the cattle raiders with Crón.

There was a silence as the young warrior, still displaying his surly arrogance, led, almost dragged and propelled, the unfortunate Móen into the room. Fidelma noted with satisfaction that at least Crítán had continued with his attempts to keep Móen clean and with a semblance of human dignity. She could feel sympathy for the poor creature as he was pushed into the room for his face showed abject fear, not knowing, not understanding, what was happening around him.

Crítán forced him to be seated and he half-sprawled in the chair, head to one side. Crítán glanced at them with a smirk.

'Well?' he demanded. 'What now? What tricks are you going to make him perform?'

Gadra moved forward, his breath an angry hiss. For a moment, Fidelma thought the old man was going to physically strike the arrogant youth.

Then a curious thing happened.

Móen began to sniff, raising his head and scenting the air. For the first time, Fidelma saw an expression of hope form on his features and he started to make a soft whimpering sound.

Gadra went straight to his side, seated himself on an adjacent chair and gripped his hand.

Fidelma could not believe that the creature's face could become

181

so altered. It lit up in recognition and joyful pleasure. She saw Gadra grasped the young man's left hand. It seemed, at first, a ritual, for Móen held his hand palm outward, straight and upright. She watched with surprise as Gadra began to trace motions of his hand on the young man's palm. Then, with equal surprise, the young man gripped the hand of Gadra and began to make the same motions back. Fidelma realised that this was what the young man had tried to do with her hand in the stables. There was little doubt in her mind that an entire conversation was now taking place. The finger gestures flew fast and furious.

Suddenly, Móen began to groan as if in physical anguish, rocking back and forth on his seat as if in pain. Gadra put his arms around the creature's shoulders. He looked up sadly at Fidelma.

'I have just told Móen of the death of Teafa. He regarded her as his mother.'

'How did he take the news of the death of Eber?' asked Eadulf.

'Without surprise,' replied Gadra. 'I think he knew of that. I have told him what has happened and what he is suspected of.'

'Told him?' It was Crítán who spoke, his voice a bark of cynical laughter. 'Come now, old one. A joke is a joke but . . .'

'Quiet!' Fidelma's voice was icy. 'You will leave us now. You may remain outside until we send for you.'

'I have been placed in charge of the prisoner.' The young warrior flushed angrily. 'It is my duty to . . .'

'It is your duty to do as you are told.' Fidelma's voice was testy. 'Go and tell Dubán, your commander, that I do not want you near this prisoner again. Go now!'

'You cannot . . .' began Crítán indignantly.

It was Eadulf who rose and, with studied gentleness, took the young warrior by the arm. Only the sudden gasp of pain and tightened jaw showed them just how much pressure Eadulf exerted.

182

'Yes, we can,' Eadulf said pleasantly. 'You are no longer required here.'

He propelled him to the door almost in the same way that Crítán had brought his prisoner in. When Eadulf closed the door behind the young warrior he found Gadra grinning at him.

'Pragmatic, indeed. I am sure that I like you, brother Saxon!'

Fidelma had taken no further notice but was gazing thoughtfully at Móen. She turned to Gadra.

'While he is composing himself, I would like to know what method you are using to communicate with him. I must know whether this communication is genuine.'

Gadra grunted in annoyance.

'Do you think I have invented all this, child?'

Fidelma gave a swift shake of her head.

'No, I did not mean that. But I must rightly seek an assurance that this is a genuine communication from the boy for if I have to present it before a court of law then I must have a full understanding of it.'

Gadra regarded her for a moment or two and shrugged indifferently.

'As an advocate you probably know something of the ancient Ogam alphabet.'

Fidelma's eyes widened.

'You use the Ogam alphabet to communicate?'

Ogam was the earliest form of writing among the people of the five kingdoms and consisted of short lines drawn to, or crossing, a base line representing the twenty characters of the alphabet. The ancients claimed that the god Ogma, patron of literacy and learning, had come to the south-west of Muman, the place of all primal beginnings, and instructed the wise ones in the use of the characters, so that they could journey through the land and even across the seas to show people how they might write. The alphabet was often inscribed on wands of hazel or aspen and many grave markers of stone were inscribed in Ogam. It had fallen into disuse with the introduction of the new Latin learning and alphabet into the kingdoms. Fidelma had studied the old system and alphabet as part of her education for many texts were still to be found written in the archaic form.

She could suddenly see how such a simple form of alphabet might be used as a means of communication by manual gestures.

Gadra was watching her changing expression as she realised the simplicity of the form.

'Do you want to test it for yourself?' he asked.

Fidelma nodded eagerly.

Gadra turned to Móen and there was a quick exchange.

'Take his palm. Hold it upright and use the line of the second digit as the base line down to the heel of the hand. Introduce yourself by writing your name in the Ogam characters.'

Fidelma cautiously took the youth's hand.

Three strokes to the right of the base line for 'F'; five dots on the base line with the tip of her finger for 'i'; two strokes to the left of the base line for 'd'; four dots on the line for 'e'; two strokes to the left for 'l'; a diagonal stroke across it for 'm' and a single dot for 'a'. She made the movements fairly slowly and cautiously. Then she paused, awaiting a response.

The young man, an eager smile on his lips, took the left hand, which she offered him, and held it palm up. Then came his finger against the palm. A diagonal for 'M'; two dots on the line for 'o'; a slight pause before four dots for 'e' and then four strokes to the right for 'n'. Móen.

It was so simple. And this sentient creature had been treated as if he were no more than an animal. Fidelma felt a thrill of outrage as she realised the enormity of it.

Slowly Fidelma began to spell out on Móen's palm.

'I am an advocate of the courts, come to investigate the murder of Eber and Teafa. Do you understand?'

'Yes. I did not kill them.'

'I want you to tell me what happened so far as you know.'

At once the youth began to use his fingers rapidly against her palm. So rapidly that she had to interrupt him.

'You are too fast. I am unused to this means of communication. Speak with Gadra here and he will translate what you have to say more rapidly.'

'Very well.'

Fidelma sat back and explained to Gadra who immediately took over. The door opened abruptly. Fidelma glanced up as Dubán entered and stood watching the proceedings in amazement. He stirred uneasily as he caught her inquiring gaze.

'Crítán has protested to me that you . . .' he began but Fidelma cut him short.

'I am well aware of what Crítán might have reported,' she said.

Dubán grimaced.

'I am not without an understanding of that young man's faults. I will see to it that he no longer stands guard over Móen, if that is your wish.' He glanced towards Gadra and Móen. 'It is true, then. Can he really communicate?'

'As you see, Dubán, we can communicate with him and he with us. Would you mind waiting outside? We must accord Móen the same privacy in this interrogation that any one of us is entitled to under the law.'

Though disappointment showed on his face, the commander of the guard jerked his head in agreement and left the room.

Fidelma and Eadulf now turned back to watch with some awe and amazement as Móen's fingers worked rapidly over Gadra's palm. The old man would halt the flow now and then and presumably asked a question for the sake of clarification. As he did so, he began to interpret between Fidelma and Móen.

'Tell us, Móen, did you kill Teafa or Eber?'

'I did not.' A pause. 'I loved Teafa. She raised me as my mother.'

'Will you tell us what happened that night, the time when you were made prisoner?'

'I will try.'

'Take your time and try to put in as much detail as you can remember.'

'I will try. I sometimes have difficulty in sleeping. It is then I rise and go for a walk.'

'A walk at night?'

'Night or day makes no difference to me.'

Fidelma with a start realised that Móen was actually smiling at the joke that he had made.

'Did you do so that night?'

'I did.'

'You do not know at what hour this was?'

'Alas, I do not. Time is meaningless to me except I know when it is hot and when it is cold, when I scent certain flowers and when I scent others. I can only tell you that it was cold when I went for my walk and there was a scent of dampness but no flowers. I rose and went to the door of our cabin. I am adept at moving about quietly.'

Fidelma realised that this could be a mark against Móen. She decided to ask for amplification.

'How well could you move around the village by yourself?'

'Unless someone has left some object discarded on the paths, something which should not be in the way of the passes between the buildings, then I usually have no difficulty. Once or twice I have fallen over a box or something of that sort which has been left lying about. Then I rouse the dogs and people get angry. Usually I manage very well.'

'Where did you go for your walk?'

'I cannot tell you. I can show you by repeating it, if you like.'

'Later. What did you do on your walk?'

'I did little except I sat by the water where the scents are often so beautiful and caress your mind and body and soul. But there were no scents at that time.'

'You sat by the water?'

'Yes.'

'Flowing water?'

'Yes. Teafa calls it a river.'

'Have you done this before?'

'Many times. It is an enjoyment in life especially when it is warm and there is a scent upon the air. I can sit there and just reflect.'

Fidelma swallowed at the sensitivity of the young man who everyone thought was a mere animal.

'Then what did you do?'

'I began to return to the cabin.'

'To Teafa's cabin?'

'That is so. It was when I was at the door that someone reached for my arm. They thrust a piece of wood into my hand. They took my other hand and ran it along the wood. I think they did this to make sure I understood that there was writing on it.'

'Writing?'

'The carved symbols in the manner in which we are speaking now.'

'Do you know who it was?'

'I do not. Their scent was unknown to me.'

'What did the symbols say?'

'It said, "Eber wants you now." Meaning I was to go to Eber.'

'What did you do?'

'I went.'

'Did you not think of waking Teafa to tell her?'

'She would not have approved of my going to Eber.'

'Why was that?'

'She thought that he was a bad man.'

'And what did you think?'

'Eber was always nice to me. Several times he gave me food and tried to communicate with me. I felt his hand on my head and face but he did not have the knowledge. I once asked Teafa to instruct him on the means of communication but she would not.'

'Did she explain why she would not?'

'Never. She simply said he was a very bad man.'

'So when you received the message, you must have thought that he had discovered the means of communication?'

'I did. If Eber could use the symbols to communicate by the stick, then he had obviously found the means.'

There was no faulting the logic.

'So what did you do with the stick?'

There was a pause.

'I dropped it, I think. No, I must have caught it on something for it seemed to be pushed out of my hand. I do not think I bothered to bend down to search for it. I was intent on going to Eber.'

'So then you found your way to Eber's apartments?'

'It was not hard. I can find my way very well.' He paused.

'Continue,' Fidelma pressed.

'I went to the door. I tapped on it as Teafa has taught me. Then I lifted the latch and went in. No one approached me. I stood for a while, thinking that if Eber was there he would make himself known. When he did not, I moved forward, realising that there must be another chamber. I moved along the boundary of the wall and eventually found the second door and I tapped on this. The door did not open and so I sought out and lifted the latch on it and managed to enter.'

'What then?'

'Nothing. I stood for a while, expecting Eber to approach me. When he did not, I wondered if there was yet another chamber. I began to move along the wall. Holding one hand out before me. I had not gone far when my hand encountered something hot, uncomfortable. I believe it to be what you call a lamp. Something which burns by which you are able to see in the dark.'

Fidelma nodded and then realising the futility of it responded: 'Yes. There was a lamp alight on the table. What then?'

'I moved around the table and my feet encountered something on the floor. I recognised this as a mattress. I decided to crawl over it and continue my journey using the wall as my guide on the other side of the room. I was intent on finding a door to another chamber. I went on my hands and knees and began to climb over what I thought was the mattress . . .'

The tapping fingers paused. Then: 'I realised that there was a body lying there. I touched it with my hand. It was wet and sticky. The wet had a salty taste and made me feel ill. I reached forward again to touch the face but my hand encountered something cold and also wet. It was very sharp. It was a . . . a knife.'

The young man shuddered.

'I knelt there not knowing what to do. I knew Eber's scent. I smelt that this was Eber before me and the life had gone from him. I think I moaned a little. I was making up my mind to seek a way out and rouse Teafa when rough hands gripped me. I feared for my life. I thrashed out. Other hands hit me, hurt me, and I was bound. I was dragged somewhere. It smelled vile. No one came near me. No one tried to communicate with me. I spent an eternity in purgatory not knowing what to do. I worked out that Eber must have been killed with a knife, the same that I had found and held. I also worked out that those who had seized me were either his killers or, worse, that they must have thought that I had killed Eber myself.

'I tried to find something to carve a message to Teafa on. I could not understand why she had abandoned me. Now and then I was thrown scraps of food. There was a bucket of water. Sometimes I managed to eat and drink but often I could not find the scraps they threw me. No one helped me. No one.'

There was a pause before the finger tapping continued.

'I do not know how long had passed. It seemed forever. Finally, I smelled a scent, the scent I smell now . . . The person called Fidelma. After that, hands, though rough, cleaned me, fed me and gave me water. I was still shackled but I was given a comfortable straw palliasse and the place smelled sweeter. Yet the time sped on. It is only now that I can talk and only now that I realise fully what has taken place.'

Fidelma gave a long sigh as Gadra finished the translation from the tapping, moving fingers of the young man.

'Móen, a great injustice has been done,' she said at last. Gadra dutifully translated. 'Even had the guilt been yours you should not have been treated like an animal. For that we must beg your forgiveness.'

'You have nothing to be forgiven for, Fidelma. It is you who have rescued me from this plight.'

'Not rescued yet. I fear that you will not be rescued until we have proved your innocence and identified the one who is guilty.'

'I understand. How can I help you?'

'You have helped enough for the present, though I will talk with you again. You will return to live in the cabin which you shared with Teafa, as this will be familiar to you. If Gadra is willing, he will be there to take care of you until our search for the guilty one is over. For your own protection I would urge you not to walk abroad unless you are accompanied.'

'I understand. Thank you, Sister Fidelma.'

'There is one more thing,' she suddenly added, as the thought struck her.

'Which is?' prompted Móen through Gadra after she had paused.

'You say that you were able to smell me?'

'That is so. I have had to develop the senses that God left me. Touch, taste and smell. I can also feel vibrations. I can feel the approach of a horse or even a lesser animal. I can feel the course of a river. These things can tell me what is happening round me.'

He paused and grinned, looking, so it seemed, straight towards Brother Eadulf.

'I know you have a companion, Fidelma, and that he is a male.' Eadulf shifted awkwardly.

'This is Brother Eadulf,' interposed Gadra, and turning to

Eadulf, said: 'If you do not know Ogam, squeeze Móen's hand in acknowledgment.'

Cautiously, Eadulf reached forward, took the young man's hand and squeezed it. He felt an answering pressure.

'Blessings on you, Brother Eadulf,' Móen's finger movements were quickly traced by Gadra.

'Let us return to your sense of smell,' cut in Fidelma. 'Cast your mind back, Móen. Remember the time when the person grabbed your hand and placed into it the stick with the Ogam instructing you to go to Eber? You said that you did not recognise the scent. Can you confirm that there was a scent?'

Móen thought for a while.

'Oh yes. I have not thought of it since. It was a sweet scent of flowers.'

'A scent of flowers? Yet it was cold, as you say. To us this would be night and judging from the time you were found at Eber's apartments, this certainly seems so. There are few flowers that give out scent in the early hours of the morning.'

'It was a perfume. At first I thought the person who handed me the stick was a lady by the scent. But the hands, the hands that touched mine were coarse and calloused. It must have been a man. Touch does not lie; it was a man who passed me the stick with the writing on.'

'What type of perfume was it?'

'I can identify smells but I cannot give them labels as you know them. However, I am sure that the hands were those of a man. Rough and coarse hands.'

Fidelma exhaled softly and sat back in her chair as if deep in thought.

'Very well, Gadra,' she said eventually to the old man, 'I am placing Móen in your custody. You are to look after him and confine him to Teafa's house for the time being.'

Gadra regarded her anxiously.

'Do you believe that the boy is innocent of the crimes which he stands accused of?'

Fidelma was dismissive.

'Believing and proving are two different things, Gadra. Do your best to see he is comfortable and I shall keep you informed.'

Gadra assisted Móen to his feet and led him to the door.

Dubán was still standing outside. He stood back to allow Gadra and his charge to pass after Fidelma had told him her wishes.

'There will be some in this *rath* who will not like this decision, Fidelma,' the warrior muttered.

Fidelma's eyes flashed angrily.

'I certainly expect the guilty to be unhappy,' she replied.

Dubán blinked at her sharp tone.

'I will inform Crón of your decision about Móen. However, I came to inform you of some news which may interest you.'

'Well?' she asked, after he had paused.

'A rider has just come into the *rath* with the news that one of the outlying farms was attacked early this morning. I am taking some men immediately to see what assistance we can render. I thought that you might be interested to know whose farm it was which was attacked.'

'Why?' demanded Fidelma. 'Get to the point, man. Why would I be interested?'

'It was the farmstead of the young man Archú.'

Eadulf pursed his lips in a soundless whistle.

'A raid on Archú's farmstead? Was anyone hurt?'

'A neighbouring shepherd brought us the news and reported that he had seen cattle being run off, barns set alight and he thinks someone was killed.'

'Who was killed?' demanded Fidelma.

'The shepherd was unable to tell us.'

'Where is this shepherd?'

'He has left the *rath* to get back to his unattended sheep.'

Eadulf turned to Fidelma with a troubled look.

'Archú told us that there was only himself and the young girl, Scoth, working the farm.'

'I know,' Fidelma replied grimly. 'Dubán, when are you and your men leaving for Archú's farmstead?'

'At once.'

'Then Eadulf and I will accompany you and your men. I have grown to have an interest in the welfare of those young people. Has the whereabouts of Muadnat been established? I would have thought that he could well resort to attacking Archú and throwing suspicion onto your cattle raiders.'

'I know you do not like Muadnat but I cannot believe that he would do anything so stupid. You misjudge him. Besides, we have seen the bandits with our own eyes.'

Eadulf was thoughtful.

'It is true, Fidelma. You cannot deny the presence of bandits.'

Fidelma glanced scornfully at him before returning her gaze to Dubán.

'We did, indeed, see the horsemen. But, if you recall, they were heading south and we saw no cattle with them. All we saw were asses loaded with heavy panniers. Where were the cattle if they were cattle raiders? Come, let us ride for Archú's farmstead.'

Chapter Thirteen

Dubán had gathered half a dozen riders; all were well armed. Fidelma was relieved to see that the arrogant young Crítan was not one of them. Fidelma noticed that neither Crón nor her mother, Cranat, came to observe their departure from the *rath*. In a column of twos, with Fidelma and Eadulf bringing up the rear, they turned through the gates of the *rath* and proceeded at a gentle trot along the river's southern bank towards the eastern end of the fertile valley of Araglin with its grain fields and grazing cattle herds. Dubán did not hurry the pace but kept the column moving at a steady rate.

They had not gone more than a few miles when the track came to a bend in the river which looped in such a way as to create a sheltered peninsula with the river forming a natural barrier on three sides. It was a small haven of land that also had the protection of trees. Flowers grew in abundance here and rising on the land was a picturesque single-storeyed cabin built of wooden logs and planks. There was a garden before it. Standing in this garden, watching them pass, obviously disturbed in the process of tending to the flowers, was a small, fleshy blonde woman.

They passed too far away for Fidelma to note the details of her features. The woman stood making no effort to raise her hand in greeting but continued to watch them as they rode by. Fidelma noticed with curiosity that a couple of Dubán's men exchanged sly, grinning glances and one of them even gave an audible guffaw.

Fidelma eased her horse towards the front of the small column to where Dubán rode.

'Who was that?' she asked.

'No one of importance,' replied the warrior gruffly.

'This no one of importance seems to create an interest among your men.'

Dubán looked uncomfortable.

'That was Clídna, a woman of flesh.'

'Woman of flesh' was a euphemism for a prostitute.

'I see.' Fidelma was thoughtful. She pulled her horse out of the line and waited while the other warriors rode by. Eadulf caught up with her and she eased her horse alongside his. She briefly passed on the explanation. He sighed and shook his head sadly.

'So much sin in so beautiful a spot.'

Fidelma did not bother to reply.

At the end of the large valley they began to ascend through the shelter of the surrounding forests but here the track was well cut and broad enough for wagons. They ascended the steep gradient between two hills, climbing upward into a second valley on a higher elevation. As they moved into this, Fidelma pointed wordlessly and Eadulf followed her outstretched hand. A column of smoke was rising some way away across the shoulder of the hills.

Dubán turned in his saddle, and noting that Fidelma had already seen the tell-tale sign waved her to come forward.

'This is the valley of the Black Marsh. Where that smoke is rising is Archú's farmstead. To your left, the valley lands belong to Muadnat.'

Fidelma noted the cultivated fields, the cattle and deer herds and rich pastureland. It was a farmstead that was worth far more than seven *cumals*, she noted. Muadnat's farm was clearly a rich one. She placed it at five times the value of the land which he had been forced to give back to Archú.

The road ran alongside the boundary of Muadnat's farmstead, slightly above it on a track worn in the side of the rolling hills. It was sometimes lined with trees and scrubland while at other times open to stretches of grassland which had been shortened by deer herds or other herbivores. In the valley below there seemed no sign of activity on Muadnat's farmstead.

'I would imagine Muadnat and his farm hands have already ridden to Archú's,' explained Dubán, guessing what was passing through her mind.

Fidelma smiled thinly but made no other comment. Certainly the column of smoke would have been easily seen from Muadnat's farmstead.

Dubán ordered the pace to increase to a canter.

The column of horses moved rapidly along the hillside track, which twisted down the slopes moving with the contours of the hill.

Fidelma realised that the part of the valley in which Archú dwelt almost constituted a separate valley to the area occupied by Muadnat. This area seemed to twist off from the main valley of the Black Marsh at a forty-five degree angle, hiding much of its lands from the track along which they had come. Soon the descent to the valley became so precipitous they had to slow down to a walk.

'How well do you know this area, Dubán?' called Fidelma.

'Well enough,' replied the warrior.

'Is this the only track in or out of this valley?'

'This is the only easy route but men, even with horses, might find a way over the peaks.'

Fidelma raised her eyes to the rounded hilltops.

'Only in desperation,' she observed.

Eadulf leaned forward.

'What are you thinking?' he asked.

'Oh, just that a band of men on horseback riding to Archú's farmstead must surely have ridden across or by the land of Muadnat and have been observed.'

They came as quickly as they could down to the valley floor. The main group of farm buildings were easily recognisable; a dwelling house, a kiln for drying corn standing just beyond it.

There was a barn and a pigsty. A little way beyond these was the smoking ruin of another barn, charred and blackened, from which the spiral of smoke was still ascending.

There were a few cattle in a pen, one of which was giving vent to an irritated lowing.

Dubán made directly for the dwelling house.

'Halt! If you value your lives!'

The voice was almost a high-pitched scream.

It caused them all to jerk upon their reins and come to an unceremonious halt before the main building.

'We are armed,' called the voice, 'and many of us. Go back from whence you came or . . .'

Fidelma edged her way forward.

'Archú!' she shouted, having recognised the voice of the youth. 'It is I, Fidelma. We have come to assist you.'

The door of the main building opened abruptly. Archú stood there staring at them. All he held in his hand was a rusty sword. Behind him the young girl, Scoth, peered fearfully over his shoulder.

'Sister Fidelma!' Archú gazed from her to Dubán and the rest of the company. 'We thought the raiders had returned.'

Fidelma swung herself down, followed by Dubán and Eadulf. The other men remained mounted, staring suspiciously about the countryside.

'We heard that bandits had raided your farmstead. A shepherd rode to the *rath* to bring word.'

Scoth pushed forward.

'That was Librén. It is true, sister. We were not even awake when they attacked. Their shouts and the lowing of our cattle disturbed us. We managed to barricade ourselves in here. But they did not assault us; they rode off with some cattle and set fire to one of the barns. It was barely light and we could hardly see what was going on.'

'Who were they?' demanded Fidelma. 'Did you recognise them?'

Archú shook his head.

'It was too dark. There was a great deal of shouting.'

'How many raiders were there?'

'I had the impression it was less than a dozen.'

'What made them break off their attack?'

Archú frowned at Dubán's sudden question.

'Break off?'

'I see only one barn burnt down,' the warrior observed. 'You have several cattle still in the pen there and I hear sheep and pigs. You are unharmed and so is your house. Obviously the raiders decided to break off their attack.'

The young man looked wonderingly at the warrior.

Fidelma gave Dubán a glance of appreciation for making a logical observation.

Scoth's mouth compressed for a moment.

'I wondered why they made no attempt to break into the farmhouse or even burn it down. It was as if they merely wanted to frighten us.'

'Perhaps it was the shepherd, Librén,' Archú suggested. 'When he saw the flames of the barn from the hillside, he sounded his shepherd's horn and came running down to help us.'

'A brave man,' muttered Eadulf.

'A foolish man,' corrected Dubán.

'Yet still brave,' affirmed Eadulf stubbornly.

'It is thanks to him they only made off with two of the cattle,' Scoth pointed out.

'Two cattle? And all because a shepherd comes running to your help?' Dubán was cynical.

'It is true,' insisted Archú. 'When Librén sounded his horn, they herded the cattle before them and rode off.'

'That is all? Two milch cows?'

Archú nodded.

'Which path did they take?' Eadulf asked.

Scoth immediately pointed down the valley in the direction of Muadnat's farmlands.

'Librén said they disappeared in that direction.'

'That is the path that leads through the bogland, the Black Marsh itself. It only goes to the lands of Muadnat,' Dubán explained uneasily.

'It certainly leads nowhere else,' Archú grimly assured him.

'Where is this Librén, the shepherd?' Fidelma asked.

Scoth turned and pointed to the southern hillside.

'Librén tends his flocks above there. He came and stayed with us until dawn, in case the raiders came back. Then he borrowed one of our horses, for Archú did not want to leave me, and rode to the *rath* to tell you of the raid. He returned just half an hour ago and told us that you were on the way.'

'Why didn't he wait?'

'He had neglected his flocks since this morning,' Archú pointed out. 'There is no need for him to stay now.'

Fidelma was looking around as if searching for something.

'This Librén said that someone was killed. Who was killed and where is the body?'

Dubán clapped a hand to his forehead and groaned.

'Fool that I am. I had forgotten.' He turned to Archú. 'Who was killed?'

Archú looked uncomfortable.

'The body is over there, by the burnt-out barn. I do not know who it is. No one saw it happen. It was only when we were trying to douse the flames later that we discovered it.'

'A man is killed on your farm during a raid and you know nothing about it?' Dubán was still cynical. 'Come, lad, if it is one of the attackers then you have nothing to fear in punishment. You were only acting in self-defence.'

Archú shook his head.

'But truly, we did not kill anyone. We did not have the weapons. We barricaded ourselves in during the attack and saw nothing.

Librén, also, was surprised and did not recognise the man.'

'Let us examine this body,' Fidelma urged, realising that there was nothing to be gained from talk.

One of Dubán's men had already discovered the corpse. He pointed wordlessly to the ground as they approached.

The body was that of someone in their thirties. An ugly looking man with a scarred face and a bulbous nose, flattened as if by a blow. The eyes were dark, wide and staring. The clothes were bloodstained and covered in a curious fine white dust. His throat had been cut, almost severing the head from the neck. It reminded Fidelma of the way a goat or some other farm animal might be butchered for its meat. One thing was for certain, he had been killed in no skirmish but had been deliberately murdered. She looked at the wrists and saw the burn mark of ropes there. The man's hands had been tied together until recently. She glanced at Dubán with raised eyebrows.

'I have never seen this man in Araglin before,' he interpreted the implied question correctly. 'He is a stranger to this valley so far as I am aware.'

Fidelma thoughtfully rubbed her chin.

'This gets more confusing. There is a raid. The raiders kill a strange captive or one of their own. They depart with only two milch cows and make no further attempt at pillage. Why?'

'Easily explained if they were Muadnat's men,' observed Scoth resentfully.

'Why do you think this body was a captive or one of their own men?' asked Dubán, examining the corpse.

'It seems a likely assumption,' Fidelma responded. 'He had his hands tied behind him until recently which might explain how his throat was cut without him putting up a struggle, for there are no other wounds. That he was a captive of the raiders or one of them is also obvious. He certainly did not appear out of thin air, did he?'

She suddenly bent down and examined the man's forearms and hands with a frown.

'What is it?' asked Eadulf.

'This man is one used to rough work. Look at the callouses on his hands; look at the scars and the dirt under his fingernails.'

She suddenly peered closely at the dead man's face and turned to Eadulf.

'Does this man remind you of anyone, Eadulf? Someone we have met in the last few days?'

Eadulf peered closely and then shook his head negatively.

Fidelma glanced up at Archú.

'I am right in thinking that it has not rained since yesterday?' The youth looked bewildered but nodded in agreement.

Fidelma returned to examining the clothes of the corpse carefully. Eadulf saw that Fidelma seemed interested in the fine layer of stone dust on the clothes of the man. Then she stood up.

'Araglin is truly becoming a place of many mysteries,' she observed softly. 'Now I think we should ride to Muadnat's farm.'

'Are you saying Muadnat is behind this?' Dubán asked with a frown.

'It is logical to begin our questioning with him,' Fidelma replied, 'especially after what has happened so far.'

'I suppose I agree.' Dubán was almost reluctant. 'If we were to assume that it was a band of raiders, then it seems odd that Archú's farmstead was raided and Muadnat's was not. Muadnat's farmstead is more accessible and richer in cattle than Archú's lands.'

Dubán ordered one of his men to stay behind to help Archú and to assist him in burying the body. The rest of them mounted up and began to trot back along the track towards Muadnat's farmstead.

As they began to move Eadulf caught Fidelma's eye and hung back at the end of the column of mounted warriors.

'Is it wise that we get involved in this matter?' he said softly so that only she heard.

'Wise?' She was surprised. 'I thought we were involved.'

'You have been sent to investigate the death of Eber, not to entangle yourself with some kind of feud between Archú and his cousin.'

'True enough,' Fidelma agreed, 'but I cannot help feeling that there is much more to the mysteries of Araglin than we are led to believe. Look how Dubán and Crón conceal their relationship. Outwardly it was claimed that Eber was respected, but secretly it is admitted that he was hated. Where is the truth to be found? And Muadnat's dislike of his young cousin . . . is this part of some hatred in this valley or is there something which connects these aspects, a spider's web which links so many points to one central evil thing that waits in the middle?'

Eadulf suppressed a sigh.

'I am but a stranger in a strange land, Fidelma. I am also a simple man. I do not see the subtleties of which you speak.'

He realised it was an easy excuse to avoid making any positive suggestions. Fidelma perceived as much and said no more.

Dubán, once they had turned back into the main area of the valley, led the way down from the mountain track through the cultivated fields towards Muadnat's farmstead. Almost immediately they could see some farm hands running towards the buildings. Obviously, they had been spotted. A familiar figure appeared abruptly. It was Muadnat's chief herdsman and nephew, Agdae.

He stood, feet apart, hands on hips, and inspected them as they drew nearer. Some of his men had come forward threatening with weapons.

'Is this a way to greet visitors, Agdae?' Dubán called as they came up.

'You ride here with armed men,' replied Agdae, unperturbed. 'Do you mean us ill or well? Better to make sure before we lay weapons aside and greet you all as brothers.'

Dubán halted his horse before Agdae.

'You should know the answer to that question,' he replied.

Agdae gestured to his men to lower their weapons and disperse.

He turned to Dubán with an insincere smile: 'What is it you seek here?'

'Where is your uncle, Muadnat?' demanded Dubán.

'I have no idea. But I am in charge here while my uncle is away. What do you seek him for?'

'There has been a raid on Archú's farmstead.'

Agdae's expression flickered momentarily.

'Am I supposed to feel sorrow for Archú when he has cheated Muadnat out of that land?'

Fidelma was about to intervene when Dubán raised a hand to stay her.

'Do you see that column of smoke behind the shoulder of the hill yonder?' he inquired.

'I see it,' replied Agdae blandly.

'You see it and yet you did not feel it necessary to ride to Archú's aid? We are a small community in these valleys of Araglin, Agdae. A raid against one of our farms is a raid against us all. When has it been the policy of the men of Araglin to refuse to help one another?'

Agdae raised his shoulders and let them fall in an exaggerated shrug.

'How was I to know that the smoke meant the boy was under attack?'

'The smoke itself should have told you,' replied Fidelma quickly.

Agdae turned and glowered at her.

'Alas, I have not your training in reading between the lines, *dálaigh*; of seeing things which are not plainly evident. To me, smoke is simply smoke. Why, Archú might have been burning fields to rid them of chaff. If I had gone running to find out what was wrong every time I saw fire on a farmer's land then I would have spent half of my lifetime doing so. Besides, if I had gone to Archú, because he has highly placed friends in legal circles, I might find myself having to pay compensation for unwelcome attentions.'

'A slippery tongue often leads to a fall,' snapped Fidelma, realising that Agdae was possessed of a sarcastic tongue. 'But having heard that a raid has taken place, you will perhaps tell us where Muadnat is.'

Agdae stood, still smirking at her but saying nothing.

Dubán repeated the question in a harsher tone.

'What can I tell you? Muadnat is not here.'

'But where is he?' insisted Dubán. 'Where has he gone?'

'All I can tell you is that he took himself off hunting yesterday and will return when he returns.'

'In which direction did he go?' insisted Dubán.

Agdae shrugged.

'Who dares to foretell in which direction a hawk will fly in search of prey?'

'Very prettily said.' Fidelma was in ill-humour. 'Let us hope that the hawk does not meet with a flock of eagles.'

Agdae blinked and stared at her, trying to read the meaning in her words.

'Muadnat is able to take care of himself,' he said defensively.

'Of that I have no doubt,' Fidelma assured him. 'Are all your field workers accounted for?'

'So far as I know,' Agdae was suddenly curious about her question. 'What do you mean?'

'Someone was killed at Archú's farm whom we have not been able to identify. Killed by the raiders.' Dubán described the man.

Agdae shook his head.

'All our men are accounted for save Muadnat. Presumably it was not he otherwise you would not be searching for him.'

'And Muadnat is hunting in the hills?'

'Just as I have said.'

'Call your men before me, Agdae,' demanded Dubán.

Agdae hesitated and then relayed the order.

The dozen or so farm hands gathered nervously under his scrutiny. They looked a sorry sight for most of them were elderly, sinewy and with strength for the plough and the sickle but not for the robust life of a cattle raider. Dubán looked at Fidelma and shrugged.

'These men will not be counted among the raiders,' he said. 'Shall we search the farmstead further?'

Fidelma reluctantly shook her head.

'Is it worth picking up the trail which Archú indicated and following the path of the raiders?' she suggested.

Dubán chuckled dryly.

'The route which was pointed out to us lay through a swamp land. Indeed, this is why this area is called the Black Marsh. Apart from the track which leads here, the other trails are dangerous. There is no way of following a trail through that treacherous bog.'

Brother Eadulf abruptly leaned forward from his horse and addressed Agdae.

'I have a question for you,' he said softly.

'Then ask away, Saxon,' Agdae replied complacently.

Eadulf pointed across the fields.

'Behind your farmstead there is a path which apparently leads up into the northern hills. It seems to lead in the opposite direction to the track that would take us back to the *rath* of Araglin. I thought there was only one way in and out of this valley?'

'What of it?' demanded Agdae.

Fidelma had raised her gaze towards the spot Eadulf had indicated and saw that he was right. There was a path there. She had not noticed it before. It was a recognisable track that rose across the northern hills, along the high meadows and clumps of woodland, towards the edge of the forests which spread across the hills on the far side of the valley.

'Where does that route lead?' queried Eadulf.

'Nowhere,' replied Agdae shortly.

Dubán took up the idea at once.

'We are told that the raiders rode in the direction of your farmstead. If they did not take the track leading back into the main valley of Araglin then the only path is that one. So where does it lead?'

'No spot in particular,' Agdae insisted. 'I told the Saxon no lie.'

'What?' Dubán let out a roar of laughter. 'Every path must lead to somewhere.'

'You know me, Dubán. I know every path and every dell within these valleys. I tell you that the track leads nowhere. It loses itself on the far side of the hills.'

'I will accept that he tells the truth,' replied Eadulf and sat back apparently satisfied. 'It does not matter. If the raiders took that path then they would have been seen by someone on this farmstead. Isn't that correct, Agdae?'

The man looked disconcerted for a moment and then jerked his head in agreement.

'You speak the truth, Saxon. They would have been seen.'

Fidelma was slightly perplexed. She wondered why Eadulf had asked about the path if he was not prepared to insist on the logical assumption that the raiders might have escaped by that route and suggest that Dubán take his men in pursuit. She quickly deduced that there was another reason to Eadulf's question.

Dubán was not persuaded.

'I will send two of my trackers to check the path. If they find any sign of the raiders then we shall go in pursuit.'

Agdae sniffed in displeasure.

'They will find nothing.'

Dubán motioned to two of his men who set off at a canter in the direction of the pathway.

Agdae was looking sourly at Fidelma.

'It seems that you are determined to paint my uncle Muadnat as a villain, *dálaigh*.'

'Muadnat is capable of painting his own image,' replied Fidelma without concern.

'Dubán, there is a horseman approaching!' It was one of Dubán's men.

They all turned in the direction to which the man was pointing. A horseman was certainly approaching from the direction of the main track to the *rath* of Araglin. It did not take long to recognise the slight form of Father Gormán.

'What is happening here?' called the priest as he rode up.

'You startled us, Father,' rejoined Dubán. 'You seemed to appear from nowhere.' He glanced at the priest's attire and added: 'It is cold weather to be abroad without a riding cloak.'

Father Gormán shrugged.

'It was warm when I started out this morning,' he said dismissively. 'But what is the matter?'

'Have you not heard that Archú's farmstead has been attacked? That is why we are nervous about horsemen in this area.'

The dark-featured priest looked uneasy.

'An attack? This is shameful. These cattle raiders again, I suppose?' He paused and shrugged. 'I was on my way to Archú's place anyway. But if there are raiders still about perhaps I should take care to go in company.'

'Oh,' Fidelma was sardonic, 'the raiders are long gone but surely you have your Faith to guard you from harm. Still, I am sure you would be welcomed at Archú's farm. There is a corpse that stands in need of your blessing.'

Father Gormán glowered in annoyance.

'Who has been killed?' he demanded.

'No one seems to know,' Dubán confessed. He was about to add something else when his two men came back.

'We have examined the path. The ground is far too stony to define any tracks so far as we climbed it. We went about a mile.'

Dubán was disappointed.

'I do not want to waste time in fruitless chases,' he muttered. 'If the track leads nowhere then it is a waste of time. I will accept what you say, Agdae, but tell your uncle that I, Dubán, wish to see him when he returns. I do not think we can do any more here.'

He glanced towards Fidelma, as if seeking her approval, and she inclined her head in agreement.

They left Father Gormán talking with Agdae, and turned back towards the *rath* of Araglin. It was after they had ridden away from Muadnat's farmstead, heading back along the track out of the valley, that Fidelma turned to Eadulf and quietly asked him what had prompted him to ask his question about the path if he was simply prepared to take Agdae's word about where it led.

'I wanted to see his reactions because I saw someone on the path as we rode up to the farmstead. I think everyone must have had their attention on Agdae and his men for it appears no one else noticed the figure but myself.'

'I did not even see the path,' agreed Fidelma. 'Certainly no one has said that they saw a figure on the hills.'

'Well, I saw someone riding swiftly along the path and vanishing into the trees behind the farmstead.'

'Who was it? Muadnat?'

Eadulf shook his head.

'No. The figure of the rider was not male. It was the slighter figure of a woman. I saw her shape clearly in the sunlight as we came up to the farm buildings.'

Fidelma raised her eyebrows in exasperation. She always felt irritated when Eadulf prolonged his pronouncements for dramatic effect.

'Did you recognise who it was?' she demanded as patiently as she could.

'I believe that it was Crón.'

Chapter Fourteen

Looking out from the window of the guests' hostel, Fidelma saw a horse and rider galloping through the gates of the *rath* of Araglin. It was morning and she and Eadulf had just finished breaking their fast. They had returned to the *rath* late the previous evening without any resolution to their visit to the farmstead of Archú. Dubán had decided to send a second man back to the farmstead after they had left Muadnat's farm as protection. But Dubán was convinced, however, that bandits were responsible for the raid. Even as Fidelma and Eadulf had sat down to breakfast, they had seen Dubán and a group of his warriors ride out and presumed that they had set out in another searching sweep of the countryside.

Eadulf's identification of the rider on the path behind Muadnat's farmhouse was, at Fidelma's insistence, a matter between them. In fact, when Fidelma pressed Eadulf as to why he was so sure of the rider's identity at that distance, Eadulf told her it was only by means of the parti-coloured cloak which he had seen Crón wearing in the hall of assembly.

The thunder of hooves on the wooden planking of the bridge was the first sound to alert Fidelma to something unusual. She moved to the window in time to see the single horse and its rider racing into the *rath*. Fidelma was surprised to see that it was Muadnat's nephew Agdae. He flung himself from the beast and went racing towards the hall of assembly.

'What now?' demanded Eadulf gloomily.

Fidelma looked composed as she resumed her seat to finish her meal.

211

'I have a feeling that we will discover the answer to your question soon.'

Indeed, it was only a few moments later that Dignait arrived to summon them to join Crón in the hall of assembly. The face of the young tanist was grim.

'It is Muadnat,' she announced as they entered the hall.

Fidelma drew a breath of annoyance.

'I suppose our litigious friend is now charging young Archú with burning down his own stable. What is it now?'

'It may well be that Archú will be charged with a serious crime, Fidelma,' replied Crón. 'But it will not be Muadnat who does the charging.'

'I think you need to explain further,' Fidelma suggested softly.

'Muadnat has been found dead. He was found hanged on the high cross of Eoghan that marks the road into Araglin.'

Fidelma's eyes went wide. She remembered Eadulf pausing to admire the cross as they arrived at the valley of Araglin.

'If memory serves me right, the high cross is not on the road to Muadnat's farmstead but stands by the road which comes into the valley in the opposite direction. Who discovered his body?'

'Agdae. The high meadow beyond the cross belongs to him. Agdae said that Muadnat left his farm yesterday afternoon to go hunting. It was only early this morning that Agdae realised that Muadnat had not returned home. He went in search of him. And found him dead at the high cross. Muadnat often went hunting in the hills beyond there. Agdae rode here to get help and has now returned there with some men.'

Fidelma made a cynical grimace.

'Doubtless Dubán has told you of our visit to Muadnat's farmstead yesterday?'

Crón nodded.

'It seems that Agdae did not think of directing us to that quarter at that time when we were looking for Muadnat.'

'Is that important?'

'We shall see. But Agdae did not know where Muadnat was to be found when we inquired for him yesterday. However, this morning, when he became worried about Muadnat's absence, he was able to go directly to that spot.'

'Well, Agdae is already accusing Archú of this murder.'

'On what grounds?'

'Because Archú is the only person in Araglin who has been at enmity with Muadnat. He says that Archú, through you, blamed Muadnat for the raid on his farmstead yesterday.'

'That is not quite accurate.' Fidelma turned to Eadulf. 'We'd better ride out to this cross and see for ourselves.'

He was in agreement and asked Crón: 'How long will it be before Dubán returns?' Adding: 'It may be that we shall have need of his services in protecting Archú from the wild accusations of Agdae.'

Crón was annoyed.

'Why should you spend time on this matter? It has nothing to do with the death of my father, Eber, or Teafa. Surely you should be devoting yourself to uncovering the murderer if, as I believe you now claim, it is not Móen . . . though I think it will take much persuasive power to convince the people of Araglin that he is innocent.'

Fidelma suppressed a passing feeling of exasperation.

'I find it is better to keep an open mind when conducting an investigation. There is much secrecy in Araglin. I have been told things which are not true. I do not know whether the death of Muadnat has anything to do with the deaths of Eber and Teafa. If you know differently then perhaps you would share your knowledge with me?'

Crón had difficulty in controlling her features and, with grim satisfaction, Fidelma saw uncertainty and even fear in her eyes. After a moment or two, Crón controlled her emotions.

'No, I do not have such information. I only make what I consider a logical observation. If you must ride out to the big cross, then you must. But I think your investigation into this matter is taking an overly long period to complete.'

'It will take as long as it takes,' replied Fidelma resolutely. 'People must have patience.'

'Agdae may not have patience. He has sworn to find Archú and exact vengeance.'

Fidelma looked sharply at her.

'Then I would advise you to send after Dubán and have him restrain Agdae unless you want to see one injustice follow another. Perhaps Archú and Scoth should be brought here to this *rath* for their own protection until I can investigate the matter properly.'

'Agdae was kin to Muadnat, as, indeed, I was. He will not let his killer escape justice,' Crón said coldly.

'Then,' replied Fidelma equally icily, 'we must ensure that the killer is found – whoever he or she is.'

She turned and strode quickly from the assembly hall with Eadulf trailing in her wake. In a short while they were riding at a rapid pace uphill towards the distant high cross.

The young warrior Crítán was already there with a couple of burly men, farm workers by the look of them. Nearby stood an ass which had obviously been prepared to receive the body of Muadnat. The purpose of the gathering seemed to be a preparation for the taking down of the body. Muadnat was hanging by his neck by a rope which had been passed over the cross-bar of the granite cross. His feet were little more than a few inches above the ground. Yet Fidelma could immediately see the stains of blood over the front of the man's shirt as if massive wounds had been inflicted while he was alive.

One of the farm workers who had been about to place a ladder against the back of the cross suddenly saw the approach of Fidelma and Eadulf and paused, muttering something to his two companions. They turned and regarded the two religious with hostility.

Young Crítán moved forward disdainfully.

'You are not welcome here,' he greeted.

Unperturbed, Fidelma halted her horse and dismounted.

'We do not ask a welcome,' she said calmly.

Eadulf also slid from his mount and hitched his reins together with those of Fidelma's horse.

Crítán stood hands on his hips. He gazed resentfully at Fidelma. His was a character which would never forgive her for apparently humiliating him. Now he made his aggression clear.

'It would be well if you left here, woman. Twice you have exonerated Archú in his feud against Muadnat. Now see where this has led. This time Archú shall not succeed. Nor will your attempts to conspire with that creature of the Devil and let him go free after he has murdered Eber and Teafa.' His tone of menace matched his words.

Fidelma did not appear troubled, standing hands demurely folded in front of her, even smiling at the youth.

'I am an advocate of the courts of the five kingdoms, Crítán,' she said pleasantly enough. 'Do you dare threaten me?'

Arrogance and inexperience combined in Crítán to cause stupidity to replace even his natural cunning. He thrust out his jaw.

'This is Araglin, woman. You do not have the protection of your church or of your brother's warriors here.'

He was disconcerted to see Fidelma's smile broaden.

'I do not need them to exert my authority here,' she replied.

The two farm hands had stood hesitantly, allowing Crítán to be their spokesman. Now the one with the ladder, realising that the young warrior might have gone a little too far with his threats, put down his burden and came forward.

'It is true that you are not wanted here, sister,' he said, with slightly more respect in his voice. 'Our kinsman,' he jerked a thumb over his shoulder to the high cross, 'has been slain and we know who must pay for it. You should be about your own business.'

'You appear to have made your mind up about the identity of

the person who you want to punish for Muadnat's death whether they are guilty or not,' observed Eadulf dryly. 'Is it not better to wait until you find the real culprit?'

'No one asked for your interference, Saxon,' snapped Crítán. 'Now be gone, the both of you. It is a fair warning that I give you.'

Fidelma's mouth turned down almost in a wistful expression. It was always a dangerous sign with her but only Eadulf realised that fact. She had noticed that the youth's words were studied, the face flushed, eyes bright and gestures exaggerated. It was obvious, now that she had a chance to observe him more closely, that the young man had taken drink to bolster his courage that morning.

'I will overlook your ill-manners, Crítán, for this time I shall take into account your youth and inexperience. Now I mean to examine Muadnat's body and I do so by the authority I hold.'

Crítán, having used verbal force and found it not intimidating, was somewhat taken aback. He glanced at the two farm hands for support. They were looking embarrassed. Now Crítán saw that he was being humiliated again in front of others.

'These are kinsmen of Muadnat,' he said stubbornly. 'We will not allow you to bend the law to allow Archú to escape our justice.'

'And are they your witness to this murder?' Fidelma demanded, turning to the two men. 'You,' she suddenly pointed to the one who had adopted a more reasonable tone with her, 'did you see Archú kill Muadnat?'

The man flushed.

'No, of course not, but . . .'

'And you?' Fidelma wheeled sharply to the second man.

'Who else but Archú would do this?' replied the man resolutely.

'Who else? Isn't that a matter to be considered by the law before you exact vengeance on someone who may be innocent?'

Crítán intervened with a sneering laugh.

'You are good at playing with words, woman. But we have had

enough of words. Be gone from this spot before I force you to leave.' His hand fell on his sword. The gesture needed no interpretation.

Eadulf came forward, his movements purposeful, but Fidelma reached out and held his arm firmly. Even so, Eadulf was flushed with anger.

'Would you dare threaten a woman?' he growled ominously. 'A woman of the cloth?'

In fact, Crítán had drawn his sword as soon as Eadulf had moved towards him. The youth's face was red, his eyes bright.

'Stand back, Eadulf,' cautioned Fidelma.

One of the farm hands, the one who had tried to appear reasonable, was regarding Crítán somewhat nervously. A verbal threat was one thing but to physically threaten a female religieuse, and an advocate of the courts at that, was something beyond him.

'Perhaps we had better let her examine the body,' he suggested anxiously.

The idea of losing face before this woman made the arrogant youth even more stubborn.

'I will say what is to be done,' he insisted almost petulantly.

'Crítán,' the other rejoined, uncertainly, 'she is not only a religieuse but . . .'

'She is the one whose pretty serpent tongue allowed Archú to usurp that which belonged to Muadnat. She is also responsible for his death!'

'Crítán!' It was Fidelma who addressed the youth in a voice that was soft but clear. 'Put up your sword and return to the *rath* and sleep off the effects of the alcohol you have consumed. I will forget the discourtesy you have shown me.'

The youth's rage only seemed to increase. He almost shook with his rage.

'If you were a warrior . . .' he scowled.

Fidelma's eyes became slits.

'If you are prepared to threaten me with physical violence, I should not let that fact hinder you.'

'Crítán!' protested the man who had been carrying the ladder as the young man raised his sword and took a threatening step forward.

Fidelma held up her hand to silence him and gestured for everyone to stay back. Eadulf could see the anger on her brow. He noted the way that she planted her feet apart and let her arms hang relaxed at her side. Her voice had become soft and sibilant.

'Boy! You have now overstepped the mark. Youth and drink are no longer an excuse. If you wish to use your sword, do so. Even a woman bowed down with years could best a little child such as yourself.'

The words were coldly spoken and were designed for an effect. They succeeded.

Crítán gave a howl of rage. He ran forward, sword upraised. Fidelma just seemed to stand there awaiting his onslaught. Eadulf was torn between leaping in front of her to defend her and staying where he was for he had a suspicion of what was about to happen. He had seen Fidelma display her unusual talent once before in Rome. Fidelma was an adept at an art which she described to him as *troid-sciathagid*, battle through defence. She had told him that when the Irish religious journeyed far and wide, travelling to preach the word of the New Faith, they did so often alone and unarmed. Believing it wrong to carry weapons, they developed a form of self-defence against robbers and bandits without the use of weapons.

The combat, if such it could be called, was over within a matter of seconds.

The boy was rushing forward with raised sword upon Fidelma one moment and the next he was sprawled on his back on the ground with Fidelma standing one foot firmly on the wrist of the hand which had grasped the sword. She had barely moved, swaying back, and seeming to throw him over her shoulder. Eadulf knew

218

that there was a science to it. The momentum of the youth himself had propelled his body forward. He lay stunned and gasping for breath.

The two farm hands were staring at the fallen youth in amazement.

Eadulf moved forward, bent and picked up the boy's sword. He gazed down at Crítán's recumbent form. He could smell the intoxicating fumes and shook his head sorrowfully.

'*Plures crapula quam gladius*,' he rebuked. 'As you have no understanding of Latin, boy, it means that "drunkenness kills more than the sword".'

Fidelma had turned to the farm hands.

'I require one of you to take this boy back to the *rath* of your tanist and ensure that he sleeps off the effects of the drink. When he sobers, you may inform him that his pretensions to be a warrior are over. Tell Crón, the tanist, that I have said this. He should find work tending herds or tilling the soil. He will not bear arms in the kingdom of Muman again. It is only because of his youth and intoxication that I shall overlook his assault on me.'

One of the men moved forward and hauled the still befuddled youth to his feet. He held out his hand to Eadulf for the boy's sword but Fidelma intervened.

'Sharp knives are not for children to play with,' she said decisively. 'Keep a hold on that toy, Eadulf.'

The man who had been carrying the ladder muttered. 'Do not associate me with the folly of that boy, sister. I seek only the truth.'

Fidelma said nothing but stood watching as the other man half carried, half hauled the boy back along the road towards the *rath* of Araglin.

Eadulf grimaced sourly after them.

'At least Crítán will be sober by the time he gets to the *rath*.'

Fidelma gave a brief sigh and turned back to the body hanging on the high cross.

'I shall need your ladder for a moment,' she told the remaining farm hand.

The man helped her place it against the high cross and she climbed up while Eadulf assisted him holding it in place.

She could see, in spite of the congealed blood and rope, that the throat of Muadnat had been cut with one quick professional cut, almost severing the head from the neck. It was not a pretty sight. It reminded her of the slaughtered carcass of some animal. The effusion of blood indicated that his throat had been cut before the rope had been fixed around his neck and then the body had been hauled up on the cross. Why had the dead man been hanged afterwards? It struck her that it was almost as if some dark ritual had been enacted. She looked carefully at the body but could see nothing that presented any other information. The rope itself was unremarkable, an ordinary strong fibre rope. One thing she did notice, there was no sign of the knife which had inflicted the first fatal wound. After some moments she climbed down.

'You may take down the body,' she told the farm hand.

Eadulf helped him lower the body of the thickset Muadnat to the ground.

While this was being done, Fidelma wandered around the cross in ever widening circles, her eyes fixed upon the ground as if searching for something. After a while she suddenly halted and drew a breath.

'Eadulf!'

Eadulf went immediately across to where she stood.

She pointed downwards. Eadulf stared at the grass, unsure what he was meant to see. There were flecks upon the blades.

'Blood splatters?' he hazarded.

She nodded.

'Observe them carefully.'

Eadulf knelt down and saw that the blood had dried on the leaves of the grass and on a broad leafed plant.

'Do you think his throat was cut here?'

'It seems a reasonable assumption,' Fidelma replied. 'Anything else?'

Eadulf had been about to rise to his feet when he paused and looked, then he uttered a short exclamation and reached forward.

'What do you make of it?' Fidelma prompted.

'It is a tuft of hair.' Eadulf rose holding it in the open palm of his hand.

'Coarse red hair,' Fidelma agreed. 'Human hair.'

'Do you think it has any connection with the murder.'

'It looks as if it was dragged out by the roots. See the ends of the hair?' she answered without replying to his question.

After he had examined it, she took the hair carefully and placed it in her *marsupium*, the leather pouch she always carried at her waist.

'Now I think that we'd best get back to the *rath*, Eadulf. There is little to do here. I want to question Agdae.' She suddenly pressed her lips together in irritation. 'Agdae! Why isn't he here?'

She turned to where the farm hand was securing the body of Muadnat across the back of the patiently waiting ass.

'Did Agdae return here after he had sought help at the *rath*?'

'No, sister,' the man replied immediately. 'He left Crítán and my friend and me to take down the body and transport it back to Muadnat's farm. But I think he rode off directly in search of Archú.'

Fidelma groaned a little.

'Did you say that you were also a kinsman of Muadnat?' she asked, recovering her poise.

The man nodded.

'I am. But then so are most of the people in this valley, including the tanist.'

'If Muadnat has so many cousins, why does he hold one cousin, young Archú, in such low esteem?'

The reply was without hesitation.

'He hated Archú's father, a foreigner. Muadnat felt that

Artgal, Archú's father, had no right to steal the affections of his kinswoman, Suanach.'

'Steal the affections?' Fidelma pulled a face. 'That is an interesting turn of phrase. From whom were Suanach's affections supposed to have been stolen? It implies that the woman was an unwilling partner in the relationship. Was she so unwilling?'

The man looked uncomfortable.

'Muadnat had arranged a marriage to Agdae. But Suanach did not want to marry him. No, in fact Suanach was very much in love with Archú's father Artgal.'

'So the fault of the dispute lay with Muadnat's own distorted view of the relationship?'

'I suppose so.' The man was reluctant to go further. 'It is best not to speak ill of the dead.'

'Then let us speak of the living. Let us speak of Archú and Agdae. Let us help to prevent injustice to the living,' replied Fidelma.

'Has the dislike of the father been passed on to the son?' Eadulf asked curiously. 'Is that it? Is Archú suffering for Muadnat's dislike of his father? If so, that is an unjust attitude.'

The farm hand looked uncomfortable.

'There is probably a great injustice here but no reason for Archú to kill Muadnat,' the man replied stubbornly.

'Are you so sure that he did so?'

'Agdae said as much.'

'Does that make Agdae's story true? Agdae, you have just told us, has as much cause to hate Archú, if not more cause, than Muadnat.'

'Agdae is also the adopted son of Muadnat, not just his nephew. Should he not know the truth?'

'The adopted son?' Fidelma was intrigued. 'So Muadnat has no wife or children of his own?'

'None. None that I know of. Agdae was a nephew. But Muadnat raised him from childhood.'

'Agdae stands to inherit Muadnat's farmstead?'

'I suppose so.'

Fidelma turned towards her horse, calling over her shoulder as she went.

'You may take the body back to Muadnat's farm. I have done now. If you see Agdae before I do, warn him against any action which will bring down the displeasure of the law upon him. You and he will know what I mean.'

Eadulf followed her into the saddle and did not speak until they began to move down the hill.

'Where now?'

'To Archú's farmstead, of course.'

'But do you think that this death is connected with those of Eber and Teafa?'

'It seems extraordinary that this pleasant valley of Araglin, which appears not to have boasted a suspicious death within years, in just a matter of days witnesses several such violent deaths. We have raids on farmsteads that were previously safe and well protected. We have cattle run off, though, curiously, only a few cattle at a time. But, above all, the deaths of Eber, Teafa, Muadnat and a strange man whom we cannot identify, cannot all be merely coincidence. I confess, Eadulf, I am no great believer in coincidence. I prefer to examine the facts and only if it is proved to be coincidence beyond any shadow of doubt will I believe it as such.'

She paused and then kicked her horse into a canter.

'We need to get to Archú's quickly in case Agdae is really intent on seeking vengeance on the boy.'

Eadulf had difficulty keeping up with Fidelma for she was an excellent horsewoman. Fidelma had a good memory for places and there was no hesitation as she led the way along the river, passing the cabin of the prostitute, Clídna, and began to climb along the snaking track through the rounded hills towards the unusual L-shaped valley of the Black Marsh which Muadnat had dominated for so long.

Fidelma had been riding since she could remember. When she rode it was as if the horse became a mere appendage of her body and will, moving to her orders almost as the thought originated, responding to her slightest pressure. Fidelma loved the freedom that it brought her. Leaning slightly forward in the saddle, the breeze tugging at her hair, the road rising with her, the country unrolling with speed that sent a thrill through her. The sound of the horse's pounding hooves echoed the rhythms in her body, lulling her into a gentle meditative state.

For a while it was as if she had become divorced from the world of petty human vindictiveness; as if she had become part of nature, breathing the warmth of the spring air, scenting the smells of the woods and fields, feeling the gentle heat of the sun. She almost closed her eyes in the sheer pleasure of sensual relish.

Then she roused herself almost with a sense of guilt.

People were dead and she had a duty to discover why they were so and who was responsible.

Her eyes flicked open. She became aware of two riders on the road ahead of them. She immediately recognised Dubán and one of his men.

She drew rein and awaited them. Eadulf halted by her side. She was about to speak when Dubán cut her short.

'I have already heard the news, sister. Crón sent me word. I have left a couple of my men with Archú and Scoth. They refuse to leave their farmstead. But they are in safe hands.'

'You have not seen Agdae then? I was told that he was riding this way.'

Dubán shook his head.

'I doubt whether he will try to harm Archú knowing that my men are with him. It is probably a passion which will eventually ebb. He will come to his senses and realise that Archú is not responsible for the death of Muadnat.'

Fidelma looked slightly puzzled.

'You seem so sure? I am only prepared to say that I think it unlikely that Archú killed Muadnat.'

'I know he did not,' replied Dubán solemnly.

Fidelma's eyebrow involuntarily arched.

'You *know*?'

'Surely. That is easy. Last night I left two of my men with Archú and Scoth. They are witnesses to the fact that neither left the farm at all.'

Fidelma smiled contritely.

'How stupid of me not to remember that. Well, at least that saves time in trying to prove Archú's innocence. But we must now discover who is guilty.'

'I am on my way back to the *rath*,' Dubán said. 'I am surprised that Crítán is not escorting you. He is supposed to be in charge of the guards this morning.'

Briefly, Fidelma told him what had happened. Dubán did not appear unduly surprised.

'I suppose I knew that the lad did not have the true spirit of a warrior. He had ambition without dedication.'

'The trouble is that he has a warrior's skills and little of a warrior's morality. He is like an arrow that has been loosed from the bow but with no controlling flights,' Fidelma said.

'I understand that well enough, sister. I am not yet in my dotage and realise that he might be a danger. I will discuss this matter with Crón.'

'I hope she takes your advice in this as in other things.'

Dubán's eyes narrowed suspiciously as he studied her expressionless face. He seemed to ask a question and, after a pause, she said: 'I am not simple-minded.'

'I did not think you were,' admitted Dubán.

'Good. Remember it well. Speak with Crón and advise her that it is better to speak the truth; better truth than half truth or complete lie.'

She turned and gestured for Eadulf to follow her. They

continued to ride along the hillside track and after a while Eadulf called to her.

'They have gone. What was the meaning of that exchange?'

Fidelma halted her horse.

'I was merely planting a seed,' she confided cheerfully. 'It is about time that the half truths and lies that are being spread are stopped and someone told me the truth.'

'But aren't you giving Crón and Dubán warning that you are suspecting them of involvement?'

'Sometimes to flush out a fox you must start to dig into its lair.'

'I see. You expect them to react in some way?'

'We shall see whether they do or not.'

Eadulf sniffed disapprovingly.

'It is often a dangerous practice for if a fox is cornered it will sometimes turn and rend its tormentor. Anyway, where are we going now? Surely Archú can tell us no more?'

'We are not going to Archú's farmstead now we know he is safe and there is no sign of Agdae there.'

'Then where?'

'The path you saw yesterday. I want to see where it leads.'

Eadulf looked dubious.

'Wouldn't it have been better to have an escort then? What if the path does lead to the lair of the cattle raiders?'

Fidelma smiled gently.

'Have no fear, Eadulf. I am not going to put myself deliberately in the way of danger.'

'It is not deliberate actions that I fear,' muttered Eadulf.

For the first time in a long while she chuckled with genuine amusement and then signalled for him to follow her. They eventually came to the track overlooking the valley in which Muadnat's farmstead lay. Fidelma halted and examined the fields and buildings with a searching look.

'I don't really want to be observed by anyone at Muadnat's farm,' she said.

'I cannot see any other means of joining the path than going through the track which lies between the farm buildings,' Eadulf pointed out.

Fidelma shook her head and held out her hand.

'Beyond those fields is a small depression that traverses the valley. I think it is a ditch or stream. Here and there, you can see that trees and brush grow along its banks. If we can find a way down into it we can probably keep below the level of any prying eyes from the farmstead until we get on the far side of the valley and can join the path.'

Eadulf appeared doubtful but observing that she was so determined he insisted that he lead the way, giving his horse its head to pick a path down the steep incline, skirting some cultivated fields and moving steadily towards the shelter of some trees through which the ditch ran. Fidelma had been right, the depression concealed a small stream, no more than six feet across in places. The stream lay at the bottom of a ditch which gave concealment to them as they followed its shallow running waters across the valley floor.

It did not take them very long to traverse the valley and move upwards, this time emerging overlooking the back of the farm buildings. Nothing was moving below them, they could not even see any workers around the barns or in the fields.

It was some time before they finally joined the second track and began to follow its course up into the northern hills.

'Well,' Fidelma exclaimed, as she examined the track carefully, 'it can't be claimed that this is unfrequented. Dubán's men obviously did not search this path long enough. It may be stony at the bottom of the hill but up here, where there is less stone, you can plainly see the marks of horses and asses, even a cart.'

The Saxon religieux looked concerned.

'Shouldn't we return for Dubán's warriors?'

Fidelma gave him a withering look.

In silence they followed the track and it began to turn around the side of the steeply sloping hill, away from the valley of the Black Marsh, until Eadulf pointed out that it had doubled back on itself.

'We are on the far side of the hill to Muadnat's farmstead now.' He pointed upwards. 'Do you see where the sun is?'

'This is a circuitous route indeed,' agreed Fidelma.

What was more interesting was that the path was now completely level, keeping at the same elevation along the hillside. They continued on, with the pathway leading directly due eastward and then swinging abruptly due south almost on a high plateau.

'I don't understand. We have doubled back on ourselves entirely,' Fidelma said.

'Not just doubled back,' Eadulf smiled, 'I think we have worked around parallel to the area of the valley where Archú's farmstead is.'

Fidelma did not understand and said so.

Eadulf pointed to the slope of the hill on his right side.

'If we climbed over the top of this hill and looked down from the summit we would be looking down onto Archú's farmlands, perhaps onto the farm itself.'

Fidelma accepted his reckoning without comment.

They had gone about half a mile when the hillside became a vast wooded vista, the trees moving over the summits of the hills, growing closely together. The track plunged straight into the woods but still kept its widely spaced borders along which a vehicle had apparently moved regularly. There were ruts caused by wheels easily discernible in the track.

'We seem to be going on for ever,' grumbled Eadulf in protest. 'Perhaps we should return to the *rath* now for we cannot continue much further and expect to be able to return there before nightfall.'

'Just a little bit further,' cajoled Fidelma. 'I think we may be coming to . . .'

She halted abruptly and signalled Eadulf to do likewise.

'Let's get our horses away from this track and proceed on foot,' she instructed. 'I think there is something up ahead.'

Eadulf was about to protest again but decided to follow her orders. They dismounted and led the horses a short distance from the track but far enough into the forest so that anyone passing along it would not spot them. Then, with Fidelma leading, they began to make their way through the wood, keeping parallel to the track.

They had not gone far before they realised that they were coming to a clearing. A sudden banging sound made them both start. It took them a few moments to realise that it was the sound of someone chopping wood. They came to a cautious stop on the edge of the clearing.

It was a wide space set against the hillside, an area of wind-blown grasses with grey granite rocks thrusting up here and there. There was a group of horses in a small makeshift corral composed of a rope fence. Alongside these horses were a dozen asses, sturdy little pack animals. A wagon stood nearby. Close by the wagon was a fire on which a hank of meat was roasting with a sizzling, spluttering sound as the fat dropped onto the eager flames. A man, a stranger whom they did not recognise, was chopping wood. There were also a few other men about the area apparently engaged on various tasks. Fidelma examined them closely, frowning slightly.

She laid a land on Eadulf's arm and pointed to the far side of the enclosure. There was another smaller enclosure in which a few cows stood patiently chewing the cud and ignoring the fate of their erstwhile companion who was about to provide the men with a meal.

A little way up on the hillside stood a small cave mouth, the entrance high enough to take a full grown man standing. Surrounding the cave was bare grey-blue granite. It was protected by an overhang, a green dome and grey granite forehead, jutting over the mouth of the cave.

It was in this clearing that the mysterious track ended. Of that there was no doubt. They had come to the lair of the cattle raiders.

Fidelma and Eadulf exchange a glance. Eadulf was clearly perplexed but Fidelma, observing some of the tools which lay placed against the wagon, was beginning to see a light. She was about to signal him to withdraw when there was a movement from the cave entrance.

A tall, burly man emerged, blinked in the light and yawned, stretching his arms skyward. He had a coarse red beard and long shoulder-length hair.

This time there was no mistaking the ugly features of Menma, the chief stableman at the *rath* of Araglin.

Chapter Fifteen

They had ridden back to the edge of the forest in silence. Fidelma's brows were drawn together in concentrated thought. Eadulf did his best to fight down the numerous questions which kept tumbling into his mind. Finally, as they emerged out of the shade of the forest, he could keep silent no longer.

'What do you think it means, Fidelma?' he demanded at last.

'If I knew that, then I might have the answer to this entire mystery,' she replied impatiently. 'However, at least we have discovered the lair of the men who have been raiding the farms of Araglin.'

'Why would Menma and these outlaws be hiding in that cave? And why should Menma be associated with cattle raiders?'

For a moment Fidelma's lips parted in a grin.

'I do not think that they are cattle raiders neither are they are exactly hiding.'

'What then?' demanded Eadulf.

'Didn't you see the tools lying about in the glade?'

'Tools? No. I was too busy watching the men. What tools?'

Fidelma sighed gently.

'You must always remember that observation and the analysis of that observation is essential to the art of truth seeking. There were several tools by the wagon. They told me that the cave must undoubtedly be a mine.'

Eadulf was astonished.

'A mine?'

'It is not unusual to find mines in this country. Had we left Lios Mhór and travelled due west along the Abhainn Mór we would come on a plain called Magh Méine, or the Plain of Minerals, where copper, lead and iron are mined.'

'I seem to have heard of that place before.'

Fidelma looked at him pityingly.

'The hostel keeper, Bressal, mentioned that he had a brother who was a miner at the Plain of Minerals,' she said softly.

'Of course. But what was Menma doing at this mine, if such it is?'

'That we must discover for ourselves.'

'And why would . . .'

'It is no good asking questions to which we do not have sufficient evidence to even make a guess at answering.'

'Perhaps we should have made our presence known and demanded an explanation,' suggested Eadulf. 'After all, you are an official of this kingdom.'

Fidelma smiled broadly.

'Those men are up to no good. Do you think they care for my office?'

'We might have been able to surprise them, disarm them . . .'

'There is a line in Horace's *Odes*, my good friend. *Vis consili expers mole ruit sua*.'

Eadulf nodded slowly: 'Force without good sense falls by its own weight,' he repeated.

She peered up at the summit of the hill above them, shading her eyes against the sun.

'You said earlier that if we climbed across the summit we should find ourselves above Archú's farmstead. Is that correct?'

Eadulf frowned at her abrupt change of subject.

'It is,' he agreed stiffly.

'Do you want to see if you are right?'

Eadulf thought she was jesting with him. She was not.

'But the slopes are far too precipitous for horses,' he protested. 'On foot we could climb the hill but . . .'

She pointed silently upwards.

Further along the hill Eadulf saw a movement. The red brown of an animal. He screwed up his eyes to focus. It was the sleek, muscular figure of a stag, herding his deer before him.

Fidelma grinned quickly.

'Where a stag may lead his herd, there might a horse and rider go. Are you willing?'

Eadulf raised his arms in unwilling surrender.

'There is something like a path just up ahead.' Fidelma turned. 'I think it is the deer run over the hill. Look!'

Eadulf could just see a worn strip of land, stretching through the fern and furze.

'We cannot ride along that,' he protested again.

'No, but we can lead our horses,' Fidelma assured him. She slid from her horse and took its bridle, picking her way carefully up the tiny animal-trodden path towards the shoulder of the rounded hill before them.

Eadulf groaned inwardly, then he, too, slipped from his horse and began to lead it after Fidelma. In truth, Eadulf had no liking for high, exposed places and so he kept his eyes closely on the path before him.

'I cannot see why you wish to use this short cut to Archú's place. We could have easily returned along the main track,' he complained, more to keep his thoughts occupied as they ascended than with the desire to argue with Fidelma.

'This is quicker. And we do not want to alert anyone at Muadnat's farm who are in league with our friends back at the mine.'

'I cannot see how any of this ties in with Eber's murder.'

Fidelma did not bother to answer him.

A wind was gusting across the hills and the horses were getting skittish. It required all their strength to keep a tight rein on them. In front, Fidelma saw the herd of deer making slow progress, grazing as they went. The wind held no fears for them or for the great antlered stag who paused now and then, like some impressive statue, staring down at them as if anxiously watching their progress as they climbed steadily upwards. The stag would pause for a while and then turn, with a curious barking bellow, and urge his charges to increase their pace. They would bound upwards for a while before pausing once more to graze.

The path was almost indistinguishable from the grazed grassy inclines around them but Fidelma pressed on, moving at an easy pace around the shoulder of the rounded hill. The winds were bluff and Eadulf found himself bending his head, not only to avoid contact with the wide open spaces but to meet the onslaught of the strong gusts. He prayed that his horse would not become too skittish for he did not know whether he would be able to hold on to the beast.

Suddenly he was aware of Fidelma halting.

'What is it?' he demanded.

'See for yourself,' she replied.

Eadulf plucked up courage for a quick nervous glance.

The L-shaped valley stretched away below them. He had an impression of some buildings far below and he dropped his gaze as soon as he could.

'What is it?' he asked again. 'Archú's valley?'

Fidelma turned and gazed at him thoughtfully.

'Do heights bother you, Eadulf?' she asked in concern.

Eadulf bit his lip. There was no point denying it.

'Not heights exactly,' he replied. 'It is a fear of being on high exposed places, not so much of falling downwards but of falling outwards. Does that sound strange?'

Fidelma shook her head slowly.

'You should have told me,' she rebuked softly.

'I would not be of use to anyone if I confessed this fear.'

'My mentor, Morann of Tara, once said that a mouse can drink no more than its fill from the stream.'

Eadulf was puzzled.

'That sounds like an obscure philosophy.'

'Not so. We must recognise our weaknesses as well as our strengths. Only then shall we know the strength in our weakness and the weakness in our strength.'

'Are you telling me that I should have accepted my fear and told you?'

'What else should you have done? Had I been forewarned then I might have been prepared if anything had happened.'

Eadulf sighed impatiently. He disliked talking about his weaknesses.

'This is not the time and especially not the place to debate my failings.'

Fidelma was immediately contrite.

'Of course,' she said consolingly. The contriteness was not suited to her character but it seemed genuine enough. 'I am not thinking clearly. From now on we shall be descending. You were right. Below is Archú's farmstead. This is the valley of the Black Marsh.'

Eadulf set his shoulders.

'Then let us set forth,' he said irritably. 'The sooner we begin the descent then the sooner we shall reach the bottom.'

Fidelma continued to lead the way carefully. The deer herd had drifted off some way and Fidelma observed that they had left the main track. While steep, it was not impossible to move along at a reasonable pace. Only now and then did they have to pause to negotiate some sheer part of the path, where a drop of only two feet caused the elevation to seem more precipitous than it actually was. At one or two points, they had to twist and turn and double back on themselves several times within a space of a few yards. But eventually they came to the more gentle lower slopes of the hill where clumps of ash trees and briars formed a boundary marker through which they found a reasonable pathway.

As they emerged from the copse of ash and beech they found two horsemen waiting for them. They were both armed with bows, arrows drawn.

'Sister Fidelma!'

The startled voice of Archú halted them. Fidelma supposed that the second man was one of the men Dubán had left behind. Archú immediately put down his bow and was apologetic.

'We did not know who you were.'

'We saw two figures coming over the shoulder of the hill. A strange route,' muttered the warrior with him.

'Strange and dangerous,' sighed Eadulf, wiping the sweat from his brow.

'We have been watching you for the past hour for my companion here spotted you soon after you appeared over the hill. Why were you taking that precipitous path? It is only sheep and deer that I have seen upon the mountain.'

'It is a long story, Archú,' Fidelma replied. 'And if Scoth could provide us with some refreshment we shall tell it to you.'

'Of course,' Archú agreed eagerly. 'Forgive me. Let us ride up to the farmhouse.'

The warrior was still looking suspiciously up at the mountain.

'Were you being followed, sister?' he asked.

Fidelma shook her head.

'Not that I know of. Did you see anyone following us?'

'No. But we must be careful. Have you heard that Muadnat has been killed?'

'Yes. We came here some hours ago and saw Dubán on the road. He told us that he had left you and another man to guard young Archú in case Agdae decided to do something foolish.'

Archú turned to his companion.

'Perhaps, you should stay here a while and check if anyone else comes over the hill. But I shall take Sister Fidelma and Brother Eadulf to my house.'

The warrior accepted the instruction without comment.

Fidelma and Eadulf followed Archú towards the distant farmstead.

'This is a bad, bad business, sister. If Dubán had not left his men behind yesterday, so that they were witness to the fact that I had not stirred from the farmstead, then I have no doubt that I would be in grave trouble.'

Fidelma did not bother to answer. That much was obvious.

'I knew Muadnat all my life and although he hated me, I cannot say his death leaves me unmoved. But he was my cousin. May he rest in peace.'

'Amen to that,' agreed Eadulf, having recovered his spirits a little.

'And how do you stand with Agdae? Did you know he was Muadnat's adopted son?'

Archú grimaced.

'That I did. He is also my cousin. His parents were killed in some pestilence many years ago. Agdae survived and Muadnat brought him up in his own home. My mother told me that Muadnat wanted her to marry him but she rejected Agdae for my father. We did not like each other, I confess it freely. He was raised with Muadnat's lack of tolerance and dislike of me.'

'And you dislike him in turn?'

'I cannot say that I could feel other than dislike. Agdae is not a likable person.'

'Who do you think killed your cousin?' Fidelma asked the question sharply.

Archú was silent for a time; for such a long period, in fact, that Eadulf thought he was refusing to answer the question. But then the young man gave a long sigh.

'I do not know. Nothing makes sense any more. The deaths of Eber and Teafa were distant to me. Their deaths did not really concern me. But Muadnat's death was closer to me, even though I disliked him. I do not understand it.'

Scoth greeted them at the farmhouse door.

The second warrior whom Dubán had left behind had come forward to take their horses.

Archú led the way inside.

'There is cider to drink,' Scoth said, going to fetch a jug and mugs.

Eadulf smiled appreciatively.

'A blessing on you for that,' he said. 'My throat is shrivelled for want of a drink.'

Archú bade them be seated while Scoth poured the drinks and offered a bowl of fruit.

Eadulf finished most of his mug in a single draught with a deep gasping sigh while Fidelma sipped more gently and appreciatively at her drink.

'I would have a care, Eadulf,' she admonished as her companion allowed his mug to be refilled. 'This is a potent distillation.'

Archú grimaced mirthlessly.

'At least Muadnat had the goodness to leave a few barrels of this cider behind.'

Scoth was deprecating.

'Well, it was my own hands that brewed it on his behalf. Better is it that I taste the fruits of my own labour than Muadnat had quaffed it all.'

Fidelma took another sip and turned her gaze to Archú.

'Have you spent all your life in this valley?'

Archú was surprised by the question.

'Yes. I was born in this very farmstead and raised here until my mother died. Then Muadnat took over and I was sent to sleep in the barns with the animals until I reached the age of choice and brought my claim to Lios Mhór. I knew nowhere else apart from this valley until I came to Lios Mhór. Why do you ask?'

'How about the land on the other side of the hill?'

'You mean the hill which we saw you riding over?'

'I do.'

'I know that the hill belongs to this farm.'

'I thought the farm consisted of seven *cumals* of valley land?'

'There are only four *cumals* in the valley itself. There are three divisions of land on the farm: the arable land which you see around the farm; the land of the three roots—'

Eadulf looked up from his drink fascinated.

'The what?' he asked. 'I have never heard of that expression before.'

'You'll find it in our laws,' Fidelma explained. 'According to our ancient classification you will see that the richest soil of a farm is known by the presence of three weeds remarkable for their large roots; that is the thistle, ragwort and the wild carrot. If the land is rich enough for them to grow, then it is highly prized land and can produce many things.'

Eadulf shook his head in bewilderment.

Fidelma was turning back to Archú.

'But that hill belongs to the farm, you say?'

'It is the part of the farm called the axe-land. If anything is to grow on the hill apart from the furze and trees, it would require much labour to clear it for cultivation.'

'But the hill does belong to this farm?'

'Oh yes. Even Muadnat would not dispute the boundary of it.'

'I see. Do you know the hill well?'

'I know it.'

'But have you explored it?'

Archú sat back clearly bewildered.

'Why would I want to explore it?'

'It rises on one side of your arable land and is part of your farmstead.'

'I have only just been granted leave to run this farm, as you know, sister. When have I had time to explore the hills surrounding it?'

'When you were a child?'

'A child?' He shook his head. 'I did not wander over those hills as a child.'

'What do you know of caves in this area?'

To Archú the question seemed an abrupt change of conversation. He shrugged.

'I have heard of caves to the north of here. There is the Cave of the Grey Sheep which my mother used to tell me about. She told me that once a grey lamb came forth out of the cave and was reared by a local farmer. The lamb grew into a sheep and the sheep eventually produced her own lambs. But the day came when the farmer decided to slaughter one of her lambs for food and the sheep gathered her remaining lambs and vanished with them into the cave. They were never seen again.'

Fidelma was impatient.

'How about mines? Did you ever hear of mines in these hills?'

Archú thought carefully before shaking his head.

'There may be mines but I could not point you to one. What is all this about?'

'We found . . .' began Eadulf but winced on receiving a sharp kick under the table from Fidelma.

Archú and Scoth gazed at Eadulf in surprise.

'We found that we wanted to know some of the geography of the area,' Fidelma said before turning to regard Eadulf with concern. 'You appear to have had a sharp pain, brother. Did I not warn you that the cider was potent?'

Eadulf grimaced in annoyance.

'It is nothing,' he muttered. 'Perhaps a cramp from walking.'

'It has been a long day and we have not eaten. We should return to the *rath*.'

'But you must stay and eat with us,' Scoth invited.

Reluctantly, Fidelma shook her head.

'Alas, we cannot. If we don't leave now we shall not return until after nightfall. Not a time to be abroad on unknown roads.'

They made their farewells and began to ride back towards Araglin.

'You did not have to kick me so hard, Fidelma,' admonished Eadulf sulkily. 'You should have told me if you did not want the young ones to know what we had discovered on the hill.'

'I am sorry, Eadulf. But it is best that we keep our own counsel for a while. It is clear that someone wanted to keep that mine a secret. The logical answer is, as it is on Archú's land, that Muadnat was trying to operate the mine without anyone knowing, especially young Archú. The path to the mine leads from his land. So have we stumbled across the real reason why Muadnat was so desperate to cling to ownership of his cousin's property?'

Eadulf whistled softly.

'I see. Muadnat was trying to keep the land in order to exploit the mine.'

'A mine belongs to the person on whose land it is. The permission of that person must be given before it can be worked by anyone else,' agreed Fidelma.

'Yes, but that does not get us anywhere near solving the mystery of the murder of Eber and Teafa.'

'Perhaps not. But it is strange that Menma seems to keep appearing in this mystery and . . .'

She halted so abruptly that Eadulf wondered if she had spotted some new danger and anxiously searched the surrounding countryside.

'What is it?' he demanded after a while.

'I am a fool!'

Eadulf was quiet.

'I should have spotted this before.'

'Spotted what?' Eadulf tried to keep his curiosity in check

'Menma. Remember how I said it was Menma who led the attack on Bressal's hostel?'

'Yes.'

'And now Menma appears at the mine?'

'Yes. But I do not see . . .'

'What was the connection between Bressal and mines?' demanded Fidelma.

Eadulf appeared to be thinking carefully.

Fidelma almost ground her teeth with frustration at his slowness.

'Bressal had a brother . . .'

Memory returned to Eadulf.

'Morna who was a miner. He had a collection of rocks . . .'

'More importantly,' interrupted Fidelma, 'Morna had returned home recently saying he had made some discovery which would make him rich. He took Bressal a rock.'

Eadulf rubbed his chin.

'I am not sure that I follow.'

Fidelma was patient.

'I believe that the rock came from the cave on Archú's land. That was the spot which Morna had found contained gold and which he believed would make him rich. I believe that Menma attacked Bressal's hostel in order to recover the rock.'

'Why?'

'Because the find was meant to be kept a secret. Bressal's brother Morna betrayed the secret.'

'Are you saying that Menma is in charge of this mine? I would not have thought him intelligent enough.'

'I think you are right. Someone else is behind this affair. It comes back to Muadnat. Menma was merely ordered to ensure that whatever Morna had told and shown his brother Bressal remained a secret. It was a coincidence that we were at the hostel at the time and were able to drive off the attack.'

Eadulf shook his head as he digested this.

'I had suspected that the attack was inspired by Muadnat to get rid of Archú,' he said. 'For Muadnat would have known Archú would have been staying there that night on his return.'

'I thought of that at first but then Muadnat knew that Archú and Scoth had no money to stay in a hostel. Also, being on foot, they would hardly have reached the hostel that night. But we carried them on our horses. Remember that I also paid for their lodgings? No, there was another motive and we have found it.'

'Then the reason was simply to keep the secret of whatever riches have been discovered in that cave?'

'I am sure. I think that I became sure yesterday.'

Eadulf looked helpless.

'You have lost me, Fidelma,' he confessed.

'Yesterday we discovered an unknown body on Archú's farm. It was a body of someone who was neither farmer nor warrior. The calloused hands, the dust of hewn rock which lay on the man's clothing told me that he belonged to one particular profession.'

Eadulf's eyes lit up.

'You recognised that he was a miner?'

'I also asked you whether he reminded you of anyone.'

'He did not.'

'You should be more observant, Eadulf. He had the same features as Bressal. The unfortunate corpse was Morna, the brother of Bressal, the hostel keeper.'

Fidelma lapsed into a contemplative silence as they continued their journey through the valley of Araglin to the *rath*.

Crón appeared to be anxiously awaiting their arrival, standing by the door of the assembly hall to receive them.

Chapter Sixteen

Crón hailed them immediately they entered the *rath*. Fidelma and Eadulf dismounted and Eadulf led the horses off to the stable. Fidelma joined Crón at the door of the hall of assembly. There was no one about except the old servant Dignait, who was tidying up the hall.

'Leave us, Dignait,' Crón called.

The old woman glared suspiciously at Fidelma, turned and left through a side door.

Fidelma sat down on a bench and the tanist, hesitating a moment, sat near her. For a few moments no one spoke and then Fidelma prompted her.

'You wish to see me?'

Crón raised her ice blue eyes to Fidelma for a moment and then dropped them.

'Yes.'

'Dubán has spoken to you, I suppose?'

Crón coloured hotly and nodded.

'I have told Dubán that I am no simpleton,' Fidelma said carefully. 'Did you think that you would be able to feed me on half truths for ever? I know that you hated your father. I want to know why?'

'It was a matter of shame,' Crón replied after a short pause.

'Best if the truth were out, for suspicion and accusation fester in dark secrets.'

'Teafa also hated my father.'

'Why?'

'My father abused his sisters.'

245

Fidelma had already expected such an answer based on the information Father Gormán had told her.

'Did he physically abuse them?' she asked for clarification's sake.

Crón sniffed: 'If by physical abuse you mean that he made them lie with him – then, yes.'

'Was it Teafa who told you this?' Fidelma solicited.

'Some years ago,' she agreed. 'There; I have said why I hated my father. But I did not hate him enough to kill him. Truly, it does not seem that you are any closer to solving the murder of my father or Teafa.'

'Oh, but I am,' smiled Fidelma. 'In fact, what you have told me means . . .'

'Am I disturbing you?' The soft male voice cut in as Fidelma was about to lean forward confidentially.

Father Gormán stood on the threshold.

Fidelma caught the warning look in Crón's eyes which told her that no further mention was to be made of the matter. She suppressed a sigh of irritation and stood up.

'I was about to leave anyway. I have had a long, tiring day. I will speak with you tomorrow about this, Crón, after I have rested.'

The breakfast had already been brought to the hostel when Fidelma emerged from the wash room. Eadulf was seated and doing the meal full justice. Fidelma moved to her seat, said a silent *gratias* and examined the plate of bread, cold meat and garnishes. She picked up her knife.

Eadulf said: 'We must hasten back to the mine today with what men Dubán can spare. Perhaps we will be able to resolve all these mysteries?'

Fidelma was sunk into her own thoughts. She was only half concentrating. Yet some part of her mind found itself being drawn to the dish of mushrooms on the table. Some distant alarm bell was ringing in the back of her mind. The mushrooms had pale yellowish brown skins with sponge-like cups all over the cap. She had often eaten *miotóg bhuí*, the species of edible fungus which grew in the long grass in damp riverside meadows in spring. They were usually presented, however, having been blanched in water, for the raw taste was sharp. Blanched they were considered a delicacy. Why had they been served raw?

A cold feeling suddenly ran down her back making her shiver violently as she examined the pieces more closely. Whereas she had thought the yellowish head had merely darkened with age, she realised now that this was not so. The mop-like head had been brown. She glanced in alarm to where Eadulf was about to place a piece of the fungus in his mouth, reached across and slapped it out of his hand.

He started back in surprise, smothering an exclamation.

'How much of that have you eaten?' she demanded.

He gazed at her stupidly.

'How much?' she thundered again.

'Most of what was on my plate,' confessed Eadulf, bewildered. 'What's wrong? I know what it is, we have it in the land of the South Folk. It's called morel.'

'*Dia ár sábháil!*' cried Fidelma, springing up. 'It is false morel.'

Eadulf paled visibly.

The false morel, which looked so like the edible morel, was deadly poisonous when eaten raw.

'God save us, indeed.' Eadulf was aghast.

Fidelma was on her feet.

'There is no time to lose. We must purge you, make you vomit. It is the only way.'

Eadulf nodded. He had not studied at the great medical college of Tuaim Brecain without learning something of the working of poisonous fungi.

He rose and made his way to the *fialtech*, the 'veil house' or privy, even forgetting in his haste to genuflect before entering to ward off the wiles of the Devil who did his best work in such places.

'Drink as much water as you possibly can,' Fidelma called after him.

He did not reply.

Fidelma turned to gaze at the plates.

This was no mistake. Someone had deliberately tried to poison them both. Why? Were they so near the solution to the deaths in Araglin that they had to be eliminated? In anger she scooped up the plates of food and took them to the door of the hostel, throwing them out. She did the same with the mugs of mead which had been provided.

She could hear Eadulf retching in the *fialtech*.

Her lips thinned angrily and she strode off to the kitchens in search of Grella who usually brought their food. The kitchens were deserted. She went into the hall of assembly and saw the young girl engaged in her cleaning tasks.

The girl seemed flustered as Fidelma came up to her.

'Tell me, who brought the food to the guests' hostel this morning?'

'I did, sister, as I always do. Was there something wrong?'

The guileless eyes of the girl told Fidelma that she would have to look elsewhere for the culprit.

'Who prepared the food this morning?'

'Dignait, I suppose. She is in charge of the kitchen.'

'Did you see her prepare the food?'

'No. When I arrived Dignait was in the hall of assembly talking with the lady Cranat. Dignait told me that I should go straight to the kitchen where I would find the tray ready with your breakfast and that I should take it straight to you and the Saxon brother.'

'So, as far as you know, Dignait prepared the breakfast?'

'Yes. You frightened me, sister, what is wrong?'

'Do you recall what the meal consisted of?'

'The meal?' She was surprised at such a question. 'Did you not eat it?'

Fidelma grimaced a little bitterly.

'What did it consist of?' she repeated.

'Colds meats, bread, oh and some mushrooms and apples and a jug of mead.'

'The mushrooms were poisonous. They were false morel.'

The girl paled. There was shock in her features but no sign of guilt.

'I did not know,' she gasped in horror.

'Where is Dignait?'

'She is not here. I think she went to her room after breakfast. Shall I show you where her cabin is?'

The girl turned and scurried fearfully before Fidelma, leading her from the hall of assembly, through some more buildings to a ramshackle cabin of wood.

'This is where she dwells.'

Fidelma called through the door.

There was no answer.

She hesitated a moment before trying the handle. The latch lifted easily and she pushed into the single-roomed building. She was surprised at the shambles which met her eye. Bedding and items of clothing were strewn here and there among personal possessions.

Grella exclaimed in amazement as she peered over Fidelma's shoulder.

Fidelma stood on the threshold and peered around with keen eyes. Someone had been looking for something. Was it Dignait who had made the untidy search of her own chamber? Or was it someone else? If so, where was Dignait? Her eyes dropped to a table. They narrowed suddenly. There was a thin smear of red across the edge of the table. Fidelma did not have to examine further to realise that it was blood.

There was little else that could be learnt from Dignait's deserted room.

She turned to where Grella was standing, open-mouthed with agitation.

'You'd best get back to your work, Grella. When you have finished I want you to go and stay with the Saxon brother. He may need your help. He has eaten some of the poisonous morel.'

The girl let out a soft exclamation and genuflected.

'He is already taking a purge,' explained Fidelma, 'but he might need someone to help him later. I must be in search of Dignait and do not want him left alone. When you have finished your work here, go and stay at the hostel and watch him carefully. Do you understand?'

Grella signalled her compliance with a jerk of her head and scurried away.

Fidelma closed the door of Dignait's chamber and made her way back to the hostel.

Eadulf was sitting with a pale face, still drinking water.

She glanced at him with an unarticulated question. He nodded slowly.

'How do you feel?' she asked softly.

Eadulf shrugged ruefully.

'Ask me that in a few hours' time. That will be when the poison takes effect if it is going to. I hope I have vomited most of it out. You never can tell.'

'Dignait is missing. Her room is in disorder and there is a stain of blood on her table.'

Eadulf's eyes widened.

'You think that Dignait . . . ?'

'She is a logical person to question as it was she who apparently prepared the food and told Grella to bring it to us. I have asked the young girl to keep an eye on you while I am away.'

'I am coming with you to find Dignait,' Eadulf protested.

Fidelma gazed at him almost tenderly and shook her head firmly.

'My friend, you must sit and continue to purge yourself. I will go to find out what I can.'

Eadulf began to object but observing the steely glint of fire in Fidelma's eyes thought better of it.

Fidelma found Crón in the hall of assembly looking morose. She straightened up a little as Fidelma approached her.

'Is it true?' she demanded. 'I have just spoken with Grella.'

'True enough,' replied Fidelma. 'Do you have any idea where Dignait might have gone?'

Crón shook her head.

'I saw her earlier today. Grella says that you have already searched her apartment?'

'She seems to have disappeared. Her chamber is deserted and in disarray and there is a smear of blood on the table there.'

'I do not know what to advise. She must be somewhere within the *rath*. I will ask that a search be made immediately.'

'Where is your mother, Cranat? I am told she knows Dignait better than anyone and she was speaking with her earlier this morning.'

'My mother has gone for her usual morning ride in the company of Father Gormán.'

'Let me know when she returns.'

Fidelma's next stop was at the cabin of Teafa.

Gadra opened the door, saw Fidelma's worried expression and silently stood aside so that she might enter.

'You are abroad early, Fidelma, and bear an expression of ill-favour on your face.'

'How is your charge?'

'Móen? He is still asleep. We were late to bed for we were discussing matters of theology.'

'Discussing theology?' She was startled.

'Móen has a profound grasp of theology,' Gadra assured her. 'We were also discussing what might be his future.'

'I suspect that he does not want to stay here?'

Gadra chuckled cynically.

'After all that has happened?'

'I suppose not,' agreed Fidelma. 'But what will he do?'

'I have suggested to him that he might like to find sanctuary from the evils of the world in a religious cloister – perhaps at Lios Mhór. He needs the order that a life among the religious can give him and many will be able to communicate with him there for, as you yourself have shown, a knowledge of the ancient Ogam can quickly be adapted to a method of communication.'

'It sounds a reasonable idea,' agreed Fidelma. 'But one that hardly fits in with your philosophy.'

'My world is dying. I have already admitted this. Móen needs to be part of the new world, not the old.' Gadra suddenly frowned. 'But I can see that you are preoccupied. You did not come here to talk of Móen. Has anything else happened?'

'I fear for the life of my companion, Eadulf,' Fidelma said curtly. 'Someone tried to poison him and myself this morning.'

Gadra's face registered shock.

'Tried? How so?'

'Poisonous mushrooms.'

'Most people can easily recognise the poisonous varieties.'

'Agreed. But false morel can easily pass as morel.'

'But it is only in a raw state that it is highly toxic. As morel is never eaten raw there is little chance . . .'

'It was the fact that the *miotóg bhuí*, the morel, was raw that made me glance at it twice. I did not touch it but, unfortunately, Brother Eadulf had already begun to eat the noxious fungus before I recognised it.'

Gadra looked serious.

'He should be purged immediately.'

'He has vomited and I have made him drink as much water as he can to increase the vomiting.'

'Is it known who is responsible for this attempt to poison you?'

'It seems likely that it is Dignait. But Dignait does not appear to be in the *rath*. She has disappeared. Her room is in uproar and there is blood on her table.'

Gadra raised his eyebrows in concern.

'It will be your duty to ask a question of me. I shall answer it now: neither I nor Móen have left this dwelling this morning.'

Fidelma grimaced.

'I did not suspect that you had.'

Gadra turned aside to his *sacculus*. The bag lay on the table. He drew out a small bottle.

'I carry my medicines about with me. This is an infusion which is a mixture of ground ivy and wormwood. Tell our Saxon friend to drink it all down mixed in a little water, the stronger potion he can drink, the better it will be. It will help him in ridding his stomach of the poison.'

Fidelma took the bottle hesitantly.

'Take it,' insisted the old hermit. Adding with a smile: 'Unless you believe that I am seeking to poison him.'

'I am truly grateful, Gadra.' Fidelma felt churlish.

'Go quickly, then. Let me know if there is anything else I can do for him.'

Clutching the bottle in her hand, Fidelma returned to the guests' hostel.

Eadulf was still sitting, looking considerably paler. There was a bluish tinge round the eyes and mouth.

'Gadra has sent this for you. You must drink it at once mixed with water.'

Eadulf took the bottle suspiciously from her hand.

'What is it?'

'A mixture of ground ivy and wormwood.'

'Something to cleanse the stomach, I suppose.'

He took off the stopper from the bottle and sniffed, screwing up his face as he did so. Then he poured the contents into a beaker and added water. He stared at it distastefully for a moment then opened his mouth and swallowed.

For a moment he was consumed by a paroxysm of coughing.

'Well,' he said, when he could manage to speak. 'If the poison does not finish me, I am sure that this infusion will do so.'

'How do you feel?' asked Fidelma anxiously.

'Sick,' confessed Eadulf. 'But it takes an hour or so before the poison has a real effect and . . .'

His eyes suddenly bulged.

'What is it?' cried Fidelma in alarm.

Hand to mouth, Eadulf leapt to his feet and disappeared in the direction of the *fialtech*. She could hear his terrible retching through the door.

'What can I do, Eadulf?' she asked in concern when he finally re-emerged.

'Little, I am afraid. If I find Dignait, if she has made me suffer thus, I shall . . . oh God!'

Hand to mouth, once more he returned to the anguish of the privy.

There was a knock on the door and Crón entered.

'It has been confirmed that Dignait is no longer in the *rath*,' she said. 'It seems to confirm her guilt.'

Fidelma regarded the tanist moodily.

'I expected as much.'

'I have sent a man to look for Dubán to inform him of what has happened,' Crón added.

'And where is Dubán now?'

'He is up in the valley of the Black Marsh. There is still the matter of Muadnat's death to be considered.' Crón hesitated and sighed. 'It is difficult to believe that Dignait would attempt to poison you.'

'At the moment there is nothing to believe or disbelieve,' replied Fidelma. 'We will not know what part she has played in this matter until she is found and questioned.'

'She has been a good servant of my family.'

'So I have been told.'

Eadulf re-emerged, saw Crón and contrived to look self-conscious.

Crón examined his pale features with apparent distaste.

'You are ill, Saxon,' the tanist greeted him dispassionately.

'You are perceptive, Crón,' Eadulf replied with an attempt at humour.

'Is there anything that I can . . . that we . . . ?'

Eadulf seated himself, outwardly cheerful.

'Only wait,' he cut in. 'Perhaps I can do that alone?'

Fidelma smiled apologetically to him.

'You are right, Eadulf. We are bothering you too much. Rest now. But I have asked the young girl Grella to look in on you from time to time.'

She turned and led Crón gently but firmly from the guests' hostel.

'Where is Crítán, incidentally?' she asked when they were outside. 'Has he sobered up after yesterday?'

'He was not so intoxicated that he did not remember what happened. You humiliated him and he will not forgive you.'

'He humiliated himself,' corrected Fidelma.

'Anyway, after raging before me last evening, just before you returned to the *rath*, he took his horse and rode off, saying that he would sell his services to a chieftain who appreciated his talent.'

'That is what I fear. His talent lies in arrogance and bullying. There are unscrupulous men about who wish to use such talents. Anyway, you say that the young man is no longer in the *rath*?'

Crón's eyes widened.

'You do not think that he conspired with Dignait to . . . ?'

'I do not waste time in speculation without facts, Crón.' A thought suddenly struck her. It did have something to do with Crítán. She was about to act upon it when she suddenly caught sight of Menma, the stableman, riding out of the *rath*. He was mounted on a sturdy mare but leading an ass on a rope behind him. There was a heavy pannier strapped to the animal's back.

'Where is he off to?' demanded Fidelma suspiciously.

'I have asked him to go to the southern highlands to round up some stray horses,' replied Crón. 'Did you want his services? Shall I call him back?'

'It does not matter for the moment.' Fidelma was reluctant to be distracted from her immediate thoughts.

There was, however, a further distraction with the sound of horses entering the *rath*, across the wooden bridge. It caused them to turn. It was Cranat and Father Gormán. They passed Menma without acknowledgment.

Crón crossed to her mother immediately and began explaining what had happened. Sister Fidelma held back, observing the interplay between mother and daughter with interest. There seemed a curious distance between them. A formality which could not quite be explained.

Father Gormán, who had been listening, had dismounted and, while someone came to take charge of his horse, he approached Fidelma.

'Brother Eadulf is a follower of Rome,' he said abruptly. 'If his life is in danger I should tend to his needs.'

'His needs are well tended to, Father Gormán,' replied Fidelma with some amusement. 'We can only wait now.'

Father Gormán coloured.

'I meant his spiritual needs. A last confession. The last rites of our church.'

'I have not quite consigned him to the Otherworld yet,' she replied. '*Dum vita est spes est,*' she added. While there is life there is hope.

She turned towards Cranat who was about to move off.

'Cranat! A word with you.'

The haughty woman turned, flushing in annoyance.

'It is usual to request . . .'

'I have no time for etiquette, as I told you before,' Fidelma said. 'We are speaking of life and death here. I believe that you saw Dignait this morning. Did you observe her preparing breakfast for the guests' hostel?'

'I do not busy myself in kitchens,' sniffed Cranat.

'Yet you saw Dignait this morning?'

'I saw her while I was crossing the hall of assembly. She came from the kitchen. I paused to speak to her on a domestic matter. I do believe that the servant Grella came in and Dignait instructed her to go to the kitchen and take the breakfast tray to the guests' hostel. That is all.'

'Dignait needs to be found. Do you know where she might go?'

Cranat returned Fidelma's look with distaste.

'I am not in the habit of busying myself with the personal affairs of servants. Now, if that is all . . . ?' She stalked off before Fidelma could reply.

Father Gormán was still determinedly standing his ground and he now took his opportunity.

'I insist upon seeing the dying Saxon brother,' he said. 'You must take a portion of the blame on yourself for this death, sister. You released that spawn of Satan knowing full well that our lives might be in danger still.'

Fidelma turned irritably to him.

'Are you sure that you are an advocate of the Christian doctrine?'

Father Gormán flushed.

'More so than you, that is obvious. The Christ himself said: "If your hand offend you, cut it off; it is better for you to enter into life maimed, than having two hands to go into hell, into the fire that never shall be quenched; where worm dies not and the fire is not quenched." It is about time that we cut off this offence. Destroy and drive out the evil in our midst!'

Fidelma clenched her jaw for a moment.

'Brother Eadulf will never stand in need of your blessing, Gormán of Cill Uird,' Fidelma replied in a quiet voice. 'He will not die yet.'

'Are you God to decide such things?' sneered the priest.

257

'No.' Fidelma shook her head. 'But my will is as strong as Adam's!'

Father Gormán looked as if he were about to argue further but then he turned, mouth compressed, and stormed back to his chapel.

Crón looked from the banging door of the chapel back to Fidelma in bemusement.

'Let me know if there is anything I can do . . .' she said, before she turned into the hall of assembly.

Fidelma began to return to the guests' hostel.

'Sister! Sister!'

Fidelma saw the little servant girl, Grella, running towards her. She could see from the girl's face that something was amiss and her heart skipped a beat.

'Is it Brother Eadulf?'

'Come quickly,' cried the girl but Fidelma had already increased her pace in the direction of the guests' hostel.

'I had only just gone in, as you instructed me to,' gasped the girl, trying to keep up with her. She did not finish for Fidelma was already entering the hostel. Grella followed on her heels.

Eadulf was lying in his cubicle, sprawled across his palliasse on his back. He seemed to be shivering, the body twitching but his eyes were closed and beads of perspiration stood out on his face.

Fidelma dropped to her knees and reached for Eadulf's hand. It was hot and sweaty. She felt for his pulse; it throbbed with a jerky motion.

'How long has he been like this?' she demanded of Grella, who hovered behind her.

'I came in here only a moment ago, as you requested, and found him so,' the girl repeated.

'Get Gadra the Hermit quickly!' When the girl hesitated she snapped: 'At the house of Teafa. Quickly now!'

She turned back to Eadulf. It was clear that he had entered a fever and was no longer conscious of what was going on around him.

She stood up and hurried to the main room where a pitcher of water stood on the stable. Seizing this and a piece of cloth used for drying the hands after washing, she dampened it and returned to Eadulf and started to wipe the sweat from his flushed face.

A moment later, the old man entered followed by Grella. He gently drew Fidelma to one side. He felt Eadulf's forehead and the pulse and stood back.

'There is little we can do now. He has succumbed to a fever which he must either pass through or depart with.'

Fidelma found her hands clenching spasmodically.

'Is there nothing else we can do?'

'The poison must have its way. It is to be hoped that he cleansed himself of as much of it as might be life threatening and this is but the result of a small residue which will trouble him for a few hours. The temperature of his body is rising. If it breaks, then we will win. If it does not . . .'

He shrugged eloquently.

'When will be know?'

'Not for a few hours yet. We can do nothing.'

Fidelma felt an unreasonable rage as she gazed at the yellowing sunken face of Eadulf. She realised how bleak her life would become if anything happened to him. She recalled how troubled she had been after she had left Eadulf in Rome to return to Ireland and the months of loneliness which followed. She had remembered how she had returned to Ireland with the curious, almost unfathomable emotion of loneliness and homesickness. It had taken a while to resolve those emotions.

For Fidelma it was hard to admit to an emotional attachment. She had fallen in love with a young warrior named Cian when she had been seventeen. He had been in the élite bodyguard of the High King at Tara. At the time she had been studying law under the great Brehon Morann. She was young and carefree and very much in love. But Cian had eventually deserted her for another. His rejection of her had left her disillusioned with life. She felt bitter, although the years had tempered her attitude. But she had never forgotten her experience nor really recovered from it. Perhaps she had never allowed herself to do so.

Eadulf of Seaxmund's Ham had been the only man of her own age in whose company she had felt really at ease and able to express herself. She had challenged him at first and those intellectual challenges became the basis of their good-natured, easy relationship for their debates over theology and cultural attitudes, contrasting their conflicting opinions and philosophies, would be a way of teasing each other. And while their arguments would rage, there was no enmity between them.

Fidelma had felt loneliness for a year and had scarcely been able to conceal her exhilaration when she had discovered that Brother Eadulf had been sent as an emissary from the newly appointed archbishop of Canterbury, Theodore, who was now the Holy Father's representative to the Anglo-Saxon kingdoms. That Eadulf was now at the court of her brother, Colgú of Cashel, was as if Fate had ordained a path in her life.

Could Fate be so cruel as to take Eadulf away; away so finally and irrevocably?

'There is nothing that you can do here, Fidelma,' Gadra was repeating. 'Let me look after the poor brother while you do your best to find who is responsible for this outrage. I will send word to you as soon as there is any change.'

Reluctantly, Fidelma looked down at the ailing features of her friend and nodded slowly. She tried to control the slight twitching at the corners of her mouth. Her face had hardened unnaturally.

'Thank you, Gadra,' she said. 'Grella here will help you, won't you, Grella?'

Grella was standing wringing her hands. 'Oh, sister, shall I be punished for this?'

'Why should you be punished?' she asked absently.

'It was I who brought the food to you and the brother,' the girl reminded her.

Fidelma realised the anguish the young girl was going through and shook her head with a sad smile.

'You will not be punished. But I must go to find Dignait and discover who is responsible for placing the poisonous fungi on the plates. Gadra here will require your help. Will you help him?'

'I will,' agreed the young girl, mournfully.

Fidelma cast one final glance at Eadulf's shivering, unconscious form, and turned to leave the hostel. It was only when she had gone several yards that she realised, for the first time in her life, she was walking without a purpose. She paused, undecided what to do.

Chapter Seventeen

Fidelma dismounted outside the single-storey cabin which was built entirely of wood. She had left the *rath* with only a vague idea in her mind. Her mind was turning over the idea which had occurred to her with the mention of Crítán. It was a line from Virgil; from the *Aeneid*. *Dux femina facti!* She was not sure why she kept thinking of this line until she passed along the road to the valley of the Black Marsh and saw the small cabin in the bend of the river.

A woman stood outside the door, where she had apparently been tending plants in a small patch of garden. She watched Fidelma's arrival with curiosity. She was a well-proportioned woman; a woman past her youthful years. She was a short, fleshy, blonde with pronounced cheekbones. Her taste in clothes was garish, their clash of colours denied their suitability.

Fidelma tied the reins of her horse to a hitching pole.

'Good day to you, sister,' greeted the woman. 'You are welcome here but I should warn you – do you know what place this is?'

Fidelma smiled briefly.

'I am told that it is the house of Clídna. Have I been misinformed?'

The fair-haired woman shook her head.

'I am Clídna but this place is a *meirdrech loc*.'

'A brothel? Yes, so I have been told.'

'Those of your calling do not usually come to visit a woman of secrets, such as myself, unless they wish to attempt to convert us to a new path in life.'

Fidelma grinned at the euphemism 'woman of secrets' as a

263

term for a prostitute, though it was widely used within the five kingdoms. It suddenly seemed appropriate for her.

'*Dux femina facti*,' she said the phrase aloud. 'A woman was the leader in the deed. It is because you hold so many secrets that I have come to you, Clídna.'

The prostitute looked puzzled a moment but gestured towards the cabin.

'Will it offend you if I ask you to come inside and partake of some hospitality?'

'It will not.'

'Then enter my house, sister, and let me offer you something to drink. Alas, my means are modest so I do not have grand wines or sweet meads to offer.'

She turned and led the way into the cabin and, once inside, indicated a seat for Fidelma while she turned to where a pot was simmering over a wood fire.

'I have just prepared this woodsman's tea,' Clídna told her. 'I think you might like it. It is plain and simple.'

'How do you prepare it?' asked Fidelma, sniffing the aroma. It had an odour of the forests about it.

'Easy to say,' smiled the woman. 'I tap a birch and drain off a quantity of the sap. Then I heat the sap infusing it with pine needles. When it is heated, I strain the mixture through sedge leaves.'

She handed Fidelma an earthenware mug.

Fidelma sipped cautiously. There was an unusual tang to the taste but it was not unpleasant.

'It is very good,' she pronounced after she had taken another sip.

'Not compared with the beverages you drink in the palace of Cashel, I'll be bound?'

Fidelma raised an eyebrow.

'So you know who I am?'

'I am a woman of secrets.' There was humour in Clídna's eyes.

'Where else do whispers and rumours come to rest but in the ears of such as I?'

'Will you tell me of yourself? How did you come to follow this calling?'

'I was the daughter of hostages. My parents were of the Uí Fidgente, taken prisoner after the battle of the Ford of Apples where Dicuil son of Fergus was slain by the men of Cashel.'

Fidelma knew that hostages had no rights in society and were made to work until ransom was paid or the next generation were freed automatically.

Clídna seemed to read her mind.

'I was born before my parents were captured. Therefore I was not a free woman. I had no rights within the clan and this is why I am as you see me now. A woman of secrets. Without honour-price, without status, without bride-price. Without property.'

'Who owns your cabin then?'

'It is on the land of Agdae.'

'Ah. Agdae of the Black Marsh?'

Clídna smiled briefly.

'I pay him rent, of course.'

'Of course.'

'I am not ashamed of my life.'

'Did I imply that you should be?'

'Usually those of your calling, Father Gormán for example, would have me scourged and driven out of this land.'

'Father Gormán is extreme in his views.'

Clídna looked at Fidelma with some surprise.

'You cannot tell me that you approve of me?'

'Approve of you, or approve of the profession you have undertaken?'

'Are they separate?'

'It depends on the individual. My mentor, Morann of Tara, told me never to measure another person's coat on my own body.' Fidelma paused. 'However, I have not come to discuss the manner of your life, Clídna. I came because I would be glad if you could assist me with information.'

The woman shrugged.

'There is little in this place that I do not know.'

'Just so. *Dux femina facti!* You might well have heard secrets whispered on the air.'

'But not the secret you wish to uncover. There are too many people who disliked Eber. Enough to wish his health would fail. I am not sure how many would go so far as to undertake the task of killing him.'

'Perhaps Agdae has sufficient motive, for example?'

Clídna shook her head quickly, a flush on her cheeks.

'Anyway, he was at Lios Mhór at the time Eber was killed. You must know that,' she said, her cheeks colouring.

Fidelma knew this fact well enough but something prompted her to test Clídna because of the tone of voice she had used when referring to Agdae as her landlord. Fidelma felt that her tone expressed something more than a professional relationship.

'He would not be capable of hiring someone else to do the deed?'

'He is not like that. He is a man of impetuous temper and was often led astray by his loyalty to his cousin, Muadnat. But he is not a violent man.'

'Yet, perhaps, even as we speak, Agdae is out trying to devise a way of killing young Archú. That is what he is reported to have threatened.'

Clídna threw back her head and laughed.

'Then you are not well informed!'

Fidelma raised her eyebrows in query.

'Are you so certain?'

Clídna rose, still smiling, and went to a door at the back of the cabin. It opened into another room which was in darkness. She motioned Fidelma to come forward. Warily, she did so. Clídna gestured for her to look into its gloomy depths, placing her finger against her lips.

A strong smell of stale alcohol wafted out of the room, which was obviously a sleeping chamber. She heard a raucous snoring sound and saw a figure stretched out on a small wooden cot.

Clídna moved silently across the floor and pulled back a wooden shutter to allow some strong light to flood the room. There was a slight moan from the figure. Fidelma peered forward. She had no trouble recognising Agdae's features. After a moment, Clídna pulled back the shutter and led Fidelma from the room.

'He has been here since the death of Muadnat and scarcely sober since that time,' Clídna explained. 'The death of his cousin has affected him. He is not capable of violence. That I know.'

Fidelma sat down again, sipping her beverage thoughtfully.

'Did Eber ever come here?'

Clídna laughed and shook her head as she returned to her seat. Laughter seemed to come easily to her.

'I was not to his taste for I was not a young girl neither was I related to him,' she replied. 'No, he had other outlets.'

'You said many people hated him?'

'He was to the people of Araglin like a raven to a bone,' reflected Clídna.

'Why was this reputation for kindliness and generosity, for gentleness and courteousness, spread about?'

'Because Eber sought power in the king of Cashel's assembly. He claimed to be a friend of everyone in order to enhance his reputation to win a seat in the assembly.'

'Woe unto you when all men shall speak well of you,' muttered Fidelma. She smiled at the disconcerted woman. 'It comes from the Gospel of the Blessed Luke. In other words, as Aristotle wrote, a man who claims many friends, has no friends. Tell me about the people who disliked him.'

'Where should I begin?' Clídna asked sceptically.

'Start within his own family circle?'

'A good enough place,' she agreed. 'Everyone in it hated him.'

'Everyone?' Fidelma leant forward with interest. 'Then let us be more specific. What of his wife?'

'Cranat? Yes, she hated him. There is no doubt. If you have spoken to her, you will know that she considers herself to be badly treated. To have married below her station. A princess of the Déisi. She disliked having to live in Araglin. Her arrangement was purely for money. You spoke a line of Latin earlier. I learnt such a line once from . . .' she hesitated and smiled, ' . . . from a friend. It was – *quaerenda pecunia primum est virtus post nummos.*'

'A line from Horace's *Epistles*,' Fidelma recognised it, 'and well remembered. Money is to be sought after first of all, virtue after wealth. So Cranat married Eber, seeking wealth before virtue?'

Clídna smiled agreement.

'And Crón is her only child by Eber?'

Clídna rubbed the side of her nose with a forefinger and nodded. Then added: 'She is.'

'When did Cranat cease to live with Eber?'

Clídna shook her head.

'That happened when Crón was about twelve or thirteen years old. There was talk of course.'

'Talk?'

'That Eber preferred his own daughter to the company of his wife.'

Fidelma sat back and looked long and thoughtfully at the prostitute.

'More of this tea?' asked Clídna, unperturbed at the effect that she had.

Fidelma nodded automatically, holding out her mug.

'Let us speak of Crón, then. How did she feel about her father?'

'I am told that she had a close relationship with him. She worked closely with him and, indeed, she had barely come to the age of choice when she was made his tanist. We are a rural community here, sister, and there was some anger at this.'

'Anger?'

'Oh yes. A young girl being heir-elect to the chiefdom.'

'It is not unusual,' Fidelma pointed out. 'Women can aspire to all offices in the five kingdoms.'

'But are rarely elected among farmers. Anyway, there was another problem. Muadnat was already the heir-elect.'

Fidelma fought to control her surprise.

'Muadnat?'

'Yes. Didn't you know that he was cousin to Eber and as Eber had no immediate male heirs, he was appointed tanist a long time ago? When Eber disinherited him and caused his own daughter to be elected tanist, there was talk that Eber paid much in bribes for that support.'

Fidelma's mind was racing.

'Wake Agdac for me!'

Clídna frowned and was about to protest but she recognised the resolute expression on Fidelma's face.

It took some moments to bring Agdae round. The man sat on the bed blinking and rubbing his eyes. He was clearly not yet sober.

'Listen, Agdae,' Fidelma's voice was harsh, 'listen carefully. I want you to tell me the truth. If you do not, then your life might be in danger. Do you understand?'

Agdae groaned in befuddled protest.

'When was Muadnat deposed by the *derbfhine* of the house of the chieftains of Araglin?'

Agdac screwed up his eyes as if trying to focus on her. He gazed at her blankly.

'When?' persisted Fidelma.

'When?' echoed Agdae stupidly. 'Oh, three weeks ago.'

'Only three weeks ago? And were you one of the *derbfhine*?'

Agdae rubbed his tousled head and nodded reluctantly.

'Give me a drink.'

'Were you a member of the *derbfhine*?' Fidelma raised her voice sharply.

'I was.'

'Did you vote for Muadnat to remain tanist?'

'Of course, why I . . .'

'Who else voted for Muadnat . . . who else?'

Agdae's head rolled back as if he wanted to go to sleep.

'Who else supported Muadnat at that assembly?'

She shook him by the shoulders.

'All right! Enough!' he protested. 'Only Cranat, Teafa and myself . . . oh, and Menma. No one else.'

'So Menma was a member of the *derbfhine*?'

'The stableman is a cousin and entitled to a voice in the *derbfhine*,' interposed Clídna.

Fidelma let Agdae collapse in his stupor back onto the bed. She stood for a moment deep in thought before returning to the other room. Clídna followed her, shutting the bedroom door softly. Fidelma sank back in her chair. Cautiously, Clídna reseated herself.

'So Crón was elected tanist only three weeks ago?' Fidelma reflected. 'I know that there is a relationship between Crón and Dubán. What of Dubán's relationship to Eber?'

Clídna pulled a face.

'That is easy. It was rumoured that Dubán hated Eber.'

'Yet he was commander of his bodyguard. Did Eber know of his hate?'

'Eber was wrapped in a cocoon of self-absorption. He was susceptible to flattery and even when he found enemies, his method was, as I have said, of buying them off. When Dubán returned after many years away from Araglin and offered his services to Eber, Eber was flattered that a renowned warrior in the fight against the Uí Fidgente would offer his services to him.'

'I see.' Fidelma was thoughtful.

Clídna regarded her expression.

'If you suspect Dubán of killing Eber, I would advise against it. Dubán is an ambitious, single-minded person but he is also a warrior with a code of honour. He would slaughter Eber in single combat but never sneak up on him in the night and cut his throat.'

'I have known the most unlikely people resort to means that are out of character.'

'Well, of all the people in Araglin, I would say that Dubán, in spite of his dislike of Eber, would be the last to resort to murder.'

'Do you know why Dubán hated Eber?'

'Ah, that is a story lost in the past. I think something happened when Dubán was a young man here, something which prompted his going to join the armies of the Cashel kings.'

'You said that if you were considering this matter, you would place other people before Dubán. Such as who?'

Clídna grinned awkwardly.

'You will not be offended if I speak my mind?'

'Why should I be?'

'You may not like what I have to say.'

'Like or dislike may not enter into it, if it places my footsteps on the path to truth. Truth is what we seek in whatever direction it lies. *Vincit omnia veritas*.'

'Father Gormán hated Eber. He was a fanatic about what he believed to be moral. He was always threatening people with hell and fiery furnaces. He threatened Eber and Teafa.'

'How do you know this?'

'I learnt it from that little conceited boy who pretends to be a warrior. He was often a visitor here.'

'Crítán?'

'The same. He was drunk here one evening and in his cups he told me Father Gormán had denounced both Eber and Teafa in the most vehement fashion. He called him a vile whoremonger who would burn in hell and said that Teafa was no better. Father Gormán accused them of many sins, so many that he claimed hell was not hot enough, nor eternity long enough, to punish him.'

'When was this?'

'Two weeks ago, according to Crítán. Eber was so outraged by Gormán that he struck him.'

'Eber struck the priest?' Even Fidelma was surprised.

'It is so.'

'Were there witnesses?'

'According to Crítán he witnessed this himself for it took place in the stables. They did not see him because he was in the hayloft.'

'What was the row about?'

'You should ask Crítán.'

'I doubt that he would tell me. Don't worry. If you tell me what Crítán said I shall see that you are not implicated if any of the information needs to be acted upon.'

'Crítán was in the hayloft of the stables. He was apparently asleep there. He was awakened by the sounds of an altercation. It was the priest with Eber and Teafa. He could not hear precisely what the argument was about except that Father Gormán was censuring them both for their lack of morality. Crítán said something was mentioned about Móen. It was then that Eber actually struck the priest.'

'What happened then?' prompted Fidelma when the woman paused.

'Father Gormán fell to the ground. Crítán said that he cried out words to the effect that Eber would be struck dead in return for that blow.'

Fidelma leant forward with interest.

'He said those very words?'

'According to Crítán.'

'What were the exact words . . . according to Crítán?'

'I think he said that Father Gormán cried out – "Heaven will strike you dead for that blow" – or something like that.'

'Ah, *heaven*. He did not say that the blow would be struck by himself?'

Clídna shook her head.

'Well, I shall not implicate you in this. Tell me, though,' Fidelma smiled briefly, 'is Agdae a good landlord?'

'No better or worse than any other man,' Clídna was self-consciously offhand.

'But you like him more than any other man?'

'It is nice to dream beyond one's station in life,' she admitted.

'What can you tell me about Muadnat?'

'Hot-headed. He was always used to his own way.'

'Did Muadnat and Agdae both frequent your . . . your house?'

Clídna laughed humorously.

'They and half of Araglin. I am not ashamed. It is what I do.'

'Did you ever hear either of them speak about a mine?'

'A mine? Do you mean a mine here in Araglin?'

'Yes. Or in the Black Marsh, on Muadnat's land, for example.'

'No. Nor anywhere else in this land.'

Fidelma was disappointed.

Clídna was rising from her seat when she suddenly turned round, frowning.

'Mind you . . . it may be nothing . . .'

Fidelma waited expectantly.

'Menma said something once.'

Fidelma was patient but her mind fully alert at the mention of the red-haired man.

'Menma said something about a man who found a rock which would make him rich.'

'What?'

'I did not understand then neither do I understand now, sister. Menma is often here and often drunk. Some weeks ago he was talking in his cups about extracting riches from the earth. I had no idea of what he was talking about. Then he said something about a man knowing the secret of making rock turn to wealth and wealth buying more power than even Eber could imagine.'

'Did he mention who this man was?'

'It was a name like Mór . . . Mór something.'

'Morna?' queried Fidelma.

'I think so. Now that you have mentioned mines. Don't the rocks yield up precious metals?'

'Have you heard any other talk? Did Muadnat ever say anything?'

'Nothing. One interesting thing, though, during this same period Menma and Muadnat appeared to become close friends. Muadnat had never been friendly with the stableman before. It was curious. I know because Agdae once complained to me that Muadnat and Menma often went hunting in the hills and he felt excluded.'

Slowly, thoughtfully, Fidelma rose from her seat.

'I am most grateful for all the information you have given me, Clídna. You have been of much help to me.'

Clídna grimaced sceptically.

'I cannot see how, sister.'

Fidelma handed her back the empty pottery mug.

'I thank you for your hospitality. May you be happy in your life.'

Fidelma mounted her horse and headed towards the valley of the Black Marsh, deep in thought.

Chapter Eighteen

Her first plan had been to set out in search of Dubán to see if he had discovered where Dignait might have fled to. But she was troubled. Even though Clídna had told her that there were others in Araglin whom she would suspect of murder before the burly warrior, Fidelma was suspicious. If he hated Eber, why had Dubán returned to Araglin and taken service with him? And if he loved Crón, the death of Eber was of benefit to them both. She had already become suspicious of the pair of them because of the lies that they had told her. She found herself unconsciously guiding her horse directly over the hills towards the mine.

The journey was tedious for several times did Fidelma think it was better to hide herself from the occasional traveller, or to give buildings a wide berth, rather than allow herself to be observed. She had a strong feeling that things were beginning to draw together like the strands of a spider's web, closer and closer to the centre where the shadowy figure of one great manipulator sat, tugging on the various threads.

Fidelma reached the stretch of forest in which she and Eadulf had discovered the cave entrance and seen Menma emerging from it. She wondered how close she could get without being spotted, how many workers were there around the cave? But she knew, instinctively, that the cave was going to provide her with one of the keys to unlock this curious mystery.

Her senses sharpened as she rode through the forest, through sombre oaks whose catkins were yellowing, inconsequentially noticing the white and red, and even pink flowers of the sturdy hawthorns, and the yews which had just ceased flowering. All the beeches stood out with their leaves a brilliant green. It seemed so peaceful, so idyllic. It was hard to imagine that mayhem and death lurked in this pleasant land.

Her horse suddenly shied nervously and, from nearby, came the curious high-pitched bark of a fox in search of its prey.

It was wise to remember that even in an idyllic setting such as this there were also predators searching for their weak victims.

She drew near the spot where she and Eadulf had previously tethered their horses and decided it would be best to repeat the exercise and approach on foot. It was just as well for as she reached the edge of the woods she heard the sound of hooves and slunk down into the undergrowth. Not far away, along the trail, a horse galloped by from the direction of the glade. Fidelma saw a slight figure crouched low over its neck, a bright parti-coloured cloak flying in the wind. Then the horse and rider were gone. Fidelma paused a moment. She thought she suddenly heard a cry from the glade and turned, moving carefully towards it. Soon she was staring across into the open glade against the side of the hill, where the cave entrance was. Two horses were standing patiently tethered there. She crouched low behind the cover of the bushes.

There was no sign of the heavy wagon which had been there previously and the fire was now a charred, blackened patch, although the tools were still stacked nearby. She listened carefully but it was quiet save the trill of bird songs arising from the forest and the gentle whisper of a breeze against the mountain slopes. Fidelma examined the horses carefully. They were saddled and were certainly not farm horses, more the sort of beasts that warriors would ride. One of them was particularly familiar and she rebuked her memory that she could not recall where she had seen it and who was riding it.

She was about to rise and move nearer the cave when it happened so fast that she could scarcely draw breath before it was all over.

One moment she was trying to recall why the horses were so

familiar and where she had seen them before and then the next she was pole-axed by a curious wailing scream. Her eyes darted towards the cave mouth. A dishevelled figure appeared. It paused for a moment, gave a sobbing gulp of breath and began to run towards the horses.

It was the red-haired Menma. The stableman had almost made it to his horse when a second figure appeared at the cave mouth. It strode leisurely from the dark with a bow and an arrow strung to it.

'Menma!'

The voice was low but the intensity carried across the glade.

The man spun round. Even from this distance, Fidelma saw the terror on his face.

'For the love of God!' he almost jabbered. 'I can pay you! I can . . .'

Then he made a grab for a sword hanging from his saddle and turned round to face his pursuer. He began to run forward swinging the blade in desperation.

The second figure unhurriedly raised his bow. Menma was running forward full pelt now, trying to close the gap. There was a dull thud. Menma jerked back on the ground, his sword flying out of his hand. The shaft of an arrow was protruding from his chest. He struggled for a moment and lay still.

The second figure walked slowly up to his inert form and gazed dispassionately down. He touched the body with the toe of his boot, as if to make sure that the man was dead. Then he reached down and pulled the arrow out of his chest. Even from this distance, Fidelma saw the little fountain of blood gush forth as the arrow was pulled. Calmly, the second figure put the arrow back in his quiver, unstrung his bow and turned to his horse, untying the reins and swinging himself up. He then leant forward, untied the reins of Menma's mount and proceeded from the glade, leading the second horse after him.

Only when he had disappeared along the forest path, did

Fidelma give a long, shuddering exhalation of breath. She felt chilly with shock.

The second figure had been that of Dubán.

It was some time before Fidelma rose from her hiding place and moved slowly forward to where the body of Menma lay. She could see that he was beyond earthly help and so she genuflected and muttered a blessing for the repose of his soul. She had no liking for the ill-smelling stableman but she wondered whether such a death was deserved. What reason had Dubán to shoot the red-haired man down in such a callous manner?

Her eye caught something tucked into the stableman's waistband, something she did not quite equate with him. She bent down and tugged it out. It was a piece of vellum with writing on. As she tugged at it something else fell out. It was a small plainly wrought gold Roman crucifix. She picked it up. The gold was rich and red from an admixture of copper in the ore. She turned to the vellum. The writing on it was in Latin. She translated it easily enough. 'If you want to know the answer to the deaths in Araglin, look beneath the farmstead of the usurper Archú.'

She frowned as she stared at it. It was simple Latin but clearly expressed and grammatically correct. She glanced down at Menma's body. He had tucked the vellum in his waistband and clearly Dubán had not noticed it. It was no good asking what it meant at this stage. She folded it carefully and put it into her *marsupium* together with the gold crucifix.

'*Terra es, terram ibis,*' she muttered as she gazed down at the body. It was true enough. In a world of uncertainties it was the only dependable eventuality. We all came from dust and to the dust we would all return some day.

She turned towards the cave entrance. She was sure that now Dubán had departed there was no one else around. The cave was dark and silent. There were tools in the entrance and she saw an oil lamp with flint and tinder nearby. It was the work of a moment to light the lamp and move on into the darkness. There were signs that the cave had been recently worked.

She had not gone far when she observed the confirmation of her suspicions. There was a spot where there was a concentration of tool marks; a glittering stream along one wall almost at shoulder height. She moved towards it and reached out her hand to touch it. It flickered red gold in the light of the lamp.

A gold mine.

So was this what the mystery was really about?

She examined the stream of gold carefully. She had some knowledge of gold for it was mined in several parts of the five kingdoms, even at Kildare, in whose great religious house, founded by Brigid, she had spent most of her life as a religieuse. It was said that the Tigernmas, the twenty-sixth High King who ruled Éireann a thousand years before the birth of Christ, was the first to smelt gold in the land. Whether it was true or not, gold had almost replaced cattle as a unit by which goods, services and obligations could be measured. Gold, because of its durable quality, had many advantages over the traditional barter system. It was a common form of currency along with other metals such as silver, bronze and copper. Whoever exploited this mine would gain much wealth.

Indeed, things were beginning to fit into a pattern but there were still several pieces missing before she could fit them into a whole. Morna, the brother of Bressal, had been a miner and his knowledge had exploited this mine. Now Morna was dead. This was why Muadnat had so desperately tried to cling on to this land. But he was dead. Menma? Menma had apparently worked for Muadnat. But he did not really have the brains to exploit this mine on his own. And now Menma was dead. And what of Dubán who had killed Menma?

She turned hurriedly from the cave and made her way out into the welcoming daylight.

Menma's body still lay on its back in the glade. The sun still shone and the song of the birds remained undiminished. It seemed so unreal.

What madness was passing through the valley of Araglin?

Fidelma crossed the glade and hurried into the shelter of the forest, making her way quickly towards her horse. The next step lay at Archú's farmstead, she decided. For the second time, within a comparatively short space, she found herself pulling her horse over the rounded shoulder of the hills which separated her from the L-shaped valley of the Black Marsh in which Archú dwelt.

It was late afternoon when she began to descend towards his farmstead.

Scoth came running forward and greeted Fidelma with a warm smile.

'It is good to see you so soon, sister. Where is Brother Eadulf?'

Fidelma told her, trying to keep her voice unemotional but the girl saw through the veil at once and reached out a hand.

'Is there anything that can be done?'

Fidelma tried to shake herself free of the gloomy foreboding.

'Nothing. Nothing until the fever breaks . . . if it breaks. Where is Archú?'

'He is up at the top meadowland repairing a fence with one of Dubán's warriors. There is news of a ravening wolf hereabouts and . . .'

Fidelma was disapproving and anxious.

'It is not right that you should be left here alone. Surely one of the warriors should be here to guard you?'

'The other is within call,' Scoth assured her. 'I do not think I need have any fear. Archú is easily able to observe if any strangers enter the valley.'

'I came up over the hill. He has not appeared to have noticed my entrance.'

'He saw you coming over the hill half an hour ago and told me to expect you,' Scoth replied brightly. 'I am not neglected. But you are here for a purpose, sister. I can see it in your eyes.'

'Let us go into your house for a moment,' suggested Fidelma.

'Is it something to do with Archú?' demanded the girl anxiously.

Fidelma guided her by the arm into the farmhouse.

'It is probably nothing but . . .' She reached into her *marsupium* and pulled out the piece of vellum. 'Can you read Latin, Scoth?'

The girl wistfully shook her head.

'I was only a kitchen servant. Archú says that he will teach me my letters when we are settled. His mother taught him.'

'Well, this is a message in Latin. It tells me that if I require answers to the deaths in Araglin I should start looking here.'

Scoth coloured angrily.

'That's wicked. Who would try . . . oh,' the girl broke off. 'I suppose it was Agdae.'

'Agdae?' Fidelma shook her head. 'I doubt if Agdae is capable of such a literate clue.'

'A what?'

'I do not think he wrote this. Why would he write it in Latin?'

'I think it is part and parcel of the same plot to drive us off this land.'

'What is?'

It was Archú standing at the door of the farmhouse regarding Scoth and Fidelma with a frown. He hesitated a moment and then continued. 'I saw you arriving. I was finishing a fence in the high meadow. Is there more trouble?'

'Someone has written to Fidelma telling her that we are responsible for the deaths in Araglin.'

Fidelma corrected her immediately.

'That is not quite what I said, Scoth. I found a piece of vellum, Archú. Can read Latin?'

'My mother taught me to decipher it,' admitted the young man. 'But I am not well versed in it.'

'What do you make of this?' She handed him the vellum. Archú took it and held it up.

'If you want to know the answers to the deaths in Araglin look beneath the farmstead of the usurper Archú,' he read in a hesitant fashion.

He looked at Fidelma in perplexity.

'What does it mean?'

'That is why I am here – to find out. I found it on the body of . . . a dead man.'

'A dead man?' he repeated bewilderedly.

'Yes. Menma.'

The young farmer showed his astonishment.

'But Menma was here this morning with a message.'

'What was this message?' Fidelma leant forward in surprise.

'Something about Dignait being missing. I was to warn Dubán's men to look out for her.'

'Is this another attempt to blacken our name and drive us from the Black Marsh?' demanded Scoth, clinging to Archú's arm.

'We must presume that some trail has been laid for me to follow. Let us see what we can find.'

'By all means search the farmstead.' Archú threw out his arms eloquently. 'We have nothing to hide.'

Fidelma took the vellum from his hands and rolled it up.

'The message appears specific when it says "look *beneath* the farmstead", Archú,' she pointed out. 'What lies beneath the farm-stead?'

The young man thought for a moment.

'Nothing lies underneath the farmstead.'

'Is there no area of recently dug earth that you have noticed? Perhaps . . .'

Archú suddenly startled them by snapping his fingers.

'I think I know what is meant.'

'What?' demanded Scoth.

'I have remembered something my mother told me about a sub-terranean chamber. This farmstead was built on an ancient site when, in the times past, they built underground chambers for storing food to prepare against any period of hardship or inclement weather.'

'Have you ever seen it?'

'I can't remember it. My mother said it was closed when I was a few years old because one of the children of a servant here was caught down there and died. Father Gormán was visiting at the time and it was he who fetched the child out and suggested the chamber be sealed up. So far as I know, it has never been opened since then. I had almost forgotten all about it until you prompted me.'

Fidelma sniffed slightly.

'It seems that the author of this letter has not. We must search out the entrance to it.'

'That is impossible. I do not know where to start.'

'Not so impossible. Our letter writer expects us to find it. Therefore it must have been in use recently.'

The floor of the farmhouse was stone-flagged and some time spent tapping the stones revealed nothing. There was no hollow sounding echo nor was there any looseness of the flags.

'Perhaps it is outside?' Scoth suggested.

They walked around the farmhouse but nothing seemed to invite them to investigate further.

'What of that barn?' demanded Fidelma, pointing to a nearby outhouse. It stood next to the one that was now a charred ruin.

'It has not been cleaned and converted yet,' Archú assured her. 'It was used for keeping pigs in.'

'Then this might be the best place to look,' Fidelma suggested, leading the way to it.

The place stank and the obnoxious odours caught at her throat. Archú had been right when he said that it had been used as a pigsty and barely cleaned.

In spite of the fact that it was daylight, the place was gloomy and dank.

'I have moved the pigs out and have been meaning to clean the place,' Archú explained as Fidelma stood hesitating in the gloom.

'Best get a lamp.'

'I will get one,' offered Scoth.

It was some moments before she returned.

Fidelma, holding the lamp high, entered the foul smelling barn and peered about. The floor was similarly flagged with stones. They seemed firm enough but then Fidelma noticed that in a corner of the straw covered floor there was a raised area of planking. Scraping the wet straw away with her foot she discovered it was a trapdoor. Bolts held it down to the floor.

'This must be the entrance,' she observed in satisfaction. 'Hold this lamp, Scoth. Give me a hand, Archú. Let us clear this area and open the trapdoor.'

It took them a while before the large wooden square was unbolted and raised back against one wall. Below, as she had guessed there might be, was a flight of rough hewn stone steps leading downwards. The man-made cavern was lined with dry stone walling surmounted by large lintels forming the roof.

Fidelma took the lantern from Scoth and descended without a word. The steps led into a main passage, too low to stand up in but not so low that one would have to crouch on all fours. As Archú had said, in olden times these places were called *uaimh talamh*, an underground cave in which food was placed for storage to be used in hard times. The main passage was called a 'creep way' from which little chambers led off. The place smelled vile and its lack of use was certainly evident.

Fidelma did not have to go far to see what she had come for. She was expecting something but was still not quite prepared for the body which revealed itself in the light of her lamp.

It was Dignait. Her throat was cut. It needed no expert to see that. The wound was still red and gaping, even though the blood was congealing. Dignait had been dead for some hours. Fidelma forced herself to examine the wound carefully. It was but a single wound caused by a sharp implement almost severing the head from the neck. She had seen this type of wound twice before and again she was reminded of the slaughter of some animal.

Archú helped extract the body from the underground storage space. Its removal was difficult but they finally hauled it up the stone steps and into the pigsty. Scoth had gone to fetch a lantern and by its light Fidelma carefully examined the body for anything which might explain this gruesome mystery. There was nothing.

It was obvious to Fidelma that Menma must have brought the body of Dignait to this spot. She recalled how he had ridden out of the *rath* early that morning leading the ass with the heavy pannier on its back. She ground her teeth. Dignait's body must have been in that pannier.

'Was Menma left alone while he was here?' she demanded.

'After he delivered the message to Dubán's men, who were with me in the high meadow, he came back to the buildings here on his own. But Scoth was here.'

'I was in the house,' Scoth affirmed. 'Menma came to the house to make his farewell.'

'Did you observe him arrive from the high field?'

Scoth shook her head.

'I was doing some washing and did not notice him until he called out to me.'

'Then plenty of time for him to come back from the high meadow, see he was not observed and take Dignait's body from the pannier and put it into the underground chamber before calling out to Scoth.'

Scoth stared in horror at Fidelma.

'The body was in the pannier? But how did Menma know where to put it? He must have known where the underground chamber was.'

'Menma was related to Muadnat,' Archú pointed out. 'Muadnat knew this farm as well as his own.'

They were interrupted by the sound of a horse cantering along the track.

Archú swung round nervously but he immediately relaxed.

'It is only Dubán,' he said, adding unnecessarily, 'that is why his men did not warn us of his approach.'

Fidelma had an immediate feeling of unease as she saw the burly warrior approaching. She was still unsure of his motive for killing Menma.

Dubán swung off his horse and greeted them with a warm smile. Then he saw the body at their feet.

'What happened?' he demanded. 'It's Dignait!'

'We found her in an underground storage space,' Archú announced.

The warrior crouched down to examine the body. Then he straightened up.

'Well, that ends one mystery,' he breathed softly. 'I was told this morning that Dignait had disappeared after, apparently, feeding the Saxon poisonous mushrooms. What does this mean, sister?'

Fidelma forced herself to appear at ease with the warrior.

'Your guess is as good as mine.'

'How did you make the discovery?'

'I discovered this piece of vellum.' Fidelma hastened to explain before anyone could mention Menma. She held it out to Dubán, watching his face closely. It seemed clear from his lack of reaction that he had not seen it before.

'I do not understand,' he commented. 'This tells you to come here to search. But how does the discovery of Dignait's body explain the mystery of the deaths in Araglin?'

'Perhaps,' Fidelma carefully retrieved the vellum, 'perhaps I am supposed to believe that Dignait was responsible for the deaths.'

'Well that can't be,' Dubán pointed out. 'It is obvious that the same hand who killed Muadnat also slew Dignait. The knife wounds are too similar for it to be a separate hand.'

'You are observant, Dubán,' Fidelma agreed quietly.

'War and death are my profession, sister. I am used to observing wounds. But whoever wrote that vellum gave us an unintentional clue.'

'A clue?'

'It is written in Latin. Few people in Araglin know Latin.'

'Ah, just so,' mused Fidelma. 'And certainly, as I pointed out to Scoth, Agdae does not. So that rules him out. Do you know Latin, Dubán?'

The warrior did not hesitate.

'Of course. Most educated people know some. Even Gadra knows Latin as pagan as he is.'

Fidelma turned to Archú.

'I want you and Scoth to come into the *rath* at noon tomorrow,' she told him and while he was attempting to protest she went on. 'Dubán will instruct his warriors to escort you.' She turned to Dubán. 'And you will also instruct your warriors to bring in Agdae . . .'

'We have not been able to find Agdae,' protested Dubán.

'You will find him at the brothel of Clídna. Make sure he has been sobered up by the time he reaches the *rath*. Oh, and bring Clídna with you as well.'

Dubán was shocked.

'Do you know what you are requesting?' he demanded.

'Exactly. Tomorrow I think we will be able to sort out the entire mystery.'

Dubán's eyes widened perceptibly.

'Is this so?'

Fidelma smiled without humour.

'Will you instruct your men now about escorting those I have mentioned?'

The warrior hesitated then inclined his head in agreement before moving off into the gloom hailing his men as he went.

Fidelma turned quickly towards her horse.

'Wait, sister!' called Scoth. 'Surely you do not mean to leave us. Why it is dusk. You will not get back to the *rath* until long after nightfall.'

'Do not worry about me. I know the way by now. And there

are things that I must do. I will see you and Archú at the *rath* tomorrow at midday.'

She swung into the saddle and sent her horse into the enveloping gloom, urging it forward in a quick trot.

She had not ridden more than half a mile into the darkness when she heard the sound of galloping behind her. She glanced about seeking shelter but the road here was long and open. There was not even a hedgerow behind which she could find cover.

'Hóigh! Sister!'

It was Dubán's voice. Reluctantly she halted and turned in her saddle.

Dubán drew up sharply alongside her.

'It is not wise to ride off in the darkness,' he admonished. 'The finding of Dignait's body does not make this valley safe.'

Fidelma smiled thinly but her expression was lost in the gloom.

'I did not think it would be,' she replied.

'You should have waited. I am going back to the *rath*, anyway. We will go together.'

Fidelma would have preferred her own company rather than have to proceed in Dubán's after what she had witnessed at the mine but there was no excuse. She must accept Dubán's company or challenge him with her suspicions and her knowledge that he had killed Menma.

'Very well,' she said. 'But I can handle most two-legged predators.'

'So I have heard,' Dubán agreed with a laugh. 'However, I was thinking of four-legged beasts. Archú tells me that there has been trouble from wolves in the last day or so through the Black Marsh.'

'Wolves are the least of my trouble.'

They began to walk their horses leisurely together.

'Ah, you are thinking of Agdae . . .'

'More of Crítán,' she spoke abruptly. 'Remember, I had a fight with that young man and he may wish revenge.'

Was there a hesitation in Dubán's tone when he finally spoke?

'Of course. I had forgotten. You need have no fear of Crítán. I am told that he has left Araglin for Cashel. Do you really mean it when you say that you think matters might be resolved after tomorrow?'

'I usually mean what I say,' Fidelma replied waspishly.

'Then that will be a relief to Crón.'

'And doubtless you . . .'

What she was about to say was cut short by a plaintive lowing of nearby cattle. It was an odd, frenzied cry of fear.

Dubán reined in his horse abruptly and gazed across the hillside into the twilight. Fidelma halted her mount beside him.

She could see the shadows of the shaggy haired cattle moving restlessly in the semi-gloom and hear their curious protest.

'What is it?' she asked, finding herself whispering.

'I do not know,' confessed Dubán. 'I think something is worrying them. An animal, perhaps. I'd better have a look.'

He slid from his horse and handed the reins to Fidelma.

She sat watching the warrior move cautiously off towards the cattle into the gloom.

It was chilly and she drew her cloak firmly around her shoulders. After a moment she became aware of Dubán's horse snorting and tugging against its rein.

'Whoa!' she called irritably. 'Hold still, beast.'

Then, without warning, her own mount reared back on its hind legs, causing her to lose her grip and go tumbling over its flank, hitting the ground with her shoulder. It was lucky that the turf was soft and springy for it cushioned her fall and she lay winded for a moment, feeling more indignant than hurt that she had taken the tumble. She raised herself to her knees and began to rub her right arm which had taken most of the impact. She felt embarrassment that she had allowed herself to fall like some novice who had never been astride a horse in their life.

'Hey!' she cried, as both mounts began to trot off into the descending darkness.

She took a hesitant step after them and a sudden coldness gripped her. Her ears detected the soft rustle of undergrowth nearby. Was that the sound of a low growl that she heard?

She stood perfectly still.

A long, low black shape emerged from the nearby underbrush and stopped. The eyes glinted in the gloom and its muzzle drew back showing sharp white canine teeth.

The wolf stared up at her and let forth a deep throaty growling.

Fidelma knew that if she made the slightest move the mighty animal would be on her, its great jaws seeking her throat, ripping and tearing. She tried to prevent herself from blinking; from even breathing. Fidelma had seen wolves before, had even been threatened but always when she was able to out-pace them on horseback or had some other means of protection. Wolves were the commonest predator in the five kingdoms but they usually kept to the mountain fastness or forest passes and attacked only when disturbed or found an unfortunate unarmed wayfarer on foot. There was easier prey in the country than humans such as the better tasting meat of farm animals or wild game like the deer herds.

But here she was alone on foot with no weapons and only yards separating her from a large animal in search of prey. Her rational mind, working alongside the fearful emotions which swept through her, recognised the animal as a bitch, a hungry mother needing food to bring to its whelps.

It seemed that an eternity passed as wolf and human stood gazing upon one another. Fidelma felt her body begin to shake and she knew that any sudden movement would be fatal.

Then she felt something fly past her. Something seemed to hit the wolf for it uttered a terrible cry, a wild yelp, a rough hand caught her and propelled her aside, and even as it did so she saw the wolf turning and disappearing into the undergrowth.

Then she swung round and was facing Dubán in the gloom.

'Are you all right?' the warrior demanded. His voice was anxious.

She gave a nervous laugh.

'I am not sure that I shall ever be all right again,' she confessed. She breathed deeply several times to recover her equilibrium. She rubbed her arm carefully where he had grasped her. 'You have rough hands for a warrior.'

Dubán chuckled.

'Leather gloves, sister. They save callouses. Now, we'd best find the horses. That wolf might bring the pack back in search of us.'

'I am sorry.' Fidelma was contrite.

'For what?' demanded the warrior.

'For being such a fool as to lose the horses.'

Dubán shrugged indifferently.

'Even the best horseman cannot provide for every contingency, sister. The wolf was unnerving the cattle. It must have been circling through the underbrush behind you and suddenly startled the horses. I heard the cry and came hurrying back. Thank God there were a few stones on the ground and I let fly with them. You did well not to move for any movement would have been fatal.' He paused and added. 'But you were not hurt in the fall?'

'Only my dignity is hurt,' smiled Fidelma in the gloom. And the sense of pride in my own logic, she added silently. Had Dubán been the sort of person she was suspecting him to be then she would be lying back there with her throat ripped out by the ravening wolf.

'Thank God it was only that and nothing more,' replied Dubán. They turned and began to walk across the springy turf.

'Do you really think the wolf might come back?' Fidelma asked.

'From the size of it, it was a bitch.' Dubán confirmed her own estimate of the wolf's sex. 'She'll be back looking for food for her hungry cubs.'

'Do they often come this close to the farmlands?'

'More often in winter than in spring or summer. Sometimes they have been known to break into the *rath* itself and make off with chickens and even a piglet as I recall.'

He halted and pointed.

'Look, there are our horses standing by those trees. They did not go far.'

Fidelma utter a silent prayer of thanks. She did not fancy a long trudge through the night.

The two horses actually seemed pleased to see their erstwhile riders and moved towards them. They allowed themselves to be caught and mounted without any fuss.

After a while, as they began to ride on Fidelma said: 'You saved my life there, Dubán.'

The warrior shrugged. He seemed embarrassed.

'I took my warrior's oath before Máenach, when he was king of Cashel, and swore to protect those in need.'

Fidelma regarded him with interest. It meant that Dubán was a warrior of the ancient order of the Golden Collar. It was said that a thousand years before the birth of Christ, Cashel sent a High King to rule over the five kingdoms of Éireann. He was Muinheamhoin Mac Fiardea, the eighth king to rule after Eber the son of Mile. And it was this High King from Cashel who instituted the order of the Golden Collar among his warriors.

'I did not know that you were a warrior of the order of Cashel,' Fidelma said quietly.

'I do not often wear my golden chain of office,' he confessed. 'I returned to Araglin only a few years ago when I felt I was no longer young and virile enough to serve the kings there. Eber had need of an experienced man to be his commander of the guard.' He sighed. 'It was not an onerous position. But maybe I should have stayed in Cashel.'

Fidelma frowned at the inflection in his voice.

'I understand that you did not like Eber?'

'Eber the kind and generous?'

Dubán's tone was cynical.

'You doubt it?'

292

'Someone should tell you the truth about Eber, sister.'

'Perhaps you should tell me.'

'I am not ready to prove my accusations. And if I cannot then I may lose what security I have made here to last me into old age.'

Fidelma was studied.

'I have no wish to harm your prospects of a peaceful life, Dubán. But if it is security you wish, I am sure my brother, as king of Cashel, and therefore hereditary head of the order which you have taken an oath in, would not see you suffer for fulfilling your oath to tell the truth. I have already warned you that I know that the truth has been distorted. Why did you kill Menma?'

Her question came sharply, like an arrow from a bow. She heard his sharp intake of breath.

'You know . . . that?'

He was silent for a moment. Then he replied.

'I followed Menma to that cave. I had been out searching for Dignait when I came across Menma with some other men and a heavy wagon at Muadnat's farm. They did not see me. I recognised the men as some of those who had passed us on the trail. The cattle raiders. Menma was giving them orders and left them to ride alone into the hills along the track that Agdae told us led nowhere. Naturally I followed.'

'Where did the other men go?'

'They headed south. I followed Menma to the cave. There was someone already at the cave.'

'Who was it?'

'I couldn't see. Menma and this other person were inside the cave talking as I arrived. The other person was giving Menma instructions to kill someone in order to silence them.'

'You did not see who this other person, the person giving instructions, was?'

'I did not. But a battle fury descended on me when I heard. Forgetting I had only my bow in my hand, I pushed into the cave and challenged them. Menma fought back fiercely while the other person, no more than a dark shadow in the gloom of the cave, fled by me. I heard them gallop away while I was struggling with Menma. He broke loose and managed to flee to his horse. I could not let him escape. You saw what happened.'

'I did. And I can confirm that someone else fled from the glade.'

'Who?'

'That I did not see. But you heard their voice.'

'I did not recognise it.'

'Was it male or a female?'

'It was a whisper but deep. I think it was male.'

'Tell me why you hated Eber? The truth, on your honour.'

In the gloom she saw Dubán's hand go to his neck as if expecting to find the golden chain of the order of warriors there.

She saw his lips compress a moment.

'You do well to remind me of honour, Fidelma,' he said. 'Maybe these last few years in Araglin I have forgotten what honour really means.'

'Because you have spent too long mixing with young ruffians who think they are warriors? Thugs like Crítán?'

In the gloom ahead they could see lights across the valley.

'There is the *rath*. We shall soon be there,' muttered Dubán.

'Then it is best you tell me what is on your mind, Dubán, before we reach it.'

'Eber was not what he claimed himself to be. He was a chieftain without honour.'

'In what way?'

'He was morally corrupt.'

'Moral corruption may take many forms. Can you be more specific.'

'Have you asked why his wife quit the bed of her husband? It is rumoured that he was like a stag on heat and any deer of the herd which crossed his path was subject to his abuse.'

'I see . . .' murmured Fidelma.

'No, I do not think you do. I mean . . . *any* deer of the herd. Even within his own family,' muttered Dubán.

'You mean that he sexually abused members of his own family?' Fidelma said quietly. She knew the allegation but wanted to hear Dubán's version.

'I cannot prove it. Neither can I prove the other thing that I know within my bones . . . that Eber was a murderer.'

Fidelma was surprised at this assertion.

'You may speak in confidence with me, Dubán. You must tell me why you suspect Eber of murder.'

'Very well. I was in love once with Eber's young sister.'

'With Teafa?'

'No. Not Teafa. She was a year older than Eber. Tomnát was the younger sister. She was fearful of her brother. When I tried to persuade her to accompany me to Cashel as my wife, she said she could not for the shameful thing that was on her.'

'Did she explain what she meant by that?'

'No, neither did I understand at the time. But within a day or so Tomnát had disappeared from the *rath*, indeed, from the very valley of Araglin, and was heard of no more. It was my belief that Eber had her killed lest she reveal the evil of his mind and soul.'

'How can you say this? You must have something which makes you suspicious.'

'I knew that the night before Tomnát disappeared, she and Eber had a terrible row.'

'You witnessed this row?'

'I heard their voices raised. I was on guard and could not enter Eber's private chambers. After a while there was silence and the next morning Tomnát had vanished. I loved Tomnát. She was as attractive as Crón is today.'

'And you said that there was a widespread search made for the missing girl?'

'For months everyone made inquiries for Tomnát. Teafa eventually came to me and told me that it was best for me to forget her sister. Teafa was the only other person who knew my feelings for Tomnát. She told me that ever since Tomnát was a little girl, Eber had forced her to sleep with him. She was never found and eventually I went off to Cashel and pledged myself in the bodyguard of the king, Máenach.'

'Did Teafa claim that Eber had killed her sister Tomnát?'

'No, she did not.'

'When did this happen?'

'Over twenty years ago. No, I can be more precise. It was a few months before Teafa adopted Móen.'

'Did you not challenge Eber, or report your suspicion that Eber had murdered Tomnát?'

'I? What could I have done alone without proof?'

'What of Teafa, who told you of this sexual abuse?'

'Teafa felt she could not betray her brother nor bring shame on her sister. I could not bring any accusation unless I had proof. I left Araglin, as I said, hoping to search out a new life. It is true what the ancient bards say – if you destroy your life in one small corner of the world, you have destroyed it in every small corner. I did not realise it until I found myself aging in the service of Cashel. I had not been able to get this place out of my mind. I dreamt of one day finding Tomnát. And though over twenty years have passed, I finally returned.'

'You have returned, Dubán, but for what purpose?'

'Easy to say; I returned for vengeance.'

Fidelma tried to examine his features in the dark but gave up.

'Vengeance is an ugly thing, Dubán. Did you seek vengeance or justice?'

'It is true that I have been seeking some evidence of what I know in my heart to be the truth. But I will be honest – I wanted vengeance. An eye for an eye, a tooth for tooth, a burning for burning. Exactly as Father Gormán teaches in his chapel.'

Fidelma held her head to one side.

'You realise what you have told me, Dubán? You have said

that you had every reason to kill Eber. And, being on guard that night, you also had the opportunity.'

Dubán nodded gravely.

'This is true, sister. There is no man I would have rather killed. The motivation for returning here and seeking service with the chieftain of Araglin was to eventually find out what happened to Tomnát and punish him if I could. If that makes me suspect, Fidelma, then I am suspect and willingly so. Treat me as you will. Though I would prefer that you discover the truth.'

'Do you deny that you killed Eber?'

'As much as I admit to seeking vengeance and weeping no tears of remorse when I heard the news of Eber's death, I confess that mine was not the hand that struck down that foul man. Nor had I reason to kill Teafa, who had been an honourable lady.'

'Could Eber not have reformed his personality? Especially after Tomnát disappeared?'

Dubán almost spat.

'Reformed? Once a wolf always a wolf. They cannot change their natures.'

'You have changed your nature,' Fidelma pointed out.

'I do not understand.' Dubán was bewildered.

'You have transferred your love for the long lost Tomnát to Eber's daughter Crón.'

'I do not deny that either.' The warrior was defensive. 'One cannot love a memory forever. It is true that when I came here, I came to seek vengeance for a lost love but I discovered another.'

'So are you telling me that twenty years and more has assuaged your hatred for Eber?'

'No. I do not tell you that. I merely say that in Eber's daughter I have found a new love. I can assure you that I did not kill Eber. And if I did not, and that poor deaf, dumb and blind idiot did not, then someone else did. And that someone might be one who also knew the truth about Eber's real character. Find the person who hid in the gloom of the cave with Menma and I think you will find the murderer.'

Fidelma was silent for a while and then she finally said: 'Perhaps you are right, Dubán. Eber has paid the price for his evil deeds and God forgive him.'

'God may forgive him, but I shall not,' declared Dubán in an uncompromising tone.

'But you truly thought that Móen was guilty when the murder was discovered?'

'I had no reason to believe otherwise. God moves in mysterious ways, sister. I truly believed that God used the unfortunate creature as an instrument of His greater vengeance.'

'It has become obvious that Menma was also somehow involved in this. Do you agree that he was an instrument of someone more powerful than he was?'

Dubán nodded agreement immediately.

'Menma was ambitious but he was a simple man. He took orders; he did not give them. So it was the person in the cave who was giving Menma orders. It was that person who wrote the vellum and is manipulating the evil that spreads in this valley.'

'That is the truth of it,' agreed Fidelma. 'On no account tell anyone yet at the *rath* of how you dealt with Menma nor of what we have discussed.'

They were getting quite close to the *rath* now. The guard dogs began to howl as they sensed the approach of Fidelma and her companion.

Chapter Nineteen

Fidelma left Dubán at the stables having unsaddled and seen to her horse's wants before making her way as quickly as she could to the guests' hostel.

Gadra was waiting by the door. She tried to guess whether the news was good or bad from his solemn expression.

'I think he is over the worst of it,' he greeted her.

Fidelma shut her eyes, swaying a moment, and then let out a deep sigh.

Gadra went on impervious to her reaction: 'He is asleep now. He has passed through the sickness and fever. I believe that your God guided you to seek my cure at an early stage. We have been able to purge the poison from him.'

'Will he be all right?' she demanded.

'I believe so. But he needs rest now.'

'Can I see him?'

'Do not wake him. Sleep is always a great healer.'

'I shall not.'

Gadra stood aside and she went into the guests' hostel. Eadulf was lying on his back on his mattress, his features pale but relaxed in a natural sleep of exhaustion. Fidelma moved forward and knelt beside his bed, raising her slim hand to gently touch his brow. It was still fairly warm; doubtless the fever had only just subsided. She felt a sudden tender feeling for the Saxon which she could not define. She had come near to losing him. She closed her eyes and uttered a silent prayer of gratitude.

A moment or so later she rose and found Gadra in the main room of the hostel.

'How can I ever thank you?'

The old man examined her with his ancient pale eyes.

'The young girl, Grella, helped a lot. I have only just sent her to her bed. Give your thanks to her.'

'But without you . . .' protested Fidelma.

'If you would give me thanks, make sure that the truth prevails in this place.'

Fidelma inclined her head slightly.

'I am near to the truth, old one. One question to bring me nearer. Was Tomnát the mother of Móen?'

Gadra's expression remained inscrutable.

'Truly, you have a perceptive mind, child.'

Fidelma allowed herself to smile.

'Then the truth shall prevail.'

When Gadra had gone, Fidelma went into the *fialtech* to wash and prepare herself for a night's repose.

Tomorrow was going to be a busy day.

Fidelma was alone in the forest.

Alone and afraid.

Around her mysterious shapes slunk through the woods on either side, the undergrowth rustled and quivered. Everything was dark.

She was calling. She was not sure to whom she was calling. Her father? Yes, she must be calling to her father. He had brought her to the forest and now he had deserted her. She was only a child. Alone and lost in the forest.

Somehow, somehow in her reasoning mind, she realised that this could not be so. Her father had died when she was a baby. Why should he have brought her here and left her?

She stumbled on through the threatening darkness of the forest. Pushing her way forward. But the forest trees seemed to grow closer and closer the more she moved forward. Finally, she could not move at all and she paused and peered up.

It was strange how the trees resembled the stems of mushrooms, giant mushrooms, great fungi towering above her.

The threatening shapes were pressing closer and closer.

She called out.

It was then she realised that it was not her father who had brought her here and deserted her.

It was Eadulf to whom she was calling.

Eadulf!

She started forward, stretching out a hand . . .

She groaned as bright flickering sunlight greeted her open eyes.

She found herself stretching forward on her bed, one hand held out before her.

She blinked rapidly and gathered her thoughts.

It was well past dawn and she was in her bed in the guests' hostel.

She heard a movement in the adjacent cubicle.

She swung out of her bed and drew on her robe.

Gadra was seated outside. He smiled as she joined him.

'A good morning, sister.'

'Is it so?' she queried, glancing toward's Eadulf's cubicle.

The old man nodded solemnly.

'It is so.'

Fidelma immediately went inside. Eadulf was still lying down but his eyes were open. He remained pale, and there were little wrinkles of pain around the corners of his mouth. But the dark eyes were clear and untroubled.

'Fidelma!' he greeted in a croaking voice that was weak with exhaustion. 'I thought that I might not see another dawn.'

She knelt beside the bed, smiling reassuringly.

'You should not give up so easily on life, Eadulf.'

'It was a struggle,' he admitted. 'One I have no wish to repeat.'

'Dignait is dead,' she announced.

Eadulf shut his eyes for a moment.

'Dignait? Was she responsible?'

'It would appear that Dignait knew who prepared the poisonous dish.'

'Then who killed Dignait?'

'I believe I know. But I need to discover the answers to a few more questions first.'

'Where was Dignait found? I thought she had disappeared from the *rath*?'

'In an underground chamber on Archú's farmstead.'

Eadulf showed his surprise.

'I don't understand.'

'I am calling everyone who is concerned into the hall of assembly at midday when I will reveal who the killer is.'

Eadulf smiled grimly.

'I will make myself strong enough to attend,' he averred.

She shook her head.

'You will remain here with Grella until you are well.'

The fact that Eadulf did not bother to argue showed that he was still very weak.

'Are you suggesting that there is one killer for all the deaths which have happened?'

'I suspect that there is one person responsible,' she replied enigmatically.

'Who?'

Fidelma gave a small laugh.

'Get yourself well, Eadulf. I'll come to you as soon as I am sure.'

She reached forward, took his hand and squeezed it.

Outside Gadra was checking some pungent broth for Eadulf. The odour was powerful. The young girl Grella had brought it from the kitchen. She looked nervous in Fidelma's presence but Fidelma smiled encouragement, thanking her for all she had done.

Grella bobbed nervously.

'I will bring your breakfast now, sister.'

While Fidelma washed the food was bought so that she was able to dress and finish eating by the time Gadra had finished giving an unappreciative Eadulf the herbal soup. By the sound of it, he was not a particularly good patient for his protests at the taste echoed through the hostel. Fidelma put her head into the cubicle.

'Shame on you, Eadulf. Unless you make yourself better, I shall not tell you what happens at noon.'

Gadra looked up with a frown.

'What happens at noon?'

'I have told Eadulf that at noon everyone concerned with this matter will gather in the hall of assembly. That will mean you and Móen. Is the young man all right?'

'He has been much cheered by what you have done for him,' Gadra replied. 'He is a bright, sensitive young man, Fidelma. He deserves a chance in life. We shall be there at noon.'

It was half an hour later that she crossed to the church of Cill Uird and strode inside. A figure was kneeling before the altar in an attitude of prayerful contemplation.

'Father Gormán!'

The priest started up in surprise.

'You have interrupted me at prayer, Sister Fidelma.' His voice was filled with irritation.

'I have urgent need to speak with you.'

Father Gormán turned to the altar, genuflected and climbed slowly from his knees.

'What is it, sister?' he asked wearily.

'I thought you should know that Dignait is dead.'

The priest visibly winced but he did not seem unduly surprised.

'So many deaths,' he sighed.

'Too many deaths,' replied Fidelma. 'Five deaths already in this pleasant valley of Araglin.'

Gormán looked at her uncertainly.

'Five?' he queried.

'Yes. A stop must be put to this carnage. *We* must put a stop to it.'

'We?' Father Gormán seemed nonplussed.

'I think you can help me.'

'What can I do?' There was almost a suspicious note to his voice.

'You were Muadnat's soul-friend, weren't you?'

'I prefer the Roman term – confessor. And, indeed, I was confessor to most people here in Araglin.'

'Very well. However you describe your role, I want to know whether Muadnat ever mentioned gold to you?'

'Are you asking me to break the sacredness of the confessional?' thundered Father Gormán.

'It is a confidentiality that I do not recognise but I respect your right to believe in it. Let me put some questions to you. I believe that Dignait had been a servant here for many years?'

'Dignait? I thought you wanted to ask me about Muadnat?'

'Let us concentrate on Dignait for a moment. She had been here since Cranat came here to marry Eber, hadn't she?'

'That is so.'

'Did you notice to whom her loyalties lay?'

'Why to this house of Araglin.'

'Not to one person? Cranat for example?'

Father Gormán hesitated and looked awkward.

'And didn't Dignait hate Eber?' pressed Fidelma.

'Hate?' Father Gormán shook his head. 'She did not respect him but that is not hate. She was closer to young Crón than her mother and would do anything for her.'

'She would do anything for Crón?' repeated Fidelma thoughtfully.

'No crime in that,' Gormán observed.

'No. No crime in that in itself.' She paused. 'You don't like Dubán, do you?'

This question was asked abruptly.

Father Gormán was annoyed.

'What have my likes and dislikes to do with this matter?' he demanded.

'Just an observation,' she conceded. 'I have seen you arguing with him. I simply wondered why you disliked him.'

'He is a man with ambition. I believe he wants to be chieftain of Araglin. Do you know that he is trying to beguile young Crón?'

'Beguile? Now that is a strange word to use. Allure, enchant or deceive. Is this what you mean?'

Father Gormán thrust out his chin.

'Observe his relationship for yourself.'

'Oh, that I have.'

'I feel sorry for Cranat. She was the wife of a chieftain without moral scruples and mother to a young woman whose innocence blinds her to the ambitions of a man old enough to be her father.'

'I recall that you hated Eber as well.'

'True, I could barely tolerate him. Eber was a sinner before God and man. There is no forgiveness for such a man who has transgressed against his fellow man and his God.'

'As a priest, you should have compassion. Instead I find much hate in you. It is for you to be forgiving. Did not Paul write to the Ephesians saying: "Be kind to one another, tender hearted, forgiving one another even as God, for Christ's sake, has forgiven you"? If God can forgive, so can his priest.'

Father Gormán stared at her for a moment. Then he grimaced in anger.

'You should have read further into that epistle to the Ephesians. Paul said: "For this you know, that no whoremonger, nor unclean person, nor covetous man, who is an idolater, has any inheritance in the kingdom of Christ and of God." Eber will have no inheritance in the afterlife.'

'And because he lay with his own sisters or even worse?'

'All I say is that this world is better off without Eber of Araglin. The sooner this valley is purged of evil, the better.'

'So it is not purged yet in your eyes? Did you know that Muadnat had a gold mine?'

Father Gormán bit his lip. 'How much do you know of this?'

'You will find out. Be in the hall of assembly at noon.'

Fidelma left the chapel abruptly with Father Gormán standing staring after her. He stood absolutely still until she had gone and then turned hurriedly towards his sacristy.

Outside the chapel Fidelma met Crón.

The young tanist acknowledged her with a grave face.

'How is Brother Eadulf this morning?'

'Well enough, thanks be to God,' replied Fidelma.

'I spoke with Dubán this morning,' the tanist went on slightly uneasily. 'He says that you are near to discovering who has put such misery onto the people of this valley?'

'Oh yes. In fact, I was coming to find you to request the use of the hall of assembly at noon today. I am asking all those I feel concerned in this matter to attend so that I may reveal the names of those responsible for the effusion of blood in this valley.'

Crón seemed visibly shaken.

'Then you must know who killed Eber and Teafa?'

'I believe I do.'

'Believe?' Crón looked dubious.

'I shall demonstrate my belief at noon.' Fidelma was almost cheerful. 'Will you ask your mother if she will attend? I am sure she will want to hear who is responsible for the slaughter of her husband?'

'I will,' the young tanist agreed.

Fidelma walked on unconcerned by Crón's curious expression.

Chapter Twenty

The hall of assembly seemed crowded. Crón had taken her chair of office. Fidelma had requested that she do so because, as tanist, it was her right. She was wearing her parti-coloured cloak and doeskin gloves of office for the occasion. Next to her sat her mother; the older woman's face was haughty and staring determinedly into the middle distance as if the proceedings were of no concern to her. On a seat below the dais, just to one side, Brother Eadulf reclined uncomfortably, still pale, his eyes shadowed but at least he was showing some signs of improvement. He had risen from his sick bed in spite of all Fidelma's protests. Next to him sprawled the burly figure of Dubán, leaning forward, so that he rested with forearms on his knees. In the well of the hall sat Archú and Scoth. Next to them was Gadra the Hermit with Móen at his side. Gadra was leaning towards Móen interpreting what was happening, fingers drumming on the young man's raised palm. Agdae fidgeted irritably on a bench on the far side of the hall next to Father Gormán. At the rear of the hall, seated alone, was Clídna, 'the woman of secrets', her chin raised defiantly as if waiting for someone to challenge her right to be there. A few seats from her was Grella, the young servant girl. A few of Dubán's men were stationed at the doors of the hall.

Fidelma took her stand before Crón, just below the dais, to the left of her chair.

'It seems that we are all here,' she observed.

'Are you prepared to start?' demanded Crón, leaning forward. Agdae called from his seat: 'But Menma is not here. Should he not be here? After all, he discovered Eber's body and identified Móen as the killer.'

Crón seemed perturbed.

'I sent him to round up cattle yesterday. It is strange that he is not here. Perhaps we should wait?'

Fidelma smiled broadly.

'I fear it would be a long wait, tanist of Araglin. No; we shall make a start for I did not expect Menma to be in attendance.'

'What do you mean? Do you accuse Menma . . . ?' began Cranat, forgetting her feigned indifference.

Fidelma raised her hand.

'All in good time. *Vincit qui patitur.* He prevails who is patient.'

There was an expectant silence in the hall as they regarded her slight, calm figure with anticipation. Fidelma examined their upturned faces, studying each carefully in turn.

'This has been one of the most difficult investigations I have undertaken. Difficult in that when a person is killed, there is usually one murder to address and one set of circumstances. In this pleasant valley of yours I found five killings to examine, and, at first, they did not all seem related. Indeed, it seemed to be that there were several different events happening all at the same time, each one unconnected with the other. In this initial assumption, I was wrong. Everything was connected; connected to one central point like the threads of a giant spider's web, all coming together to where one dominating creature waited, manipulating those threads.'

She paused to let the ripple of their surprise rise and ebb away.

'Where shall we begin to unravel this silken web of deceit which clings to so many lives? I could start at the centre of the web. I could make a lunge for the spider waiting there. In doing so, however, I might leave the spider a path to scuttle from the centre, along some strand of the web where it may yet elude me. So I shall begin to unravel the web from the outside, slowly but surely destroying the outer strands until there is nowhere for the spider to run.'

Crón leant forward with scepticism on her features.

'This is all very poetic, Sister Fidelma. Does your rhetoric have some purpose?'

Fidelma turned quickly to her with a look of appraisal.

'You have seen my methods, Crón, and have expressed your appreciation of them. I do not think I need defend my procedure.'

The young tanist flushed and sat back. Fidelma confidently turned back to her audience.

'Let us start with the first thread. This thread is Muadnat of the Black Marsh.'

'What has Muadnat to do with the murder of my husband?' Cranat demanded in a dry, rasping tone. 'He was Eber's friend and once his tanist.'

'By patience you will have a linen shirt from the flax plant,' replied Fidelma good naturedly, uttering an old saying that had been a favourite of her mentor, Morann of Tara. 'My involvement in this affair actually began with Muadnat, so it is fitting that I should start with him. Muadnat in recent times became possessed of a gold mine. He found it on the land which he had tried to claim from his cousin, Archú.'

There was an immediate expression of surprise from the young farmer.

'Where was this?' demanded Archú. 'I have never heard of a gold mine in the Black Marsh.'

'The mine is located on the far side of the hill whose land was too poor for cultivation. You dismissed it as axe-land. I should say that it was probably not Muadnat who made the discovery but a miner named Morna. He was brother of a hostel keeper named Bressal, who keeps a hostel not far from this valley on the western road which leads to Lios Mhór and Cashel.'

The young farmer looked astonished, glancing to Scoth at his side.

'Do you mean the hostel where we stayed?'

'The same,' confirmed Fidelma. 'Remember that Bressal spoke about his brother Morna who had brought him a rock which he claimed would make him rich? That was from the cave on your land which had begun to yield up gold.'

'It's a lie!' Agdae intervened angrily. 'Muadnat never mentioned a gold mine to me. You all know that I was his nephew and his adopted son.'

'Muadnat wanted to keep his mine a secret,' went on Fidelma, unperturbed. 'The problem was that he had a cousin who was claiming the land as his own. This cousin, Archú, decided to take the matter to law. Muadnat fought desperately to keep hold of the land. You see, Muadnat believed in bending laws for his own purpose but not breaking them entirely. The matter was embarrassing. Muadnat had a piece of luck, however. Archú took the matter to Lios Mhór rather than have the case heard before Eber. Eber was a crafty man and might have asked too many questions about why Muadnat was keen to hang on to the land.'

Agdae looked sour.

'Why didn't Muadnat make me a partner in his gold mine?'

'You were not ruthless enough for the enterprise,' called Clídna.

Fidelma saw Crón about to rebuke her for daring to speak in the hall of assembly and interrupted.

'Clídna is right,' she confirmed. 'Agdae is not the sort of person who would be mixed up in illegal mining. Muadnat wanted someone who would obey orders without questions asked. He chose his cousin Menma.'

'Menma?' frowned Agdae. 'Was Menma working with Muadnat?'

Fidelma regarded him sadly. 'Menma was his overseer. Menma ran the mine, recruited the miners, saw that they were fed and ensured that gold was shipped south where it would be held securely. How do you secretly feed and house a group of hungry miners in a peaceful pastoral valley without the local farmers knowing about them? A place to hide was no problem. The mine itself provided shelter. But what of food?'

'What you do is carry out raids on farms and carry off the livestock,' replied Eadulf triumphantly. 'Not too much, a cow or two here and there, perhaps.'

'But Muadnat had a rich farm,' Crón pointed out. 'He could have fed those miners without resorting to such subterfuge as cattle raids.'

'That would mean that Agdae would come to know what was happening. You forget that Agdae was Muadnat's chief herdsman. Agdae would know if Muadnat was killing more cattle and supplying food to a source which he could not account for. And if Muadnat dismissed Agdae from that job it would look very suspicious. After all, Agdae was Muadnat's closest relative.'

Agdae was flushed in mortification.

'What made you think that the cattle raids were not genuine?' demanded Dubán.

'I have heard of cattle raiders, of outlaws, running off cattle. But, as Eadulf pointed out, never in ones or twos. Outlaws seek cattle to sell. That being so they would move entire herds or certainly enough cattle to make the sale worthwhile. I suspected that these cattle were being taken for food only. This was confirmed when we encountered some of the raiders when we were coming back from Gadra's hermitage. They were moving south, with asses loaded with panniers. The panniers were doubtless filled with gold.'

'Some of the raiders?' queried Dubán.

'Menma was not with them and neither were others we will identify shortly,' explained Fidelma.

'But I do not see the connection between Muadnat's gold mine and the death of Eber and Teafa?' Agdae protested sullenly.

'We will eventually get there, following the strands of the spider's web,' Fidelma assured him. 'Muadnat's wish was to hang on to the mine. He did his best to do so. Perhaps even against the advice of his partner.'

There was a silence.

'Muadnat would never take Menma's advice about anything,' sneered Agdae.

Fidelma chose not to ignore the jibe.

'Even while he was at Lios Mhór, Muadnat's partner had probably decided that he would take over the gold mine,' Fidelma said. 'The reason was that Muadnat was drawing too much attention to himself in arguing law with Archú. The mine was meant to be secret. More importantly, Muadnat had fallen out of favour with Eber.

'Muadnat had been Eber's tanist until a few weeks ago. He had been due to be chieftain when Eber died. But suddenly he found himself dispossessed. Eber had persuaded the *derbfhine* of his family to accept his daughter Crón as tanist instead of Muadnat.

'The raid on Bressal's hostel, for example, was probably conducted without Muadnat's knowledge. The raid was led by the man I later recognised as Menma. He had been told that Morna, Bressal's brother, the miner who had discovered the mine, was being too free with his tongue. In fact, Morna had taken a rock to his brother, a rock which contained a gold trace, and told his brother that he would grow rich by it. It was not realised that Morna had not passed on any specific information. By chance we happened to be there and thwarted Menma's attack.'

'What happened to this miner named Morna?' demanded Dubán. 'Was he killed?'

'He was, indeed. He had been captured, killed and was later left at Archú's farm where, it was thought, he would simply be regarded as an outlaw killed in the raid. His relationship to Bressal was only obvious to me by the similarity of the features of the two brothers.'

'Are you saying that Muadnat knew nothing about the raid of Bressal's hostel and the slaughter of Bressal's brother?' asked Eadulf in surprise.

'I do not see how this story of Muadnat's gold mine relates to the murder of my father,' Crón insisted impatiently.

Fidelma allowed herself to smile briefly.

'I have but unravelled the first thread of the spider's web. Muadnat's death became inevitable because of two old human emotions – fear and greed. Menma killed him, of course. Menma slaughtered Muadnat as one might slaughter an animal. It was the same way he had slaughtered Morna. It was the cold professionalism that pointed to Menma. One of his tasks was to slaughter meat for his chieftain's table. I am not sure whether it was his idea to have Muadnat hanged on the cross after the act. Presumably this was a method of distracting me. Menma made one mistake. Before dealing the death blow, Menma allowed Muadnat to grasp some strands of his hair and pull out a tuft by the roots. It was left at the scene.'

'What would Menma get out of slaughtering his partner Muadnat?' asked Father Gormán. 'It does not make sense to me. Agdae would have inherited Muadnat's wealth anyway.'

'But, as we have heard, Agdae did not know about the mine and, as it was secret, the partner would continue to reap the benefits whether Agdae took over the farm or not.'

'Are you claiming that Menma is responsible for all the deaths in Araglin?' demanded Dubán. 'I have difficulty following this.'

'Menma was responsible only for the deaths of Morna, of Muadnat and of Dignait . . . for they were all slaughtered in the same manner. Menma killed his victims with the same professionalism of a slaughterman killing a lamb.'

'But why was Dignait killed?' asked Father Gormán.

'A simple reason, and the same reason as Morna was killed,' replied Fidelma. 'It was to ensure her silence. Dignait did not prepare that dish of poisonous mushrooms which nearly killed Brother Eadulf. A professional cook would know there are better ways to poison someone than to present a dish of false morel which anyone would have recognised.'

'The Saxon did not,' Crón pointed out with a sceptical humour.

'I know morel is usually blanched. I was a stranger in your land and thought this was your way of preparing the dish,' Eadulf replied defensively, the colour rising to his cheeks. 'That was why I was not on my guard against false morel.'

'Dignait would have had a more effective way if she had meant to poison us. No. Dignait was killed for the simple reason that she had seen the real would-be assassin.'

'And who was that? Menma?' Grella found the courage to speak up. 'Menma was about the buildings that morning as usual.'

'I'll tell you in good time. Let us continue to unravel the spider's web first. Let us turn now to the killing of Eber and Teafa. What made this case difficult is that most people here had a reason for killing Eber. He was a hated man. But Teafa was different. Who hated her? I saw that there was a better chance of tracking down the murder of Teafa than of Eber. If the same killer had slain both then we could eliminate some of the suspects.'

She paused for a second and then gave an eloquent shrug.

'I arrived here having been told a simple story. Eber, the chieftain of Araglin, had been slain and his murderer had been caught. I was told to investigate and to make sure that the law was followed in the prosecution of the murderer. It sounded easy enough. Except that it was not so.

'The murderer, so it was claimed, turned out to be one who is deaf, blind and dumb. I speak, of course, of Móen. What was more, he was also alleged to have killed the woman who had raised him.

'I was initially told that Eber was kind and generous and made no enemies. A paragon of every virtue under the sun. Who else would kill him but some crazed animal? That was how Móen was presented to me.'

Móen let out an angry growl as Gadra interpreted what was being said. Fidelma ignored the interruption.

'Let us proceed along this thread logically. It became apparent that Eber was not the paragon of virtue that everyone first insisted that he was. It became obvious that Eber was a strange, demented man. It is not my task to comment on what forces twisted Eber's mind. I was told he also drank and was verbally aggressive. He assuaged those he offended by bribes. His faults were overlooked as he was chieftain. But he and his family hid a dark secret . . . there was incest among them.'

Crón went white and could not suppress a soft hiss of breath. Cranat, beside her, made no effort to comfort her daughter but sat stiffly, eyes fixed on some distant object.

'This incest went back a long way, Crón,' Fidelma said compassionately. 'It went back to the time Eber was a boy reaching puberty and his two sisters were of similar age. Several people here knew, and others perhaps suspected, about that incest. It was let slip to me in conversation that one person knew that Móen was a child born of incest.'

There was a sudden hush in the hall. Crón cast a glance towards where Móen was sitting. Her face was ghastly.

'Do you mean that he . . . that Teafa . . . his mother? That Eber . . . ?' She could not articulate properly and gave up with a shudder.

'I have no doubt that Teafa suffered from Eber's molestation,' Fidelma continued calmly. 'But there was another sister named Tomnát.'

Dubán was on his feet, his face suffused with anger.

'How dare you bring her name into this!' he exclaimed. 'How dare you suggest that she was mother to a . . . a . . .'

'Gadra!' Fidelma, ignoring his outburst, turned to the old hermit. 'Gadra, who was Móen's mother?'

The old man bowed his head, his shoulders slumped in resignation.

'You know the answer already.'

'Then tell everyone, so that they may know the truth.'

'It was the year before Eber married Cranat that this happened. Tomnát became pregnant with Eber's child. Teafa knew of it.'

'Tomnát loved me!' Dubán cried, his voice cracking with emotion. Crón was staring at him unable to believe his outburst. 'She would have told me if this had been true. She disappeared. Eber killed her, of that I am sure.'

'Not so,' replied Gadra sadly. 'The secret was kept between Tomnát and Teafa. They knew that if it was known, if either Eber or Father Gormán heard of it, then the child might have been killed. Eber to hide his shame and Father Gormán because he is of an intolerant faith. Gormán approves the custom of many Christian lands in which such children born of incest are put to death in the name of morality. There would be no help from Father Gormán for poor Tomnát if she had tried to turn to him.'

'Why didn't Tomnát turn to Dubán. He protests that he loved her and that she loved him.' Fidelma's lips thinned. 'Surely, if this were so, she would have turned to Dubán for help?'

'Not so,' the old man replied. 'If it is the truth you want, then here it is. Tomnát knew that Dubán was far too concerned with his ambition to go to Cashel and receive the golden collar of a warrior. In spite of his professed love, Dubán would never have endangered the fulfilment of his ambition. Could she trust him to accept the child, the child of her own brother?'

Dubán leant forward, head cradled in his hands.

'So she turned to you, Gadra?' quietly prompted Fidelma.

'Before her condition became noticeable, Tomnát left Araglin. She came to join me in my hermitage where she knew that she would be safe. Only Teafa knew where she was.'

'If Tomnát could not tell me, why didn't Teafa tell me?' cried Dubán. 'I spent weeks scouring the valley, thinking that Eber had killed her.'

'Teafa kept faith with Tomnát's request,' the old man said.

'Go on,' urged Fidelma. 'What happened?'

'When her time came, Tomnát died giving Móen life. Teafa was with her and she resolved to take the baby and bring it up, claiming it to be a foundling. She did not know until later that

the child was handicapped and then she refused to give him up
having sworn an oath to her dead sister.'

Eyes were turned on the young man whose face creased in
anguish as Gadra translated what he had been saying.

Fidelma looked round the hall with a contemptuous expression.

'You are a farming community here. Farmers! You know about
inbreeding. You know that the offspring of closely related animals
usually have a magnification of certain traits of their parents in
behaviour or health. Some of these traits may be favourable ones
— they could lead to higher intelligence — but other traits could
develop; ones that are detrimental and unhealthy. Traits that give
rise to deafness, blindness and the inability to give voice.'

Crón interrupted, her voice full of distaste.

'So are you saying that we must accept Móen as the son of my
father . . . his own uncle? That he is my . . . my half-brother?'

She shivered as she said it.

'Tomnát died and left a living child,' confirmed Fidelma. 'Teafa,
as we all know, pretended that he was a foundling, discovered
while she was hunting in the forest. At first it was not suspected
that the child was unlike other children. But then Teafa realised
that things were wrong with the child. She sent for Gadra and
Gadra, being a wise man and healer, realised the problem. He
could not heal the afflictions caused by the incest but he taught
Teafa a means of communicating with Móen. Apart from the
physical problems, the child was highly intelligent and able to
learn. Teafa raised a talented boy.'

'Are you saying that Eber did not even know that Móen was
his own son?' asked Agdae.

'By all accounts he was kind to the boy,' Fidelma replied. 'Of
all the people here, all who hated Eber, only Móen did not.'

She turned once again to Gadra.

'Ask Móen whether he knew that Eber was his father.'

Gadra shook his head.

'No need for that. He has suffered much. I will tell you, however, that Teafa never told the boy. It was for his own protection. Nor was Eber told that Móen was his flesh and blood, so far as I know.'

'In fact, Eber was eventually told,' Fidelma said quickly. 'There was a row one day which was witnessed by the youth Crítán. We will come to that later.'

'Why is my father's . . . sexual life,' interrupted Crón, pausing a moment and then reforming her thoughts. 'While this may be of interest, it does not tell us who is responsible for Eber and Teafa's death.'

'Oh, but it does.'

'Please explain then,' invited the tanist coldly. 'Are you saying that you now believe Móen to be guilty? That he found out who his real father was? That he hated him for the wrong which Eber had done to his mother and himself?'

Fidelma shook her head.

'I dismissed the charge that Móen was the killer at an early stage of this investigation. Even before I had spoken with him, I knew Móen was not the killer.'

'Perhaps you will explain why?' Father Gormán asked dryly. 'It seemed perfectly clear to me.'

'The original accusation was that Móen had killed Teafa and then made his way to Eber's apartments and killed him. There were certain things wrong with this idea. Firstly, from the haughty young Crítán I learnt that he had seen Teafa alive after Móen went to Eber's apartments. To be responsible for both murders, Móen would have had to kill Teafa first and then Eber.'

'Why couldn't he have done that?' demanded Agdae.

'Because Menma claimed that he had found Móen bending over the body of Eber, knife in hand, having just killed him. The whole essence of the charge is that Móen was caught almost in the act.'

They greeted the point in silence. Then Crón said: 'But Menma has already been condemned by you as a murderer and therefore a liar. Perhaps he lied.'

'He told lies right enough,' agreed Fidelma impassively. 'But not in this instance. His discovery of Móen at the scene of this crime was a gift. It could not have worked out better. But Teafa was still alive when Móen entered Eber's apartments. Crítán, returning from Clídna's establishment, saw Móen on his way to Eber's apartments and then saw Teafa still alive standing by her cabin with a lamp. For a moment, when he was telling me this story, I think Crítán recognised the illogic of it. But he wanted Móen to be guilty, so he ignored it.

'Móen had been for a walk in the early hours of the morning and was just entering the cabin of Teafa when someone handed him an Ogam stick. Ogam is the method by which one communicates with Móen. Móen told me that someone with calloused hands, but whom he had thought, by the rich perfume he detected, was a female, had pressed the Ogam stick into his hand. It told him to go to Eber's apartments at once. He did so and, having stumbled over the body, it was there that Menma found him. The person who pressed the Ogam stick into Móen's hands was the killer who meant him to be discovered and condemned.'

'What proof have you of the existence of this fabled stick, instructing Móen to go to Eber?' asked Father Gormán.

'Proof? I have the stick itself.' Fidelma smiled complacently. 'You see, Móen thought he dropped the stick at the door. It was knocked from his hand before he set off to Eber's. The killer did not want the evidence found. They had already killed Eber. Just as the killer was going to recover the stick, Teafa, who had been awakened by the encounter, came out. She was holding a lamp and had discovered Móen was missing. She saw the Ogam stick and picked it up. At this point she was seen by Crítán. She asked Crítán if he had seen Móen. The boy lied and went on his way. The killer, who had to wait in the shadows until Crítán moved on, was faced with a dilemma. Teafa had gone back into her cabin to read the faked Ogam message. So now she had to be killed. The oil lamp which Crítán had seen in Teafa's hand was knocked to the ground in the struggle and caught fire. That had to be extinguished because the killer wanted to ensure that Móen could also be accused of the murder. The Ogam stick with the instructions on it was thrown into the fire but not entirely burnt. There is still enough on it to compare with Móen's excellent memory. He recalled that the stick said: "Eber wants you now." The letters ER and WANTS remained.'

Brother Eadulf was smiling at the simplicity of Fidelma's reconstruction.

'Móen did another impossible thing,' he offered. 'When Menma found Móen leaning over the body, he said it was just before sunrise. And the lamp was lit by Eber's bedside.'

'Well? What is wrong with that?' asked Dubán. 'It would be dark before sunrise.'

Eadulf chuckled.

'Why would Móen need to light a lamp? This disposes of the accusation that Móen entered by stealth and stabbed Eber to death as he lay there asleep.'

'Exactly,' agreed Fidelma approvingly. 'Unless we are to believe that a blind person had need to light a lamp to see what they were doing.'

'Eber could have lit the lamp himself,' Agdae pointed out. 'He could have lit the lamp to let Móen in and . . .'

'Of course!' Fidelma was sarcastic. 'Eber was awake, lit the lamp and let Móen in. He then obligingly went back to bed and waited while Móen felt his way to where he kept his hunting knives, selected one, found his way to the bed and stabbed him to death. The easier answer is Móen's version of what happened. That when he entered the room he found Eber already dead. The killer had already struck. The killer then went to divert Móen to Eber's apartments and then found that they had to deal with Teafa. Eber was not slain in his sleep. He was killed by someone he knew very well; someone he had no suspicion about. He had lit the lamp and allowed that person into his bed chamber.'

'Who would Eber trust enough to allow into his bed chamber?' demanded Agdae. 'His wife?'

Crón let out a gasp.

'Are you accusing my mother?'

Fidelma looked at Cranat thoughtfully. The widow of Eber was sitting disdainfully watching her.

'I was waiting for you to reach me with your foul allegations,' Cranat said sibilantly. 'Sister Fidelma, I remind you that I am a princess of the Déisi. I have powerful friends.'

'Your rank and friends mean nothing to me, Cranat. The law applies to us all in equal measure. But we have finally come to the spider in the centre of its complicated web.'

Crón was staring aghast at her mother.

'It cannot be.'

'Cranat has never made a secret of the fact that she wanted money and power,' sneered Agdae.

'You cannot prove that Cranat had cause to murder her own husband,' Father Gormán protested to Fidelma.

'Prove cause? Let me try. Since Crón was thirteen years old Cranat was prepared to put up with her hatred of Eber so long as he supported her. When Teafa told her what Eber was doing, she simply withdrew from his bed but continued to live as chieftainess – wealth before virtue. Eber seemed prepared to tolerate the situation. Perhaps he just wanted a wife for the sake of appearances? Dubán informs me that a few weeks ago there was another argument between Teafa and Cranat when Crón became tanist. The argument included mention of Móen. That was when Cranat learnt the truth about her husband's son. Did she now plot a day of vengeance?'

Fidelma paused. No one said anything.

'Virtue after wealth. *Quaerenda pecunia primum est virtus post nummos.* Cranat might have left Eber's bed but, ironically, she had began to have an affair with Muadnat. With Eber gone she might become the wife of the new chieftain.'

Brother Eadulf bent forward, excitement on his face.

'Móen said that the person who gave him the Ogam stick had calloused hands like a man. But he scented perfume and thought it was a woman. Dignait had calloused hands. Dignait was close to Cranat because Dignait was of the Déisi and had come here as Cranat's servant when she married Eber.'

'Only ladies of rank wear perfume,' corrected Dubán. 'Dignait would not have worn perfume.

Crón was shaking her head with disbelief.

'Are you saying that my mother was Muadnat's partner in the gold mine and that she decided to kill my father to marry him?'

'Cranat had reason to hate Eber and Móen. Teafa had told her about the relationship.' She paused and glanced at Crón. 'You have good Latin, don't you?'

'My mother taught me,' replied the tanist.

'She taught you well. Actually it was the Latin on a piece of vellum that set in motion the final pieces to this puzzle. Menma, having killed Dignait in her room to prevent her speaking about whom she had seen putting the false morel on the trays in the kitchen, was told to dump the body at Archú's underground store. Then he was to give me the vellum with the clue written in Latin on it. It was good Latin.

'Am I accused because my Latin is good?' sneered Cranat.

'Is your Ogam also good?' inquired Fidelma. She went on before Cranat could reply. 'It is wise to remember the words of Publicius Terentius Afer that no one ever drew up a plan where events do not introduce the necessity of modification. Dubán had followed Menma to the mine, having observed him with the so-called cattle raiders. He reached the mine entrance and heard Muadnat's partner giving Menma some final instructions. Dubán entered. Menma waylaid him and allowed his chief to get away. I was there as well, and I saw the figure flying along the path.'

'You saw the figure?' sneered Cranat. 'Do you swear it was me?'

'It was a figure clad in a parti-coloured cloak, a cloak of office.'

Crón grimaced with an attempt at a smile, pointing to the cloak of office that she was wearing.

'But I wear such a cloak.'

'Truly,' called Eadulf. 'And I saw such a figure wearing a similar parti-coloured cloak climbing on the track across the hills to the mine on the day we were at Muadnat's farmstead.'

'I am now confused. Are you accusing Cranat or her daughter?' cried Father Gormán.

'Some time ago Crón told me that this same parti-coloured cloak is worn by all chieftains of Araglin and their ladies. You wear one too, don't you, Cranat? And you also wear a strong perfume of roses.'

The widow of Eber scowled at her but Fidelma turned to Gadra.

'Gadra, tell Móen I want him to smell something. Bring him here.' She turned to the others. 'Móen, to make up for deficiencies in his other senses, has a highly developed sense of smell which I have previously observed.'

Gadra did as she bid him, leading Móen, shuffling forward, to the front of the dais.

'Father Gormán, will you come forward and witness this procedure? It must not be claimed later that Móen was in doubt.'

Somewhat reluctantly the priest came forward. Fidelma then turned to Gadra.

'Instruct Móen to smell as I direct and then identify if he has ever detected the same scent before. Tell him that I want to see if he perceives the same scent as he did when he was handed the Ogam stick.'

She thrust out her hand allowing Móen to sniff at it. Cranat had risen to her feet.

'I shall not let that beast near me!' she protested, backing away.

'You will have no choice,' Fidelma assured her, signalling Dubán to come forward and stand behind her. Móen had shaken his head at Fidelma's wrist. Fidelma motioned to Crón to hold out her hand. Móen sniffed at it. He turned and made some signs on Gadra's hand.

Gadra shook his head.

Cranat put her hands resolutely behind her back.

'Father Gormán,' Fidelma instructed, 'as Cranat is reluctant to hold out her hand to the boy, will you help her? Perhaps she will not object to a priest's hand being laid upon her.'

'I am sorry, lady,' muttered Father Gormán, with evident distaste, reaching and firmly taking her left arm. Cranat pulled her head away in distaste as Móen sniffed at her wrist.

There was excitement in the hall as he turned and made rapid signs on Gadra's hand. The old man looked shocked.

'It is false!' screamed Cranat. 'You are in some plot to discredit me!'

But the old man was not looking at Cranat.

'It is not the scent of the woman which he identifies,' Gadra said slowly, staring aghast at Father Gormán. The priest had gone white.

Dubán had automatically stepped forward and gripped the priest by the wrist. Then he frowned disconcerted as he stared at the man's struggling hand.

'But Móen said that the person he sniffed at Teafa's door had calloused hands. This priest's hands are as soft as a woman's.'

Fidelma was unperturbed.

'You are not wearing your leather gloves today, Father Gormán?' she remarked. 'You see, Dubán, yesterday you gave me the answer that I was looking for when I thought your hands were calloused but, in fact, you were simply wearing leather gloves.'

With a sudden cry Father Gormán wrenched himself free of Dubán's grasp, leapt from the dais and began to push from the hall. He barely reached half way across the hall when he was overpowered and led away. His features were distorted in a frenzy of rage. He began shouting unintelligibly: 'And Christ said – "you serpents, you generation of vipers, how can you escape the damnation of hell?"!'

'A most appropriate text,' muttered Eadulf to disguise his astonishment.

Cranat collapsed back into her chair, her face flushed, her breathing heavy. She was regarding Fidelma with hatred.

'You have some explaining to do before we can believe in this fantastic charge,' she said quietly.

Chapter Twenty-One

Fidelma was still standing quietly before the dais and regarding them all with a sombre expression.

'There are few places in these five kingdoms where I have encountered so much hatred, so much deceit and so much sadness,' she began slowly. 'Gormán and Menma might be guilty of taking human lives but that which stimulated them to do so is an evil inherent in this valley.

'Was Eber the instigator of this malignancy or was he also a victim? We shall not know. Tomnát was certainly a victim. She might not have been had she been able to trust at least one person in this valley other than her fellow victim and sister; one person might have saved her.'

She turned and regarded Dubán without a change of expression.

The warrior lowered his gaze before her fiery green eyes.

'Teafa had also been a victim but she had saved some of her self respect as well as her sister's son. Móen was the saddest victim of them all.'

'And wasn't I a victim?' demanded Cranat harshly. 'I was a princess of the Déisi and yet I was forced to reduce myself in wedlock to this depravity?'

'Forced? You were prepared to put up with it. Even when Teafa first came to warn you years ago that your husband was continuing his degeneracy and had encouraged your own daughter into his bed when she was only twelve or thirteen!'

'That's not true!' gasped Crón, starting forward, her face draining of blood.

'No?' Fidelma grimaced sourly. 'You have already confessed

as much. Better these dark secrets should now be made known. Teafa saw Eber's vileness starting all over again with you, Crón. You became a victim too. She went to warn Cranat to leave, to divorce and take you with her. But Cranat was content to merely remove herself from her husband's bed and continued to live here because here was wealth and security. She left her daughter to fend for herself. It was not Cranat who then refused to speak further with Teafa but Teafa with Cranat.'

There was a deathly silence in the hall of assembly.

Fidelma turned to Crón and regarded her sorrowfully.

'Yes, Crón, you were a victim but you also made yourself mistress of the situation. You used your father's lascivious desires to wheedle yourself into power. Muadnat had been your father's tanist. A few weeks ago you felt yourself strong enough to be able to demand that your father nominate you as tanist and then use his power to ensure the *derbfhine* support you. Indeed, because of Eber's bribes only four people stood against you. Your own mother and Teafa, who both knew the price that you were paying; Agdae, Muadnat's nephew; and Menma who was bound to Muadnat not only as a relative but by the power of Muadnat's gold. You are unfit to hold office.'

She swung round again on Dubán.

'And without office, Dubán, how long will you declare your love for Crón? Tomnát recognised that relentless ambition in you twenty years ago, when she felt that she could not confide her terrible secret. Now that Crón's secret, the same secret, is out, will you remain faithful? No!' She raised her hand as he made to answer. 'No protestations now. Do not answer me until after the meeting of the *derbfhine* has declared whether Crón is to be chieftain of Araglin or not.'

Fidelma turned to the hall, sweeping everyone with her passionate gaze.

'Morann of Tara once said, evil can enter as a tiny seed and, if unchecked, grows into an oak tree. A forest has grown here. The hope of Araglin lies in the innocence of youth, of boys like Archú and girls like Scoth.' She smiled suddenly at Clídna. 'And if any single haven of morality exists in this place, it is to be found here within this woman.'

Clídna blushed and hung her head.

Agdae rose slowly to his feet.

'Your judgment on Araglin is harsh, sister,' he said quietly. Then, with an awkward glance to the silent Cranat and her daughter, he added: 'But it is not unjustly spoken. However, tell us how you came to identify Father Gormán? You also built up a good argument against Cranat.'

'I knew it was unlikely that Cranat had killed them for a simple reason: if she had been the murderess then she would not have sent to my brother at Cashel to send a Brehon to make a formal investigation.'

'Why did she do that?' asked Eadulf.

'Above all things, as we have learnt, Cranat is a princess of the Déisi. She did not want any finger of suspicion to be pointed at her house. She thought that the presence of a Brehon would lend moral weight to the matter. I believe that she really thought that Móen was guilty having discovered the truth of his birth.'

She gazed sorrowfully at Eadulf. 'There was one point which destroyed the case against Cranat, which I presented purposefully to allay Gormán's suspicion about where I was leading. Everyone failed to question it. That was good, otherwise Gormán might have been put on his guard but I am surprised some of you did not spot it.'

'What was that?' demanded Agdae gloomily.

'You forgot the maxim – *summa sedes non capit duos* – the highest seat does not hold two. Crón had become tanist before her father's murder. Muadnat was no longer tanist so Cranat could not have killed Eber with the hope of becoming wife of the new chieftain.'

'Then what made you suspect Gormán?' asked Gadra.

329

'Easy to say,' acknowledged Fidelma. 'At Lios Mhór I first heard that Gormán was a fanatical advocate for Rome. As it turned out, he was simply a fanatic, an intolerant zealot, whatever he believed in. I learnt that he had built a chapel at Ard Mór and, I was informed, attracted much wealth to furnish it. His chapel here, Cill Uird, was equally opulent. Unlike most priests, he had money to equip and ride a horse.'

'Wealth is not a sign of guilt,' muttered Cranat.

'It depends on where that wealth came from. Gormán had become the partner in a secret gold mine with Muadnat. How or why the partnership developed, perhaps we shall never know. My guess is that Muadnat, to exploit his mine and escape paying tribute to Eber, decided Gormán was a means of disguising where the gold came from. Gormán could pretend that it came as gifts from those who supported his beliefs. The gold was converted into riches stored in the chapels at Ard Mór and Cill Uird. What Muadnat overlooked was man's inherent greed. Just because Gormán was a priest it did not mean that he was not a man.'

'But why did he kill Eber and Teafa?' demanded Crón, overcoming her resentment at what Fidelma had revealed about her relationship with her father.

'I have said – he was an intolerant fanatic. Once he learnt that Eber was the father of Móen he was incensed against the immorality of it. Eber must be despatched to Gormán's concept of hell and Móen, as a child of Eber's incest, was to be punished by being accused of the murder. I have already explained that Teafa was killed to keep her silent about the evidence of the Ogam stick. The motive with Eber was no more complicated than Gormán's zealous morality.'

'But how did he learn that Móen was Eber's son?' asked Crón. 'Even I did not know of it before you told us.'

Fidelma looked hard at Cranat.

'I think that you can answer this question. Two weeks ago Dubán saw you and Teafa arguing. You left that argument and went directly to see Gormán. When Teafa found out that Crón had used her relationship with her father to become tanist, she went to you to argue further why this thing must not be so. She told you that Móen was the child of Eber's incest?'

'As priest here, Father Gormán had a right to know,' replied Cranat.

'But Gormán was a fanatic and that knowledge led directly to their deaths. After Cranat had told him, Gormán went in fury to accuse Eber and Teafa. Crítán witnessed the confrontation and saw Eber strike the priest. That was when Gormán decided to kill him.'

'But what if Móen had not picked out the perfume of the church incense?' Eadulf reflected. 'I would have thought that such incense would have been a common enough odour to Móen to have recognised and identified it with the chapel before this?'

Fidelma shook her head sadly at Eadulf.

'Don't you remember that Gormán told us that he refused to allow Móen into the chapel? That he avoided him? Móen was, therefore, not able to identify the perfume before today.'

'But why did Father Gormán kill my uncle, Muadnat?' asked Agdae. 'He was his partner in the illegal mine.'

'I mentioned the reason briefly before. As Muadnat began to draw more and more attention to himself, trying to legally wrest the land back from Archú, Gormán became fearful. This behaviour could lead to the discovery of the mine because people's attention was being focussed on the area. Menma was Gormán's man, not Muadnat's. He had Menma kill Muadnat to preserve the secret. For the same reason, he had Menma kill Morna and Dignait. And Gorman's simple greed played the prime part.'

'What made you realise that Menma served Gormán?'

'That there was some collaboration between Gormán and Menma became obvious to me. I saw them arguing together once. When Archú told Gormán he wanted to bring Muadnat to court over his land dispute, Gormán told Archú to take his case to Lios

Mhór. I found this curious until I realised that this would prevent Eber being involved in the case. Eber might have questioned Muadnat too closely. Gormán instructed Archú to go by a longer route to Lios Mhór. Perhaps the reason for this was so that Archú would not encounter the gold being transported to Ard Mór along the quicker route.

'Gormán then found that one of the miners he was employing, Morna, had taken a piece of rock from the mine to his brother Bressal. Menma was told to kill Morna and also destroy the hostel. The excuse of outlaws in the district would serve as a covering for these acts.

'There were several things that now drew my attention to Gormán. Eadulf had seen a slight figure wearing a parti-coloured cloak at Muadnat's farmhouse. The figure vanished. Moments later, Gormán appeared but without a riding cloak. I knew Gormán had possessed such a cloak for I had seen the parti-coloured cloak in Gormán's sacristy. Gormán's clothes were also impregnated with a heavy scent from the incense he used in his church. Gormán wore gloves. The implication of these facts, I have already explained.

'On the night before poor Brother Eadulf took the poisonous mushrooms, Gormán had overheard me expressing confidence to Crón that I could name the murderer by the next day. He slipped into the kitchen early the next morning and placed some false morel on the plates. Dignait had seen him in the kitchen and he realised that when word of the poison became known, she would not hesitate to point the finger at him to absolve herself. Or perhaps he had always meant to lay the blame on her. Menma was sent to silence her and told what to do with her body. Gormán was one of the few people who knew about the underground storage chamber on Archú's farm for he had, as Archú told me, been there when someone died by accident and it was Gormán who suggested, at that time, the chamber be sealed. Gormán also wrote good Latin and Ogam. The parts of the puzzle were joining together.'

Fidelma paused and spread her hands expressively.

'But, when all these facts were placed together, one main factor fitted the pieces of the puzzle into a frame. Gormán had been told that Móen was born of Eber's incestuous relationship with his sister. He let the fact slip out when he was talking to me. His creed of intolerance could not accept it and for that he killed Eber and Teafa in an act whose motives were unrelated to the illegal gold mine.'

Three days later Fidelma and Eadulf stopped at Bressal's 'Hostel of the Stars' to break the news of his brother's death. The plump keeper of the hostel was shocked but resigned.

'I suspected that death had overtaken him when he did not return. My brother spent his life searching for wealth in order to spend the rest of it doing nothing. He would not have been happy doing nothing. But it is sad that he could not have discovered that fact for himself.'

Fidelma nodded. '*Auri sacra fames* – the cursed hunger for gold destroys more than it creates. Did not the blessed Matthew write: "Lay not up for yourselves treasures upon earth, where moth and rust do corrupt and where thieves break through and steal"?'

Bressal smiled in agreement with the sentiment.

'Say a prayer for Morna's soul, sister.'

They rode on through the woods towards the main road which would lead them to Cashel. In the three days that they had been waiting at the *rath* of Araglin, since Fidelma's relevations, news had reached her that the mineworkers had been rounded up and Gormán's store of gold in the chapel at Ard Mór had been confiscated by the local Brehon, pending the result of the trial of Gormán at Cashel. But the trial would not take place. Fidelma had generously allowed Gormán to be imprisoned in the sacristy of his own chapel. On the day following his internment, Gormán ate a secret store of false morel and died within four hours. It was, remarked Brother Eadulf, still feeling delicate in health, a fitting end.

Agdae was appointed temporary tanist of the Araglin by a special meeting of the *derbfhine* of the family of Eber. Only Crón protested. It was obvious that she would not be confirmed as chieftain of Araglin. Dubán had not even waited for the results of the meeting but saddled his horse and vanished into the mountains. Cranat had also taken what possessions she could and ridden back to the land of the Déisi.

It was Eadulf who voiced Fidelma's sentiments as they rode along.

'I shall not be sorry to leave this place. I feel I need to find some good clean water to bathe in after all that has happened.'

It was as they came to the cross roads that Fidelma saw two familiar figures on foot trudging along the road to Lios Mhór. One of them was young but being led by the hand by the elder of the two, an elderly man whose slightly stooping shoulders marked the passing of many years.

'Gadra!' called Fidelma, easing her horse forward.

The old man paused and looked round. They saw his fingers drum against the hand of Móen, doubtless explaining why he was halting.

'Blessings on your journey, Fidelma,' he smiled at Fidelma and then turned to Eadulf, 'and on your journey, my Saxon brother.'

Fidelma swung off her horse.

'We wondered why we had not seen you both these last few days. You should have bidden farewell to us. Where are you and Móen bound?'

'To Lios Mhór,' the old man replied.

'To the monastery?' asked Fidelma in surprise.

'Yes. You needn't look confounded,' Gadra chuckled. 'Would not an old pagan like myself be welcomed there?'

'There is a welcome for everyone in the house of the Christ,' replied Fidelma solemnly. 'Though I must confess that your decision to go there does surprise me.'

'Well.' Gadra rubbed a forefinger against the side of his nose. 'If the choice were mine, I would continue a while longer to live in my mountain dwelling. But the boy has need of me.'

'Ah,' Eadulf sighed. 'It is a laudable thing you do for the boy. The confines of a cloister are better protection than the mountain fastness.'

Gadra shot him an amused glance.

'More importantly, he needs the company of those who can communicate with him. The holy house at Lios Mhór contains members of your religious who have knowledge of the old writing. I can quickly teach them the way of using it. Once Móen is able to communicate with several people then I will have fulfilled my duty to Teafa and Tomnát. I will be able to move on to my destiny and leave him to his.'

Fidelma smiled.

'That is a generous gesture.'

'Generous?' Gadra shook his head. 'It is no more than is my sacred duty to the intellect which is Móen's. The boy has demonstrated his sense of smell and guided in the right way I am sure that this quality can be employed.'

'To what end?' Eadulf asked with interest.

'There are any amount of things to do for a person who can sense the aroma of things, from mixing perfumes to identifying herbs in the right quantity or to the making of medicines.'

'So you and Móen will reside at Lios Mhór?'

'For the time being.'

Fidelma grinned mischievously

'And, who knows, even you might become a Christian under such holy influence?'

'That I never will,' Gadra chuckled sourly. 'I have seen too much of your Christian love and charity to want to be part of it.'

'I am sure that if you listen to the Word, preached by the brothers and sisters at Lios Mhór, you will come to accept that the Word is the Truth,' declared Eadulf stoutly.

'Your Word or Gormán's Word? How can you be so certain that your Word is the Truth for everyone or, indeed, whether it is a Truth at all?' asked Gadra, good naturedly.

'One must have Faith or the Truth will elude you,' Eadulf was stung to reply.

Gadra shook his head and raised his hand to the blue canopy of the sky.

'Has it ever occurred to you, my Saxon brother, that when the moment comes for that door to open for us to pass into the Otherworld, either one of us might find that these things, about which we argue so vehemently, might be nothing more than some great misunderstanding?'

'Never!' snapped Eadulf, outraged.

The old hermit regarded him sadly.

'Than your faith is blind and you have abrogated your own free will which is against the spiritual order of this world.'

Fidelma laid a hand on Eadulf as she sensed an angry retort.

'I understand you, Gadra,' she said, 'for we are sprung of the same common ancestors. But customs change, just as the days roll by. We cannot bid them halt nor can we return to the point we started out from. But I recognise in you the same virtues that we all have.'

'Bless you for that, sister. After all, do not all the tracks lead to the same great centre?'

There was a silence and then Móen demanded attention.

'He says that he is sorry that he did not bid you farewell properly before we set out but he felt that he had imposed too much on your good office. He thinks you know how he feels. He owes you his life.'

'He owes me nothing. I am a servant of the law.'

'He says, he feels that the law is like a cage which traps those who do not have the power to secure a key.'

'If anyone can disprove that statement, it is he,' replied Eadulf indignantly.

'It was not the law but the lawyer which provided the key,' interpreted Gadra.

'The blessed Timothy wrote in holy scripture that the law is good if it is used lawfully,' replied Fidelma. 'And a learned Greek, Heraclitis, once said that a people should fight for their law as if it were their city wall against an invading army.'

'We will have to disagree. Law cannot dictate morality. But I thank you for what you have done. Farewell, Fidelma of Kildare. Farewell, my Saxon brother. Peace attend you on your road.'

They stood watching the old man leading Móen away through the forest path.

Fidelma felt suddenly very sad.

'I wish I could have convinced him that our law is a sacred thing, the result of centuries of human wisdom and experience to protect us as well as to punish. If I did not believe it I would not be an advocate.'

Eadulf inclined his head in agreement.

'Didn't someone once say that it is not laws which are corrupt but those who interpret them?'

Fidelma swung up on her horse.

'Many years ago Aeschylus wrote that wrong doing must not win by the technicality of the law. By that means we have to submit the law to our own judgment. I think this is what the blessed Matthew was really warning about when he wrote "judge not lest ye be judged".'

They turned their horses north along the road to Cashel.

SHROUD FOR THE ARCHBISHOP

ARCHBISHOP

A Sister Fidelma Mystery from the author of
ABSOLUTION BY MURDER

Peter Tremayne

Wighard, archbishop designate of Canterbury, has been
discovered garrotted in his chambers in the Lateran
Palace in Rome in the autumn of AD 664. The solution
to this terrible crime appears simple as the palace
guards have arrested an Irish religieux, Brother Ronan
Ragallach, as he fled from Wighard's chambers.

Although Ronan denies responsibility, Bishop Gelasius,
in charge of running affairs at the palace, is convinced
the crime is political; Wighard was slain in pique at the
triumph of the pro-Roman Anglo-Saxon clergy in their
debate with the pro-Columba Irish clergy at Whitby.
And there is also the matter of missing treasure . . .

Bishop Gelasius realises that Wighard's murder could
lead to war between the Saxon and Irish kingdoms if
Ronan is accused without independent evidence. So he
invites Sister Fidelma of Kildare and Brother Eadulf of
Seaxmund's Ham to investigage. But more deaths
follow before the pieces of this strange jigsaw of evil
and vengeance are put together.

'The Sister Fidelma stories take us into a world that
only an author steeped in Celtic history could recreate
so vividly – and one which no other crime novelist has
explored before. Make way for a unique lady detective
going where no one has gone before!' Peter Haining

FICTION / CRIME   0 7472 4848 6

The Holy Innocents

A Roger The Chapman Medieval Mystery

KATE SEDLEY

As Roger the Chapman, novice monk turned pedlar, makes his way towards Totnes, he learns that a gang of cutthroats is terrorizing the surrounding district. After he himself is playfully ambushed by some country women, he is inexorably drawn into the spider's web of a local tragedy.

Rescued by the handsome Grizelda, he is told of the terrible fate of the Skelton children. Recently deprived of their wealthy mother, they were left to the care of their unpopular stepfather who by chance becomes Roger's temporary landlord. For Roger is given charge of the very town house from which the two youngsters mysteriously vanished.

But how had they left this house? Why had they left it? And were the outlaws really responsible for their dismal deaths? These are the questions that will increasingly haunt the chapman.

'Compares well to Ellis Peters's Brother Cadfael tales' – *Publishers Weekly*

'Sedley skilfully interweaves romance, intrigue, and authentic period detail' – *Booklist*

'An attractive hero and effective scene setting' – *Liverpool Daily Post*

FICTION / CRIME 0 7472 4665 3

A selection of bestsellers from Headline

ASKING FOR TROUBLE	Ann Granger	£5.99	☐
FAITHFUL UNTO DEATH	Caroline Graham	£5.99	☐
THE WICKED WINTER	Kate Sedley	£5.99	☐
HOTEL PARADISE	Martha Grimes	£5.99	☐
MURDER IN THE MOTORSTABLE	Amy Myers	£5.99	☐
WEIGHED IN THE BALANCE	Anne Perry	£5.99	☐
THE DEVIL'S HUNT	P C Doherty	£5.99	☐
EVERY DEADLY SIN	D M Greenwood	£4.99	☐
SKINNER'S ORDEAL	Quintin Jardine	£5.99	☐
HONKY TONK KAT	Karen Kijewski	£5.99	☐
THE QUICK AND THE DEAD	Alison Joseph	£5.99	☐
THE RELIC MURDERS	Michael Clynes	£5.99	☐

All Headline books are available at your local bookshop or newsagent, or can be ordered direct from the publisher. Just tick the titles you want and fill in the form below. Prices and availability subject to change without notice.

Headline Book Publishing, Cash Sales Department, Bookpoint, 39 Milton Park, Abingdon, OXON, OX14 4TD, UK. If you have a credit card you may order by telephone – 01235 400400.

Please enclose a cheque or postal order made payable to Bookpoint Ltd to the value of the cover price and allow the following for postage and packing:

UK & BFPO: £1.00 for the first book, 50p for the second book and 30p for each additional book ordered up to a maximum charge of £3.00.

OVERSEAS & EIRE: £2.00 for the first book, £1.00 for the second book and 50p for each additional book.

Name ....

Address ....

....

....

If you would prefer to pay by credit card, please complete:
Please debit my Visa/Access/Diner's Card/American Express (delete as applicable) card no:

Signature .... Expiry Date..............